# THE RAIDERS AND THE CROSS

## *Jox McNabb Thrillers*
## *Book Two*

## Patrick Larsimont

*Also in the Jox McNabb series*
The Lightening and the Few
The Maple and the Blue
The Vulcan and the Straits

# THE RAIDERS AND THE CROSS

Published by Sapere Books.

24 Trafalgar Road, Ilkley, LS29 8HH

saperebooks.com

Copyright © Patrick Larsimont, 2023

Patrick Larsimont has asserted his right to be identified as the author of this work.
All rights reserved.

No part of this publication may be reproduced, stored in any retrieval system, or transmitted, in any form, or by any means, electronic, mechanical, photocopying, recording, or otherwise, without the prior written permission of the publishers.
This book is a work of fiction. Names, characters, businesses, organisations, places and events, other than those clearly in the public domain, are either the product of the author's imagination, or are used fictitiously.
Any resemblances to actual persons, living or dead, events or locales are purely coincidental.

ISBN: 978-1-80055-911-0

*For my girls, Lily and Melody for whom I do this.*
*Also, my writing gangs — The Thursday Morning Club, the Pencil Pack,*
*the History Quill, the AUB Scribblers, Writing the Past, Cornerstones and my fellow Sapere authors.*
*You are all precious to me.*

It had taken all of Melanie's courage to face the prospect of returning to Scotland to tidy up her grandfather's lodge on the Dundonald Estate in the southern Highlands of Perthshire. She'd been making excuses that it was too far from London, but in truth she was frightened of the ghosts of happier, innocent times and how they might affect her barely contained grief.

When she closed her eyes, she was transported to halcyon days playing hide and seek through the verdant fields and woods of the estate. Her task was always to hide and his to find her, but in their version of the game, he would sneak up on her once spotted and give her a delicious fright by roaring, 'Bang-bang-bang'. Her squeals of delight would see them dissolve with laughter, especially if he'd 'got her good'. The name had stuck — Grandpa Bang-Bang.

The estate belonged to a family of foreign aristocrats. The factor, Angus Dundonald of that ilk, once explained that the land had belonged to his family, but had long since been sold to pay death duties. He told Melanie that his employers had 'a great debt of honour' owed to her grandfather and the lodge was gifted to him and his descendants in perpetuity with their eternal gratitude. Angus said he'd only ever met 'His Lordship', as he insisted on calling him, half a dozen times during the salmon season, fishing the Isla that bordered the estate. With his advancing years and increasing infirmity, he came less often, but Angus had fond memories of Jox and the laird enjoying whisky-fuelled nights and baying lustily at the moon together.

'Aye, they were grand old pals,' he recalled. 'Close as brothers.'

Melanie was back in this familiar space, so full of treasured memories. It was hard to take the stale metallic tang of ash in

# PROLOGUE

## *Scotland, Autumn 1990*

Melanie McNabb's grandfather had always been the constant in her life. The anchor against whatever t might throw at her.

He was there when her father left and when her r grandfather's only daughter, unravelled, her drinki her irrational, inconsistent and frankly terrifying environment for a timid adolescent to grow up in.

He was always there, saying, 'Don't worry, my l your top cover. Just look up and you'll see. I'm alv She didn't understand what he meant until she was yes, her Grandpa Bang-Bang had always been overwatch throughout her life. Her hero, her eye in t

He was gone now and it had taken over a year to g the grief, containing it where it could do no harm. that time to learn about his part in the Battle of Brita found the remains of his most implacable foe, th fighter ace *Hauptmann* Otto Werner who had so v vanquished him early in the war. She'd unco circumstances that saw young Pilot Officer Jer McNabb awarded the George Cross and the Dis Flying Cross, but most intriguing of all, she was on t Alice, the mysterious woman he'd almost been court- for and for whom he'd held a candle throughout hi wasn't Melanie's grandmother, so who was she and become of her?

the wood burner or the musty mildew in the rooms she'd abandoned for almost two years. Feeling guilty, she drifted forlornly from room to dark room, the melancholy familiarity of everything crushing. It was just the skeleton of the past with all the flesh and sinews of life long gone.

Walking up the creaking stairwell, she found dozens of images of her younger self on the wall: pink and windswept on some sunny beach, blonde hair in a bird's nest and eyes shining with youthful exuberance; proudly holding a baby tooth that had required her grandfather's string and door trick to shift; an awkward teenager, blushing in her first proper frock, bought for her leaver's ball from boarding school at St Leonard's in Fife; and a more confident twenty-something in her graduation gown, posing hand-on-hip for her grandfather's camera. Each and every chapter of her life was captured and displayed here, and yet so much of Jox's own life remained a mystery.

There were so few pictures of him. Those he allowed were black and white group-shots of men in uniform. As a child, she'd played an early form of 'Where's Wally?' trying to find a young Grandpa Bang-Bang in the sea of faces. The largest picture was over the mantelpiece, a squadron portrait annotated 'Montrose 1941'. The men were grouped in front of a sleek black Spitfire, its huge propeller and outstretched wings looming over them like a protective mother raptor over her eaglets.

The earnest faces of these determined young men had stared at her all her life, always challenging her to do better and be worthy of their sacrifice. She recognised some, like Uncle Pritch for example, but others were unknown. It was her desire to know more of their stories that had driven her interest and eventual studies. She had decoded the nicknames inscribed in the margins of the picture, which she knew by heart: Pete,

Badger, Pritch, Cam, Miro, Ghillie, Wee Brotch, Bubbles, Solly, Big Stick, Mogs, Kanga, Roo, Wally, Axel and Otmar. A strange collection, like the heroes of a Tolkien tale. Reciting their names had often soothed her to sleep or calmed pre-exam nerves. They were so familiar that they became the unexpected catalysts that drove her to academic achievement through to her PhD and career as a military historian and curator with the Imperial War Museum.

In time, she had discovered the fate of some of the men, but others were reduced to a solitary line in dreary wartime reports or a statistic on the websites of aviation enthusiasts. Some had disappeared without a trace, lost and forgotten, and perhaps still lying beneath the sod or sand of some lonely foreign clime. There were survivors, of course, like her grandfather and Uncle Pritch, but none of them were left untouched by what they'd seen, endured and suffered as young airmen. Some scars were visible, others weren't, and perhaps these were the most painful of all.

At first, it was frightening to wake in the middle of the night to the sound of Grandpa Bang-Bang's screams. He would call out, warning unseen friends of unseen foes. In time, she'd got used to it and realised it was just her grandfather having another one of his dreams. He was always back the next morning, smiling and kind, and always there for her.

Melanie decided she would start by sorting through his clothes. He didn't have that many, always a man keen to avoid excess. He would joke that he was just a tight Scotsman, but it was typical of a wartime generation for whom thrift and economy became second nature through necessity rather than desire.

When dressed casually, he favoured a combination of Perthshire farmer's tweed and army surplus serge and denim.

Melanie always pictured him in green, army green, the colour of the 'pongos' he so enjoyed taunting. He wore V-neck jumpers from faithful old M&S or Aitken & Niven, but always with holes at the elbows, a tattersall shirt and sometimes a cravat. 'Reminds me of my flying days,' he'd say with a wink and smile.

At the other extreme, his wardrobe contained all manner of formal wear: kilts, mess tunics, black tie, white tie and a surprising number of Nehru-collared velvet frockcoats in various hues and Paisley patterns. Laid out on the bed, they were boy-sized — surely too small for a war hero of Group Captain Jeremy McNabb's stature, and the larger-than-life protector of her childhood. Inside, though, she guessed that he was still always just 'wee Jox'.

After the war, he'd stayed on in the service, serving in various quasi-honorary roles in Aden, Malaya and the Caribbean, but he had eventually left, missing the adrenalin of wartime flying and hating the petty politics of peacetime aviation. Ultimately, it was the post-war appeasement of Stalin and the Soviets, and the corresponding betrayal of so many of his wartime comrades from Poland, Czechoslovakia and elsewhere, that had sickened him beyond quiet acquiescence, so he'd voted with his feet.

For the next few decades, he'd worked in the fishery and tourism industries, supplemented by a reasonable RAF pension that a grateful nation had bestowed on one of her most faithful wartime servants and heroes. He'd also inherited a healthy legacy from his estranged father, who had done rather well in the Far East but hadn't survived beyond the war, succumbing to liver disease brought on by alcohol and an aggressive liver fluke that he'd contracted after drinking some dodgy water.

Melanie sometimes feared alcoholism might be hereditary and had skipped a generation between her great-grandfather and her own mother. It wasn't something she liked to dwell on, but occasionally the fear was enough to stop her from that extra glass and had saved her from many a hangover.

Seeing Jox's finery laid out on the bed, she marvelled, not for the first time, at the dazzling array of gallantry medals and campaign ribbons. She recognised their significance from her studies but knew scant little of what he'd done to earn them. There was no doubting his long and very active war, as demonstrated by the bewildering array of stars and ribbons, including the 1939-45 and Atlantic stars, the Air Crew Europe with two clasps, the Africa, Italy, France & Germany stars, the War Medal and even the Canadian Volunteer Service Medal with a Dieppe clasp. More unexpectedly, they also included the French *Chevalier de la Légion d'Honneur*, the Belgian *Croix de Guerre* and even the Royal Albanian Hero's Star.

Jox had been everywhere and must have done exceptional things to merit them, but Melanie couldn't help but wonder what it was that had pushed him to do so much. What demons had driven him to fight and keep on fighting?

His uniforms and medals would go to the Imperial War Museum, as was right and appropriate. There she could choose what would go on display and what should be preserved for posterity. She carefully packed everything up for shipping down to Lambeth.

Academic research could only take her so far; she wanted a more human, organic telling of Jox's story. So many witnesses from that time had already passed, and whilst there were recordings of testimonies at the museum, including her grandfather's, she wanted more than that.

She decided she needed to see her Uncle Pritch. He was still alive, but he wasn't very well, according to the Royal Star & Garter Home in Richmond, London, where he was a long-term resident. But perhaps the maimed and blind old man, once such a formidable and vital ladies' man, could still tell her what she needed to hear.

Melanie walked into the Royal Star & Garter Home a few days later. Her Uncle Pritch had been a resident for a dozen years, since the death of his French wife, Amandine. The couple had always been her favourites, not least because as a child with little or no family, she had called them *Parrain* and *Marraine*, godfather and godmother.

Pritch had been larger than life and desperately good-looking, the epitome of a swashbuckling pirate captain, with an eye patch and a single right arm. Amandine had had startling pale blue eyes and dark flyaway hair that she'd always struggled to tame. They'd never had any children, so Melanie became their surrogate daughter. Regular visits from France were always accompanied by a deluge of *joli cadeaux*; always clever, intricately wrapped, and well-considered toys when she was younger, then oh-so-chic fashions when she got older. The contrast between the utilitarian apparel that her grandfather bought her and their *à la mode* gifts was stark and always very welcome.

It was a closeness that made Melanie feel terribly guilty about not visiting Uncle Pritch for the last few years. She'd seen him at her grandfather's funeral, but had been too distraught to pay him the attention he deserved. She was ashamed of her behaviour, considering how frail he was and the fact that he'd come all the way from London. She recalled how terribly thin and confused he'd been, not at all the vibrant old warrior of her childhood.

Melanie entered through the imposing metal doorway of the home, beneath the Red Cross medallion set in the carved stone mantel. The Union Jack hung listlessly from a pole between towering sandstone columns. She was nervous, intimidated by the grand edifice, the home of heroes before they embarked on their final journey.

After checking in at the reception desk, Melanie was shown to a grand but worn room with several tatty floral sofas. Squadron Leader Pritchard would be brought to her, she was told, accompanied by his friend Nancy, one of the other residents at the home. She was one of the few people who could still get through to Pritch. Melanie was warned that he wasn't always very lucid and could sometimes be aggressive and rude.

'Please don't expect too much, Miss,' said the orderly.

Pritch was wheeled in, crumpled and tiny in striped pyjamas, a burgundy dressing gown and monogrammed slippers.

His companion was a short, wide-faced lady with silver hair in a bob and bright red lipstick. She pushed Pritch's wheelchair along determinedly, carefully positioning him beside Melanie before applying the brake. When she looked up, her gaze was direct, perhaps challenging, but at the same time somehow haunted. Her smile and piercing dark eyes didn't seem to match.

'Hello dear, my name's Nancy Forward. You can call me Nancy.' She spoke in a soft Antipodean accent, and compared to Pritch's sallow skin tone she was the picture of rude health. The only thing betraying her age was the tremble in her hands, accentuated by the bright vermillion of the varnish on her fingernails.

Melanie introduced herself and explained why she was there.

'I knew your grandfather very well,' Nancy said. 'We met several times at the Victoria Cross and George Cross Association meetings over the years. A charming man, who always reminded me of my late husband. John was an RAF pilot too.' She patted Pritch's shoulder with an affectionate hand. 'That's what first got us talking, wasn't it, Pritchy, my darling?'

He moved for the first time, his head jerking as he raised his frail right hand.

'Come on, let's sit down and see whether we can have a nice convo. That'll be lovely, eh, Pritchy? I've asked them to bring us some tea, dear.'

'Melanie, my Melanie,' he said, pointing.

'*Bonjour, Parrain* Pritch,' said Melanie, her voice beginning to crack.

'There, there, dear,' said Nancy. 'Try not to get upset, it only sets him off. Speak nice and loudly, calm and clear. He understands everything you say.'

Pritch nodded and reached out his hand. It was as Melanie remembered — paler, thinner and with longer fingernails, but still the hand of a pianist. Jox had always said that before losing the other hand, Pritch had loved to play.

'How have you been, Uncle Pritch? I'm so sorry I've not been to visit. I was really sad for a long time when Grandpa died.'

'Brave Melanie,' he nodded. 'Miss him too. Jox, my friend.'

Emotion was welling up within Melanie and she was struggling to keep it contained.

'I'll see Jox soon. Big party, me and him, and the Treble Ones. All the boys waiting for me.'

'*Parrain*, please don't say that,' said Melanie in the voice of a little girl who didn't want to be orphaned. 'Please don't leave me all alone.'

'Not alone. Always here. Ghosts of yesterday. I miss my friends and I'm tired. So tired. It's no fun, is it, Nancy?'

She shook her head sadly.

He brightened and a glimpse of the old Pritch returned to his rheumy eyes. 'I'd have chased you around the table back in the day.' He gave a wheezing laugh, dissolving into a hacking cough.

'I'd have let you catch me, Pritchy darling,' replied Nancy.

They were still chuckling when the tea was brought in. Melanie served, and she noticed that Uncle Pritch held his cup more steadily than his friend Nancy.

'I wanted to ask you a question, Uncle Pritch,' said Melanie. 'I've been sorting through Grandpa's things and found some items that I know nothing about. Photographs and letters from people I don't recognise.'

Pritch smiled. 'Jox had many secrets.'

'Secrets about someone called Alice? Who was she?'

'I was the best man, instead of George.'

'I know that name. There's a picture of Grandpa with a dog called Georgie.'

'No. Georgie was my dog. Big George died at Montrose. Jox got the medal.'

Melanie wasn't following what he was saying.

'I think he means the George Cross. Your grandfather was awarded the George Cross for trying to save someone called George,' said Nancy.

Pritch nodded. 'George Cross, like Nancy.'

'You were awarded the George Cross too?'

'The George Medal. I was an ensign in the First Aid Nursing Yeomanry, but you don't want to hear about me. What were you saying about the best man, Pritchy?'

'I was best man for Jox.'

'He was going to marry Alice? What happened?' Melanie asked.

'London's burning, London's burning,' he croaked, then was silent. He crumpled back into his chair. It was as if a door had slammed and he was stranded behind it. She asked again, but he stared blankly.

'I'm afraid he's gone,' said Nancy. 'I'm very sorry, dear. He fades in and out. It's as if he gets tired of remembering and withdraws somewhere safer. Sometimes it lasts for days and then he'll just pop back. I'll keep asking the questions, and I'll write to you and let you know if I learn anything.'

'You're so very kind, Nancy. Uncle Pritch is lucky to have a friend like you.'

'Don't worry, dear, he helps me too. I've got more than enough of my own demons. We all do in this place. The war did a lot of damage, even after all these years.'

'I'm so grateful he has you. I haven't really been there for him. He deserves much better than that. He meant so much to me when I was a child.'

'Stop that!' said Nancy, with sudden steel in her voice. 'It's not for the young to heal the wounds of the previous generations. He loves you and always will. Hold onto that. It's really all he can offer now. I promise, I'll let you know if he says anything more about Jox or this Alice, but hopefully you have something to go on.' She glanced at Pritch, who was asleep again. 'I think I better get him back to his room. He's tuckered out. I'll get the orderly to see you out.'

The same woman who had shown Melanie to the room appeared. Melanie tried to give her godfather a kiss on the cheek, but he was completely unresponsive.

'Please don't take it to heart, dear,' said Nancy. 'He's not really in there anymore. He's probably already with his dear Treble Ones. He often talks about Wheelie Ferriss, Wolfie McKenzie and David the Bruce. Do you recognise those names?'

'Wheelie Ferriss sounds familiar. I think he was Grandpa's mentor during the Battle of Britain. He once told me that he organised Wheelie's funeral. It was a sad memory that stayed with him for a long time.'

'Perhaps they're all up there, waiting for old Pritch to arrive and get the party started. If you believe in such things, I guess Jox will be there too.'

'You don't believe it, Nancy? I find the idea comforting.'

'Comfort? Maybe for some, but I've always been too practical and bloody-minded to put faith in that sort of thing. It would have been my dearest wish to see my first husband again, after everything he suffered for me, but I can't have faith that will happen. I've seen far too much darkness to think there'll be light at the end. No, better not to dwell on such things. Goodbye, it was so lovely to meet you. I do hope we'll see you again.'

Once back at the reception area, Melanie said to the orderly, 'What a remarkable woman, so very gentle and kind.'

'You mean Nancy? I wouldn't exactly describe her as that. She's far too deadly.'

'Deadly? But why? What do you mean?'

'That's Nancy Wake, the "White Mouse". During the Second World War, she was the deadliest Special Operations agent in the whole of occupied France.'

'What? That little old lady?'

'She wasn't always old, but yes, that little old lady. She strangled a strapping SS trooper with her bare hands, apparently. It's funny that you should underestimate her; in fact, her favourite expression about that time is that "they couldn't see what was right in front of their noses". I think it was her unthreatening appearance that duped the enemy. She once told me that the first thing she did when she landed by parachute was put on some heels and fresh lipstick. The Nazis never imagined this pretty dollybird could be dangerous, but she actually led over seven thousand Resistance fighters and had a five-million-franc bounty on her head as the Gestapo's most wanted.'

'My Lord, what a remarkable woman,' said an incredulous Melanie. 'And so lowkey about everything, just wanting to help my uncle. In retrospect, she did perhaps seem somewhat haunted, but I never would have guessed what was behind that.'

'She hides it well, but she has suffered a great deal. Her first husband, a Frenchman, was captured and tortured by the Gestapo, then executed when he wouldn't divulge her whereabouts. She has struggled with the guilt over the years. By the war's end, thanks to her, over five thousand airmen and soldiers were rescued and she's one of the most decorated women of the Second World War, with medals from five different nations. Nancy Wake is a true legend.'

For the next few days, Melanie was busy in her office at the Imperial War Museum. Fifty years ago, on the 29th of December 1940 at the peak of the London Blitz, London had come as close to destruction as it ever had. The museum was marking the anniversary with a series of events to demonstrate what had been lost and how the city's landscape had been changed forever. The bombing raid that had occurred that night had come to be known as the Second Great Fire of London.

Melanie had been asked to curate an exhibition to commemorate that terrible night. The ditty her Uncle Pritch had started singing kept churning through her head, as she planned the exhibition:

*London's burning, London's burning,*
*Fetch the engines, fetch the engines,*
*Fire, fire! Fire, fire!*
*Pour on water, pour on water.*

It was giving her a headache and she was getting nowhere. She needed to clear her thoughts, so she decided to go for a walk. Picking her coat and beanie hat up to protect her from the chill, she left her office, deep within the IWM building, ready to face the elements.

Whilst Melanie was out, a yellow Post-It note was left on her desk. She recognised the spidery handwriting of Mrs Cohen, one of the museum's volunteers:

*Mrs Cunningham from the Royal Star and Garter home called. Please call her urgently. She said you have the number. I'm sorry dear, but it sounds quite serious. I hope everything's all right. Love, Mrs C*

Melanie's blood ran cold. It was the call she'd been dreading for weeks.

# CHAPTER ONE

## *London, Spring 1941*

The Heinkel throbbed in the night sky like a malevolent locust. The rest of the swarm were scattered in the clouds, amongst the twisting smoke rising from the burning city. Brilliant white flashes strobed shadows against the clouds like spooling celluloid at the end of a projection.

Flying Officer Jox McNabb looked away, keen to avoid burning out his night vision. It was the most precious asset in his armoury, and staring at the giant grasshopper perched on the blazing headlight of the city in flames was a bad idea. He eased the nose of his matt black Supermarine Spitfire Mk VB down a touch. It bore a discreet RAF roundel and his identifying letters in a muted blood red. Barely visible, only his glowing exhaust manifolds could betray his presence, but only to a very sharp-eyed enemy gunner.

Jox had been following the bomber stream for about twenty minutes. He was a veteran at this and had the ribbons on his chest to prove it, but stalking his quarry in the pitch dark was new, as was the elegant Spitfire he was in. It was proving a worthy replacement to the Hurricane, the trusty warhorse that had seen him through the chaos of France and England's skies. This new steed already bore his signature JU-X, the emblem of a Scottish claymore held aloft, and the name '*Marguerite IV*' etched in a childish scrawl. This was in memory of a little French girl he'd been unable to save, but in whose name he had fought through the Battle of Britain. Later, it was for the many friends he'd lost, but now things were personal. His broken heart demanded savage retribution, and this glass-nosed bastard would be the first to pay.

Initially, he was guided towards his target by ground radar, but it was then up to him to find the raiders in the shrouded sky. He'd found them low over the Thames Estuary, heading upstream like migratory fish, laden with deadly spawn to unload on the sleeping city. He'd positioned himself at twenty-five thousand feet, high above the serried ranks of twin-engine Heinkels, picking a target amongst their lumbering forms. He was just a fleeting shadow against the full moon reflecting off the sea.

He dropped the Mark V through the formation, then edged towards the vulnerable belly of his intended victim. He held his breath, hoping the manoeuvre would go unnoticed, then exhaled slowly into his facemask, the cold chamois leather expanding. He reached up a hand and gave it a squeeze, feeling ice crystals fall away, landing against his chin. He'd been up for a while and the Spitfire was notoriously chilly, since the tight cockpit didn't allow for any bulky clothing. His next breath was a metallic hiss from the oxygen bottle, and he rubbed his legs with gloved hands, trying to get his circulation going. His feet were cold, and he adjusted their position on the rudder pedals. His left foot was dark blue, not from the cold but a prank in the mess a few weeks ago. Jox smiled bitterly at the memory, an innocent time, now long gone. He glanced up, hoping to catch the raider silhouetted against the clouds, lightened by the burning city.

The darkness was punctured by a bright arc of fire. The rings of his targeting sight were on the swollen body looming above him. Jox let rip with the full force of four .303 Browning guns and a pair of 20mm Hispano II cannons, each with a spring-loaded sixty-round drum magazine. The murderous weight of fire hurled at the raider was vastly superior to anything he'd had at his disposal last summer and he was impressed by the devastation it wrought. A series of explosions ripped open the belly of the bomber, flaring into the night sky so that Jox could make out the black crosses on the bomber's elliptical wings and the hooked swastika on its stocky tail.

Jox wondered how many of the five-man crew had survived his blistering attack. Were they terrified, battling the flames and the drag of G-force inside the plummeting aircraft, desperately trying to get out? In the darkness, there was no way of telling since any blossoming parachutes were instantly snatched away by the roaring slipstream. How many would end up as prisoners or simply die out there in the cold? In his heart, he wanted them dead, burning in that falling wreckage. Christ, what kind of a beast had this war made of him?

A second clattering burst arched from the Spitfire's wings, shaking him out of his dark musings. He remembered Sailor Malan's second rule of air fighting, drummed into their heads at flight school: 'Whilst shooting, think of absolutely nothing else.' He hadn't even realised he'd fired again, so he dropped his nose to clear the disintegrating target from the Spit's notorious blind spot. He watched his victim fall away, a sulphurous yellow tail of flame blazing from ruptured fuel tanks. Like a fiery comet, it was an unexpected thing of beauty.

Lit up now, all pretence of stealth gone, the startled gunners of other Heinkels blazed away at his shadow. Jox leant the steering column sharply to the right, spiralling away from the grasping tentacles of red tracer bullets. He grunted at the crushing effect of G-force as he fell, levelling out when he saw another Spitfire engaging a struggling Heinkel about half a mile away.

The rest of No.111 Squadron were out there somewhere. Jox wondered how David Pritchard and Cameron Glasgow were getting on. Glasgow was his wingman, but in the chaos of smoke and cloud he'd lost him. He reached for his R/T switch but recalled that radio silence had been ordered, when it was realised that enemy bombers were monitoring the British channels to counter the recent successes of radar-controlled searchlights. Tonight, the probing beams had been of little use to the hunters, other than ruining their night vision when caught in the blinding glare.

Jox climbed, searching for a second victim. A lumbering candidate loomed in the half-light, only visible because its bomb bay doors were opening. Rising steadily, he slipped behind the unsuspecting raider, too preoccupied with keeping straight and level so as to allow its bomb aimer to peer through his sights. None of the gunners in the nose, dorsal, ventral, beam or gondola positions spotted Jox's sleek Spitfire. They became aware of his presence only when he opened fire, then the panicking rear gunner desperately tried to counter, but far too late.

The illuminated gunsight traced a stream of cannon fire and bullets through the target, raking the entire length of the aircraft from rear to front. In his wandering thoughts, Jox could see Mike 'Wheelie' Ferriss's earnest face and his signature tactic of attacking the greenhouse-nosed He 111s from the front. What he was doing was effectively the reverse. Poor old Mike, his teacher and dear mentor, another comrade lost along the way. There were far too many.

The Heinkel reared like a wounded stag, exploding into a ball of fire and oily smoke. The Spitfire punched through the boiling mass of flame, the clear sides of the cockpit streaking with something dark, wet and liquid. A gory slug trail slid from the clear Perspex as a soggy fragment of a German airman slipped off the canopy.

Jox levelled off and scanned the horizon, already lightening to a familiar shade of Aberdeen granite-grey. In aerial combat, action was often over quickly, and a crowded sky became remarkably empty. Below him, the flames raged on as he tapped his fuel gauge to check the accuracy of the reading. He was running low and had used up most of his ammo too. The butcher's bill of two kills for the night barely sated his hunger for revenge, but it would have to do.

Jox was hit by a wave of grief and utter exhaustion. It was a physical pain in his chest, and he struggled to breathe. He was far too young to be feeling like this. He knew it came from having nothing more to live for. His destiny now was to become his enemy's angel of destruction, until the day when the flames would mercifully come for him too.

There was nothing else; it was simply his fate.

# CHAPTER TWO

It was bitterly cold as Jox and his sweetheart WAAF Alice Milne walked hand in hand between the weathered headstones that marked the airmen's section of Sleeping Hillock Cemetery near Montrose. The stones, once perfectly aligned, leant this way and that, shifted by the persistent strong winds off the North Sea. It was as if they were trying to see past one another to discover who was coming to visit.

Since the dawn of military aviation in Scotland, airmen had been buried here. Flight was a deadly mistress, and the bleak conditions at RAF Montrose made it a cruel place to learn, as the visiting pair knew all too well.

'Good morning, my darling,' said Alice, her voice cracking as they reached her brother's headstone. 'Look who I've brought to see you.'

'Hello there, old chum,' said Jox. 'It's been a while. I'm sorry it's taken so long to come.' His sky-blue eyes tracked the lettering cut into the stone:

*PILOT OFFICER*
*G. A. E. MILNE*
*PILOT*
*ROYAL AIR FORCE*
*19TH MARCH 1940 AGE 20*
*REST NOW DARLING BOY*
*WITH OUR EVERLASTING LOVE*

It was the grave of George Milne, one of his few friends and certainly one of the best. There had been such a terrifying succession of deaths since the beginning of this awful war. The intensity of those friendships was at the utter mercy of the unpredictability and wantonness of war. Dear sweet naïve George, tall and gangly with those remarkable cow eyes had been one of the first to die. Now, Jox was here to tell him that he hoped to make his sister a bride. Jox looked to Alice. Her eyes were so like George's.

'The thing is, old boy, there have been a lot of changes up here, what with the war and everything,' stammered Jox. 'Of course, I knew you had a sister, but well, Alice and I met at your funeral. Not exactly the best of circumstances, but you know…'

'It's such a shame we never spent any time all together,' said Alice.

'If George hadn't died, we probably wouldn't have met.'

'Oh, I think we would have. He was always talking about you.' She nodded encouragingly. 'Go on, Jox.'

'You see, George, we met again down south during the battle. I was stationed at Croydon, and Alice was a controller at Kenley. We've been through an awful lot together. It was a terrible, but also a precious summer for us. The weather was glorious, but that only meant that Jerry came over in droves. You remember old Pritch? He got shot down over Dunkirk and hurt his leg. So did I, as it happens. The thing is, George, Alice and I have become very close, and well, we're getting married.'

Jox paused, nervously examining his hands. They were still lumpy with the scars from the burning wreck of the Harvard Mark 1 trainer that he'd pulled George from just a few miles from here. All that felt like such a long time ago, but it had been little more than a year.

Jox and Alice were in their RAF uniforms with the wind tugging at them. Alice wore her Women's Auxiliary Air Force great coat over her skirt and stockinged legs. Her shoulder-length curly blonde hair was tucked in a bun under her cap, and she stood as tall as Jox. He was in his RAF tunic, the azure rings of his rank on his sleeves, pilot wings on his chest alongside the ribbons of the George Cross and the Distinguished Flying Cross. The former had been awarded to him for trying to save poor George and the latter for downing eight enemy aircraft over France and the South during the previous summer and autumn.

'We've been down to the farm to ask for your father's permission, George,' said Jox. 'He's been very sad since you died. We have his blessing, but he told us to come and ask for yours.' Jox took a deep breath. 'So, here I am, George, asking you for Alice's hand.' He was feeling rather foolish talking to a mute stone but was moved by the solemnity of what he was asking.

They stood quietly before George's grave. He was taking his time over the answer.

High above, a seagull wheeled and gave a plaintive cry. With a thunderous splat, a fishy mess streaked down George's headstone, showering the pair in their pristine uniforms. They jumped back, thoroughly splashed. Jox was horrified, but Alice was letting out peals of laughter.

'That's so bloody typical of Georgie,' she cried happily. 'He's telling us he approves, but that you'd better watch your step.'

Jox was very glad the moment hadn't been completely ruined for his bride-to-be and spluttered, 'Not exactly the sign from God, or George for that matter, that I expected, but I'll take it.' He looked down the untidy row of stones and realised that the gulls routinely used them for target practice. He gingerly flicked off a persistent lump sticking to his pilot wings. 'George doesn't seem terribly impressed by my wings. Perhaps he's cross he never got that far...' Jox caught himself, cursed, then quickly added, 'Well, perhaps he did. A rather finer pair than mine.'

Alice smiled forgivingly; her eyes filled with happy tears as she took his hand again. 'Oh, he's here all right, and as usual he's teasing me. He was always the one to have the last laugh was my brother.'

RAF Montrose hadn't changed. It was still bloody bleak, raining most of the time and always, always windy. Busier than Jox remembered, there were many more training courses being held than when he was last here as a fresh-faced trainee. In truth, he was still rather fresh-faced; tomorrow would be his twentieth birthday and the boys were throwing him a party in the mess. Sadly, it was 'the boys' that had changed most of all.

Jox, Pritchard and the rest of No. 111 Squadron, the Treble Ones, were back at No.8 Flying Training School, RAF Montrose for conversion from their trusty Hurricanes to sleek new Spitfire Mark Vs. Like most Hurricane pilots they were rather protective of their current steeds, especially since all the newspapers and the wireless always made such a fuss about Spitfires. It was as if the little fighters had won the Battle of Britain on their own, when any pilot worth his salt knew that it was the old Hurricane that had done most of the heavy lifting. Jox really wasn't keen to swap, but if it meant a change from the endless coastal patrols over the Firth of Forth from RAF Drem, and now over the northeast of Scotland from RAF Dyce near Aberdeen, then he was up for it. The only excitement he'd had over the last six months were the occasional high-altitude interceptions of reconnaissance aircraft, more often than not long fruitless chases with little resulting action.

At Montrose, the Treble Ones would not only be converting to Spitfires, but their role was changing: they were to become night fighters. They were to train in a new tactic, codenamed SMACK. Britain's cities were being battered by the Luftwaffe's nightly bomber raids, operating with relative impunity. Since the 7th of September 1940, London alone had been bombed for over forty nights in succession. The plan now was that the new SMACK procedure would vector Spitfire interceptors onto the raiders, guided by earth-bound radar-controlled searchlights pointing in the direction of flight of the bomber stream. Once the codeword CONE was signalled, several search beams would converge, locking onto a detected bomber, illuminating it for the stalking Spitfires to find and destroy.

In theory, the tactic was sound, and Britain's cities could certainly do with respite from the nightly raids. In practice, though, the Spitfire was proving hard to take off and land in the dark, its notorious blind spot to the front and powerful torque-producing Merlin engine swinging the aircraft off its line. It didn't bode well that the squadron had suffered several aircraft damaged in training and had tragically lost two pilots in a mid-air collision.

The faces of the squadron had changed enormously from the ragged men who'd survived the trying days of last summer. Squadron Leader John 'Tommy' Thompson, their charismatic CO, had been promoted and moved on to become Acting Wing Commander i/c Flying Training for 11 Group HQ. He was now the Station Commander of RAF Southend. Jox missed the bear-like former rugby player, who had become a surrogate father figure to his young subordinate, as so many of their friends and comrades had fallen during the meatgrinder summer of the Battle of Britain. Thompson had been by his side when His Majesty the King had decorated them both at Buckingham Palace, watched proudly by Alice and Thompson's chatty wife, Sylvia.

Since then, Squadron Leader Arthur J Biggar, an old India hand, had led them for five months, swiftly replaced by a Kiwi, Johnny McLean, who had lasted just six months before moving on too. Their latest Commanding Officer was George 'Wee Brotch' Brotchie, a veteran of France who had missed much of the Battle of Britain through injury, then serving as an instructor. He was a good-looking little man with a clipped moustache but was known to be a bit of a martinet with a chip on his shoulder for not being one of 'The Few'. His low kill count compared to some of the aces in the squadron also grated.

Since the Battle of Britain, the squadron had been reorganised into four sections of four aircraft each. Referred to as a 'finger four' squadron, on patrol now each section flew in a formation like the fingernails of the right hand, spread across a frontage of two hundred metres. This approach had been shamelessly copied from the Luftwaffe once the weakness of the RAF's previous tactics had become obvious. The routine losses of the aircraft at the rear, the exposed 'Tail-end Charlies', often the least experienced pilots, had provided damning evidence.

The Battle of Britain had certainly taken an atrocious toll on No.111 Squadron, like so many others, and the RAF was simply struggling to fill the gaps. This was despite the flurry of highly motivated foreign pilots from many invaded nations and Britain's Dominions that had flocked to the ranks.

The squadron's duty roster certainly looked very different. The 'old lags' included Jox, leading A Flight with trusty Flight Sergeant Cameron Glasgow as his wingman. Miroslav Mansfeld, an experienced Czech pilot, led the second element, with a replacement sergeant pilot under his tutelage.

Squadron Leader Brotchie's wingman was David Pritchard, Jox's best friend, who'd been through basic training with him. He was also to be Jox's best man at his forthcoming wedding. Red Section's second pair was led by *Chevalier* Olivier de Ghellinck, a Belgian aristocrat known as Ghillie, who had proven his deadly worth during the autumn's onslaught. He was also waiting for a replacement wingman.

Pete Simpson, the most senior of Thompson's surviving flight leaders, led B Flight. He was backed by South African Tom Wallace, a skilled ex-officer broken to Sergeant Pilot for disciplinary issues involving a girl. He was also recovering from wounds and steadily making his way from under the cloud of his court martial. Yellow Section's second element also needed replacements, as did Green Section.

From when Jox first joined the squadron at RAF Northolt in May 1940, only Pritchard, Glasgow, Simpson and the adjutant, Badger Robertson, were familiar faces. The Treble Ones had lost well over a hundred percent of its personnel in little more than twelve months. What was left of the hard-won combat experience lay in the hands of some shockingly young men, prematurely labelled as veterans. Only Badger Robertson, Cam Glasgow and Miro Mansfeld were older than twenty-three, and the adage that war is declared by old men, but it is the youth that fight and die, was never more apt.

# CHAPTER THREE

Jox really wasn't looking forward to the birthday party planned in his honour and was only going because Pritchard had put so much effort into it. It was also an opportunity for Alice to meet the new faces in the squadron.

She was on leave after her previous posting at RAF Kenley, which she'd left under a bit of a cloud following her engagement to Jox. There was also the fracas with a certain scar-faced Squadron Leader, the Kenley controller and her boss, who'd had his own designs on her. Jox had put a stop to that, but it had involved blows; certainly 'conduct unbecoming' between officers. Jox had escaped a court martial, receiving only a reprimand, thanks to Thompson and the fact that he had been about to be decorated for valour by His Majesty the King.

Alice's new posting was as a plotter at the Cabinet War Rooms in central London, an opportunity she was looking forward to, but which concerned Jox since she would be in the eye of the storm. The Blitz was continuing to take a devastating toll on the city and its exhausted inhabitants. She would brook no discussion, though, determined to do her part in the war effort. Jox couldn't fault her for that and as ever he loved her spirit, recognising that she was also trying to make up for her brother's tragic early demise. Previous generations of the Milnes had done their duty in the muddy hell of the trenches during the Great War, and in George's absence, she felt it was up to her to do her bit.

Earlier that day, Jox had left her at their boarding house in Montrose, as she made party arrangements with Pritchard. He was taking his role as their best man very seriously. Jox took a cargo flight up to RAF Dyce to rendezvous with two new replacements for Yellow Section, with orders to shuttle them back to Montrose in a trio of squadron Hurricanes that had just completed their two-hundred-hour services. He'd volunteered for the duty, knowing there wouldn't be many more opportunities to fly his trusty Hurricane, *Marguerite III*, once the Treble Ones had completed their conversion to a night fighter role on new Spitfire Mark Vs.

Upon landing, he caught up with his ground crew in the maintenance sheds at Dyce airfield, where they were finalising routine technical inspections before handing over their beloved Hurricanes. They were led by red-headed Flight Sergeant Barnes, a tall rigger responsible for his aircraft's airframe, with Dublin-born Corporal Black, whose domain was the aircraft's excellent Rolls-Royce Merlin engine and finally Leading Aircraftman Tech 'Smithy', his plumber, as the armourers were known. Together, they'd seen him through the Battle of Britain, saving his skin on more than one occasion, and he trusted them like few others.

'Don't worry, the old girl's doing fine, sir,' said Barnes. 'Just a few fissures in the wood-braced fuselage near the wing struts and a couple of worn-out fabric panels that need replacing. All sorted now. Blackie found an oil leak too, but then again· Blackie always finds one.'

The grimy Irishman grinned from his position, flat on his back beneath *Marguerite III*'s oily propellor housing.

'Smithy tells me that the rifling in one of the guns is worn out too. It's firing completely skew-whiff, so he's replaced it. No one's ever going to say the Treble One engineering crews handed over any lame ducks.'

'I don't think anyone would ever dare do that, Flight,' said Jox with real affection for his doughty rigger and crew chief. 'How are things going with the new Spits?'

'I'll be honest, sir, I'm not a great fan,' replied Barnes. Jox was surprised to hear this verdict when so many air personnel involved with Spitfires raved about them. 'For a start, I know they're faster than the Hurricane, with that all-metal aluminium monocoque business, but if one of them Snappers or a canny gunner in a Jerry bomber catches a piece of you, you'll know all about it; the metal of this bird will get all twisted up. The old Hurricane can take a lot more damage with its doped fabric over a wooden frame, without falling to bits.' The big rigger laughed. 'But who am I telling? You've taken on more than your fair share of hits, sir. What are we on now, *Marguerite II* or *III*?'

'This one's my third,' said Jox sheepishly. 'I guess the Spit will be number four.'

'Same paint job on the Spit, sir?'

'Yes please,' replied Jox. 'Maybe tone things down a bit for night fighting. Don't want a lot of bright colours giving me away when I'm trying to creep up on one of those big bastards.' He reached instinctively for the porcelain doll's arm that he kept in his tunic pocket. It had belonged to Marguerite, a little refugee he'd met and lost by the roadside in beleaguered France. Her name had been on his aircraft ever since.

'Righto, sir, but you know that's not really the problem with the Spit,' continued Barnes. 'During the Battle of Britain, we could turn around old *Marguerite* here in less than ten minutes, nine minutes max. That's a complete service, mind — re-arm, refuel and a new oxygen bottle rigged up, ready for you to get back up there. You remember we even slept in the blast pens to get things done as fast as we could.'

'Yes, and your ground crews paid the price,' said Jox, remembering the five killed when RAF Croydon was bombed on the 15th of August during the height of the battle.

Barnes stood mute for a moment, then shook his shaggy red head to chase away the memories. 'No, the problem is the fastest we've been able to turn around a Spitfire has been twenty-six minutes, almost three times longer than the Hurricane.'

'Strewth, I had no idea.'

'You know, sir, if we'd only had Spits and no Hurricanes, I really don't think we could have withstood the Jerries last summer,' said the thoughtful rigger. 'One of the warrant officers from the engineering branch told me that we only had about five hundred Hurricanes and three hundred Spitfires facing over two and half thousand Jerry aircraft. If the numbers of our fighters had been reversed, we wouldn't have stood a chance. We just couldn't have got enough up in the air to fight them off.'

'Well, we've got a lot more now and our job is to get Jerry off the backs of the civvy population, rather than protecting our shipping, radar stations and airfields like last summer. I'm certainly more invested in getting stuck into protecting our people than installations.'

'We're with you on that, sir,' replied Barnes. 'Blackie's got family in Kilburn, and Smithy's people live by the river down in Chelsea, which has taken a real pasting. They've been bombed out twice, but thankfully no one was killed.'

Jox cast his mind back to his first flight over London, flying from RAF Northolt, when he and Pritchard had just joined the squadron. He'd loved the freedom and privilege of seeing the capital from the sky, flying low over the length of the Thames. He recalled how obvious the enormous chimneys of the power stations at Battersea and Chelsea were on the skyline and could well imagine every bomber aiming for the giant landmarks.

'Kilburn?' he asked. 'Blackie, I thought you were from Dublin?'

'Born and bred, sir,' came the disembodied voice of the Irish fitter from under the engine canopy. 'But you'd be surprised at the number of Paddies down old Kilburn High Street. It's a regular O'Connell Street, so it is. We get everywhere, the Irish.'

Jox laughed. 'Yes, I suppose you do, and I for one am very grateful for that.'

'Right you are, sir, but you may live to regret that!' he added with a cackle. They all laughed. Blackie was a bit of a rascal and never far from trouble.

'I can't be hanging about just chin-wagging with you lot. I'm here to pick up two new chaps and fly these kites back to Montrose. When d'you think you'll have them ready, Flight?'

'Not long now, sir,' replied Barnes. 'Blackie's just closing up, and *Marguerite* will be fit for take-off in about twenty minutes.'

'I better go find those new chaps, then,' said Jox. 'Hope they're not too green. Seen any lost pilot-types?'

'I think I saw one young gentleman waiting at the squadron office. He looked like he was missing his mother,' said Barnes with a wink.

*Oh Christ*, thought Jox, remembering just how inexperienced he'd been when first reporting for duty to Badger Robertson. The equally young face of the impossibly keen 'Jugs' Carmel-Connolly also came to mind, all white-blond hair and rosy cheeks. The schoolboy rower had been shot out of the sky with four other No. 111 Squadron comrades, lost over the muddy waters of the Thames estuary on the 11th of August 1940. The Treble Ones' blackest day of the Battle of Britain.

Jox crossed the crisp, frosty grass that separated RAF Dyce's three concrete runways, overlapping like on a Union Jack. He'd often used the pattern to find his way to the airfield in the dubious weather common to northwest Aberdeen. It was cold and clear today, with some high-altitude cloud. Part of 13 Group, Dyce had been the Sector Operations Room with fighter squadrons providing cover from enemy raids from occupied Norway during the Battle of Britain. Now, it was mainly a photographic reconnaissance airbase, plus a training facility for anti-shipping operations for Coastal Command and convoy escort duties.

No. 111 Squadron still had an office on the airfield to manage the transfer of personnel and aircraft down to Montrose. Jox entered the timber dispersal hut, not recognising the corporal behind the desk, who jumped to his feet.

'Calm down, Corporal, no need for that,' said Jox. 'I'm here to pick up two replacement pilots for the Treble Ones. My orders are to fly them down in three Hurricanes that have just passed their inspections. My ground crew tell me they'll be ready for the off in about half an hour, so I want to get cracking. I've got a bit of a do tonight back at Montrose.'

A female voice called out from behind the back of the petrified-looking corporal, 'Good morning, Flying Officer McNabb. Lovely to see you again.' Jox recognised her as Maureen, who ran the squadron office for Robertson with a rod of steel, but also with kindness, as betrayed by her big brown eyes peering over a formidable black typewriter. He hadn't seen her since the squadron had moved north, but she'd been with them during the worst of times at RAF Croydon, when several of her WAAF colleagues had been killed during raids on the airfield.

'Hello Maureen. Lovely to see you back with us. How have you been? What have you been up to?' asked Jox.

'I'm well, thank you. Things have been a little tough. I was on compassionate leave for a bit with some family matters to sort out.'

'I'm sorry to hear that, Maureen,' said a concerned Jox. 'Was it a close family member?'

She nodded, trying to compose herself. 'Yes, I'm afraid it was,' she replied flatly. 'My entire family: both parents, grandmother, twin sisters and my baby brother. We lived in Thames Haven on Canvey Island. My dad worked for the oil refinery, with a house down the road.' Her soft Essex accent was cracking. 'The Jerries raided in September and with all that oil in them big tanks, the whole lot went up. Burned for days, they did.' She fell silent, visibly shaking as she told her story. 'My family were in the Anderson shelter in the garden, just like they were supposed to be. A wall of flame came rolling down the street and burned all the air up. They suffocated, tucked up in that shelter.'

'I'm so sorry, Maureen,' said Jox, crossing past the embarrassed corporal to give her a hug. 'Come on, have a seat. Corporal, get a cup of tea on the go!'

Maureen rubbed her tears away with the back of her hand, smudging her eye makeup in the process. 'My apologies, sir. I don't know what's come over me. I'm all right, truly I am. It's just that seeing you again has brought that time back.' She patted his hand. 'You was always one of my favourites. You don't want to be hearing about my woes.' She made an effort to appear more cheerful. 'I heard you're getting married. She's a very lucky girl.'

'Yes, to Alice. She's a WAAF too,' he replied, glad for the chance to change the subject. 'Actually, we're having a bit of a party for my birthday down in Montrose this evening. If you could make it…' He realised that she would have no way of getting there.

'That's awfully kind,' said Maureen, more brightly. 'I've only just arrived in Aberdeen myself, so I should probably stick around. I'll be moving down there with the rest of the squadron soon enough, once Jenkins here and I get the office packed up. I hear the weather's often pretty grim down there.'

'I'm afraid it is. Can make for some treacherous flying conditions.'

'All the more reason to stay here, but thank you, sir. Like I said, she's a lucky girl,' concluded Maureen. 'Now, what can I do for you?'

Grateful to be back on safer ground, Jox replied, 'I'm due to collect two replacement pilots and ferry them back to Montrose. Any sign of them?'

'Yes, well, one of them. Sergeant Pilot Broughton has been here for a while. I've sent him over to the mess hall to get a butty and a cup of tea. Should be back any minute.'

'What's he like?'

'I'd say he's quite young, nervous, but keen to do well. I think he was one of the cadets from around here. A local boy, kept calling me "Ma'am", which was nice but made me feel terribly old.'

'What's he look like?'

'Young, slim. About five eight. Dark hair, dark eyes and quite pale, I'd say.'

'What about the other chap? Any sign of him?'

Before she could answer, Corporal Jenkins piped up, 'He called while you were out back, Sergeant,' he said, with eyes darting between Jox and Maureen. What on earth was making the corporal so nervous? 'His shuttle from RAF Wick has been delayed by fog. He's going to be several hours late.'

'Oh damn. Well, I can't wait. He'll have to make his own way down to Montrose.'

'That shouldn't be a problem. He's an experienced flying officer like you, sir,' said the corporal. He stopped himself, worried he'd overstepped the mark. 'I ... I'll get that tea, then.' He bolted for the door.

'What the devil's wrong with that chap? Why is he so twitchy?' Jox asked.

'You make him nervous, sir.'

'Me? Why on earth is that?'

Maureen smiled. 'You're a big deal in this squadron, sir. There aren't many George Cross awardees around here. I don't suppose there are many as decorated as you in the whole of 13 Group. You're pretty special to us erks, you know, sir.'

'That's ridiculous. I'm just doing my job. I'm only nineteen, for Christ's sake.'

'Twenty, actually.'

Jox frowned. 'How do you know that?'

'You've just invited me to your birthday party, remember?'

The door of the timber hut housing the squadron office clattered open. A self-conscious sergeant pilot stepped through, a grey duffel bag slung over his shoulder.

'Ah, here he is,' said Maureen. 'Flying Officer McNabb, this is Sergeant Basil Broughton.'

The sergeant dropped his bag, came to attention and saluted. 'Sergeant Pilot Broughton reporting for duty, sir.'

Jox smiled and extended his hand. 'Welcome to the Treble Ones, Broughton. Please call me Jox.' They shook hands. 'They must have given you a nickname on your training course. What should we be calling you?'

'The boys often call me Bubbles, sir.'

'Bubbles? That's classic,' laughed Jox and was pleased to see that Maureen did too.

'Basil Broughton. B-B. Bubbles,' said the sergeant.

Jox liked him already.

They took off within half an hour, two stubby-winged, humpbacked Hurricanes rising through the cold air of grey Aberdeen. The weak wintery sun shone on the striped varnished surface of their doped canvas skins, flaring through the domed Perspex canopies. It was only a short hop to Montrose, but Jox had already warned Broughton that he wanted to have a final stooge about in *Marguerite III*. He told the young sergeant pilot to do his best to keep up and to only resort to the radio if they lost contact. The aerobatics that Jox planned were strictly unauthorised, but he reasoned they would provide a good opportunity to see what the kid had in his tank. When he said kid, he realised Broughton was just a couple of years younger than he was, and he was doing a good job keeping up after a textbook take-off. The sergeant was doing very well, in fact rather better than Jox had at his age.

All things considered, this young Broughton was looking very promising indeed.

# CHAPTER FOUR

Jox showered and shaved after his flight down from Dyce and put on his smartest uniform. It was questionable whether it was a wise thing to do, given the likelihood of high jinks in the mess tonight. He hoped the boys would keep a lid on it, not wishing to embarrass Jox before the prospective Mrs McNabb. He could count on Pritchard to keep things on track, but he also knew that George Brotchie, the new CO had an evil sense of humour that Jox had seen others suffer from.

Jox pushed through the mess doors anxiously and was greeted by a loud cheer from the group assembled at the bar. Most of the faces were familiar, others less so, either because they were new to the squadron or were simply hangers-on from other units, who sensed a good party in the making.

Front and centre came David Pritchard, his closest friend from their earliest training days and the many adventures since. He was limping, the result of a lost kneecap after being shot down over Dunkirk. He'd recovered sufficiently to get back into the cockpit, his motto being that if Douglas Bader could fly with no legs, he could bloody well fly with a single patella. Pritchard was Jox's rock and had been since the beginning of the war.

Invitations to tonight's celebration in the officer's mess had been extended to the squadron's NCOs, so Flight Sergeant Cameron Glasgow was standing beside Pritchard, observing Jox's evident embarrassment. Glasgow was his wingman and guardian angel in the sky, a role he'd taken over from his twin brother, Anthony, who'd been shot down and was reportedly a prisoner of war somewhere in Austria. The dour twins were supremely technical fliers and astute instructors. Cam Glasgow was the jollier of the two and had saved Jox's skin on more than one occasion, as indeed had his brother before him. They were like protective uncles, critical, but always supportive. Jox had been there for Glasgow when he'd lost his nerve after his twin had been reported missing, so he in turn was there for Jox in every circumstance.

With so many faces beaming at him, Jox didn't know where to look. He spotted de Ghellinck, the enigmatic Belgian aristocrat raising his glass. Beside him was the broad face of Sergeant Miroslav Mansfeld, nodding amiably. Jox was glad to see that young Broughton was with them, looking nervous surrounded by so many officers and grizzled veterans. Mansfeld was older than most of the others and an experienced combat pilot from Czechoslovakia. He was well placed to bring on his young number two, once Broughton had worked out Mansfeld's creative interpretation of the English language.

Also at the bar was Flight Lieutenant Pete Simpson, the squadron's second-in-command, raising his pipe in Jox's direction. He had kind blue eyes in a square face that betrayed the pain of seeing too many comrades lost over the last year. Simpson was the squadron's oldest hand, having joined the Treble Ones in November 1939, way before Jox or Pritchard had even arrived. He and the adjutant, Robertson, were now the 'keepers of the flame'.

With him was Tom Wallace from South Africa, and a dark-haired chap that Jox didn't recognise. His hair was slicked into a centre parting, his eyes darting as he took in the unfamiliar surroundings. On his right breast pocket Jox saw there was an unfamiliar pilot's badge and CZECHOSLOVAKIA patches on his shoulders.

'There you are!' bellowed Pritchard. 'We've been waiting.' He grabbed Jox and dragged him across the crowded room, depositing him before their diminutive commanding officer and the adjutant. Alice was standing between them, a rose between two thorns.

She looked up at him and smiled. His heart leapt at the sight of her, and it was as if someone had switched on the lights. In her arms she was holding a furry black and tan bundle. Unusually, in Alice's presence, it was this bundle that monopolised the attention of the two squadron leaders. It was a black puppy, which Jox instantly recognised as a Border Terrier, the breed that had the run of the Milnes' family farm.

'Happy birthday, my darling,' said Alice, amused by the confusion on Jox's face. 'This little fellow is your birthday present from the Milnes, from daddy and me. We've named him Georgie and Squadron Leader Brotchie has kindly accepted him as the new official mascot of the Treble Ones. Badger tells me his predecessor, Butcher the white Staffy, was sadly killed after Croydon was bombed last summer.'

'Poor thing missed his owner, Charlie Darwood, so terribly,' said Robertson. 'You remember, Jox, the damned thing howled for days.'

'I think it's a wonderful idea, Miss Milne,' interrupted Brotchie, taking the puppy from her. 'Your dog, of course, McNabb, but I hope you'll let the rest of us have a wee play now and again. Just the thing for squadron morale. What a capital idea, Miss Milne, or should I call you Mrs McNabb? Which do you prefer?'

'I prefer Section Officer Milne, sir, but amongst friends please call me Alice, just Alice.'

'Er ... quite right,' spluttered Brotchie.

'And now I think it's time for wee Georgie to meet his daddy, don't you, sir?'

'What? Yes, of course.' He handed the puppy somewhat reluctantly to Jox, and the floppy mutt, all bright eyes, bristly face, and dark paws, licked his new parent's nose.

'He likes you,' said Alice, with a catch in her voice. 'My brother always had a nose for good fellows, and so does he. Say something, Jox. Tell me you like him, at least.'

Jox peered into the shining gaze of the terrier puppy, wriggling in his grasp and giving a baby bark. 'Like him? I love him, but I can tell he's going to be a handful.'

Little Georgie escaped Jox's embrace and began sniffing, slipping between the feet around him. Once he'd made his mind up, he cocked his leg and promptly piddled on the CO's highly burnished black lace-ups. As the puddle spread across the parquet, several 'dashing' airmen leapt aside.

Brotchie let out a bellowing laugh. 'McNabb! Your dog has just pissed on me. You may be his father, but it appears I'm the anointed one.'

Jox scooped up the wayward mutt, apologising profusely. The CO was taking it with remarkably good grace, as the squadron roared with laughter. Entirely unintentionally, Georgie had already raised the morale of the assembled group, giving the new and old faces something to laugh about. Handing the dog to Pritchard, Jox said, 'Here, hold the pooch for a second. Pete Simpson's calling me over.'

'Why am I the one left holding the baby?' asked Pritchard.

'Privilege of being the best man, old chum,' replied Jox with a wink.

Seeing him approach, Simpson put his hand on the shoulder of the thin-faced Czech officer standing beside him.

'Jox, let me introduce Pilot Officer Otmar Kucera. He's joined us from No. 6 Ops Training Unit to be my new Yellow Three.'

The Czech officer's serious expression was transformed by his smile, revealing straight white teeth. He bowed his head in the continental way and clicked his heels.

'Jox McNabb, Blue One. Glad to have you join us, Ot…Was it Otmar?'

'Otmar Kucera, sir.'

'Have you met Miro? He's Czech and my Blue Three.'

'Yes, I've met Miroslav, but you know it is embarrassing. He was years ahead of me at the Prostějov Military Aviation Academy. A very gifted test pilot attached to Czech Air Force General Staff. It is not correct that he should only be a sergeant and I am lieutenant, how you say, pilot officer? This should not be.'

'You don't need to worry; he won't stay a sergeant for long. He's clearly very experienced, and I'm sure he will be commissioned soon. I understand he's experienced at night fighting, so that'll be useful as we convert. We've given him a new wingman to train, so let's see how he gets on.'

'It will be his honour. He is a proud Czech pilot and excellent instructor.'

'So tell me, Otmar, how did you make it all the way from Czechoslovakia? I'm sure it must be quite a story.'

'Yes, a story, but not unique,' replied Kucera, a shadow crossing his handsome face.

'I'd love to hear it, but only if you want to tell it,' said Jox. 'No obligation.'

'Of course, obligation. You are a superior officer and your country gave me the opportunity to fight invaders of my country. Anything you order; my duty is to obey.'

'I admire your motivation, Otmar, but we take things a little more casually in this squadron. You'll get used to it. We fight better as friends, rather than because of orders and hierarchies.'

'Yes, we are friends. This is good. Friends and then brothers to kill many Nazis,' said Kucera enthusiastically. 'My story is not so unusual. After German occupation, I escaped on Christmas almost one year ago. I crossed many countries to reach Lebanon. There I caught a ship to France to join the Czech Air Force at Agde near Montpelier. I trained on a French fighter at Bordeaux-Merignac, but then France fell too and so I caught another ship to come to England. I went to the Czech depot at RAF Cosford, and they sent me to 6 OTU Sutton Bridge, where I learned to fly Hurricanes. Now, I have come to No. 111 Squadron to learn to fly Spitfires and can kill some Nazis now, yes?'

Simpson laughed. 'See how keen these Czech pilots are to get stuck in? Real firebreathers, every one of them. I'd be quaking in my boots if I was Jerry. Say, what's your new chap like, Jox? Seems rather young in comparison.'

'I'm afraid so. Would you believe he wants to be called Bubbles? An excellent technical flyer, though. When I came down from Dyce with him, he matched me move for move. Impressive, to tell you the truth. Miro will soon get him up to speed.'

The glass double doors to the bar clattered open with a loud bang, revealing a short red-headed officer with a large nose and a lopsided grin. He dropped his bags with a second clatter, ensuring that every conversation in the room stopped. Unworried by the spectacle he was creating, he bellowed, 'What's a man got to do to get a bloody drink in this dump?'

From his red and somewhat bleary eyes, it was clear the grinning flying officer had already had a few. Jox and Pritchard stared, dumbfounded. Standing there was none other than Morgan Chalmers. Good old Mogs, their training mate and favourite rascal, and amongst them all, the one who'd taken George Milne's death the hardest.

'Who the devil is that?' thundered Brotchie. 'He's an absolute disgrace.'

'That, my dear chap, is your new Green Section leader, Flying Officer Morgan Chalmers,' said Badger Robertson wryly. 'He was due in earlier with Jox but was delayed by fog. He's clearly spent the time in the bar. He's transferring from No. 504 Squadron, out of RAF Wick. Volunteered to join us, apparently. Can't blame him, bloody freezing up there. Has a good performance report and a solid couple of kills under his belt. A few discipline issues. Spirited, I'd say, and as you can see, he likes a tipple. Know the feeling. Whose round is it?'

Distracted by the question, the frowning CO was startled when Alice shrieked and ran into the open arms of Chalmers, who roared his delight. Jox and Pritchard grinned at how happy she was to see her late brother's best friend. Jox knew she and Chalmers had been corresponding since George's death, finding comfort in sharing their grief.

Chalmers hadn't had quite so active a war as the pair of them, stationed way to the north near John O' Groats. He'd also been deeply affected by the accidental death of another of their training mates at Montrose, Aussie Roy 'Digger' Callandar who was posted to Wick with Chalmers after they'd received their pilot wings. They'd become close after George's death and together had patrolled the cliffs and turbulent slate-grey waters of the northern coastline, on the lookout for enemy shipping, U-boats, and long-range reconnaissance aircraft.

On a solo flight in bad weather, Digger had flown into a mountain and Chalmers blamed himself for not being there. However much it was argued that if he had been, he'd probably have hit the hillside too, Chalmers felt responsible for the death of his friend. Jox had first heard this from Moose, another Montrose course mate, currently with No. 1 Squadron of the Royal Canadian Air Force at RAF Prestwick.

Alice had since shown Jox long, rambling letters, written by Chalmers when clearly worse for wear, telling of his solitary life with No. 504 Squadron. He'd avoided befriending anyone, lest he bring them misfortune. It would later emerge that it was Alice who'd encouraged him to apply for a transfer to the Treble Ones. Desperate for replacements, it was a formality to get the posting approved.

'Morgan-bloody-Chalmers! You're a sight for sore eyes. What are you doing here?' said an excited Pritchard.

'Pritch! Jox! Hello boys. Here comes trouble. I'm here to show you girls how it's really done.' Chalmers was drunk, but not so much that he did not recognise the two squadron leaders, one scowling and the other smiling benignly. He came to attention and saluted. 'Flying Officer Morgan Chalmers reporting for duty, sirs,' he slurred. 'My apologies for my late arrival.'

Robertson was chuckling as Brotchie bristled. Brotchie and Chalmers were about the same size, pocket versions of the other airmen in the bar, who were all watching to see how this particular farce would unfold.

'This is neither the time nor place to report for duty, Chalmers,' said the CO icily. 'It is after hours, and I will not abide talking shop in the mess. Tomorrow morning, you will report to me properly, and I advise you to be immaculate and on the ball. My first impression of you has hardly been favourable. Let me advise you to keep well out of my sight until then. It is only because McNabb and Pritchard appear to hold you in high esteem, and because Miss Milne is clearly fond of you, that I am giving you the benefit of the doubt. Do not disappoint me.'

# CHAPTER FIVE

It took a week for things to settle down and for Mogs Chalmers to make amends for his calamitous arrival at the squadron.

He buckled down, keen to impress, and soon had Green Section running smoothly. By then, he had also managed to get the CO on side by finding two replacements, currently supernumerary to their squadron and desperate for some action.

Two brawny Aussies duly reported to RAF Montrose with their sunny Antipodean dispositions, can-do attitudes and a healthy disdain for Pommy grub and hierarchies. Perhaps predictably, one was nicknamed 'Kanga' and the other 'Roo', but they couldn't have been more different from one another.

Chalmers knew them as friends of Digger Callendar, who'd taken the boat ride to Blighty with them, answering the call of the mother country in her hour of need. Both were attached to No. 18 Group, Coastal Command at RAF Wick, flying anti-submarine patrols in open-cockpit Fairey Swordfish torpedo bombers. A year spent endlessly patrolling the icy grey waters and finding a grand total of zero U-boats had left them bored and restless, not to mention rigid with the cold. When offered the opportunity to see some real action with a posting near metropolitan London, they both jumped at it.

Shane 'Kanga' Reeves was from Cairns in Queensland and was already an experienced seaplane pilot, ferrying supplies between the tropical islands of the Daintree Channel. He loved the sea, fishing and open-water diving, quickly earning a reputation as a madman amongst the crofting Highlanders, who saw him swimming with the seals off the cliffs of the Duncansby Stacks. Tall, rugged, and wind-chapped, he had big hands, big feet, and a red hooked nose. Oozing self-confidence, his ready laugh made him popular with the other men very quickly.

Rupert 'Roo' James was completely different. He was from the dry red interior of Australia, from a sheep station where livestock outnumbered people several thousand-fold. Quietly spoken, unusual amongst Aussies, he was also an experienced pilot. 'Without a kite, you're totally isolated in the desert. You might as well be living on Mars,' he'd explained.

He had a head of curly dark hair, a broad nose and a certain quiet spirituality. He was also very wealthy. His English emigrant father owned the vast station, encompassing hundreds of square miles and many thousands of sheep. In a wartime market desperate for meat and wool, the family were making a fortune. As different as they were, though, the two Aussies were very close 'fair dinkum' mates.

Chalmers was an experienced Hurricane pilot, but his two recruits had only trained as torpedo dive bombers. Officially they were both still sailors, wearing the dark blue of the Royal Australian Navy Fleet Air Arm. Under Chalmers' tutelage, the pair, along with the other recent arrivals, Broughton and Kucera, embarked on an intensive programme of familiarisation, overseen by squadron 2i/c Pete Simpson.

The first of six brand-new Spitfire Mark Vs were delivered by a gaggle of pretty ATA ferry pilots, who caused quite a sensation when they popped into the officer's mess for lunch. The distinctive purr of Merlin engines became more commonplace, as the sleek fighters wheeled overhead like crows, buffeted by powerful gusts from the North Sea. For Chalmers, the bleak landscape held dark memories of when George Milne's Harvard had crashed onto the same concrete runway, just moments after they'd spoken on the R/T.

He worked hard to push those thoughts from his mind, concentrating on demonstrating the manoeuvres he required of his pilots and giving terse instructions as he took them through their paces. Both he and Simpson agreed that young Broughton was the best of the bunch, confirming Jox's high opinion of him. He just needed to prove he had the killer instinct needed to survive aerial combat.

Keen to test them, Brotchie and wingman Pritchard took on the role of enemy interceptors, flashing without warning between the matt black Spitfires in their bulkier Hurricanes. From the ground, the contest between the fragile-looking Spitfires and the thundering broad-shouldered Hurricanes hardly seemed fair. Both were about the same length, and it was generally accepted that the Hurricanes were slower, but not in the hands of veteran pilots like Brotchie and Pritch.

With childish relish, the CO would nip behind, below or above one of the hapless newbies, shouting into the R/T, 'Bang-bang-bang, you're dead. Drop out of the formation and head for the showers.'

On one occasion, flying alongside, Jox watched as the CO closed in on Broughton's aircraft. The youngster applied a good deal of right rudder, then deftly skidded aside from the pursuing Hurricane. Moving too fast to react, his pursuer overshot, and Broughton swung back, smartly positioning himself on Brotchie's tail. Jox heard Broughton's reedy voice on the R/T radio.

'Bang-bang, you're dead. Time for the showers, sir.'

It was the smartest piece of air combat manoeuvring that Jox had seen in a long while.

After their rather rowdy birthday party, Alice and Jox spent the weekend at a boarding house in Montrose, scandalising the landlady as they weren't married. The only thing that drove them from the covers was hunger and wee Georgie's whining when he needed a walk.

They found a little teashop, serving fine 'Full Scottish' breakfasts, which were loaded with Arbroath smokies, black pudding, and haggis. For tea, there were also excellent 'fish suppers' fresh from the churning North Sea. Food rationing didn't appear to have reached this far north, but that was probably because all the produce came from within a mile of Montrose.

They took long walks on the blisteringly cold beach, made less grim by the fact that they were together. They even found an abandoned fishermen's bothy, where they made love, warming their frozen bodies by the fire, thrilled by the delicious threat of getting caught.

Georgie rarely left their side for very long, acting as a sort of puppy chaperone vainly protecting their virtue. They had to be careful, though, as unobserved he was quite capable of wandering off beyond the barbed wire and warning signs, onto parts of the beach mined against the possibility of invasion from Norway. Every now and then, there was a detonation as some hapless seal or herring gull set one off, leaving soggy carcasses that were quickly feasted upon by their rapacious fellows.

Lying in the dunes, they watched the gulls wheel above the sands, dicing with death every time they landed. There were two varieties: the small, swift ones with black heads and the large, mean-looking herring gulls with cruel yellow eyes. The little ones were noisy and bold, seemingly laughing at their larger cousins as they slipped and dived amongst them. The large ones, white with two-tone grey backs and yellow paddled feet, each had a bright red spot on their yellow beaks. The target, according to Alice, for their drab-coloured young demanding regurgitated fish.

Watching the gulls reminded Jox of last summer. Big, arrogant and cruel, the herring gulls were the Jerries, and their smaller cousins were the Hurricanes and Spits that had harried and tormented the invaders. Just like back then, for the gulls' violence and death were ever-present.

Disturbed by his dark musings, ornithology had lost its appeal for Jox and he got to his feet. He scooped Georgie up, hoping the pup's affection might chase the demons away. He smiled to reassure Alice. 'I'm just feeling chilly. I'll need a warm-up back at the house.'

She took his hand and smiled coquettishly. Glancing back at the birds, he knew he would never see gulls in any other way; another small pleasure dashed by the war.

Alice's leave came to an end, and Jox saw her off at Montrose station on her long rail journey south.

She was reporting for duty the following week at the War Rooms near Whitehall. She was very excited about the task and the possibility that Prime Minister Churchill might be following operations that she was tracking. It was thrilling to think that Mr Churchill and the war cabinet might be making decisions based on her work.

Jox was due to come down to London in a few weeks' time. He would arrive before Christmas and would stay on until after New Year. Alice had a plan to prove that Hogmanay could be spent outside Scotland and could be every bit as fun in London. Jox was unconvinced but was up for the challenge.

In the meantime, he was left with a long list of dos and don'ts relating to Georgie and was made to promise umpteen times to take good care of the pup.

'You will look after him, won't you?' Alice asked through the rail carriage window. Jox was on the platform, wreathed with steam from the puffing locomotive about to pull away. The pup wriggled, unsettled by all the strange noises and smells.

'I will, I promise,' replied Jox. 'I'll even remember to feed him, once in a while.'

'You bleeding better, you rotter.'

He laughed, knowing she knew that he loved the pup dearly. Alice wanted to leave something of herself with him, so he had something to be responsible for. That way, she felt he wouldn't take so many chances when flying. He was no longer alone; someone depended on him and was waiting for his return every day.

'That counts as much for me as for wee Georgie,' she declared as the shrill whistle blew, and the train juddered forward. Jox stretched to the open window, and they kissed as Georgie whined. The moving train split them apart.

'Write to me!' Jox called. 'Send me the address of where you end up. Please be careful; you're in more danger in London than I am up here in the wilds. I'll see you in a few weeks. I love you!'

Georgie started barking at what he saw as a new game, drowning out Alice's reply as the train gathered speed.

Jox spent the rest of the week chasing the delivery of the next batch of Spitfires. The first six had already been allocated to pilots and ground crews. His aircraft was being given the once-over by Flight Sergeant Barnes and his crew up at RAF Dyce and would then be sprayed to his specifications. In the meantime, he'd been tasked by Badger Robertson to find out where the squadron's three final replacements had been waylaid.

Coming up from the south was newly qualified Pilot Officer Solomon Cohen, the son of Jewish refugees from Leipzig who'd escaped Nazi oppression in the thirties. He'd learned to fly with the University of London Air Squadron and then at No.7 OTU at RAF Hawarden in Wales.

He was due to arrive with a more experienced Flying Officer Michael Longstaffe, who'd once been a tobacco merchant and weekend aviator whilst living amongst the expatriate community of the Shanghai International Settlement. He'd quit China after the bloody civil war and Japanese atrocities he'd witnessed, and his personnel file spoke of being keen to serve in a 'clean war' back in England. Jox wasn't convinced that could be accommodated, but was grateful for another experienced pilot, rather than a gormless child like he'd been at the beginning of the war.

Later in the week, Jox received a telephone call confirming the 'final piece of his puzzle' was in place. Axel Fisken was from Norway and had served his country in a Gloster Gladiator throughout the Norwegian campaign. He'd then joined the resistance and had been briefly captured, but had managed to escape the country when the exiled King had ordered his loyal troops to regroup in the United Kingdom. According to his file, he'd lost family during the invasion and two fingers to torture. Revenge was his motivation for joining the squadron, and with him, Jox's 'grid' was complete. It occurred to him that these three men had much sounder reasons to fight than he ever did when he joined the Treble Ones.

Off-duty, Jox took long walks on the beach with Georgie and occasionally took his old Hurricane *Marguerite* out for a few final flights. He flew with Cam Glasgow, or else Pritchard, but found solo forays more to his liking. It was as if he wanted to say farewell to the old girl, this Hurricane that had seen him through so much. It wasn't entirely true, of course, given her first predecessor ditched off Dunkirk and her second was eviscerated by an unknown German Me 110 ace, ending up pranged on some Kentish cliff. It reminded him of the adage of a woodsman's favourite axe: the head was replaced a dozen times and the shaft even more, but it was still his favourite old axe.

Occasionally, when flying solo, Jox would sneak Georgie into the cockpit with him. The duty ground crew he was allocated in the absence of his own weren't too bothered and enjoyed seeing the puppy. When strapped into his lap, the warmth of Jox's legs soon lulled Georgie to sleep, as long as Jox didn't pull too many aerobatics.

After one particular sortie to Fife and back, Jox landed to find Badger Robertson armed with his latest toy, a Box Brownie camera. He was taking snaps of anything that stood still long enough. Initially, Jox was concerned he would get a telling-off from the adjutant, but instead Robertson was delighted to have something new to capture. He later let Jox have a few copies, including a portrait of a smiling Jox in the cockpit with Georgie on his lap. The picture also captured the row of flowers stencilled along the cockpit edge and the name of the French girl painted on the Hurricane's nose. Jox posted a print to Alice with his first letter, providing proof that 'the little blighter is alive and well in my care'. On the back he scribbled, 'Self, Georgie and Marguerite'.

After their impromptu photographic session, Robertson asked if Jox was free for lunch. He'd been invited by the station commander but didn't fancy going on his own.

'You trained here, didn't you?'

'That's right,' replied Jox. 'No. 12 flying course at No. 8 Flight Training School. Pritch, Mogs and I were all on the same course. As was my fiancée's brother.'

'Excellent, then you're just the man.'

'I'm not following you.'

'This is all rather tiresome, but the lunch is to mark my cousin's retirement. He's Wing Commander Robertson, the station commander. You'll remember him, and I'm sure he'll be pleased to see you.'

Jox recalled the resemblance of the cousins when he'd first met Robertson.

'Well, I hope he remembers me,' said Jox. 'He must have seen hundreds of pilots passing through. He certainly made a big impact on me, when he pinned on my wings and said, "You'll do, McNabb."'

'That sounds like Bill, all right. Man of few words. Always a bit of a stuffed shirt when we were younger. Still, you might enjoy the lunch. He's gathered the great and the good together to prove to himself that he's contributed to the service by training men rather than being in the fighting. A few ex-students that have become aces are coming to tell their stories, so it might be amusing. I'm told Ginger Neil and Paddy Finucane were asked but are unavailable.'

'That's a shame, I know them both. On our course too, under Brian Carbury.'

'Carbury! That's the fellow who's coming,' exclaimed Robertson. 'Quite a big noise, I hear. My cousin tells me he got the DFC and Bar during the Battle of Britain, with No. 603

(City of Edinburgh), who he also trained. He's got fifteen enemy aircraft destroyed, two shared, two probables and five damaged to his name. That's practically a cricket score. Busy chap, I'd say, one of only four "aces in a day".'

'I'd be very pleased to see him. Carbury and my instructor Flight Sergeant Waugh are really the men that got me my flying badge. I'll always be grateful to them.'

'Come to think of it, I'm surprised Cousin Bill didn't invite you in the first place. Your George Cross and DFC punches higher than a DFC and Bar.'

'Oh, I don't know about that. In my book, Carbury certainly deserves the plaudits. Your cousin probably doesn't even know I'm back at Montrose. I've only been here a few weeks.'

'Well, maybe,' said Robertson. 'Anyway, you're coming. Let's hope Bill's table is better than his memory, because I'm bringing the Treble Ones' finest with me.'

'I hardly think I'm the finest,' spluttered Jox.

'I wasn't talking about you,' chuckled Robertson. 'I was talking about wee Georgie.'

# CHAPTER SIX

The women of the Air Transport Auxiliary were back and causing quite a stir, but this time not because of their pencilled-in stocking seams or the rouge on their pouting lips. They were delivering the second half dozen Spitfire Mark VBs to No. 111 Squadron and doing it in fine style.

It was a rare blue-skyed midwinter's day at the windswept Montrose aerodrome. For once, though, it was sunny, the perfect antidote to the endless dreich days so common during winter in this part of Scotland. The ATA pilots came in low over the choppy sea in two pristine Vic formations, spaced perfectly, both horizontally and vertically, as if on revue at an air show. The sleek Spitfires were in their black night fighter livery, incongruous in the bright blue maritime sky, approaching like dark raptors over a flock of white seabirds.

With approval from the tower they banked in unison, carefully manoeuvring into pairs and taking a curved approach to compensate for the Spits' poor forward visibility. Lining up to land on the easternmost of the aerodrome's crossed runways, the throb of six Merlin engines provided a base note to the high-pitched whirring of undercarriages lowering before locking with a reassuring 'clunk' moments before the skid of rubber on concrete.

The first two to touch down were JU-E, the nearest the squadron identifiers could get to George or Joe for the CO, then Jox's trusty JU-X, also discreetly emblazoned with her new name *Marguerite IV*. The long-nosed aircraft wheeled towards the parking aprons indicated by the 'Follow Me' ground crews waving flags. As their propellers slowed, the blades were devoid of the usual yellow tips due to their night fighter colours. Parked in a single dramatic line, the women powered their engines down. One wayward Merlin coughed in defiance, flaring a blast of flame from the exhaust stubs that lined its long nose. There was no doubting why they were called Spitfires.

The clear Perspex hoods of the aircraft canopies sparkled in the winter sun as the ATA ladies pulled them back, then dropped the side hatches. They were helped from the narrow confines of the cockpits by overattentive ground crews, rather more helpful than they usually were. The lady pilots' slim figures were eminently better suited to the confines of the aircraft cockpits than the large lumpy men that would soon be inheriting them. As if part of some post-flight drill, the six ATA pilots removed their leather flying helmets, oxygen masks and parachutes, quickly checking their hair in compact mirrors before applying a coating of fresh lipstick. They carefully positioned their dark blue forage caps at a jaunty angle on permed hair, before sallying forth across the field to meet their admiring audience.

The Spitfires ticked as they cooled in the chilly air, in spite of the bright sunshine overhead. Ground crews swarmed over them, carrying out post-flight checks, securing armament, refuelling, and wiping down the canopies. Jox took the opportunity to take a closer look at his new steed. He circled *Marguerite IV* very slowly, already finding comfort in the familiar lettering and markings that she bore. He marvelled at the sleek aerodynamic lines of the all-metal monocoque fuselage, realising there wasn't a straight line to be seen anywhere on the aircraft. It was entirely shaped by wind and airflow, with a Rolls-Royce supercharged Merlin engine delivering over one thousand horsepower, ensuring its pre-war

Schneider Trophy-winning performance. The sleek metal skin of the fluid aircraft made its fabric-covered predecessors seem prehistoric, despite Staff Sergeant Barnes's reservations about its ability to absorb damage and the time it took to turn around in the heat of battle.

Jox noted that the spatted undercarriage wheels were closer together than on the Hurricane, explaining why the Spitfire had a reputation for ending up on its nose when landing on bumpy ground. This worried Jox a little, given their new night fighter role which would often have them landing in poor light conditions. There may be trouble ahead on that account. The fact that he'd already tipped his own Hurricane onto its nose, trying to land at Kenley during a raid last summer was not forgotten. But the bomb craters in the runway hadn't exactly helped.

He indicated to the duty rigger that this one was his and asked if he could have a quick look around the cockpit. He climbed up the side of the aircraft using the handy foothold, a useful design feature missing in the Hurricane. He for one appreciated it, given that he wasn't exactly the tallest of fellows. Nevertheless, he knew that his size would be an advantage in this cockpit, as he'd heard there wasn't much room in there.

Ducking his head behind the instrument panel, he could see down the aircraft's long nose, recognising the challenge that the large blind spot would pose. For all the advantages that this reputedly fastest single-engine fighter in the service had, it appeared the winged goddess had some fairly sizeable clay feet to contend with too. Jox would be taking his first flight the following morning and would find out for himself soon enough. He felt a confusing mix of schoolboy excitement, a veteran pilot's professional curiosity with anxious trepidation and no little dread.

The next morning, flying conditions couldn't have been more different. Overnight, a table of low-level grey cloud had rolled in from the sea. For once, no brisk wind had driven it off and below the cloud, the air was unusually still, the cover acting like a protective lid over the aerodrome. Above the cloud it would doubtless still be blowy, and Jox was looking forward to testing his new aircraft in that stiff wind, as well as trying some aerobatics in the bright blue yonder.

Approaching the aircraft, he nodded to the rigger he'd seen yesterday. She was fuelled and armed, and he advised Jox to keep an eye on the gauge as the Spit only had an eighty-five-gallon fuel tank and a smaller range than the Hurricane. Jox ran his hands over the aircraft, checking the flaps and the resistance of the cables, as he went through his pre-flight inspection routine. She was cold, slight and rather tinny as his fingers glided over the metal skin and sunken rivets.

Circling the aircraft, he noted her narrow retractable undercarriage, the roominess of the domed cockpit hood, the four stubby wing-mounted guns and the larger pair of 20mm cannons projecting like twin proboscises from the leading edge of either wing. A three-propellered spinner loomed above the nacelle of her powerful Merlin engine with a large, ducted radiator scoop incised into the fuselage under the shoulder of the starboard wing. He crouched and ran a hand over the bulges on the undersides of the wings, accommodating the twin sixty-round drum magazines for the 20mm cannons. They reminded Jox of Remora suckerfish he'd once seen in a picture book at school, who attached themselves beneath sharks, large marine animals, and even ocean-going ships. It was a disturbing image, somehow sinister and pregnant with menace.

With the unnamed rigger's help, Jox climbed into the narrow cockpit, slotting the low-slung parachute hanging from his straps into the bucket seat to form a cushion to sit on. It was certainly snugger in here than in the Hurricane.

At Wing Commander Robertson's luncheon, when Jox had caught up with his former instructor, Brian Carbury, they'd talked at length about the Spitfire. His view was that a pilot didn't so much strap himself into this aircraft, rather he put it on like some large knapsack. Jox wasn't entirely convinced by the imagery, preferring the idea of strapping on wings, but he agreed that it was certainly a tight fit.

He connected the oxygen tube to his mask and plugged the jack for the R/T into the panel. The voice of Montrose tower came alive in his ears. Glancing down at the rigger, he was now accompanied by a flight mechanic manning a trolley accumulator. He gave them the thumbs-up, and the latter plugged the cable into the flap in the engine cowling to get the engine started. He gave it a few revs while somewhat disconcertingly, the rigger lay across the tailplane to hold it down. Once he had tower clearance, Jox taxied to the centre of the runway. He was an experienced pilot, but flying a Spit for the first time was still an intimidating experience. Twin-seater training Spitfires didn't exist, so all trainees, whether experienced or not, were entirely on their own, right from the outset.

Carbury had warned him about the aircraft's poor forward visibility, but also the extreme sensitivity of the controls and the tendency for the powerful torque of the engine to pull the aircraft off its flight line. He'd cautioned Jox about the radiator's propensity to boil over if the engine was overworked. When landing after a flight, for example, it was important not to lower the undercarriage too early, since it created wind resistance that strained an already hot engine. This could lead the ethylene-glycol in the radiator to boil over, spouting a white cloud over the canopy at the most crucial stage of the landing approach. Getting your aircraft down and the engine switched off was then imperative to avoid complete engine seizure.

And yet, despite all his reservations, Carbury was clearly infatuated with the aircraft and had become a master with it, as proven in spades by his many plaudits, achievements, and decorations. Jox had found him a bit distracted at the lunch, pleased to see his erstwhile pupil, but brooding darkly about 'having been put out to pasture'.

They'd discussed his remarkable run of fortune: five victories in a day, seven in a week; awarded the DFC in September and the Bar a month later. He'd been wounded in the foot and was still using a stick, but he expected to return to duties as an instructor quite soon.

'Not much chance of action for me, I'm afraid. I've probably rubbed too many people up the wrong way. Not enough of "an officer and gentleman" for the powers that be, I suppose. You know, I'm just a farm boy from Wellington who got rather good at flying a Spitfire.'

When they parted, they promised to keep in touch and Carbury asked Jox if he'd be happy to be a character witness if he ever needed one. It struck Jox as a rather odd thing to ask, given that to his mind there was no finer pilot out there than Flying Officer Brian Carbury, DFC and Bar.

Jox accelerated down the runway into the lightest of sea breezes. His wheels drummed on the concrete until the sound was replaced by whistling, as they spun in the cold air. The guage on his dashboard indicated a take-off angle of eleven degrees as the Spitfire rose gracefully. Climbing at two hundred miles per hour, Jox began pumping the long handle to the right of the cockpit to retract the undercarriage. With his right hand pumping and the left still on the control column, the aircraft wobbled in a characteristic porpoising that was apparently typical of novice Spitfire pilots. Jox gave himself a bit of a fright when he realised the aircraft was dipping when it should have been rising, so he slowed his pumping to a gentler rhythm.

Once the undercarriage indicator went from green to red, he glanced across to the fail-safe system on the wing tips where two steel indicator rods were in the down position, confirming that the undercarriage was up. Jox pulled back on the control column and the aircraft soared like a summer swallow.

With growing confidence, he began taking her through her paces, rolling, banking, and diving, then climbing high to execute a stall turn. She was spectacularly responsive and ever hungrier for greater speed and tighter manoeuvring. He took up the challenge and climbed high above the grey cloud, then fell into a steep dive from high altitude. Reaching the cloud line, the air-speed indicator passed four hundred miles per hour. Without realising it, he was travelling faster than he ever had before. Having scared himself enough, he pulled up and levelled off.

Flying in his trusty Hurricane, Jox had always felt like he was wearing a clumsy suit of protective armour. Now, it was like he'd been released to fight light, free and unfettered. It was almost as if the aircraft was flying him, rather than the other way around. The astonishing sensitivity was liberating but also utterly unforgiving. The slightest touch of the rudder, elevator or trimmer and the Spitfire leapt in eager response. You needed good muscles to haul the old Hurricane through manoeuvres, but with the Spit it was like he only needed to think of a movement for it to react.

He'd often heard the analogy of the Spitfire being the swift greyhound, compared to the stoic Hurricane, the solid dependable bulldog. Soaring through the clouds at a bewildering speed, he at first reluctantly, but then with growing exhilaration could see the truth in the comparison.

The sudden changes of speed and direction started to take their toll. To avoid blacking out Jox gulped air and bore down against the positive G, pulling the stick back hard and feeling the centrifugal force pressing down and squashing him to the bottom of his bucket seat. The harder he pulled, the heavier he felt it bearing down until he could move neither his hands nor feet due to the sensation of immense weight. Blood was being forced from his optic nerve, taking him to the edge of blackout, before he recovered control. It had been a while since he had exposed his body to these forces, and he could feel his guts complaining. He would undoubtedly need the loo as soon as he landed. The squadron medical officer had once told him that suffering from piles, brought on by excessive G-force exposure, was a common ailment amongst veteran fighter pilots. Not a prospect typically associated with dashing aces, nor one he particularly looked forward to.

The aircraft was flying level, just above the flat cloud base, a continuous sheep-wool grey. Jox remembered another aspect of the Spitfire that Carbury had warned him about. Holding the aircraft straight and at the correct angle of approach when landing was a challenge in the Spitfire, given its long nose and significant blind spot. He advised experimenting with angles, skidding sideways to get sneak forward views during practice landings. Jox used the flat surface of the clouds as a stand-in for the runways and grassy fields he would undoubtedly be called to land on in the future. After several goes, he was confident that he had mastered what was needed and was ready to give it a go for real. His fuel level was getting low in any case, and he really could do with getting to the loo.

Once through the clouds, he navigated homewards, spotting the familiar sock-shaped perimeter of the airfield. He contacted the tower for permission to land, then took a curved approach to the landing strip. He began pumping the undercarriage down until the green dash light blinked on. He opened up the radiator to keep the glycol temperature down, switching the airscrew to a finer pitch, and applied flaps. Wind resistance was pushing against the undercarriage, and the engine temperature gauge was rising as it worked harder. He landed with a small bump on the Spitfire's narrow-set wheels, fishtailing to maximise the friction to slow down. Once safely on the deck and confident that he was fully in control, he exhaled with quiet relief.

'That wasn't too bad,' he muttered. He wasn't a complete convert but had to admit he'd enjoyed stooging around in the nippy aircraft. It would take time for him to become fully confident of his ability to control the beast, but he would certainly enjoy getting there.

Together, he felt sure they'd inflict some real damage, payback for Jerry's ravages being meted out to Britain's battered cities and exhausted civilians. It would be good to be back in the saddle again too, once more at the point of the lance. Thompson's words whenever the squadron plunged into the fray came to mind.

'Tally-ho, tally-ho,' Jox whispered as he switched off the engine.

# CHAPTER SEVEN

It felt like Jox had been stuck in this carriage for most of the day, and he was starting to feel positively stir-crazy.

Taking the fast train to London at Edinburgh Waverly turned out to be an exercise in optimism, since the journey proved to be anything but rapid and his compartment companions were certainly making the stuttering progress feel even longer.

It had started innocently enough. He boarded carriage 13, compartment C, then checked that his travel warrant and ticket were tucked away in his tunic with his lucky porcelain talisman. He nodded to the shifty fellow with the thin face sitting opposite him. He was wearing a dark fedora, what Pritchard would have called 'a spiv's hat'. He looked worried at the sight of Jox's uniform but now sat smoking one evil-smelling cigarette after the next. Occasionally, he would glance up at the battered brown suitcase in the luggage rack, clinking mysteriously with the cadence of the train. Jox suspected something illicit was up there but was content to live and let live. However, he wasn't sure how long he could put up with the nicotine-stained fug the chap was producing.

Crossing the border made Jox think of his wee terrier, Georgie, left with 'Uncle Pritch' and the other fellows of No. 111 Squadron whilst he was away on leave. He couldn't wait for the Christmas break in London but knew he would miss the pup.

At North Berwick, a young boy and his mother boarded. She was the kind of woman who felt the need to provide a running commentary on everything that she or her scallywag of a son were up to. Every mundane thing was accompanied by a Cockney soliloquy along the lines of, 'Thanks ever so for everything you're doing for the country, young man. Now, don't fiddle so, Arthur. Sit like a good boy, or I shan't be taking you back home to Bow. He was evacuated, you know, all the way up here. Stayed with a lovely couple, the McMurrays, in a place called Coldstream. Strange name for a town, but they had a lovely big house. What was it called, Arthur? Hope Park, that was it. No bleeding chance of getting my Arthur to stay put, though. I've told him time and again that it's to keep him safe from Jerry bombs, but will he ever listen to his old mum? Not a bleeding chance…'

This went on for hours, and even the silent smoker appeared a little frazzled. Artie, as he told them he liked to be called, was fascinated by Jox's uniform. To have access to 'a real fighter pilot all of me own' was a thrill for the boy, who'd inherited his mother's linguistic approach to life. 'You're one of them Brylcreem Boys, ain't ya? What's that medal for? What about that one? Have you shot down any Jerries? Wanna see my shrapnel?'

It was exhausting simply trying to keep up. Thankfully his mother had brought liver paste sandwiches and some pop, which shut him up for a while, but then she picked up the baton herself.

This was becoming the journey from hell as the train began a series of unscheduled stops. It was late afternoon by the time the guard came down the carriages, advising them that there had been a raid on the yards outside Peterborough. Jox asked when they might be getting to London and he replied, less than encouragingly, 'I'm sorry, sir, I've absolutely no idea. We're in the lap of the Gods. Sit tight and let's hope that Jerry doesn't spot the train out in the open.'

Jox winced. He didn't want to be late for Alice when she came off shift at the Cabinet War Rooms.

The boy heard the drone of aircraft first. 'I can tell Jerry bombers from their noise. That one's a Junkers 88. It makes a sort of high-pitched burbling sound. Not like them old Dornier 17s rattling away like toolboxes strapped to a pump. Then there's the deep throbbing of the Heinkel 111s that always sound like they're about to give up the ghost.' Artie had a remarkably good ear, and it took Jox a moment to recognise the sound of an old adversary.

Glancing through the grimy carriage window, he spotted a twin-engine *Schnellbomber* that had so successfully executed hit-and-run raids on the RAF's airfields and radar installations last summer. They'd practically brought the service to its knees. This one was remarkably low, hugging the earth as it tried to evade a pair of Hurricanes in pursuit. It was long, sleek, and menacing, following the rail tracks as it tried to escape.

Flashing past the stalled train, the gunner in the rear-facing ventral position had a pop, letting rip with a stream of tracers in their general direction. His aim was poor, scattering gravel from between the rails, ricochets whirring and shredding trackside shrubbery. A single spent round thumped into the side of the carriage, whipping off the startled smoker's fedora and letting in a thin ray of sunshine through a perfect round hole in the wall. The spiv said shakily, 'I think we deserve a drink.'

Above them, the Ju 88's pilot jinked the aircraft, desperate to escape his dogged pursuers. There was a roar of gunfire that startled the train's passengers, muting the mother and son for an instant, as everyone threw themselves to the ground.

Jox's curiosity eventually got the better of him and he looked up at the sound of a resounding boom. He rose in time to see one of the Hurricanes perform a victory roll, recognising RF-E, the identifier letters of No. 303 Polish Squadron with the striped badge on the aircraft's humped shoulder. That 'City of Warsaw' badge had earned a hell of a reputation during the Battle of Britain, shooting down more enemy aircraft than any other, RAF or Allied.

The purr of the Merlins overhead stirred something in Jox's heart. A pall of black smoke was rising from beyond a stand of bare English oaks cresting a hillock. The smoke from the oil fire of a crashed aircraft was quite unlike that of the comforting crackling of twigs on a bonfire. It was an acrid black streak, propelled violently into the sky by the roar of burning fuel and metal. Uncompromising in its bleakness, it raced heavenwards like the ragged tail of a rocket marking the death of yet more airmen consumed by the flames.

The train jolted forwards and began to move. Artie and his mother were mercifully silent from the shock of recent events.

It was early evening as they passed through the green fields of Hertfordshire. Jox glanced out of the window. There were civilians scattered beneath tall, denuded trees, huddled along chilly hedgerows. He was reminded of the chaotic scenes he'd experienced in France. Jox was shocked to see the number of children, ragged women with babies and stooped old men amongst the cowed populace, sheltering between the vegetation and the raw ploughed fields. He saw perambulators and wheelbarrows piled high with bedding and household utensils, grubby urchins leading dogs on string leads and frail matrons, cold and pale with tabby cats on their laps. It was a damning representation of London's panicked population, uncared for by the authorities and unconsidered by sweeping political statements about how the country 'can take it'.

The scenery slipped into the suburbs. Here, bomb damage was immediately obvious. Jox had been this way many times before, barely registering the grimy Victorian tunnels and rows of terraced houses as they passed. Now, though, what was left of them marked him deeply. Charred timbers and the teetering remains of battered walls leant over unidentified piles of rubble and masonry, the remains of peoples' lives and homes. They passed a mansion block of flats with a huge slice removed, revealing private rooms within. Here there was a lady's boudoir with diaphanous pink drapes fluttering to the elements, and there a gentleman's wood-panelled commode hanging high up on a third floor.

Most marked was the pervasive stink of ash and charred wet wood that wafted into the carriage, mixed with the earthy smell of damp brick dust and a powerful sense of pity for the victims, their privacy invaded and homes shattered. It was the small things that stayed with you — the sight of an eviscerated piano, someone's pride and joy, warped by fire and soaked by hoses, standing out in a shattered suburban street. Nearby, a child's doll lay twisted in the gutter, its head missing and its juvenile owner probably buried beneath the rubble.

Reaching the terminus at London King's Cross, it was well after eight as the guard passed through the train to ensure that the blackout was observed. Another night of raids was threatening, and the moving lights of a train were the perfect bait to attract attention from the air.

Jox was cursing since he was already three hours late, but emboldened by the spiv's whisky in his belly, he hoped Alice would be waiting at the suite they'd taken at The Ritz at Green Park. This was far from his usual haunt, but encouraged by Pritchard and Robertson, he'd enquired after a reservation, making full use of the letters that he now had after his name.

What good were decorations from the king, if they could not be used to secure a decent room to spend some precious time with his fiancée? Both were serving officers, had saved up their pay and planned to have a blast between Christmas and New Year.

In the meantime, the train slowed again. It was in near darkness, the windows covered, and young Artie was filled with a mixture of excitement and fear. The drone of the bombers was clear to hear, which the boy easily identified as labouring Heinkel 111 engines.

Hiding in deep tunnels, the train pulled into Kings Cross at nine o'clock, disgorging its weary passengers onto a crowded, oddly muted platform. Overhead, there were muffled thumps of explosions reverberating through the station's ancient structures. Many of the passengers were servicemen, desperately scurrying along to make up for lost time, either reporting late for duty or keen for long-awaited passes and weekend leaves in the 'Big Smoke' to begin.

Jox bid farewell to Artie and his mother, ripping the purple and white ribbon of the DFC from his tunic and offering it to the boy. 'Here, I don't suppose any of your pals will have one of these.' His mother was appalled at the idea of Jox deliberately damaging his uniform. 'Don't worry,' he said. 'I've got another set in my bag.'

Jox shouldered his duffel and searched for signs indicating where the tube entrance might be. He found nothing in the claustrophobic darkness, but eventually identified a ticket inspector, who pointed him in the right direction. Apparently, all signage had been removed to confuse any German paratroopers that might eventually come along. Jox laughed out loud. He didn't know about Nazi paratroopers, but it had certainly confused him.

He was lucky and caught the last Piccadilly line train heading south, before the tube stations once more became dormitories for London's cowering population. Six stops later, he emerged onto the rather grander setting of Piccadilly, a stark contrast to grubby King's Cross. Despite being under the same blackout regulations, the area not so far from Buckingham Palace radiated a confidence, timelessness and Great British solidity. Across the road was Green Park, with a reputation for *al fresco* nocturnal liaisons.

Jox realised his own intentions for the evening weren't really so far removed from the giggling shadows he passed. Up ahead the blue awning of The Ritz Hotel at number 150 Piccadilly beckoned. Outside was a burning brazier and a uniformed doorman, providing a warm welcome to the hotel's elegant guests. Jox felt a little uneasy at the blinking target the brazier might provide to an observant bomb aimer, but realised there were plenty of other fires ablaze across the city.

The doorman saluted smartly and held open the brass door. 'Good evening, sir. Welcome to The Ritz London. I hope you enjoy your stay.'

# CHAPTER EIGHT

Alice was in the upstairs bar at The Ritz. She'd left word for Jox with a key to their suite so he could freshen up and get dressed for dinner.

Her things were hanging neatly in the Art Deco wardrobes, painted an elegant ivory white. Her nightdress was on the bed and he couldn't resist inhaling her scent, realising just how much he'd been looking forward to seeing her. In the sumptuous bathroom, toiletries were arranged in a neat line, and it struck him, not for the first time, how untidy he was in comparison. He would have his work cut out living with someone this fastidious but was rather banking on opposites attracting.

After a quick wash and brush-up, he dunked his head in a basin of piping hot water, an unbelievable luxury in wartime. He applied pomade to his hair, styling it in the prescribed slick RAF manner. Not for nothing were they called the 'Brylcreem Boys'.

He dug out the spare decoration ribbons from his bag, then tidied up his tunic with the silver-backed clothes brush bearing the hotel's lion crest. There was cigarette ash all over it and sniffing the shoulder, he realised just how smoky the journey south had been. He retrieved some cologne from his washbag. Pritchard had given it to him with the prophetic words, 'Got this in Paris before the war. Women love it when a man doesn't smell too much like a man.' He splashed it on liberally. With a final glance in the mirror, he decided he looked pretty sharp but just wished he was a little taller. *Ah well, can't have it all.*

He took the opulent spiral staircase carpeted in red and gold two steps at a time, reaching the wide vaulted corridor on the ground floor. Out of breath, he asked for directions from an immaculate hotel porter in striped trousers and black tails, who seemed unperturbed by being confronted by this heavy-breathing, fragrant example of one of the RAF's finest.

Jox was shown to the bar with a knowing smile. It was like stepping into a jewellery box made of dark wood and exotic leather, with Art Deco styling and lots of gold trim. The murmur of conversation mixed with the tinkling of a piano.

It took him a moment to spot Alice at the bar, sitting with an elegant pair of ladies with very dark hair and smoky eyes. Unused to seeing her out of uniform, he didn't recognise her long blonde hair curling over her shoulders, but her laughter was unmistakable. As he approached, the shorter of the glamourous women said, '*Ooh, regardez un pilote!*'

'There you are, my darling!' Alice exclaimed. She wrapped her arms around him and kissed him more passionately than he'd expected in such a public place. He rather enjoyed the admiring glances they were getting. Alice was clearly a few drinks down and her eyes, always her best features, were shiny with more than just delight at seeing him. He'd had a couple too and was enjoying this liberated side to them both.

'Where are my manners?' said Alice. 'Darling, let me introduce you to my wonderful new friends. This is Princess…'

'Please call me Ruhi,' interrupted the taller of the two. 'This is my sister, Myze.'

'*Enchantée*,' said the smaller of the pair, her dark curly hair in a side parting. She extended an elegant hand, tipped with vermillion talons and Jox realised she was expecting him to kiss it.

'This is my fiancé, Flying Officer Jox McNabb,' said Alice as he repeated the performance, brushing his lips against the back of the older sister's gloved hand. She was the more striking of the two, with dark, intelligent eyes and the demeanour of a woman used to unsettling men.

'So, you're one of the brave heroes protecting our defenceless womanhood?' she asked, arching an eyebrow with amusement.

'I very much doubt you're defenceless, Miss Ruhi,' said Jox. 'And I know for a fact that my fiancée can more than stand up for herself. She ably demonstrated that when RAF Kenley was bombed last summer and in her recent work for Mr Churchill.'

'Oh, you never told us you worked for the PM, Alice,' cooed Ruhi.

'Hush, Jox. "Loose lips sink ships" and all that,' replied Alice. 'Of course, that doesn't include you two, considering who you are and everything.'

Jox was unclear what she was talking about.

'Don't worry, your secret is safe with us,' said Myze. 'We have secrets too.'

'I'm afraid you ladies have the advantage. I have no idea what you're talking about.'

The three of them giggled, before Ruhi, clearly the leader of the little gang, replied, 'Oh, if you must know, our brother Zog is the King of Albania. Our family live here at The Ritz, in "gilded exile" as they call it. Actually, it's rather tedious and you two make a refreshing change from the sycophants who surround us. It gets really dull for all of us sisters.'

'Sisters?' asked Jox. 'There are more of you?'

They both laughed. 'Yes, six of us. We and Maxhide are the younger ones. She's around here somewhere, probably getting into mischief.'

'My word, six. That must be a sight to behold.'

'Why, thank you,' purred Ruhi. *'Qu'il est charmant*! I shall take that as a compliment.' Catching her eye, she took Alice's hand in hers. 'Please don't worry, dear Alice, I'm not flirting with your handsome beau, just teasing.' The frown on Alice's face made it quite clear that's exactly what she thought.

Seeking to defuse the unexpected tension, Myze said, 'You must come for tea. Yes, why not, tea at the Ritz! How much fun would that be?'

'So, the two of you really are princesses?' said Jox, standing up straighter.

'Look, he's a proper English soldier now. Just for us, Ruhi,' said Myze. 'Please don't do that, we're just friends having a drink together.'

'And you all live here?'

'Yes, ever since the Italians betrayed us and invaded our country,' Myze replied. 'We all have our tasks, but it can get very tedious. Our older sister, Senije, is sort of in charge and oversees the Albanian Red Cross. Ruhi takes care of arts and cultural matters, whilst I have education, women's rights and sports. Maxie, our youngest sister has tourism. It all sounds rather jolly, but there isn't much to do. There actually aren't that many Albanians in the United Kingdom and we're not allowed out much.' She sighed. 'There's such an exciting city out there, during the most momentous of times and we're stuck in here.'

Jox laughed and, considering the opulent surroundings, said, 'This doesn't seem so bad, but aren't you worried about the bombing? A stray bomb in the wrong place could wipe out the entire royal family.'

'What a cheerful thought,' said Ruhi. 'But no, apparently this is a new building, built with reinforced concrete floors inside a frame of, would you believe it, Krupp steel imported from Germany. It's one of the most solid buildings in London, we've been assured. It's even safer than His Majesty's Buckingham Palace down the road, which has been hit several times and is quite fragile in comparison. In any case, the hotel management have built us a shelter if things get really bad. There's also *La Popote* in the basement. It used to be the Grill Room restaurant but now doubles as a shelter. Actually, it's also become *the* night club for the more colourful types of London's elite. Come to think of it, that's probably where Maxie is. She seems to enjoy the company of the louche bunch that inhabit the depths of the hotel. Perhaps you might find it entertaining to join us there for a drink. I must warn you; anything goes and it's not for the easily shocked.'

'I'm not sure I follow you,' said Alice.

Jox was also struggling to imagine what could possibly be so shocking in a former barbeque restaurant.

Ruhi smiled knowingly. '*La Popote* is, shall we say, rather bohemian and hedonistic. It's been described as "notoriously queer" and you'd be surprised who you'll find down there. All manner of artistic types, aristocrats and politicians.'

Jox was beginning to understand what she was getting at. He'd been to a private co-educational school in Scotland, the oldest in the land, but had heard of the peccadillos that came out of some of the single-sex public schools. That there should be a bar dedicated to that sort of thing, in The Ritz no less, was a shock given Jox's rather sheltered upbringing.

Setting off from Montrose that morning, never in his wildest dreams had he imagined that he'd end the evening by taking his fiancée to a roué's nightspot in the company of two Albanian princesses.

After an excellent late supper hosted by the princesses, the party decided they were ready to take on *La Popote*. It had occurred to Jox during the meal that there was little or no rationing at The Ritz, nor were the diners encumbered with having to hand over food coupons. *Oh, the life of the rich.*

Approaching the notorious nightclub through darkened corridors, the crumps of muffled explosions could be heard from above, accompanied by the low throbbing of bombers' engines. As they reached an anonymous door, loud music drowned the sound of the enemy, one thumping timpani replacing the other.

Inside, the music was blaring, and it was very close and sweaty. The décor was an artistic approximation of a trench from the last war, apparently a tribute to R.C. Sherriff's *Journey's End*. The walls were packed with sandbags held in place by wooden joists and bare metal struts. Crude drawings and slogans were daubed on the woodwork and subdued lighting was provided by candles in the necks of wine bottles on rough tablecloths. A similarly makeshift candelabra lit the dancefloor, behind which there was a stage with a singer, piano and small band. On one wall there was a mural of the Western Front during the last war, opposite a caricature of Hitler and Goering dancing a passionate tango together.

The revellers were an equally odd selection of misfit couples, men dancing with men, women with women, and a smattering of more conventional pairings. Jox recognised a few politicians and the West End starlet, Pauline Tennent, dancing with an extraordinary-looking woman who was wearing men's clothes and a monocle and smoking through a long onyx cigarette holder. There were several other colourful partiers, whom Jox struggled to assign a gender to.

On stage, a stout woman in a shimmering emerald-green dress was singing. She had bright red hair, thick make-up and gaudy crimson lips. Her voice was a distinctly unladylike baritone, providing a soulful rendition of the popular Gershwin number 'Summertime'. As the singer rasped 'and the living is easy', the assembled crowd gave an almighty cheer.

The princesses were obviously habitués of *La Popote* and were shown to a corner table with a good view of the stage. Sitting there was an elegant young woman, fairer than her sisters, but recognisable as one of them. This was their 'wild child', Princess Maxhide. With her were two men, who got to their feet and crossed their right arms across their chests in an odd salute. It was a bit like the first part of a Nazi salute, but they didn't raise their arms into the air. The men peered at Jox suspiciously but were mollified when Ruhi took his arm and spoke in what presumably was Albanian. One went to the bar and the other stood discreetly behind the table, making room for the princesses, Alice and Jox.

Against the din of the music, Jox leant towards Ruhi's fragrant ear and asked, 'What was that peculiar salute?'

'It is not peculiar. It is our Albanian salute. We call it *Përshëndetja zogiste*. You try it. Put your right hand over your heart, palm facing downwards.' Jox did as instructed. 'Perfect! Now, if you meet His Majesty in the corridors, you can greet him correctly. My brother will be most impressed.'

'Isn't it quite like the German or Italian salute?' asked Jox.

'That cannot be helped. We had it first.'

Their drinks arrived and were poured out by the two burly bodyguards, usurping the club's waiters. They were noticeably friendlier now, realising that Alice and Jox were guests of the princesses. They were clearly men who could take care of themselves, with the tell-tale bulge in their white dinner jackets.

'Are these gentlemen bodyguards or Albanian soldiers?' asked Alice.

'Both, actually,' replied Ruhi. 'Aron and Ilir are captains of our brother's corps of bodyguards.'

'Are there many Albanian troops in England?' asked Jox. 'I've got chaps from all over in my squadron but haven't met any Albanians yet.'

'Not so many. Albania is a poor country, and we don't have so many aircraft and pilots. What we did have, the Italians stole from us. Tell me, where are all these new comrades from?'

'All over, it seems. At the start of the war, we were mainly Brits, but now there are chaps from the Colonies and Dominions, and let me see, we have a Belgian aristocrat, a new Norwegian chap and two excellent Czech pilots, Miro and Otmar.'

'Two Czechs? President Beneš will be pleased to hear that. He is often here having lunch with his cabinet,' said Ruhi, as if referring to a family friend.

'They're proving to be good fighters and excellent pilots. They really seem to hate the enemy. It's like they have a personal stake in the fight.'

'I'm sure they do. They've come a long way to fight for their country.'

The band were taking a short break, and the low-ceilinged room was filled with tobacco smoke and the sound of clinking glasses and conversation. There was a resounding thump, and they all felt the change in air pressure. Some dust trickled from the ceiling and there was uneasy laughter.

Unfazed, Ruhi continued, 'We learned to hate a long time ago in Albania, and we take feuds very personally. Now, it is Great Britain's turn to learn what the rest of Europe have experienced at the hands of the Axis. May God protect us all from the terrible times ahead.'

A new singer was on the stage, who began singing a calypso tune, full of sunshine and laughter.

'I live in London city,
Where the rain pours, it's a pity,
So, the girls and boys, they cry for toys,
But all they need is some sun, sun.
I am the Calypso King
Sunshine is what I bring
So, you can dance
And find romance
All in the name of fun, fun.'

He was well known to the crowd and popular. Dancers of all genders and persuasions flocked onto the dancefloor.

Maxhide clapped her hands with delight, screeching, 'It's Curly Cummings!'

He was a handsome mixed-race man with closely cropped curly hair, dark eyes and startling white teeth, visible even in the half-light. As he sang, he wiggled his hips, flirtatiously locking gazes with people in the crowd, causing many to swoon. He was indiscriminate in his attentions, enjoying the impact he had on all. For an instant, his gaze settled on Jox, but receiving no reaction he moved on to someone more receptive.

Ruhi leant into Jox's ear. 'I really don't see why my sister gets so excited. Curly is obviously not one for the girls.'

A slim white man in his twenties ran up to Cummings, wrapped his arms around him and began kissing him. His face was hidden, but he was noticeable because in addition to his dinner jacket he had a blue feather boa around his neck, was wearing full mascara and was tottering in bright red heels. The pair wriggled and danced suggestively, and the crowd roared. Jox was bemused but had to admit this was a hell of a party.

Alice grabbed his arm. 'Oh, good Lord, can you see who that is?' She tugged at Jox, pointing at the stage.

The pale fellow was still in the arms of Curly Cummings, but Jox could now see his face. Despite the make-up and smeared rouged lips, it was unmistakably Sandy Bullough, his South African friend from flight training. Last summer, he had been the Intelligence Officer at RAF Croydon and Kenley and had been instrumental in clearing up some trouble that Jox and Alice had run into with a rapacious squadron leader called Drummond, who'd had lecherous plans for Alice.

'What the devil?'

Their eyes locked and Sandy looked terrified. He bolted, running as fast as his heels permitted.

## CHAPTER NINE

'What an extraordinary evening,' said Alice the following morning.

'Not exactly the romantic break I'd imagined,' replied Jox. 'We've certainly seen the colourful side of London. I'm dreading to think what can happen between now and New Year.'

Alice pushed a strand of blonde hair behind her ear. 'Tell you what, why don't we just stay in bed for the rest of the week? Just you and me — sod the rest of them.'

'Sounds divine, but you promised me that Hogmanay in London could beat Scotland. I'm not convinced and unless you've lured me here under false pretences, I expect to see it all.'

'I think we've seen quite enough, don't you?' she replied, stirring her builder's tea.

The chipped crockery was quite a contrast to last night's cut crystal. They were having breakfast in the bustling refectory of the Piccadilly Lyon's Corner House. It was their flagship teashop, a short walk from The Ritz and just the comforting hug they needed this morning. White- and gold-fronted, it was the perfect place for a nice cup of tea and some grub at a reasonable price.

Their 'Nippy' arrived loaded with their breakfast: porridge, bacon, fried bread, toast, marmalade and a second pot of tea, all for the princely sum of 1s 6d. She wore a starched cap and a black dress with a double row of buttons, a white collar and cuffs, and a square white apron at the waist.

'There you are, my darlings. You look like you've been through the wars. Get caught in last night's raid, did you?'

Alice and Jox glanced at each other and giggled. 'Yes, something like that.'

Spotting Sandy Bullough cavorting about in drag had been quite a shock. When he'd bolted, Jox's first instinct had been to worry that he was in trouble and needed help. It wasn't the get-up that bothered him so much, nor even the unexpected behaviour with that singer chap — what had struck him was the abject look of terror in his friend's eyes.

It wasn't a long chase and perhaps predictably, it had ended in the men's loos. Jox left a startled Alice with the princesses as he bolted off. He wasn't too worried, since she'd also seen Sandy's distress and he was her friend too.

The lavatories were busy, with most cubicles occupied. The end door was shutting, but he managed to get his arm to it, knowing that Sandy was there as he could see red heels below the edge of the stall.

'No, no, I can't have you see me like this, Jox,' he screeched.

Jox pushed with his shoulder and barged his way in with a loud bang. The commotion was exactly what the majority of the occupants of the facilities were trying to avoid, so they emptied remarkably quickly.

'Calm down, Sandy. It's only me. What the hell's going on?' said Jox. His friend was smaller than he remembered, underweight, with dark hair and teeth that were too big for his mouth.

'It's … it's not what you think,' Bullough stammered. 'Well, it is, but it isn't. I can't explain here, there are too many ears.' He took a deep breath. 'I'll explain everything, or at least what I can, but not here. You and Alice must meet me at the Royal Air Force Club for lunch tomorrow. Say at one o'clock. It's just up the road at No. 128.' He passed a trembling hand through his hair. 'How do I look? Must be a frightful mess. You gave me such a bloody shock, you Scottish rascal.'

For an instant Jox recognised the old Sandy Bullough, but then the strange new version spoke again. 'I need to know that I can count on your discretion. This may all seem strange — well, actually it is — but you must know I'm still on the job, on official business. I won't deny that I'm tapping into some natural inclinations I've repressed all my life, but even dressed like this and behaving like I was out there, believe me, I'm still serving King and Country. Now, better fix my lipstick and get back out there. You wait a bit, then come out. Try to be discreet, and please don't be shocked at what I get up to.' He smiled. 'One final thing: be careful around those princesses. If they're friends of yours, warn the young one to stay away from Curly Cummings. He's a very dangerous man.'

Jox and Alice still had a few hours to kill after breakfast and before meeting Sandy. The previous night had gone on into the early hours, and despite the princesses claiming to be Muhammadans, they certainly packed away the drinks. After hours of dancing and carousing, with Bullough seemingly playing the role of court jester to the debauched crowd, Alice and Jox retired very late. They'd left Princess Ruhi with promises to meet later in the week, then made their weary way to bed. Too exhausted for anything like passion, they were asleep instantly, reassured that their leave was only just beginning and there was plenty of time.

With food in their stomachs and hangovers receding, a walk seemed in order to build an appetite before lunch at the RAF Club. Then there was the delicious prospect of an afternoon spent reacquainting themselves. They walked towards

Piccadilly Circus, searching for the familiar statue of Eros, but discovered he'd been removed for safekeeping. Only the copper base was left, covered in protective timbers. On towards Leicester Square, Cambridge Circus and bohemian Soho, they were soon in familiar territory for Alice, who'd been to prep school in the area.

There was a lot of bomb damage, and a Royal Mail pillar box she'd passed regularly during her childhood was bent like a squashed cigarette butt by the force of an explosion. The neighbourhood police box beside it was like a blue shoebox squashed by a petulant toddler's foot. At the crossroads of Rupert Street and Shaftsbury Avenue, there was an enormous crater outside the old Apollo Theatre. A Number 19 double decker bus was tipped into it like a discarded Dinky toy, windscreen submerged in a deep murky puddle.

London was grey and cold today, with winter fog thickened by the smoke of a hundred fires burning through the night. Shops and businesses were boarded up or had shattered windows like smashed ice, glistening all over the road surface. On Oxford Street, tailors' dummies and broken mannequins had been blasted out from John Lewis's windows, duping the eye into seeing pale naked bodies on the pavement.

London's timeless facades had toothy gaps that mocked the claim that 'We can take it!' Instead, the familiar face of an old friend looked like he'd been beaten by a heavyweight. Battered and bruised, he was still standing, but hardly recognisable.

Their shoes crunched on broken glass, cooling embers and the fabric of life reduced to fragments and tatters. A stink of burst sewerage wafted over them, along with the damp of doused timbers and wet brick dust, mixed with the acrid odour of melted manmade materials. They navigated their way gingerly, mindful of what they walked on, avoiding the bubbled sticky mounds and other unidentifiable lumps, some of possibly human origin. The night's dead and wounded had been taken away, but grim remnants remained.

It was sobering to think that while all this suffering had occurred, they were dancing at The Ritz. It was a thought that weighed heavily upon them, darkening their mood as they headed for their appointment.

The Royal Airforce Club had been founded in 1917, and since the outbreak of war, membership had grown considerably, as a home from home for staff whilst stationed in London. In that respect, Sandy Bullough was fairly typical: South African-born, from a wealthy family in Durban and a well-connected young man from the Dominions. He had already been a qualified pilot when he'd joined Jox and Pritchard at No. 18 EFTS (Elementary Flying Training School) at Fairoaks in Surrey. From the outset, he had clearly been very bright, in fact a bit of a 'know-it-all', which hadn't made him popular with the course instructors. Against all expectations, he'd been 'bowler hatted' out, his services no longer required by His Majesty's Royal Air Force.

Through perseverance and the influence of family members, he'd reapplied his talent and undoubted intellect to becoming an Intelligence Officer. The previous summer he'd served in that capacity at RAF Croydon and Kenley, proving to be fair but annoyingly firm with often-inflated victory claims made by his fighter pilot comrades. He was a solid and dependable friend to No. 111 Squadron in general and Jox and Alice in particular. His help in dealing with some unpleasantness relating to the squadron leader with wandering hands who'd set his cap at Alice, but who was also her commanding officer, had proven invaluable. This was why the pair sitting in the club library were nervous, having seen a completely unexpected side of their friend.

Bullough kept them waiting for almost an hour. Jox spent the time examining the sepia photographs on the walls. These were Royal Flying Corps boys from the last war, many long since reduced to dust in Flanders fields, fertiliser for the vaunted poppies. Amongst them, he recognised the face of a youthful Badger Robertson, before he'd experienced the 'frightfulness' that had permanently striped his hair. Beside him stood his cousin Wing Commander Robertson, as yet unstooped by the extreme violence and blind terror he'd experienced.

Jox drifted over to the domed hallway adorned with a collection of squadron insignia, hand-painted in vivid watercolours. He quickly found No. 111 Squadron's badge, once described by Robertson as 'two red swords crossed in saltire, a cross potent quadrat charged with three black Saxon seaxes, fesswise in pale.' That meant very little to Jox, other than a confusing jumble of swords and crosses, but the Latin motto *Adstantes* — 'standing by', ready to serve or fight — had always spoken to him.

Bullough burst through the double doors, unworried about having kept them waiting. He was more conventionally attired in a slate-blue uniform but was bareheaded. He was smiling, but the pair knew him well enough to detect a touch of nerves.

'Alice my darling, Jox old boy, thank you for coming.'

They were also in uniform and got awkwardly to their feet. Bullough had the two thick and one thin sky-blue stripes of a squadron leader on the cuffs of his tunic. As a flying officer and section officer respectively, Jox and Alice were of the same rank, but Bullough was now two ranks above. Whatever he'd been up to since they'd last seen one another, it was doing wonders for his military career.

'Let's have a seat,' said Bullough. 'I think I've got some explaining to do.' Neither of them replied, as his eyes darted from one to the other. 'Well, there are really two stories to tell: one a bit more awkward, but the other perhaps more important. I'll get the awkward part out of the way. You're both close friends of mine, and yesterday you saw a side of me that you've not seen before. That you have, to be honest, is quite a relief. It's something I've kept hidden from the world, but it's now more or less in the open, thanks in no small part to the war. You've probably worked out that I'm a man who prefers the company of men. No offence, dear Alice — socially I love the ladies, but this has been an unspoken thing for most of my life. I'm sorry I've kept it from you, my dear friends. Ironically, it's the second aspect of my story which allowed me to free myself from the constraints of the first.' He paused, giving them the chance to catch up. 'Before I explain, I must remind you of your oaths as officers and make it clear that what I will tell you is utterly confidential and must not be shared beyond the three of us. Do you understand?'

They nodded, but he waited until they realised that he wanted a spoken response. They replied, 'Yes sir,' in unison.

'It began last summer, when I observed that beyond the damage and casualties inflicted by the enemy on Croydon and Kenley, there was an unusually high level of theft, sabotage and accidents. I kept track of the incidents and became convinced this was more than simply petty theft and profiteering. It was an orchestrated campaign that was weakening the RAF's ability to wage war. Since then, I've had some success identifying those responsible, and have been making my way up the food chain of what I believe are a group of enemy agents, embedded at the highest level of British society — a *réseau* doing great harm to our war effort.'

'Where does *La Popote* fit in and you gallivanting about with that mob?' asked Jox.

'What I'm trying to explain is that firstly, that queer bunch are really *my* bunch, but amongst them are some very dangerous bad apples, whom I'm working on identifying and eliminating.'

'Who do you suspect?' asked Alice.

'I'm still not entirely sure, but I know that delicious singer, Curly Cummings, is not what he seems. He's the darling of the boys and girls at *La Popote*, and half a dozen other night spots around the West End. What better cover than being the handsome, flirtatious Calypso King of the demi-monde? He claims to be from Barbados but actually comes from the Dutch Antilles. His name is Henk Van der Wael and I believe he is an *Abwehr* agent, and a very dangerous one at that. That's why I warned you regarding Princess Maxhide. She has no idea who she is dealing with, politically or in terms of potential scandal. I suspect someone within their Albanian entourage is also acting as a foreign agent. Let's not forget that despite Italy having annexed Albania, it wasn't so long ago that King Zog was himself a general in the Austro-Hungarian Army, fighting alongside Germany in the last war. No one ever said things aren't complicated in the Balkans.' He smiled. 'I'm starving. Let's chat over lunch. What do you fancy? The devilled kidneys are really excellent.'

Over lunch, they discussed the whereabouts of people they knew in common. Jox updated him on their Canadian friend, Moose, recovering from a foot injury, courtesy of a cannon shell when jumped by a pair of new *Friedrich* series Bf 109Fs over Le Touquet with No. 1 Squadron RCAF.

'I don't think the big fella has the full complement of toes anymore,' said Jox. 'Hopefully it won't stop him getting back in the cockpit. That's two of our pals who are now "hop-alongs". Him and Pritch would make a fine dancing pair.'

'They're certainly fine-looking men,' said Bullough. 'Wouldn't you agree, Alice?'

'Oh, Sandy, you know I only have eyes for my Jox.'

'I hope he realises how precious that is, and he's a very lucky man.'

'He does,' said Jox solemnly. 'You wouldn't recognise the squadron. There are so many new faces, with a new CO and we're training for a night fighter role now.'

'We certainly need to do something about the night-time raids,' said Bullough. 'We can't seem to hit a barn door at the moment. The enemy are over London with impunity every night and the ack-ack guns make a lot of noise, but don't seem to bring much down. Tell me, what's the new CO like?'

'We've had quite a merry-go-round. The current chap is Squadron Leader George Brotchie, Wee Brotch, they call him. Bit of a stickler who gets carried away, but Badger is keeping him on the straight and narrow. I don't know if you know Mogs? Pritch and I trained with him at Montrose. Well, he's joined us now as our Green Section leader.'

'How about you, Alice? I understand you've got a new job. Working for the PM, no less.'

'How did you know that?' she asked.

'There are certain advantages to being in the Intelligence community, and I may have had a word.'

'Well, in that case, my lips are sealed.'

'Good girl,' he said rather patronisingly, but the glint in his eyes told her he was impressed. 'That's the ticket. How's your lamb?'

'Never mind that, Sandy,' she said. 'Stop circling about and tell us what you want.'

'Ha! No flies on you. As usual, you're quite right. Whilst the pair of you are here and it seems that you have a good in with the Albanian princesses, it would seem like an opportunity to understand what they and their entourage are up to. I'd like you to stay close — find out who's hanging around and trying to ingratiate themselves. Any names you can provide are useful, especially if we can establish a link to Curly Cummings, or rather Henk Van der Wael.'

## CHAPTER TEN

Jox and Alice walked from No. 128 Piccadilly hand in hand, reflecting on what Sandy Bullough had asked of them.

An early queue was forming outside Green Park tube station. Local residents were already waiting for access for the night. It was only mid-afternoon, but these Londoners were clearly wary of the nightly bombing. Many were noticeably twitchy, displaying symptoms of what the newspapers were calling being 'bomb shy'.

Reaching The Ritz, Jox and Alice were soon back in their romantic bubble. They spent the rest of the afternoon in their suite, lazy, loving and languorous. It was everything they'd hoped for after their weeks apart.

Lying in each other's arms, Alice traced her finger over the scars on Jox's muscled but slim body. His hands bore the marks of the flames from when he'd tried to save her brother. There were hard lumps in the small of his back, from when he'd nearly broken it when his back-armour had taken the full weight of a Nazi 20mm cannon shell, and he'd crashed onto the cliffs near Dover. Through his eyebrow there was also a jagged white line where he'd struck his face when ditching off Dunkirk.

'You've certainly been through the wars, my darling,' she sighed.

With evening approaching, they shared a long hot bath in the largest tub either of them had ever seen, got dressed and were surprised at how ravenous they felt, considering they'd already eaten twice. Of course, the afternoon's frolics had required no little energy and stamina.

They asked the doorman for the nearest fish and chip shop, and unfazed by the question, he provided directions to one a few streets away. As he pointed, the leaden skies rumbled and Jox could hear the low throb of aircraft. Young Artie would undoubtedly have identified them, but Jox hoped he was safely tucked away in Bow with his talkative mother. He lifted wary eyes skywards and couldn't help thinking that their room on the fifth floor was terribly exposed, irrespective of the vaunted German steel and concrete.

After a remarkably fine fried fish supper, with fat-cut chips and crispy batter scraps, eaten al fresco on a bench in Green Park, they discussed whether their impromptu picnic would be considered conduct unbecoming for 'officers and gentlemen/women'. Their playful banter was interrupted by the plaintive call of the air-raid siren at the entrance to the tube station, waxing and waning. The banshee call was designed to prompt civilians into action, but for Jox it was rather too close to the terrifying Jericho Trumpets on the Stukas he'd experienced in France. He'd also seen the destruction they'd wreaked and was even more dubious about the idea of returning to the hotel.

'Look up there on the corner of the building.' He pointed to where The Ritz faced the park. 'Those two windows, four from the corner on the floor with the flag posts. Those are our room. You know, I don't fancy our chances if they get hit. There's a shelter in the hotel, but it'll be a right palaver trying to get in. Our best bet is probably the public shelter at the tube station. What do you think? If nothing else, we can see what ordinary Londoners are experiencing every night.'

Alice agreed as the wailing sirens were already giving her the willies. They crossed the broad stretch of Piccadilly, joining a small crowd being marshalled through the doors by an ARP warden and an anxious member of London Underground's staff.

Heading down the stairs, Jox said, 'I don't suppose we'll get much of a spot. People have been queuing for hours.'

The first thing that hit them was the stench of packed humanity, uncovered latrine pails and the general fug of the underground. Alice stifled a gag, desperate to hold onto her fish supper.

A heavily pregnant woman was making her way down the stairs when she stumbled, and Jox lunged to catch her. There was a mermaid's tail tattooed on her arm, along with a Hope & Anchor motif. It was probably a love token for a Royal Navy sweetheart. She smiled gratefully, then breathing heavily, she duck-waddled through the pressing crowd.

They found a spot beside some mothers ignoring their children as they gossiped. Feral progeny chased skittish little rodents darting amongst the grey dust and balls of human hair that collected between the tube rails. Jox was unsure if he felt sorrier for the children or the mice.

Down the platform, a noisy group of soldiers were on leave, the alcohol in their veins evident from the volume of their raised voices. They were bragging of wartime exploits, despite not having left home shores. They were being watched by a grizzled RSM from the East Surreys, who had the faraway look of veterans from the last war and more recently the ragged survivors of the British Expeditionary Force. Men who had proven their mettle in combat and recognised it in one another. He caught Jox's gaze.

'You been over?'

'Yeah, how about you?'

'Escaped from St Valery by the skin of my teeth. You?'

'Shot down over Dunkirk, then again over Kent during the Battle of Britain.'

'Not having much luck, are you, son?'

'Oh, I don't know about that. I don't think two for eight is a bad trade-off.'

'Nah, that's fair enough. Check out them kids over there. Don't know they're born. Mind you, you don't seem much older yourself, but I reckon you've seen a thing or two.'

Jox nodded grimly, fingering the porcelain doll's arm in his pocket.

'They'll learn soon enough, once Jerry gets here,' said the veteran.

'Still think that's on the cards?'

'Well, we couldn't stop them in France.'

'We did last summer in the skies.'

'Yeah, I reckon you did, but listen, they're still up there now.'

As if on cue, the tube tunnels rumbled. The sound was punctuated by the thump of distant explosions, the howl of flames and the groan of collapsing masonry.

'Don't worry, we're working on that,' said Jox defiantly.

'Better get on with it, before there's nothing left to defend.'

The 'all clear' came in the early hours of the morning. Jox and Alice emerged from the tube station, blinking in the watery light of a winter's dawn. Stiff-limbed and exhausted, they stumbled for the haven of the hotel, noticing that a corner of the elegant edifice, at the opposite end to their room, was smashed in. The doorman held the door open as they entered the elegant hallway, designed for the great and the good to promenade. They shuffled to their room like malfunctioning automatons.

'Ah, there you are, Flying Officer McNabb,' said a perfumed receptionist from behind his mahogany counter. 'I've some messages for you and Miss Milne.' He handed over a buff-coloured envelope of RAF stationery addressed to him and a stiff white vellum envelope for Alice. Too tired for delicacy, Jox opened his roughly with his fingers to find a scrawled note from Moose, confirming that he would be in town over Christmas. He wasn't terribly mobile, but was keen to see them, otherwise he'd be forced to stay in Scotland to spend a lonely Christmas far from home, probably drinking too much with the other Canucks of No. 1 RCAF Squadron. Jox was pleased; he hadn't seen his big friend since he'd been wounded and was keen to catch up. There weren't all that many of them left from before the Battle of Britain, and every one of them was precious.

'Moose wants to spend Christmas with us,' said Jox. 'You all right with that?'

'Of course, but he better bring his glad rags with him. We've just been invited to a bit of a do.' Alice handed him a gold-embossed invitation card, the type known in well-to-do circles as a 'stiffy.' He scanned it and was dumbstruck.

*The High Lord Chamberlain is commanded by*
*His Majesty King Zog I of the Albanians to invite:*
*Flying Officer Jeremy McNabb & Section Officer Alice Milne*
*to a Christmas Luncheon*
*at His Majesty's Private Dining Rooms,*
*The Ritz London, 150 Piccadilly, Mayfair, London*
*On Wednesday, 25th December 1940 at 1 o'clock*
*A reply is requested to:*
*His Excellency High Lord Chamberlain Mehmet Ali*
*The Ritz London, 150 Piccadilly, Mayfair, London*
*Dress: Uniform, Morning Coat or Lounge Suit*

Attached was a handwritten note saying: *We do hope you'll come. It promises to be fun. Fond regards, Myze, Ruhi and Maxhide*

'Crikey,' said Jox. 'I wasn't expecting that. D'you think they'd mind if we brought Moose? I can't let him down, however fancy the invitation.'

'I don't know, but we're not missing out on this,' replied Alice. 'We need to RSVP to that Mehmet Ali, Lord Chamberlain chap anyway. I don't suppose there's any harm in asking. I remember one of the princesses saying the king is always keen to meet allied servicemen.'

'Let's hope it's not going to be a problem. It'll be fascinating, especially after what Sandy was talking about.'

'Problem? That's not the problem. What the hell am I going to wear?' asked Alice.

'The invitation says uniform, so what's the issue?'

'The issue is I'm not going to be the ugly duckling in my drab uniform and clumpy shoes when the room is full of princesses in stunning gowns. It's all right for you men.'

'I take your point,' said Jox, sensing her growing unease. 'But let's think about it: we're at The Ritz, and the concierge is right there. Where better to get help tackling the problem?'

The next few days were a flurry of dress fittings and long-distance telephone calls to Moose at RAF Prestwick, warning him of what to expect. Jox also heard back from the king's chamberlain that His Majesty would be delighted to meet another Battle of Britain hero, especially one wounded in combat and from the Dominion of Canada, which had been so welcoming to many of His Majesty's subjects.

Jox had agreed to meet Moose off the sleeper train at King's Cross. He wanted to catch him on his own, to help with his luggage, but also to see if he was as incapacitated as he sounded. In any case, Alice had a final dress fitting, having engaged the services of the redoubtable Madame Francoise, The Ritz's chief seamstress. Alice's friend, Stephanie, a jolly but fiery-tempered girl with aristocratic connections, who also worked at the Cabinet War Rooms, was in attendance. Alice proposed she might like to meet Moose, so they could go for dinner as a foursome. Once she'd described him, the response was an emphatic, 'Ooh, I do like the big ones.' So that was settled, but Jox felt unsure whether his limping friend would be eaten alive.

Moose was the last off the train. His bulky body tick-tocked down the platform, as he leant heavily on a stick. Steam swirled around his broad shoulders and peaked cap. The pair embraced and Jox took his duffel bag from him.

'Christ, man, you don't look too clever,' said Jox.

'Looks a lot worse than it is, eh,' replied the beaming Canuck. 'I just need to get used to walking without a big toe. Doesn't affect my flying too much, which is good news, and I was never much of a dancer.'

'It's really great to see you, pal,' said Jox, realising just how much he'd missed him. He was embarrassed at how moved he was feeling and hoped Moose hadn't noticed.

'What are you getting so soft about, eh? It's not that bad. Plenty of fight in the old Moose, you know.'

'I certainly hope so. We've got some serious partying lined up.'

'Great, tell me all about it. I was intrigued when you called and said to bring a mess uniform. It wasn't easy finding one big enough, eh.'

'You'll be pleased you did, I'm telling you. We're going to have fun.'

'Bring it on, I could do with a laugh,' Moose said as they headed down into the tube.

# CHAPTER ELEVEN

'My Lords, ladies and gentlemen, please put your hands together for the most fabulous Father Christmas in all of London,' gushed an excited Princess Maxhide.

Less convinced was the tanned face hidden behind a cottonwool beard standing behind her. With heavily mascaraed eyes and rouged lips sticking to the white fibres, he was certainly a striking Father Christmas, but for all the wrong reasons.

He was trying to sing a time-honoured Christmas carol for the bemused luncheon guests but was making rather a hash of things. His number-one fan may have described him as 'The finest voice in the West End,' but it was clear that Charles 'Curly' Cummings was regretting having ever agreed to perform.

With an exasperated flourish, he pulled off his beard and instructed his quartet to return to safer territory. He ad-libbed a Calypso tune, his usual bread and butter.

The audience was a hybrid of British and foreign cultures, merged together to form a rich but rather confusing blend of customs. At its centre were a fabulously wealthy Albanian royal family of mid-European Ottoman and secular Islamic origin, added to which was Queen Geraldine's Orthodox Catholic faith through her Hungarian ancestry. Then there was the family's interpretation of what a British Christmas lunch could or should be like, on top of which there was the unmistakable flourish of The Ritz's panache.

Alice asked Princess Ruhi how the family usually celebrated Christmas.

'Our family are Turkish Ottomans, but we like to celebrate Christmas for the sake of Crown Prince Leka. To tell you the truth, we like to celebrate any and every occasion, but we are keen on the British tradition of a big lunch on the twenty-fifth. It's far jollier than the sombre *réveillon* on the night of the twenty-fourth. Much more fun.'

One guest taking it all in his stride was Moose. He'd already spent the two previous evenings fighting off and eventually succumbing to the charms of Alice's friend, Stephanie. Now he was flirting outrageously with Princess Myze. Things had got off to a good start, when the petite princess had spotted the big Canuck limping with his cane and exclaimed, '*Regardez un éléphant blessé!*'

Having studied in Quebec, Moose spoke fluent French and was quick to reply, '*Non, votre Majesté, pas un éléphant, un élan.* Not an elephant, a moose.' He put thumbs to his temples, mimicking antlers, then twisted one downwards, as if broken. '*Enchanté*, they call me Moose.' Absolutely charmed, she hadn't left his side since, taking great pleasure in feeding him prodigious amounts of food and fine wine.

At one point in the evening, he leant over to Jox. 'I think I've died and gone to heaven. After nothing but that Spam, bully beef and boiled fish for weeks, this is paradise.'

Jox had to agree. The wine in particular was unlike anything he'd tasted before. He complimented Princess Ruhi, who smiled with pleasure.

'Albania is one of the oldest wine-producing countries in the world,' she said. 'We Illyrians taught the Romans and the Greeks how to make wine over three thousand years ago. I'm pleased you like it; wine production is one of my responsibilities as Minister for Culture and Arts. It must be considered an art form, don't you agree?'

Jox raised his crystal glass in agreement and looked down the long table laden with food, unimaginable out there where the real war was being fought. Fine linens, metal cutlery and decanters filled with wines and liqueurs were ranged down the table.

The Albanian royal family all had a marked resemblance, with fine aquiline features, pale skin, and dark curly hair. Princess Maxhide was the only exception with fair hair, but Jox was unsure whether that was achieved cosmetically. Several of their royal courtiers, including the Lord High Chamberlain, Mehmet Ali, also had similar features. A self-important peacock of a man, he spoke perfect English but insisted on addressing guests in only Italian or Turkish.

Jox was holding a weighty dessert spoon, seeing his reflection in the yellow metal. Ruhi wore an amused expression when he asked, 'Is this made of…'

'Of course,' she replied. 'Albania's gold reserve is downstairs in the vaults of the hotel. We simply asked Garrard, the kings' jewellers, yours and mine, to melt down a few bars and fashion this canteen of cutlery for the occasion. They've done a good job, don't you think?'

Jox stared incredulously at the spoon, hesitant now to finish his pudding. He'd heard of being born with a silver spoon in your mouth, but frankly this was ridiculous. Right now, he was saving up to buy wedding rings and a gift for his bride-to-be, and he realised that this single spoon would be more than enough to do that. He placed it carefully back on the crisp white tablecloth and pushed it away, removing any temptation.

Further down the table, Moose was stripped to his shirtsleeves as a succession of the king's courtiers and bodyguards took turns arm-wrestling with him. With every fresh victory, Princess Myze squealed with delight, becoming more and more excited and amorous. Jox had warned Moose about getting too boisterous when he had a drink in him, but he was being charming and delighting their hosts.

'He's quite a character,' said Ruhi, sidling up to Jox.

'One of the best,' said Jox. 'We've been through a hell of a lot together.'

'I'd love to hear about that, and so would my brother. Would you like to meet His Majesty King Zog the First of the Albanians?'

'It would be my honour,' replied Jox, unsure what he was letting himself in for.

King Zog was a remarkable-looking man. If Charlie Chaplin's recent film *The Great Dictator* was supposed to pastiche Herr Hitler, King Zog was very nearly the real thing. Most striking was that there was a permanent cloud of billowing cigarette smoke around him. Reportedly smoking over two hundred cigarettes a day, he had his family's dark eyes and a slim face with a debonair little moustache. Outdoors he favoured a gilded peaked cap worn at a rakish angle and an exquisite uniform with epaulettes, a lanyard and a gold chain with the stars of various orders dotted across his chest. Over his heart was the motif of the flying eagle. Princess Ruhi explained that Albania was the 'Land of Eagles' and the Albanian people were 'the sons of eagles'. Jox couldn't help wondering what the eagles of the Luftwaffe might have to say about that. Jox, Moose, Pritchard and many of their comrades had faced their 'maximum effort' on the infamous *Adlertag*, 'Eagle Day' in August 1940.

When he spoke, King Zog had a high-pitched voice, with an accent that sounded Italian. 'So, tell me, *Teniente*, my sister says you are an RAF ace from the Battle of Britain.'

'I had the honour of playing my part, Your Majesty,' replied Jox.

The king observed him with a blue trail of smoke rising from his lips. 'I think you are being modest. May I call you Jox? Such an amusing name. A bit like Zog, no? Short and to the point but with meaning and menace. Our enemies discover that at their peril,' he smiled glacially.

Earlier, Princess Ruhi had explained that her brother had first been a politician, had become prime minister and then president, and had then been proclaimed king. In the clan-based politics of the Balkans, he was a survivor, ruthless and vindictive, having survived over fifty assassination attempts. In a land of the blood feuds, he was a master.

'Your candour does you no credit, Jox,' said the king. 'These baubles of mine are mainly hereditary or symbolic. Yours, I can tell are earned with blood and courage. Do not speak with that false modesty that I know the British are so fond of. In Albania, we worship the brave, and fete our heroes. That is why I am proud that you are at my table. Pull up a chair and speak to me of the war. I sicken of the puffery of perfumed dandies. I enjoy the company of fighting men, like that giant of yours over there, embarrassing every one of my men.'

The coterie around the king made way for Jox. Mehmet Ali, the Lord High Chamberlain, glared at him and Jox was surprised to see Curly Cummings seated beside him, wearing a white dinner jacket like those usually worn in tropical climes. He was still in full makeup, quite shocking to Jox, but evidently nothing unusual in the present company.

'So, tell me, what is your opinion of the British fighters compared to those of Germany and Italy?' asked King Zog. 'My chamberlain remains convinced of the superiority of the enemy's aircraft in terms of design, capabilities and performance. What do you think?'

'A fair question, Your Majesty. In my opinion, the superiority is in the numbers rather than the quality of the aircraft. Both sides have lame ducks, but also some excellent ones. Some have had their time — the Stuka, for example. It spread such terror across Europe during *Blitzkrieg*, but without air superiority it has been chopped to pieces over the Channel. The same could be said of the vaunted Bf 110 Destroyers: fast, powerful and with a devastating weight of fire, but they're just not nimble enough.' He had the rapt attention of King Zog and his entourage. 'I'll admit that I was almost bested by one but have since managed to shoot down two. One was sheer luck, but the other was thanks to my developing skills. My friend Moose has also bagged a brace of them.'

'What about these armadas of terror-bombers, apparently "bombing Britain back to the dark ages?"' asked Chamberlain Mehmet Ali. 'They fly over London with apparent impunity, and the RAF seems to have no answer.'

'Once again, it is my belief that it's the numbers that count. Thankfully the bombloads they carry are comparatively light, and the bombers are easy targets during daylight raids. Entire *Staffel* have been shot down during single sorties. What has held us back is only having .303 MGs to fire, rather than cannons. Hitting them was never the issue; bringing them down was. Now that our aircraft are equipped with cannons, things will only get better.'

'What about the blasted night raids? The other day even the hotel was hit,' said King Zog.

'I'll admit the shift in focus to night raids has given the enemy a temporary advantage. I can assure you we have something up our sleeve to counter that.'

'And what might that be, my dear Jox?' asked a languorous Curly Cummings, the lilting sound of the islands clear in his accent.

'Why, Mr Cummings, that would be Top Secret.'

'Ooh, you are such a tease,' he purred.

'Be that as it may, I can assure you we are not playing parlour games.'

Chamberlain Ali snorted. 'There's little point in telling a story with no climax.'

'Perhaps, but this discussion concerns real war, not whatever this might be,' said Jox, waving his hand over the bountiful table and struggling to mask his irritation.

'Enough!' exclaimed the king. 'Apologise to *Teniente* Jox — he is the only warrior amongst you. Mehmet Ali, make yourself useful for once, and go fetch Jox's Canadian friend. I'm interested to hear his views.'

The chamberlain was shocked by the reprimand, but obeyed sullenly, giving Jox a murderous glance as he passed.

Moose arrived, grinning and still in shirtsleeves. He was covered in a sheen of sweat after his exertions. He bowed clumsily and mumbled a greeting, then limped to a chair, his balance affected by his missing toe, not to mention the prodigious amount of wine he'd consumed. King Zog was as charmed by the brusque Canuck as his younger sister, Princess Myze. She was unwilling to lose him and had followed him up the table.

'Please tell me how you were wounded, *Teniente* Moose,' said the king.

'Not much to tell, Your Majesty,' replied Moose. 'My section was on a Rhubarb mission over Le Touquet, a couple of weeks back.'

'What is this Rhubarb?' asked the king.

'An offensive operation against the enemy, searching for targets of opportunity, rather than a more defensive role like that of night fighters,' said Jox.

'So, you go to the enemy and just look for trouble?'

'That's exactly right, Your Majesty,' said Moose, like an excited schoolboy. 'But that trouble found me first. I got jumped by a couple of heavy-gunned F-series Bf 109s over Le Touquet. They chased us all the way home. My Yank buddy Otto got blown out of the sky and I lost half my foot. Real shame, that. He has such a lovely wife, Helen, and they only got married six months ago.'

Jox glanced up the table and found Alice watching and listening intently.

'This war has cost us our best men. It is the duty of those left to ensure their legacy lives on,' said King Zog wistfully.

'We do our best,' said Curly Cummings, trying to join the conversation.

This irritated Jox. 'And what is your best, Curly? What is it that you are doing? I don't see you joining up.'

The man's mascaraed eyes narrowed; any semblance of bonhomie had evaporated in an instant. 'I'm not sure how, but I appear to have offended you,' he said.

Jox held his gaze and said glacially, 'Platitudes are all very well, but there's a war going on.' He was pleased to have taken some wind from his sails, knowing what he knew of this man's activities.

Cummings blinked slowly, then caught himself. 'My apologies if I have offended you,' he said. 'It was certainly not my intention. Please, let me try again.' He smiled, this time seemingly genuinely, but still with the stare of a serpent. 'I'm hosting a calypso evening on Friday the twenty-ninth of December at the Coconut Grove on Regent Street. A sort of dress rehearsal for New Year's Eve, if you will. I'd be honoured if you and your friends would come as my special guests.'

'That's mighty kind,' said Moose, oblivious to the dangerous undercurrent. 'I'm back on duty in Scotland this weekend. I'm sorry, I can't join you. Sounds like fun.'

'I know the princesses have a prior engagement, so it will be just you and your good lady. I'd be honoured if you would agree to be my guests,' said Cummings. 'I can guarantee you will meet some interesting people.'

Was he walking into a trap? He recalled Sandy Bullough's instructions, but also the warning that Curly Cummings was a dangerous man. *Keep your friends close and your enemies closer* came to mind, as Jox replied cautiously, 'We have a dinner reservation beforehand, so we may be late, but yes, we'd love to join you. Please let the hotel reception have the address when you have a moment, and we'll be sure to join you. The Coconut Grove, did you say? I'm sure I've heard of it.'

'The doorman knows it well. He's hailed cabs for me many times. I'm delighted and so keen to get a better insight into how this great battle overhead is unfolding. As a mere entertainer, flotsam on the terrible tide, it's so frustrating being unable to help those brave boys sacrificing so much in our name,' said Cummings, seemingly genuine, but again with the eyes of a cobra. It might have been more believable if Chamberlain Ali hadn't snorted his derision.

*It'll make for an interesting evening,* thought Jox. This really was not what he'd expected when he'd sworn to serve and defend King and Country. He caught Alice's eye across the table and she nodded quiet encouragement. She was far better suited to all this intrigue and double-talk than he ever was. Not exactly what the average bridegroom might have found appealing in his bride, but it made him love her all the more.

# CHAPTER TWELVE

Christmas came and went in the warm embrace of Jox and Alice's little bubble of two. Danger rumbled and banged through the nights, but they were oblivious in each other's arms, ignoring the grim realities of life out there.

Every morning, they would emerge to find another part of London devastated by the night's raids. Familiar spots like Trafalgar Square, Horse Guards, and the Whitehall streets near where Alice worked were deserted, with anything precious or important swaddled by mounds of sandbags. It was particularly poignant to see the war memorials to those who'd died in 'the war to end all wars' scratched and pitted by the latest calamity inflicted upon the capital's weary populace.

The 29th of December was the evening they'd agreed to attend Curly Cummings' soirée. Their precious time together was slipping through their fingers, and they would soon have to face the reality of their respective worlds again. The wedding was planned for spring, but who knew what fate held in store? They dropped a note for Sandy Bullough at the RAF club, letting him know of their plans and promising to report back if they discovered anything interesting. A clipped reply arrived a few hours later: *Be careful and stay alert. Thank you for this service to your country. All best, Sandy.*

The Coconut Grove wasn't easy to find, not because it was particularly hidden, but because the familiar curved thoroughfare of Regent's Street was in pitch darkness, bar the occasional flaring in the skies. They navigated their way using the reflections on the bubbling stream of water that flowed down the middle of the street, like a peaty Scottish burn. A water main must have been breached upstream, creating the torrent and no doubt hampering fire-fighting efforts somewhere in the city.

Groping their way forward, their feet got soaked and their toes were stubbed by unseen obstacles. Finally reaching the venue, they were shown past some naked brick walls to a set of double doors. Beyond, Caribbean music was playing, and as they stepped through they were instantly in the moist heat of the tropics.

A mixed crowd were sitting at tables discreetly lit by shaded oil lamps. There were a number of uniforms, as well as dinner suits and evening dresses. A good deal of gold braid was on show and Jox could see that the Royal Navy were out in force. Wet trails of condensation ran down the walls and a number of ladies were fluttering fans before their glowing faces. It was hot and sultry, in keeping with the club's ambiance. The dance orchestra played furiously, and the floor was filled with couples, oblivious to what was raging above them in the city.

Jox and Alice were shown to a table on the edge of the dancefloor, where their host Curly Cummings was in deep discussion with a man, whom they recognised as the Lord High Chamberlain, Mehmet Ali.

'Oh great,' groaned Jox. 'That's all we needed.'

The men greeted them with reptilian smiles. Both stood, shook hands and gallantly kissed Alice on the hand. Mehmet Ali ordered some champagne, as Cummings said, 'I'm delighted you could make it. I've had so many telephone cancellations from friends cut off by the raids. Things are getting quite hairy out east, I'm told.'

'Yes, it's good to find shelter,' replied Jox. 'It's certainly a lively night in here.'

'That's kind of you,' purred Cummings. 'We're doing what we can to raise morale. It's the least I can do for all these brave boys.'

Jox couldn't tell if he was being mocked.

Cummings focused his attention on Alice, whilst Jox was cornered by Mehmet Ali. He appeared to be making an effort, being amiable, but Jox just found it unsettling. Ali poured out some champagne and toasted their good health.

'You and your Canadian friend made quite an impression on His Majesty,' said the Chamberlain. 'I hope I'm not being indiscreet by telling you that he plans to bestow an Albanian Order of Merit on the pair of you. I've been instructed to draw up the paperwork for the Military Order of Bravery. It's a five-point white cross with a double-headed black eagle on a red background, circled by a gold laurel. You'll be pleased to hear that the award comes with a monthly pension payable to the recipient and his descendants of a hundred gold francs.'

Jox was speechless.

'So, you see, my friend, I come bearing gifts,' said Ali with a curious smile.

'I ... I don't know what to say.'

'If I were you, I would graciously accept. His Majesty likes to get his own way and is fickle with his affections. Something I know all too well, I can assure you.'

'I don't even know if I'm permitted to wear it with my uniform.'

'Oh, I think you will be,' replied Ali. 'Mister Churchill's government are at pains not to antagonise His Majesty's humour. Any issues will disappear in the face of that.'

'I'm flabbergasted.'

'You should be. It's a great honour. Like I said, you made quite an impression,' said Ali. 'On me too, actually. I was interested to hear your views on the war and how the RAF are measuring up to these nightly raids. From a layman's perspective, I see London "taking it" and not much of the RAF "dishing it out".'

'As I said at lunch, there are plans to deal with the raids, but it takes time, men and training,' said Jox, more defensively than he intended. He needed to be careful how much he shared.

'Do you think London has that luxury, Mister McNabb? Seems to me the city's running out of time. Soon there won't be much of it left.'

'You underestimate the British people, Excellency.'

'Ah yes, Mister Churchill's "bulldog spirit". It baffles me why he should use a dog for that analogy. As Muslims, we see dogs as *haram*, forbidden, unclean and impure. I cannot conceive how the spirit of a filthy cur might be something to aspire to.'

'Bulldogs are tough, belligerent and never give up,' said Jox. 'They are bred to fight creatures much bigger and stronger than themselves and to prevail through sheer doggedness and tenacity. These are traits to be admired, when facing up to a bully.' Jox smiled. 'The fact that the Prime Minister looks like one too probably helps.'

Ali gave a glacial smile. 'I'm not sure this "bulldog spirit" is as pervasive as you think, Mister McNabb. In certain circles, even at the heart of your government, there are those who favour peace and an accommodation between belligerents. Voices for appeasement, if you will, voices that are growing and that need support, but also evidence of the true state of the war.' He eyed Jox carefully. 'Evidence, for example, that someone like you might provide. Someone who has seen the vast resources of the enemy and the devastation it brings. That's an insight people would listen to.' He let the words sink in. 'Of course, this dedication and desire for the truth wouldn't go unrewarded. I feel sure a decorated war hero and his charming fiancée, who already works within the government, would prove very useful to this emerging faction, who in turn would be very appreciative.'

There it was. He'd said it. Now Jox knew why Cummings and Ali were so interested in him and Alice. They were already aware she worked at the Cabinet War Rooms, a clear indication they'd been investigating the couples' background. Jox racked his brain, trying to remember if he'd said anything controversial at the Christmas lunch, a trigger for their interest, but his mind remained blank.

'Perhaps you should think about it,' said Ali.

Cummings was staring across the table. Sensing the tension, Alice quickly said, 'Come on, darling, I know you've got two left feet, but you can't bring a girl to a nightclub and not dance.'

'Yes, dance,' said Cummings. 'Enjoy yourself. I must get ready for my set.'

Cummings sauntered onto the stage in a high-waisted white suit, broad at the shoulders, cinched at the waist and with baggy trouser legs. On the streets of Harlem, it was known as a zoot suit, but in wartime London it was a remarkable thing for a gentleman to be wearing. On his head was a wide-brimmed Panama, paired with a silver pineapple-headed cane, which he twirled as he sang.

His repertoire included a string of his Calypso hits, interspersed with 'scat singing' — a form of vocal improvisation in the style of Louis Armstrong and Cab Calloway. The performance was a sensation with the bohemian crowd of the Coconut Grove, leading to wild dancing that raised the pulses of the more conservative patrons.

For Jox and Alice, it was an assault on the senses, a completely new and intoxicating form of music. Mehmet Ali watched bemused from their table, a burly bodyguard by his side. Jox recognised one of the Royal Guards he'd met at the Christmas luncheon. The Lord Chamberlain clapped his appreciation of their athletic gyrations from across the smoky room.

With a series of calls and counter calls, Cummings had the dancers on the floor whipped into a frenzy. Jox found himself parroting the 'hi-de-hi-de-his' and the 'ho-de-ho-de-hoes' with the rest of the crowd. Alice's face was flushed, and she'd never looked happier nor more beautiful.

But then, with no warning, the ceiling above the stage collapsed in a cloud of choking dust. A heartbeat before, a blinding flash had flared amongst the crowded tables. The music stopped dead, overtaken by the screams and groans of the wounded. Panic-stricken survivors surged towards the clogged exits, the more severely hurt and the dead trampled underfoot in the melee to escape the chaos.

Arm in arm when everything went black, Jox and Alice clung desperately to each other within the heaving mass, stranded in crushing darkness. Younger and more robust than most, they had the strength to strain against the press of bodies, an instinct of self-preservation fuelling a selfish determination to live.

An elegant young woman dancing beside them was lifted off her feet, blue-lipped and asphyxiated by the crush, her neck flopping like a dead chicken's. Under her, a bull of a man in naval uniform roared his defiance at all those weighing down upon him. His face got redder and redder, until something gave way and his limp body sank through the crossed limbs of the crowd as if sinking through ice floes.

One moment they were in the crushing grip of the mob, the next they were propelled onto Regent Street. The stream of water from earlier now provided some soothing muddy coolness for their parched throats and overheated bodies. Fires raged up and down the street and the earth itself was aflame. Bewildered, terrified and with all sense of direction lost, they followed the flow of the water, reasoning that it must surely drain towards the Thames, where there might be shelter from the fire and heat.

The whole of humanity appeared to be heading downstream, stepping through the debris, the wounded and the dead lying in the streets. Alice had lost her heels in the scramble to escape, so was running barefoot.

The mob represented the whole of London: grimy shift workers, dishevelled dinner-suited gentlemen, anxious young women in various uniforms, haggard matrons and bewildered children in their pyjamas. Firemen and ARP wardens, hollow-eyed with exhaustion, herded them away from the fires, the conflagration etched in the lines of their soot-blackened faces.

As they ran, the building at 177 Regent Street collapsed with a groan, entombing the remains of the Coconut Grove beneath smoking ruins. What was left was now fuel for the fires started by thousands of incendiaries falling from the skies.

Jox and Alice watched as a young girl and an older man in the baggy siren suits and flat helmets of an ARP fire party, tackled one flickering incendiary. Her pretty face was bleached white by the glare as she held a grandly termed 'self-locating bomb remover' — basically a metal clasp on the end of a broom handle. She clipped it onto the one-kilogram incendiary bomb, lifting it free of combustible debris and placing it onto harder ground. The man then extinguished it by pouring on dry sand from a heavy red pail. It took them ten minutes to deal with a single bomblet, whilst countless others continued to spread the flames.

Jox and Alice followed the crowds heading for the river, still unaware of their good fortune, having escaped the collapse at the Coconut Grove. Befuddled and awed by the inferno spreading across the city, they dumbly headed downstream. Occasionally, the clouds and smoke would part, offering a brief glimpse of cross-shaped shadows droning overhead, with probing searchlights chasing them across the heavens.

The night was filled with noise, but not just the crackling of flames, explosions and the groan of collapsing buildings. Nor was it just the shouting of firefighters, the screams of victims, and the never-ending whine of sirens. It was the terrifying sound of the fire itself: howling one instant and roaring the next. It was a ravening beast, determined to consume everything in its path.

# CHAPTER THIRTEEN

Looking east, Jox could see the reflections of the fires on the surface of the Thames. Loading cranes and tethered barrage balloons were silhouetted against the inferno raging in the docklands.

Night had turned into day, but with none of the optimism of a new dawn. Rather, it revealed things the darkness could mercifully have kept to itself: the clogged storm-drain with a lump of pale flesh attached to a woman's long hair; a child's arm, protruding dusty and stiff from brick rubble that had once been a home.

Nearing the river, there were legions of dead rats, fat from the warehouses and discarded offal of nearby Smithfield Market. They'd been caught by the rolling blast and asphyxiated. Their bodies littered the cobbles, floating like bloated beavers in the shallows along the shoreline.

Stranded on the riverbank, Jox and Alice were overtaken by a tumbling wall of debris and sparks, throwing themselves down into the river mud to escape the blast. Sweeping high over the embankment and piers, burning pieces extinguished with hisses and plops on the churning surface of the tea-coloured water. Tendrils of drifting smoke and steam twisted over the river like the city's lost souls crossing London's own version of the Styx.

In an unconvincing impression of the ferryman of Hades, a grubby Royal Navy sailor cried out, 'You and the young lady wade out to me, and I'll get you to the other side. Not saying it's much safer over there, just not so many fires.' He was balancing adroitly in a clinker-built rowboat, expertly handling a single oar and at the same time reaching for them with a boat hook. 'I'm on leave at my parents' flat near Borough Market. I saw the fires and wanted to help. Found this boat near Blackfriars Bridge, so I nicked it and I've been ferrying people across most of the night.' He had the reassuring Cockney accent of a born Londoner and was taking the sight of his hometown in flames remarkably coolly. He wore a bell-bottomed rating's uniform, with the distinctive striped collar and a dark sailor's cap with the letters HMS. He had bad teeth, a wide grin and a face grimy from the smoke. His competence and confidence were the most reassuring things they'd seen all night.

'What time is it, please?' asked Alice.

'Big Ben over there says it's gone three. I'm surprised it's still standing with half the town in flames.'

Alice followed his pointing arm and recognised the clockfaces and spike of London's most familiar landmark, jutting through the swirling clouds which flashed in various hues. She was trembling, from cold, shock or maybe both.

'Here, there's a blanket down there. Might be a bit smelly, but you're welcome to it. The name's Matt, by the way. Matt Pye.'

They introduced themselves.

Pye said, 'Listen, there's still room for a few more. Shame to waste the trip back. Tell you what, Jox, you keep your eyes peeled for stragglers and I'll row over when you spot one.'

Jox peered at the northern bank. It was darker towards the west and brighter to the east. The stink changed as they drifted downstream. Mostly it was thick and choking, oily and tarred, but every so often it carried cloying sap or turpentine from burning pine. Sometimes it was sweeter and acrid, burning sugar, molasses and rum from the wharf-side warehouses of Tate & Lyall.

Jox could see a line of vehicles parked along the embankment, long hoses running down to the edge of the water. As he'd seen on Regent Street, the bombing had burst several water mains when demand was at its peak. The loss of main's pressure also meant that these Auxiliary Fire Service trucks had to pump water directly from the Thames. Their efforts were further hampered by the low tide, the distance the water had to travel and the frustrating regularity with which the hoses became blocked with river mud.

'I think there's someone down there on the shore by the Submariner's Memorial,' said Pye. 'Let's take a quick gander before we head back to Blackfriars Bridge.' Struggling with the glare, Jox couldn't see with the brightness coming from behind the bridge's low arches.

'How do you know your way around? I can't see a bloody thing.'

'I'm in the Royal Navy, on submarines as it happens, so of course I know the monument, but I grew up on the river. Spent my childhood mud-larking and swimming around here. There's even a beach down by Tower Bridge. I bet it's quite a hot spot right about now. There, it moved again. I think it might be an animal.'

This time, Jox's fighter pilot eyes caught the movement, and as they approached, he realised it was a large dog. Collapsed in the mud, it whimpered as they approached. Against his better instincts, Jox jumped into the shallows and ran towards it. At arm's length, he could smell the animal's badly singed coat. It was so badly burnt that he couldn't tell what breed it was. Perhaps a guard dog, he reasoned, used to patrol the warehouses against pilfering. It had once had long ears and a pointed snout. It was probably a German Shepherd, and the irony wasn't lost on Jox. His heart went out to the poor beast, bewildered and suffering terribly. He lifted it gently into the boat.

'Poor thing's on its last legs,' said Pye. The dog's clawed feet scratched against the timbers of the boat, desperate to reach the water.

'I think he's thirsty,' said Alice, shaken from her stupor by the creature's suffering.

'Here, use this,' said Pye, handing over his matelot's hat. Waterproof, it held a good scoop of water, which the dog lapped up furiously, emptying more in quick succession. It panted for a while and then lay back with a groan.

'I dunno if there's much we can do for him,' said Pye. 'He's proper done in.'

'His collar says he's called Otto,' said Alice, cradling the beast's ruined head. In her tattered evening gown, trying to soothe the suffering beast, she was a touching sight. The tough sailor and airman exchanged glances; it wasn't the smoke that was affecting their eyes.

'Right, let's get Otto back to someone who can help,' said Pye. 'Hold on.'

The hound awakened only once, trying to identify who was helping him. The hairs on his snout were reduced to pinheads, eyelashes singed to bristles, with corneas opaque from the heat. Alice couldn't have been more than a shadowy figure, but somehow, he felt secure, knowing that someone cared.

It took about ten minutes to get to the south bank, landing across the river from St Paul's great dome, proud and defiant in a sea of fire and flames. How it remained unscathed when surrounded by such devastation was beyond Jox. He wasn't a particularly religious man, but he did wonder if God was protecting his own. Mind you, that didn't say much for the rest of London, currently going through what could only be described as hellfire.

On the southern shoreline, they were met by a group of Volunteer Aid Department workers providing nursing care for the needy. Otto was handed over to them, wrapped in a blanket. If any of the volunteers were surprised that he was a dog, their kindness ensured he was as well taken care of as any human victim. After all, like them he'd served as a steadfast, loyal servant of the Crown.

In his final moments, he was surrounded by care and attention, but his passing was the final straw that broke the camel's back for Alice, after everything they'd been through. She sobbed into the charred fur of the faithful hound, sobbing for the nameless victims they'd seen and for their martyred city.

Dawn was finally breaking to reveal dark plumes of smoke over the financial and publishing districts of the City of London. They had been hit particularly hard, and there were still spouting arcs of water valiantly trying to hold back the flames.

Alice was exhausted and approaching collapse. Jox wasn't doing much better. Only Matt Pye, their erstwhile saviour was unaffected, as if hewn from Portland stone, stoic in the face of whatever the enemy hurled at them. Wrapped in fresh VAD blankets and fortified by the inevitable 'cuppa char' laced with rum, the pair bade him farewell, as he was determined to get back across to Blackfriars for another rescue run.

They would need to take a longer, more circular route through Southwark and Waterloo to make their way back to Piccadilly and the comforting embrace of the Ritz. When they finally arrived, they were relieved, but somehow the luxury seemed obscene after what they'd been through. Shattered, they lay on their bed, succumbing to the sleep of the utterly exhausted. It was a fitful rest, full of dreams of encroaching fire and choking smoke, leaving them flailing, calling out, oblivious to one another.

Jox was the first to awaken, sweating and reeking of smoke. A shower was heaven-sent, and he knew he was fortunate compared to the homeless across the city. He had washed his hair several times before his fingers stopped smelling of tar. Blowing his nose and brushing his teeth didn't seem to shift the acrid taste in his throat. He felt like he had a hangover, not from drink, but from inhaling noxious fumes.

Sitting in a towel by the side of the bed, he watched Alice as she slept. With every breath, her chest rose and fell, and a smell of bonfire wafted over him. Now that he was clean, he realised just how much they'd stunk when returning to the hotel. It was a wonder the staff had even allowed them in, though the murderous expression on Jox's face would have convinced any but the foolhardiest.

Alice was talking in her sleep. A frown creased her brow as she hissed his name, 'Joxxx.' He wondered if she was waking up. 'Don't leave me… Don't leave me in the dark,' she whimpered. 'Don't leave me.'

He had never seen such fear on her face, not even when they'd faced the bombs at Kenley last summer. Her eyes opened, staring sightlessly. 'Save him from the fire, Jox. My Georgie, there's a good boy.'

'Are you all right, darling?' he asked.

She smiled and lowered her eyelids. 'Save him from the fire, Jox. There's a good boy. Okay, okay, okay.'

What a strange soliloquy. Things were muddled in her dreams but being vividly experienced. What was the war doing to her on top of the horror they'd seen last night? Alice was always so composed, much more so than him, but unguarded and asleep something deeper was playing out. He wanted to help. Was waking her the best or the worst of things to do? He settled on letting her sleep, reasoning that it was repairing the damage that was in there, perhaps offering an escape from raw and difficult memories.

Jox got dressed in his second-best uniform. Actually, it was his best now, given the previous contender was a stinking pile in the bathtub next door. Alice's borrowed evening gown, or at least what was left of it, was in there too. At least her uniform hadn't been ruined. Far less satisfactory was the state of her feet. Stripping off last night, he'd noticed how blistered and bloody they were, grimy and frozen after their night's travails. He'd escaped the shattered nightclub, ruined streets and freezing river in his black RAF shoes. She'd lost her heels at the Coconut Grove, hobbling through debris-strewn streets and the toxic mud of the Thames barefoot. Last night he'd carefully washed them off as she'd fallen asleep with her feet in the tub. He'd lifted her into bed but now wanted someone to have a look at them, as they were bruised, cut, and burnt beyond his capabilities to care for them.

Jox put a call to reception, asking for the hotel doctor. He also made an appointment to see his uniform outfitters before the end of his leave and return to Montrose. They also needed to report back to Bullough on what they'd learnt at the Coconut Grove. Christ, the Coconut Grove — that was a conversation that felt like a lifetime ago.

'I could really do with a cup of coffee,' he said to himself, louder than intended.

'Hmmm?' responded Alice sleepily.

'Sleep, my darling. I'm going to get a doctor to check your feet. My beautiful brave girl, why didn't you tell me you were struggling so?'

She yawned and smiled sadly. 'It seemed so insignificant compared to the suffering we witnessed. It's my fault for wearing those damned silly heels. It was bad enough trying to dance with them, let alone run. I swear to you, my darling husband-to-be, if I ever wear heels again you have the grounds for divorce.'

'Amen to that,' said Jox. He wasn't a fan of her towering over him. They kissed. 'Right, I'll get some brunch organised and you, my dear, need a shower. You are far too fragrant for comfort.'

'Oh, you pig,' she retorted, flailing at him with one of her sore feet.

He scampered away, grateful that she'd awoken playful and happy in spite of everything. Not for the first time, he counted his blessings for having found such a resilient partner in life, capable of bouncing back from adversity so readily.

Once Alice was up and dressed, she and Jox hurried across the road towards Marble Arch, but it was hard going with Alice's sore feet. The RAF Club stood undamaged, but either side of it, Hamilton Mews and Down Street Mews were a shambles. Both residential, it was very likely their residents had joined the ranks of the homeless, if they had sheltered in Green Park tube station last night. If not, they were probably under the steaming rubble of what had once been their homes.

Slipping through the club's discreet doorway was like a homecoming after the chaos of the previous night. The quiet efficiency of the staff was soothing and more appropriate than the obsequiousness of the Ritz staff. Jox was tiring of his gilded cage and was keen to get back to his day job. It would mean leaving Alice, but she was feeling it too, the pull of duty after everything they'd witnessed last night.

He had two tasks to complete before heading to Scotland: debriefing Bullough and, having received a vellum envelope left at reception, attending the convocation by His Royal Highness King Zog of Albania to be decorated.

# CHAPTER FOURTEEN

'Christ, you two look like you've been through the grinder!' exclaimed Bullough. 'My God, Alice, what on earth's happened to your feet? Are you all right?' He crossed the room swiftly and helped her to a chair. 'Please, sit down, sit down.'

'We got caught in the raids last night,' Alice said wearily.

'Good Lord, what happened?'

'We went dancing at the Coconut Grove.'

'The Coconut Grove? Isn't that where you were meeting Curly Cummings?'

'Exactly,' said Jox. 'He was on stage when the ceiling collapsed.'

'Christ! Is he all right?'

'I've no idea. One minute he was singing something about Calypso Kings, the next we're in the dark and in this terrible crush.'

'I really didn't think we were going to make it out of there, Sandy,' added Alice. 'It was horrendous. I lost my shoes, but that was the least of it. People were on the floor getting trampled in the panic.' She took a deep breath, trying to still the images flashing in her mind. 'I certainly didn't see any signs of "Keep calm and carry on".'

Jox added, 'There was screaming and choking dust. We lost sight of Mehmet Ali and his bodyguards.'

Bullough was shocked. 'Wait, what? You're saying Chamberlain Ali was there too?'

'Yes, actually he did most of the talking.'

'I saw you were having quite a discussion,' said Alice. 'I did mean to ask.'

'That's what I wanted to report back to Sandy,' said Jox.

'Before you do, old chum, let me make a quick telephone call,' replied Bullough. 'If Mehmet Ali was there and anything has happened to him, it could become a diplomatic incident. The Albanians will be quick to blame us if he's been hurt or killed.'

'I don't see why. He had bodyguards with him.'

'They're a fickle bunch and it'll cause a ruckus. I'd better just check,' said Bullough. He excused himself and walked to a table at the opposite end of the library with a squat Bakelite telephone on it. He was soon engaged in an animated discussion.

Bullough re-joined them. 'No casualty lists as yet, but by the sound of things, it doesn't look good. The whole building collapsed. You were very lucky to get out.'

'I think you better check those lists carefully,' said Jox. 'There were an awful lot of brass in there, especially Royal Navy.'

'I will, but you know the tars can take care of themselves. They have far more resources than we do. You know, senior service and all that,' said Bullough.

'Funny you should say that. Last night, it was a naval rating who pretty much saved our lives, getting us safely across the river. Utterly selfless chap. If anyone deserves a medal, it's him, not flipping me!'

'Oh yes, I heard about that. It was rather a surprise when the papers crossed my desk. The Albanian Order of the Black Eagle, eh? Congratulations, there aren't many of those about.'

'Completely undeserved,' said Jox. 'The whim of a king.'

'Tell you what,' said Bullough, 'if you feel strongly about it, let me have the name of that Jolly Jack Tar and I'll see what I can do. One good turn deserves another.'

'Matt Pye,' said Alice. 'He's a submariner, I think. He said his parents lived near Borough Market. That's about all we know.'

'I'll jot down the details, but in the meantime, Jox, what was Mehmet Ali so keen to discuss with you?'

'He started off by probing me about the state of the war and trying to get an idea of how I felt about how it was being run. He went on to say there are people in the government who are keen for peace and appeasement with Germany. I got the sense he was sounding me out, trying to identify a body of disgruntled RAF personnel who could provide evidence of how badly the war was going and how incompetently the powers that be are running things. His view was that the British people are being misled and need to be better informed so as to put pressure on the government for peace.'

'Well, he's not wrong about the appeasers in the government. We've got Oswald Mosley and his wife Diana bleating from Holloway Prison, then Halifax on the fringes of government sniping away, and even the Duke of Windsor seems keen for us to throw in the towel.' He tapped his index finger against his lip, thinking out loud. 'Clearly, it's in Germany's interest to get like-minded people lined up for when and if they launch an invasion. That way, there's a government in waiting and an infrastructure already in place.'

'I thought their Operation Sealion was shelved after the pasting we gave them during the Battle of Britain?' said Jox.

'Postponed, I'd say, but not shelved. Otherwise, what would be the point of the bombing we're enduring? They want us on our knees when the time comes.' Bullough pursed his lips. 'What is a new development is that Curly Cummings, who we suspect is an *Abwehr* agent, is now out in the open, and from what you're saying he has managed to recruit a senior player in Mehmet Ali, a diplomat of a foreign allied government. Just imagine if they started to gain traction with other exiled governments, not to mention the pilots and soldiers currently filling the gaps in our ranks. Didn't you say over half the replacements at No. 111 Squadron were from countries overrun by the Nazis? What if they were infiltrating rather than reinforcing? It hardly bears contemplating. It would be a catastrophe.'

'Do you think it's possible?' said a horrified Jox.

'Truthfully, no, but that doesn't mean the *Abwehr* won't be trying to make it happen. I've seen them try other hare-brained stunts. I have to admire their ambition. What concerns me is that Curly Cummings is the ringmaster of this particular circus and may well have his fingers in the pies of other exiled governments too. He and I are part of this demi-monde where the intelligence community meets the, shall we say, more colourful and liberal appetites of powerful people, aristocracy, and politicians. It's the perfect agar to cultivate a culture of espionage and intrigue.'

The telephone across the room rang shrilly, making them all jump.

Bullough strode over. 'Squadron Leader Bullough here. Last night? Yes, that's right. The address?' He glanced at Alice and Jox.

'The Coconut Grove, 177 Regent Street,' Alice replied.

Bullough passed on the details, then listened intently. He thanked his correspondent, replaced the handset, and returned grim-faced. 'It appears our concerns for this nascent circle of spies may have been premature.' They looked at him, puzzled. 'I'm afraid it's been confirmed that Curly Cummings, Mehmet Ali and Captain Aaron Ahmeti of the Royal Albanian Guards have all been killed, along with a hundred and thirteen other patrons of the Coconut Grove nightclub. Final casualty figures are still being confirmed, but the indications aren't promising. It appears that all of Curly's orchestra were killed with the exception of a single saxophonist.'

'Oh my God!' cried Alice. 'There were over a dozen of them. Jox, do you realise that could so easily have been us?'

'I know, darling, it's sobering,' said Jox. 'No-one deserves to die like that.'

'Those poor people,' said Alice. 'I can't believe we made it out of there and then didn't even realise what happened. Why us and not them? I just don't understand.'

'It wasn't our time,' said Jox. 'There's no point questioning fate. Up there, one minute you're flying, the next you're gone. Why did I make it through last summer, when so many better pilots didn't? Wheelie, Higgsy and David the Bruce were all far better men than me, but it just wasn't my time.'

It was the last day before Jox's return to Scotland. He'd managed to get to his tailors at Hawkes & Co at Number One Savile Row and had impressed them sufficiently to get a new dress uniform turned around overnight. He told them he was being decorated by the king; he just didn't specify which one.

They'd done a hell of a job, especially getting his rather grubby original 'Montrose' wings clean and then finding the appropriate replacement ribbons for his decorations. The purple striped ribbon of the DFC was fairly common and in stock, but the modest dark blue of the George Cross sent them into a bit of a tizzy, trying to find exactly the right hue.

It struck him that medals for valour always got people terribly worked up, despite the fact that the actions that won them were often purely instinctive. All he'd been trying to do was help his pal, George. Nothing more. That got him thinking of wee Georgie, his border terrier waiting with Pritchard back at Montrose. It would be a terrible wrench leaving Alice, but seeing Georgie again would be some compensation. He knew it was the very reason she'd given him the pup, and he loved her all the more for it.

The new clobber proved rather expensive, but he'd rationalised that the monthly stipend from the award would cover the cost. He had no idea how much a hundred gold Albanian *franga* a month represented, but it sounded like a lot. All the more, if it was to be paid until the end of his days and then to Alice, as his wife, and on down to any descendants. It sounded too good to be true, but when they'd re-read the official letter together, there it was in black and white, signed with a flourish by His Royal Highness King Zog.

Jox was standing in an anteroom, waiting to be called in for the medal ceremony. The collar of his sky-blue shirt and tie were tight at his throat, and his new black Grenson Oxfords were pinching. They were an extravagance for the occasion that he was already regretting. By God, he wished they'd turn down the heating!

Alice was in the other room with the princesses. Bullough was with her, uninvited but having fabricated a role for himself in the ceremony. He was accepting the decoration on behalf of Moose Grant, who had returned to operational duties, much to Princess Myze's distress. Bullough had acquired a light-blue Aide-de-Camp aiguilette, which made his unadorned uniform seem rather grander — a challenge, since he was never the most martial-looking of men, despite the importance of his department for shady dealings.

Suffering in silence, Jox wished Moose was with him, sharing in the embarrassment. The double doors opened, and the sole surviving Albanian Guards Captain Ilir Krasniqi smiled and bowed obsequiously.

Jox was announced as *'Teniente* Jeremy McNabb,' and marched forward during the recitation in a language he didn't understand, whilst several members of the audience clapped. He kept a serious face and to his relief the ceremony didn't take long, as a succession of dignitaries were also receiving awards.

His overriding memory of the king was that at first, he didn't appear to recognise him. When pinning the double-headed eagle medal to Jox's chest, he smelt strongly of cigarettes and cologne. Shaking his hand, King Zog declared, 'You are a fine young officer, an example to us all. I have lost some of my finest and it pains me dearly. We must treasure our heroes, so it is right we honour you.' He was wearing a simple black armband on his otherwise ornate uniform and was clearly upset. Several other members of the royal party, including Queen Geraldine and at least three of his sisters wore them too.

Princess Maxhide, the youngest, was dressed entirely in black, her face hidden by a veil. She'd taken the news of Curly Cummings' death rather badly and was now playing the grieving widow, a most unlikely scenario given the man's leanings in life. His funeral was organised for later in the week, after Jox had returned north. Alice had agreed to accompany the princesses. It promised to be a gathering of the most colourful and bohemian characters in London and once again, Bullough would attend, 'Purely for information-gathering purposes.'

Today the princesses Myze and Ruhi were dressed in white trouser suits, sashes, gilded belts and swords. They wore black ties and white peaked caps, giving them the look of Italian gelati sellers, but these were actually the uniforms of Colonels of the Female Youth Battalions of the Royal Albanian Army.

Following the Muslim tradition, the funerals of Chamberlain Mehmet Ali and his bodyguard Captain Aaron Ahmeti were to be held before sundown in the Ottoman section of Brookwood Cemetery in Surrey. Straight after the medal ceremony, the royal party were leaving with a long line of Daimlers waiting outside the hotel. Bullough had expressed his concerns that the ostentatious cortege of vehicles might attract the attention of marauding enemy fighters. After discussing the threat with the king, Captain Ilir Krasniqi, in his new role as royal chamberlain, relayed the king's commentary.

'Send a fighter escort if you are so unsure of having the mastery of your own airspace.'

Accordingly, two Polish Hurricanes from No. 303 'Kościuszko' Squadron were set to take off from RAF Northolt in northwest London, to fly loops over the Albanian royal convoy as it progressed. They would land and refuel during the funerals and would repeat the performance as the king and party returned to The Ritz. To Jox, it was such a monumental waste of fuel, but Bullough insisted it was a necessary diplomatic expense. He added that he'd rather waste some fuel and have two cheesed-off Poles than run the risk, however remote, of King Zog or any of his entourage being hurt by unopposed enemy action. Apparently, heads were already rolling in the Foreign Office because Mehmet Ali had managed to slip his minders and had then gone and got himself killed.

Jox stepped back from the king and saluted in the regulation manner. Zog glared at him expectantly. Jox remembered what Princess Ruhi had shown him. He crossed his right arm crisply across his chest, fingers extended like a naval salute, then placed his right hand across his heart with palm downward. The king smiled and returned the salute, as did his royal sisters. It was such a simple thing, but given their reaction it was absolutely the right thing to do.

Jox was shown to a seat beside Alice, whilst Bullough went up to receive Moose's decoration on his behalf. If King Zog expected the tall bull-necked Canuck, the contrasting slightness of Sandy Bullough couldn't have been more marked, and yet Bullough skilfully overcame any unease, quickly making the king burst out laughing with some remark.

Watching them, Jox couldn't help observing that they were engaged in a very different kind of warfare than he was used to. One of diplomacy and insincere smiles, whispers, flattery, and murky subterfuge. The identity of one's friends or enemies was always unclear, and every word and action had hidden meanings. It was a world he was weary of, and he longed for the simpler world of men and machines, camaraderie, and duty. A world where he knew his enemy and simply needed to find him in the darkness of the night.

It was New Year's Eve, his much-anticipated Hogmanay in London. Alice would have something planned, perhaps with the princesses or Stephanie, her friend from work. He really wasn't in the mood. The prospect of revelry in this time of misery didn't sit well with him anymore. He was feeling the pull of the air, of uncomplicated flight and freedom, far away from the subterfuge and whims of fate that had buffeted him over the last few days.

This wasn't how he'd expected to be feeling after his leave, but he'd seen so many startling and shocking things that he yearned for the simplicity of the cockpit. There, at least, he was the master of his own destiny.

# CHAPTER FIFTEEN

There was a letter from Alice in Jox's cubby hole when he came down for breakfast. Rather than joining the others for powdered eggs and toast, he grabbed a mug of tea and found a quiet corner. It had been a few weeks since their eventful leave together in London.

*Whitehall, W1*
*Sunday, 2 Feb '41*

*My darling Jox,*
*It feels like such a long time since I've seen you. I'd got rather used to waking up beside you and my cot feels rather cold. Our accommodation block here couldn't be more different, but at least I have my memories and the dreams of the days we'll have together.*
*I hope the trip back to Montrose wasn't too bad and that you weren't delayed. Trains these days never seem to keep to timetables. I suppose that's another thing we can blame Jerry for. I bet wee Georgie was happy to have his daddy back, although I'm sure he's been more than spoilt by the soft-hearted boys of your squadron. Don't let him get too fat; he's a working dog and needs plenty of exercise. I bet the beach at Montrose is still bleak at this time of year, but perfect for his walks. Do you remember our little fisherman's hut? I certainly do.*
*Work is much as expected, with long hours spent underground. I do find it rewarding and it's a real privilege to be working in the presence of 'No.1' (I hope the censor will allow that!). We work away like moles, coming up for meals and breaks. You'd think we'd be pale as ghosts, but the powers that be have decided we must sit under sun ray lamps for ten minutes a week, so I'm as brown as a berry. I have some awful strap*

marks, but you can't expect me to parade around in the all-together in a room full of others, can you? Mind you, doesn't seem to stop Stephanie, who is rather buxom and sunburnt in all the wrong places because of her fair complexion. You remember, she's my friend who took such a shine to Moose. She's such a wag.

When I get time off, I go for walks around tired old London town, thinking of you (don't get a big head now) and what our life will be like after the war. Roll on May, when I become Mrs Alice McNabb! It's got a certain ring to it, don't you think?

I hope Pritch and the boys are behaving. Tell him I expect the very best of him as best man and he must protect you during your stag party. Will Moose be joining you? I know he's stationed in Scotland, but I'm afraid I have no idea where. Say hello and do let him know that both Stephanie Merritt and Princess Myze have been asking after him. There's something about that big fellow that is very appealing to the ladies, but I only have eyes for my darling Jox!

Speaking of the princesses, I went to Curly Cummings' funeral. What an odd bunch. Sandy was a charming escort but was like an owl watching mice at play. Always searching for clues but being charming all the while. He's just been promoted to Wing Commander. I expect being a desktop warrior, chasing baddies with his pen and his brain has some advantages.

As you can imagine, Princess Maxhide put on a bravura performance at Curly's funeral. Would you believe she's now transferred her affections to a new cabaret singer called 'Snake Hips' Johnson, who plays at the Café de Paris near Piccadilly Circus? She really does pick them, since 'Snake Hips' has as much interest in the fairer sex as old Curly did before him. Ooh, I bet you never expected your fiancée to be such a gossip!

Otherwise, old London keeps on keeping on. We're having fewer raids. Perhaps Jerry is 'spreading the love' to other cities. From work, I can see that northern cities have been hit badly. Most recent raids here have been bigger bombs rather than firebombs. Not much comfort if your building cops one, but at least entire neighbourhoods aren't going up in flames like *before. Still, I think I'm fairly safe in my underground cell, and there's always Steph to keep up my morale. I was thinking of asking her to be my bridesmaid. What do you think?*

*Listen, love, I must leave off. I'm on the two to nine shift today, so hopefully it'll be quiet. Please, PLEASE take care of yourself. Remember, every time you take off, my fragile heart is with you. It doesn't stop thumping until I know you're back on the ground. It's such an honour for me to be your fiancée, but it's not great for my nerves. Be safe and remember you carry my dreams.*

*Yours now and always,*
*Alice xx*

Take-off at dusk from Montrose was pretty straightforward, but now that night had fallen, Jox could see little through the sides of his cockpit. It was like flying in a swirling pint of Guinness. Dundee was supposed to be down there somewhere to the west, but for the life of him he couldn't see it. The city really should have been obvious, edged by the silvery Tay of McGonagall, with the distinctive arching spans of the great curving rail bridge.

Blue Section were ordered over the city for a live practice of the SMACK interception procedure. Dundee was Scotland's fourth largest city, the capital of the ancient county of Angus and worth defending. High-powered searchlights were meant to be probing after a pair of Handley Page Halifax bombers that were doubling as the enemy, and Jox's section were vectored onto them for a guided interception.

The trouble was he could see none of it, not the city nor the bridge. By all accounts, neither could the radar operators on the ground, who had remained steadfastly silent. This was turning into a bloody disaster. Peering forward, all he could see was the dull glow of his exhaust stubs, matching the frustration burning in the pit of his stomach.

Thankfully, the sharp young vision of Bubbles Broughton at Blue Four finally found the dim edge of Dundee cut by the bank of the river. His element leader, newly commissioned Czech pilot Miro Mansfeld, an experienced night fighter, grunted his confirmation. Flying in finger-four formation, the pair should have been on Jox's starboard side, staggered behind him, but he could see neither of them. *Damn it, what a peasouper.*

'WAGON Blue Leader, this is Blue Three. I can see your tail. Blue Four, he's tight on my arse, over,' said Mansfeld in his distinctive accent.

The Scots brogue of Cam Glasgow, Jox's wingman, cut in, 'Aye, Blue Two here. I can see you too.' This was Glasgow's hometown and he'd been looking forward to the exercise. Now he was complaining in his inimitable way, 'I cannae see pish oot here.'

Jox strained to see over his shoulders and gave the porcelain talisman in his pocket a quick squeeze. He began to make out the glow of nose exhausts strobing weakly through their propellors. He realised that if they'd been enemies, he'd already be dead. Mulling over that prospect, he now began to see the outline of twinkling Dundee below. A searchlight came on, lighting up Glasgow's aircraft over Jox's left shoulder. A colourful stream of Caledonian invective came forth and the light peeled away, probing for the missing Halifax bombers. The beam cut the gloom like an usherette's torch through the cigarette fug of a busy picture house. It locked onto a blurry patch of airspace above and ahead of Blue Section's aircraft.

The codeword 'CONE' was given over the radio and two more beams switched on and converged with the first. Dark smudges appeared in the brume. Jox ordered the section to climb.

They attacked the illuminated pair of four-engine bombers. Jox and Glasgow took a swing at the portside aircraft, Mansfeld and Broughton the starboard. As they'd been taught, they aimed for the bloated underbellies of the bogeys, then spoke into their mask mics. Each in turn said, 'Bang-bang-bang,' mimicking their guns and ensuring there was no doubt amongst the bomber crews nor the ground controllers that No. 111 Squadron's night fighters had successfully intercepted the 'enemy', even in these appalling weather conditions.

Completing the manoeuvre, Jox ordered the section to climb clear of the soup they'd been flying through, bursting through the cloud cover to reveal a twinkling display of stars and the dancing green hues of *aurora borealis* across the heavens. They could have navigated home by the stars, but it was easier to follow the coordinates provided by Montrose tower.

Despite his earlier reservations concerning the weather and the efficacy of the SMACK radar tracking system, it had all worked. Glasgow summed up their collective relief. 'Aye, well, trust the Dundonians to make a hare-brained scheme like this work.'

Jox was pleased to be bringing them home in one piece and looked forward to applying their new skills to real-world interceptions, rather than these endless exercises. He was happy the mission was over and was dreaming of warming up after this awful dreich night by the fireside, chewing the fat over a few drams.

A few nights later, bombers bearing the Viking longship emblem of KGr 100 dropped payloads of small fifty-kilogram high explosive bombs, oil bombs and then thousands of incendiaries on Clydebank. Blazes were raging at the Yoker Distillery to the east of the town and the timber yards belonging to the Singer Sewing Machine works.

Up on the hill above the town, Auchentoshan Distillery was also hit, setting ablaze warehouses holding stock equivalent to over a million gallons of whisky. Scotland's own fire water now burned as it flowed into a nearby burn, a molten mass coursing downstream to the Clyde.

At street level, townsfolk were getting caught in the open. Bodies were clumped together on the streets as a terrific anti-aircraft barrage arched over, blasting blindly at the invisible but audible enemy overhead.

Clydebank's emergency services were completely overwhelmed, particularly once the control centre received a direct hit early on in the raid. A crater, thirty feet wide and twenty feet deep severed the town's principal water main, further reducing the firefighters' ability to contain the inferno.

This was the moment the Treble Ones were called into the fight. Glasgow's own No. 602 Squadron had already been sent to intercept the bombers, hunting by sight, but it was proving ineffective, as more and more raiders were getting through.

So it was with high expectations that No. 111 Squadron, trained as Ground Controlled Interceptors (GCI) and night fighting specialists were sent in. Their expertise was desperately needed to tip the balance, so they were dragged from their beds, dosed with strong coffee and hastily briefed. Scrambling off into the darkness after midnight, both veterans and combat virgins were finally being called to put their training and skills to the test.

Jox and his comrades were taking the fight to the enemy, and for many it was well past time.

# CHAPTER SIXTEEN

They took off in pairs. Brotchie and Pritchard went up first with Red Section, then Jox with Blue, Simpson with Yellow, and finally Chalmers at the rear with Green. They followed the coastline, crossing the choppy Firth of Forth at Grangemouth, the home base of No. 602 (City of Glasgow) Squadron. By the time they reached Falkirk, they could see the flames over Clydebank.

It was a clear and moonlit night, cold enough for frost to crystalise on the Spitfires' canopies. Ahead, the fires provided a pulsing homing beacon. Visibility was good as Brotchie ordered the sections to tighten up. He contacted ground control, responsible for providing their vector coordinates.

Below were the rolling hills, valleys and burns of Jox's homeland, where the people slept on, unaware that a riverside neighbour was being ravaged by fire. There was a faint movement shimmering across the glowing surface of the moon, a line that shouldn't have been there.

'Bird strike, bird strike!' came a cry over the R/T. It sounded like Pritchard. The squadron scattered like pigeons pounced upon by a kestrel. One aircraft pulled up steeply before Jox, the mantle of condensation forming across its back like the cloak of a Viking king. Aircraft tumbled and flames could be seen spouting from exhaust stubs like fiery comets.

'Red Two, Mayday, Mayday. I'm going down.'

Jox felt a hollow thud on the leading edge of his starboard wing, where the snout of his cannon jutted out. Momentarily skewered, a large bird flapped, before being whipped away. A second thumped against his canopy with a terrific bang, leaving a long, dark smear down the Perspex. Behind him, another Canada Goose struck the propeller of young Broughton's aircraft, hitting it like a meat cannon ball. It shattered the blades and covered the hood with minced gore. The boy screamed in blind terror.

Struggling to regain control of his bucking aircraft, Jox heard Cam Glasgow swearing as he avoided smacking into the back of him. Broughton was still screaming and then went silent. Mansfeld's deadpan voice reported, 'WAGON leader, this is Red Three. Wingman Red Four has a bird strike. I see a parachute; he has bailed out.'

Jox tilted his Spitfire to catch the half orb of Broughton's parachute, brightly lit in the moonlight. There was a flaming impact as his aircraft hit a dark hillside. All around them, honking in the night sky were ragged vees of wild geese, driven from the margins of the Clyde by the fiery devastation.

'WAGON Squadron, this is WAGON Leader. Red Two is down,' said Brotchie tersely. 'Green Leader, take your section back around and mark where the kites have pranged. Keep your eyes peeled for parachutes. We've seen one, but there should be another. And for God's sake, watch those bloody birds. We're down two kites and we haven't seen a bandit!' After collecting his thoughts, he said, 'Turnhouse Ops, WAGON Leader here. WAGON Squadron on station. Do you have any trade for us?'

They were approaching the fiery edges of Clydeside. On the horizon, plumes of thick smoke rose in tilting columns. Streams of tracers rose from the ground, but there was no sign of any searchlights.

'Turnhouse Ops here. The power is out over the target. Ground radar and lights are U/S. WAGON Squadron patrol at

Angels Ten for targets of opportunity. An estimated hundred plus bandits are in the area.'

'Damn,' replied Brotchie. 'After all our training, we're still going in blind. Right, WAGON Leader here. Blue Leader, take your lot south over the river. I'll look for action over the worst of the fires and then head east. Yellow Leader, you take yours north. See what you can find, but be careful, VILLA Squadron are also up here and some experimental Beaufighters with onboard radar will be here soon. Don't confuse them with bandits; they look remarkably similar. Green Leader, catch up when you can, and keep an ear open to support any section that's in contact. WAGON Leader out.'

Jox acknowledged the order and dipped his aircraft onto its portside wing, dutifully followed by Glasgow and Mansfeld. The river below them was liquid flame, with large tracts of the wooden wharfs ablaze. Taking in the horror, his mind was racing elsewhere.

Pritchard was down! One minute there, gone the next. *How will I ever manage without Pritch?*

Jox had no siblings. Those he chose to call brother were carefully selected to fill the gaps where he found himself weakest. Cam Glasgow was like his right arm: straight and true. Moose was his strength and vigour, Sandy Bullough his guile and intelligence, but Pritch was *joie de vivre*, positivity and laughter. A world without him would be very bleak indeed.

'WAGON Blue Section, Leader here. Did anyone see Pritch go down?'

Mansfeld replied, 'No, only Bubbles.'

Glasgow was more measured, realising that his young officer was imagining the worst. 'Take it easy, Blue Leader. Red Two is an excellent pilot. If anyone can get out of a jam, it's him. Don't torture yourself. We've a mission to protect those poor souls down there. Pritch is big enough and ugly enough to take care of himself.'

He was right, but Jox was horrified at the prospect of having to tell Alice they'd lost their best man. After losing her brother, the news would be crushing, and she would undoubtedly see it as a bad omen.

It was Miro Mansfeld, the wise old night owl, who saw something low, flying at tree level above a burning park. 'Have a bandit at two o'clock low.'

It was an enemy Heinkel with one engine on fire, pursued by the sleek silhouette of a Spitfire. Flames against a flaming backdrop didn't register, but flickering tracers juddering after their prey were what Mansfeld had spotted.

'Let's cover that Spit,' said Jox. 'See if he needs a hand or if there are more bandits about. Follow me. Tally-ho, tally-ho.' He heard the 'Wilcos' in his ears and Blue Section, or at least what was left of it, dropped, loosing off quick bursts as they slipped past, one after the next.

The bomber folded in half, disintegrating into components, like silvery rain. A single airman dropped from the aircraft, parachute blossoming, but he was only delaying his fate, as hot winds sucked him inexorably towards the burning timber rafters of an ancient kirk. His ashes would join those of countless Clydebankers who'd been buried here over the centuries.

They wouldn't make a claim for this bandit; a four-way split wasn't terribly impressive. The unknown No. 603 Squadron pilot, codename VILLA, had done the hard part, having found the enemy and getting in the first shots. Jox clicked his R/T.

'WAGON Blue Leader to unknown VILLA pilot. Good kill. Blue Leader out.'

They had enough fuel for about half an hour, so they patrolled further but found no sign of the enemy. A ship moored at the docks took a pot-shot at them and they spiralled away, wasting more precious fuel.

Red and Yellow Sections confirmed they had blanked too. Only Chalmers and Green Section had bagged a brace, one falling to Chalmers and the other shared between the inseparable Aussies, Kanga Reeves and Roo James. Their delay in getting to the patrol area placed them in the right place at the right time. They also reported sightings of the wrecks of both Pritchard and Broughton's aircraft, the latter observed to land by parachute. There was no sign of Pritchard.

Nearing the fuel bingo point, the squadron headed forlornly back home. Once on the ground, there were no celebrations as they were all exhausted, shocked by their losses and the devastation they'd witnessed. After a debrief with Robertson and the new Commanding Officer, some were tempted by a lacklustre breakfast of eggs and tinned bacon, but most opted for a few hours' kip. They would be on call again the following evening.

It wasn't until mid-morning, when many were still in their beds, that a grimy, pinch-faced and rather damp Broughton shuffled into the dispersal. He was carrying his Mae West and a dripping, bundled parachute in his arms. He dumped them dramatically onto the floor, then sat down, giving a very plausible impression of a drowned rat. After a restorative dram, despite the hour, he told his tale of the night.

'I heard Pritch call "Bird Strike" and then my propellor minced up a bloody great goose. It punched a hole through my canopy, smashing my targeting sight, and I got a big wet slap in the face.' He pointed to his bruised chin and the burgundy streaks down his neck. 'Guts and feathers were rattling around the cockpit and the wind howled through the hole. Couldn't see a damned thing, and my Spit was out of control. I was shitting myself.'

'You did well to get out,' soothed Glasgow.

'Racing through my mind was all those bloody hills. I didn't have much time, but I got out, landing in a freezing fucking loch.' Broughton lifted his sopping Mae West jacket. 'This thing saved my life. I managed to get to the shore and crawled onto the pebbly beach. I couldn't move — I was so cold and completely knackered. Those stones may be pretty, but they're bloody uncomfortable. Anyway, I managed to find a bothy with an old gamekeeper and his wife, Iona. She gave me a cup of tea and a dram once I'd convinced her shotgun-toting husband that I wasn't a Jerry.'

'How'd you do that?' asked Mansfeld.

'I sang "Danny Boy." That convinced them.'

'Clever laddie, that was well done,' said Glasgow. The others nodded their approval.

'Some chaps from the Argylls came by and picked me up, then brought me home.'

'You've had a lucky escape,' said Brotchie, who'd been listening quietly from the corner. 'No news of my wingman, though. The longer it takes, the more likely it won't be good news.' He glanced at Jox and Chalmers regretfully.

Badger Robertson, wiser and older than the rest, took the pipe from his mouth. 'Let's not give up on old Pritch quite yet. He's gone down before, and like a bad penny he always turns up. Chin up, boys.'

Jox reached into his pocket for Marguerite's doll's arm. He rubbed the smooth surface with his thumb furiously, silently praying for the safety of his friend.

Nothing was heard of Pritchard before the squadron were ordered back to Clydebank. It was still burning, but most of last night's survivors had been evacuated into the countryside. The enemy were attacking in force for a second night, but this time from a greater altitude and they were invisible from the ground. This didn't stop the AA gun positions that had been brought in, blasting away at the night sky assisted by radar-controlled searchlights, which were now also working. The Treble Ones could at last apply their specialist training.

It was the squadron newcomers Solly Cohen and Axel Fisken who brought down a raider apiece, pressing home separate attacks.

Arriving back at Montrose in the early hours, the squadron were satisfied they'd gone some way in avenging Clydebank.

Pritchard casually sauntered into the mess just after lunch. Like a tomcat returning from his nocturnal adventures, his face was scratched with vivid red marks, and he was limping, but probably from a flare-up of his Dunkirk wound.

The expression on his face was that of someone who knew a cracking joke and couldn't wait to deliver the punchline. The men made a great fuss of him, settling down to hear the fine tale it would undoubtedly be. When Pritchard had been handed a frothy pint of Eighty Shilling, Robertson asked the inevitable question: 'Where the bloody hell have you been?'

'Now, there's a question and therein lies quite a tale,' replied a beaming Pritchard, settling onto his barstool. 'The straight answer is up an enormous Scots pine in the grounds of Lennox castle, but I think I better explain. You see, when I hit that bloody bird, my engine flared and caught fire. I had no control in my stick and things were getting a tad hot. I took to my silk and drifted along quite nicely, seeing my kite prang into some big mountain.'

'Your wreckage was found on Meikle Bin in the Campsie Fells,' replied Robertson.

'Quite so. Well, I'm floating, pushed along by the wind, rather cold as I recall, towards a baronial mansion. It was really quite dark, and I couldn't see very well, but it was about four or five storeys high, looming large in the landscape. I thought, *right, this'll do*. Well, I couldn't have been more wrong.

'First off, I landed short, falling through the canopy of a bloody great tree. That's how I got these scratches. Stuck fast, my feet were dangling twenty feet off the ground, like some puppet on strings.' He chuckled. 'As you can imagine, I raised merry hell trying to attract attention, but nothing doing. I tired myself out and must have dozed off from the shock or the cold.

'Anyway, I woke up and it was daylight. I saw some men shuffling about in pyjamas and dressing gowns. I called down; they looked up and completely ignored me. I screamed blue murder but got nothing. They just wandered off and left me hanging, cold, hungry, and thoroughly hacked off. Another chap came along, similarly attired, so I gave the same performance. He jumped out of his skin, screeched blue murder and ran off jabbering. Must have given him quite a fright, but at least hopefully he would tell someone. Nothing doing, I was still hanging there like a plonker.

'It must have been mid-afternoon by the time a couple finally came along. He was wearing the uniform of a brown job and she was a nurse. They were walking hand in hand and in no time were under my tree, putting a blanket down and canoodling. Well, it was a bit delicate interrupting as they were getting fruity and quite frankly, after hours up there, I was thoroughly bored and things were only now getting interesting.'

Pritchard was giggling and the others could picture the scene. 'There was a lot of oohing and aahing going on, and before I knew what was what, she was on her back and you can imagine the rest. Turned out she was really quite a looker, nurse's uniform and all. Couldn't see much of him, thank God, other than rabbit buttocks.' His audience were roaring. 'Our girl was in the throes of passion when she opened her peepers and spotted yours truly. She gave a mighty shriek, and her beau thought he was really hitting the spot. She kicked him off and started covering up, which was rather a pity. She was pointing and our chap jumped up, trousers at his ankles and, shall we say, rapidly sinking to half-mast. Well, I didn't know what to say, so I blurted out, "Sorry to interrupt. I'm in a bit of bother. I don't suppose you could help me down?"

'She was off, and he was swearing and calling me a pervert. I was getting rather fed-up and roared down, "I didn't ask you to pick this bloody tree, did I, pongo? Now get me down, or, by God, I'll find you and rip that little plonker of yours right off!"

'That did the trick, and he ran off too, but a mob of nurses and chaps in white coats soon arrived with ladders. It must have been six o'clock by the time I was finally "wheels down".'

He indicated to the bar steward that he fancied another pint. 'Things got rather better after that. It appeared that I'd landed in the grounds of Lennox Castle, outside Lennoxtown in Dunbartonshire. The place is a mental asylum. The chaps I'd seen earlier were patients who obviously thought I was some figment of their imaginations and ignored me. The big house — and it really was an enormous affair with towers, castellated edges and everything — is now a nurses' home, housing a few hundred delightful young women, with their patients accommodated around the estate grounds. They patched me up and gave me a nice dinner, and some of the ladies were really rather lovely after my trials and tribulations. Mind you, I didn't see my courting couple again. Still, the lovelies asked me to stay for the night.' Pritchard smiled wickedly. 'As a man with my reputation, who was I to argue?'

'You might have telephoned to let us know,' said Robertson.

'Impossible, dear boy. My hands were completely full.'

## CHAPTER SEVENTEEN

Jox was on the duty roster to lead a trio of Spits up to RAF Dyce for servicing after the exertions of the Clydebank missions. He took the opportunity to cadge a lift into Aberdeen itself, making a beeline for Jamieson & Carry, the jewellers on Union Street that he'd been assured were the finest in town. He wanted a wedding gift for Alice, finally settling on an elegant string of pearls that cost him the best part of two months' salary.

Feeling upbeat about his purchase, he remembered that it was his stag-do that evening. The prospect filled him with trepidation. Since the triumphant return from the dead of Pritchard and Broughton, the squadron had notched up four new kills and the Treble Ones were determined to mark the occasion. These were the first scores on the board under Brotchie's command, and he was determined to celebrate vigorously.

The evening would undoubtedly involve high jinks, especially given the CO's reputation for taking things too far. Jox was justifiably nervous, in spite of the assurances from Pritchard and Robertson, who promised to take care of him.

By the time he was at the bar, his plan was to face his fears head-on. Three pints of 90 Shilling were lined up before him with whisky chasers. Taking a deep breath, he turned to his squadron mates and raised the first glass to their undisguised glee. The noise that rose from them was like the baying of hounds scenting a fox.

'Here's to a good night, my friends,' Jox said. 'You mean a great deal to me, and it's an honour to serve with you. Up there, I trust you with my life, so why would it be any different down here? If you're planning to play any nasty tricks on me, know only this: I'll be disappointed in you. Right, I've nothing else to say about that. *Slàinte Mhath*!'

His squadron mates crowded in, wishing him all good things. He knew some better than others, but all were sincere in their wishes for his impending wedding. Pete Simpson, the veteran amongst the squadron's flight leaders, tried to engage Jox in a semi-sensible conversation about what a husband might expect from a marriage, but since he wasn't married himself, Jox wondered whether he was speaking from a sense of optimism rather than experience. A sensitive, deep-thinking chap who'd only turned twenty the previous week himself, he was a little tipsy, but he was very insistent that Jox understand the seriousness of the undertaking.

Simpson looked old for his years. Combat did that. He'd been with No. 111 Squadron since November 1939, when he'd been aged just eighteen — no older than Jox when he'd joined in May 1940. *Christ, I hope the war hasn't marked me that much*, thought Jox. Good old Pete — well, actually, pretty young Pete — he really looked like he could do with a break from Ops.

The squadron's two Czech pilots, Mansfeld and Kucera, approached timidly, keen to wish Jox the best and present him with a rope garlanded with artificial flowers and intricately plaited ribbons. Kucera explained, 'In our country, this rope is strung across the doorway of the church. It symbolises the sins the groom must leave behind as he enters matrimony. Tonight, we will drink and then attach the bottles to the rope, representing your misspent youth. When you and your bride emerge from church as a married couple, you must first pay money to the church to make up for these sins.'

'*At' je váš život tvrdý jako knedlík*,' said Mansfeld. 'May your life together be as hard as dumplings. *Na zdraví*!'

Across the bar, Axel Fisken bellowed, '*Skål*!' Olivier de Ghellinck echoed, '*À la vôtre*,' and Solly Cohen gave a hearty '*L'Chayim*.' Finally, the old China hand, Mike Longstaffe leant over and added, '*Gānbēi*!' in Mandarin. There was no better illustration of the international nature the war had taken on, nor the unified effort of so many nations and creeds pitted against a common enemy. It was a humbling realisation, and Jox was grateful to be part of it.

It didn't take many rounds before things descended into chaos. The contest to place a sooty footprint on the ceiling was won by the appropriately light Broughton, who was effectively caber tossed up there by the burly Aussies, Reeves and James. Racing around the walls of the bar, without touching the floor, came down to a final between Yellow and Green Sections. Chalmers was quick and very dextrous, but experience shone through as he was beaten by the CO who'd been playing the game for a long time. Whether Chalmers cunningly let him win, was quite another question.

Winners or losers, they all drank and poor Jox was always pushed to the front of the queue. His last coherent conversation was with de Ghellinck and Axel Fisken. They were telling him the stories of the women they'd left behind in their home countries.

'My fiancée Tove and I were in the resistance after the fall of Norway,' said the fair-haired Norwegian. Unusually for a pilot, he wore little round golden spectacles perched on the bridge of his pointed nose. Despite a somewhat bookish appearance, Fisken was a veteran pilot and a killer, as demonstrated by his solo victory over Clydebank. He didn't speak very often, but when he did it was with a chilling intensity that some found unsettling.

'We were betrayed by a comrade, a Quisling traitor, and I was captured, but Tove escaped.' Fisken lifted his left hand to show two missing fingers. 'They took these trying to get me to give her up.' He smiled bitterly. 'I was lucky; the convoy taking us to the camps in Germany was attacked by British fighter-bombers. In the confusion, I managed to escape and hide in some fishing net sheds. I was found by the fisherman, but thankfully he was the head of the local resistance. When he discovered I was a fighter pilot, he arranged a passage to England. I then made my way to the *Utefronten*, the Free Norwegian forces in London, and hoped they might have information on Tove.' He stared at his missing fingers. 'Tove means beautiful in Norse. I fight to see my Tove again.' His sky-blue eyes bored into Jox. 'Look after your Tove, my friend.'

Olivier de Ghellinck joined the conversation. 'I fight for a woman too — not for a lover, but for my sister, the bravest woman I know. It was easy for aviators to flee Belgium when it fell; we just stole our aircraft and headed south. I made it to Gibraltar, then came to England and joined the squadron. My sister, Véronique, she stayed. She lost her husband Hubert during the Campaign of Eighteen Days and is now bringing up their two little children on her own. I've tried to establish contact through the Belgian embassy and have learnt she is working as a courier in the *Réseau Comète* — how you say, Comet Line? They pass allied airmen to return to England. Every day she risks her life and those of her babies, when I'm here safe in England. It is she who should be the *chevalier*, the knight, not me. She is who I fight for. For her and for Belgium.'

'What remarkable women,' said Jox, slurring a bit. 'My Alice is brave too. During the Battle of Britain, we were bombed at RAF Kenley, and over Christmas we got caught in the worst of the Blitz. London was in flames, and you wouldn't believe the destruction I saw. Simply awful. I was relieved, but rather ashamed to escape back to Montrose. She's still there, working for the Prime Minister — but, you know, shhhh, I can't talk about that.'

It was barely ten o'clock and Jox was paralytic. This was the moment Squadron Leader Brotchie chose to strike. His penchant for cruel tricks had come to the fore, and he was carrying a bucket. Jox was passed out on a sofa as Brotchie gathered his troops around him.

'Now then, gentlemen, to mark the occasion of our Jox marrying the delectable Alice, it seems appropriate to remind him of his loyalties as a true-blue fighter pilot in the RAF. A blue mark, if you will, to remind him of his duty when in the arms of his beloved. The blue of the uniforms we proudly wear.'

The men were unsure what he was on about. Pritchard glanced at somnolent Jox, then at Robertson, who was looking nervous.

'This bucket contains five bottles of blue Quink ink, dissolved in some white spirit. We're going to dip one of young McNabb's hands and one of his feet to remind him to always put his "best foot forward" and "to keep a hand on his wallet" as he enters matrimony.'

Pritchard considered the implications of what was planned and assessed the grief he was likely to get from his unconscious friend. Most importantly, though, he thought about what Alice would do to him if he let this happen. 'Hold on, hold on. This isn't on,' he said, placing his not inconsiderable bulk between Jox and the diminutive CO.

'I beg your pardon, Flying Officer Pritchard?' roared Brotchie. 'Out of my way!'

'Look, sir, I'm all for a harmless prank and I don't want to spoil the fun, but if you dip either of his hands in that ink, it's going to show in their wedding photos, which are meant to last a lifetime. He's going to wear his wedding ring over it. As his best man and friend, I cannot allow us to sabotage his wedding like that. His bride would never forgive us and, more importantly, me.'

Brotchie's face was turning puce when Robertson stepped forward and whispered into his ear. The CO considered what was said.

'Right, fine, that can work. A compromise, I see, fine.' The mood lightened. 'Right, chaps, get the shoe and sock off his left foot. We'll make a left footer of him yet,' cried the CO with renewed glee. 'Roll up his trouser leg so we don't splash his uniform. This stuff's pretty nasty, so don't wake him up and don't spill anything.'

The operation ran remarkably smoothly. With his left foot immersed, Jox frowned, then mumbled a few words. They carefully dried off his foot, ruining several mess bar towels, then got his sock and shoe back on.

The following morning, rising early as was his habit, Pritchard was in the shower room when he heard the flush of the communal urinal, then a screech, followed by a stream of invectives. No one on the dormitory floor was left in any doubt that Jox had just discovered his cobalt-coloured appendage.

A few days later, what was in doubt was the identity of the person responsible for a jar of potassium permanganate powder being dumped over the top of the aluminium partition around the bathtub occupied by Squadron Leader Brotchie. Emerging furious and rather more puce than usual, it took a few hours for him to appear bright red and rather contrite.

# CHAPTER EIGHTEEN

Stephanie was late meeting Alice outside the cinema and if she didn't get a move on, they'd miss the news reels before the main feature. Tonight's picture was the latest Tyrone Power film, *The Mark of Zorro*. Stephanie had said it was all the rage and had assured Alice that Tyrone was quite the dish.

Standing outside the picture house on her own, Alice attracted the attention of some Polish soldiers larking about on the pavement. One of them had a camera and asked that she take their picture. She reluctantly obliged but didn't really want to encourage them, so she hastily returned it. The photographer sneaked a quick shot of her, making her frown, as she didn't really like the idea of becoming some kind of barrack room pin-up. They were a fine-looking bunch of men, smart and well turned-out, but boisterous like men can be when moving in a pack.

Alice decided to go in. She bought her ticket and entered the auditorium without waiting any longer for Stephanie. The Pathé News reels were just starting, and she was keen to see if the news released to the public differed greatly from what she heard first-hand at work.

The first report was on the Clydebank Blitz, which she knew Jox had been involved in. The footage was desperate, but in truth no worse than when London was hit over Christmas. Perhaps the difference was that Londoners were familiar with what was coming but the Clydesiders had no real experience of any raids.

The next story was about the American President Roosevelt giving a speech to White House Correspondents, promising aid to Britain 'until total victory has been won'. The final report was about the big band leader, Glen Miller and his orchestra, reaching the number one spot with 'The Song of the Volga Boatmen'. The catchy number was playing when outside the air-raid sirens began to wail. The film flickered and the lights went up. A nervous commissionaire stepped up to inform the audience of an imminent raid. Patrons were advised to evacuate immediately and to seek refuge at one of the two nearest underground shelters. He provided directions and the audience began to file out in an orderly manner. Alice reached the exit at the same time as the now more subdued Poles.

Outside, it was nearing dusk, and the raids were starting early tonight. In the distance, Alice could already hear the rumble of detonations. The streets were a cacophony of noise, with the haunting wail of the sirens and booming reports from a battery of heavy QF 3.7-inch anti-aircraft guns in the nearby park. Firing big 28 lb shells to a ceiling of 35,000 feet, they were fairly inaccurate but provided some reassurance to Londoners that the city was fighting back.

Alice found the volume disorienting. The photographer from earlier grabbed her shoulder. 'Please, miss, come this way to safety.' He and his companions were headed down an alleyway alongside the cinema. It was a dead-end.

'No, this way,' she indicated, gesticulating towards the nearest shelter.

They started to follow. Alice turned the corner onto a tree-lined avenue where she knew there was an entrance to the shelter. Above them, a silent shadow loomed, a parachute carrying a dark six-foot shape. The canopy caught in the bare branches of one of the avenue's London plane trees. The load came to rest, suspended ten feet above the tarmac road.

One of the men cried, '*Niemiec! To niemiecki pilot!*' and several turned and started running towards it. Gazing up in horror, Alice realised this enemy airman was no human, but a parachute landmine.

In the half-light of flickering fires, fuelled by bloodthirsty enthusiasm, the men scrambled towards it and began tugging at the loose cords.

Alice screamed, 'No!'

There was an ominous whirring, then a loud click.

It was the last thing she would ever hear.

The telephone call to the mess came from Wing Commander Sandy Bullough. A grim-faced Badger Robertson was sent to fetch Jox, escorting him wordlessly to the office. From Brotchie's face, Jox had a deep sense of foreboding. He recognised Bullough's voice instantly.

'Look, Jox, there's no easy way of doing this. I'm afraid Alice has been reported missing. She got caught in a raid last night. She was meeting a friend at the cinema, but the friend was delayed. It appears a landmine hit the cinema and there's not much of it left. There are several casualties and I fear the worst.'

The blood drained from Jox's face and he felt faint. Robertson leapt forward to give him a steadying hand.

'I'm so sorry, Jox,' he said. 'She was such a wonderful girl.'

'Is there any hope?' Jox asked Bullough. 'Have they at least found her?'

'I'm afraid not. The only information I have is from my contact at the War Rooms. He said that according to the cinema manager, she was last seen leading a group of soldiers towards a shelter. There's no sign of them either. Some may be too injured to question yet. You have to understand, it's utter chaos down there. Those bloody things are huge. I'm so sorry.'

Grief welled up from the pit of Jox's stomach. His had been a lonely childhood, where emotions were kept in check, but Alice was his safe anchorage, the one person with whom he could let himself go. She was gone now, and he'd never felt so alone. A low keening sound was in his ears, growing louder. With a start, he realised it was coming from him.

Robertson wrapped his arms around him as Brotchie looked on, well-meaning but embarrassed. Jox began to sob — for Alice, for her brother George, for Mike Ferriss and for the many others he'd lost along the way.

He pulled back, eyes wide. 'Who's going to tell her father? After George's death, this is going to destroy him.'

'I'm sure there are official channels...' spluttered Brotchie, rubbing his finger vigorously over his moustache, a sign of his own nerves.

'No, I have to go to him. I have to be the one to tell him.'

It took almost a week before official confirmation arrived. Alice was declared 'Missing Presumed Deceased. Remains Not Recovered.' Her family had already received a telegram from the Air Ministry by the time Jox made the trip to the Milne Farm in Northumberland. He was accompanied by his faithful wingman Cam Glasgow.

Jox had telephoned ahead and spoken to one of George Senior's brothers, uncles to Alice and George. He remembered them from George's funeral at Montrose; they were surprisingly tall older men, almost identical versions of their nephew with the family's long-lashed cow's eyes.

They were seated across the kitchen table from Jox and Glasgow, having welcomed them into their home. Gaunt, red-eyed and wearing black bands on their arms, they introduced themselves as Jack and Henry.

'My sincere condolences to you and your family,' said Jox, ill at ease.

'Away now, Jox, you're one of us,' said Jack Milne. 'This is as hard for you as the rest of the family. You made our darling Alice very happy, and we were looking forward to your wedding with great joy.'

His brother nodded sadly. 'This family has certainly bled for the country, but I never believed it would take our Alice. I'm right sorry for you, lad, but I want you to make me a promise. I want you to live your life fully, for the sake of our Alice, her brother George, and our own dear brother George Senior.'

'Where is Mr Milne?' asked Jox. 'Has he taken the news very badly? Is he unwell?'

The brothers exchanged glances. They were uncomplicated men of the land, who had stared death in the face many times during the last war. Like most farmers, they were very matter-of-fact about such things.

Jack Milne cleared his throat. 'Our brother took his life two days ago. He was heartbroken when he lost George, but losing our Alice as well was just too much. We found him in the barn with a photograph of their dear mother in one hand and a twelve bore in the other.'

Jox was horrified. Beside him, Glasgow clenched his jaw so tightly that the muscle twitched. Jox could only splutter, 'I'm so sorry.'

'It's a release for our George. He saw no future without his wife and children. He had us, of course, but it just wasn't enough. He couldn't face living in the past with only his memories. We respect his decision,' said Henry Milne.

'That's what I'm trying to tell you, lad,' said Jack Milne. 'You can't be living your life in the past. You're still young. Life has so much in store for you, and you've still got a job to do. The country depends on you. Promise me this, lad: put this behind you and focus on the future. We don't want another life destroyed.' The old gentlemen looked at him imploringly.

'I promise, but it'll take time,' said Jox. 'First, I need to rid myself of this rage burning inside me. Someone needs to pay for my Alice.'

# CHAPTER NINETEEN

No. 111 Squadron re-joined No. 11 Group at the beginning of May 1941. Their new station was RAF North Weald in Epping Forest, callsign COWSLIP. It was familiar territory for the squadron's older hands, many of whom had passed through here during the Battle of Britain. The airfield had seen a lot of action, with its runways bombed several times. Most of the damage was cleared away, but the scars remained, like those visible and invisible on the veterans of Treble One.

The transfer south ran smoothly, apart from a tragic accident when two Spits flown by relative newcomers, Pilot Officer George Bain from Edinburgh and Sergeant Freddy Drummond, a Kiwi, collided southwest of Aberdeen. Drummond was killed and Bain was injured in the eye and leg, seriously enough to end his flying career.

Jox was called to the squadron office a few days after their arrival at North Weald. He was dreading the summons, knowing he'd been causing problems by flying recklessly and aggressively, and being short-tempered and distracted.

He was showing the strain. His hands shook, so when carrying a teacup, he had to tilt it to disguise the rattle. His left eye twitched before take-off, and he found himself hiccupping and burping like a set of windy bagpipes. Thankfully, once he was airborne the nerves disappeared, replaced by steely determination. He wondered if anyone was noticing that he was falling apart.

He needn't have worried. The CO was in a good mood, buoyed, he supposed, by the prospect of some imminent action. Even old Badger Robertson had a spring in his step.

'Ah, Jox,' said Brotchie. 'Thanks for coming by. How are Blue Section shaping up? All settled?'

'Yes, I think so,' Jox replied.

'How are you doing? I know it's a difficult time.'

'I'm all right, sir. Just keen to get stuck in. Getting into some action will keep my mind off things.'

'Excellent! Well, here's your chance,' Brotchie said, grinning. 'We've been given the green light to make a fighter sweep over France — to have a crack at some factory and railway targets, and to see if we can shake a reaction out of Jerry's fighters. Sort of a hit and run, to see what trouble we can rustle up. Just the thing to get back in the saddle with old Fritz after all this SMACK night interceptor business. We'll no doubt get called in for duty over London, but in the meantime, here's an oppo for a bit of action.'

'Sounds good,' replied Jox. 'Hope we don't stir up too much of a hornet's nest.'

'Can't be helped,' said Brotchie. 'I want you to take B Flight, your section and Mogs' out this afternoon. The forecast is for low cloud and a bit of rain, so it should allow you to creep up and search for targets.'

'Right, sir. I'll get the boys briefed and choose a target.'

'Good lad. I know you've had a rough time, but I need you at your best. The men deserve better.'

'Yes, sir,' replied Jox, contrite and a little embarrassed.

'Less of that sir business,' replied Brotchie sternly. Then he smiled. 'I have every confidence in you and since you'll be leading the flight, I suppose you better have some of these.' He placed a twin set of Flight Lieutenant's ribbons on the desk: two narrow blue bands on a slightly wider black band. 'Congratulations on your promotion, Flight Lieutenant Jeremy McNabb GC DFC. I know the timing is a bit difficult, but this has been in the works for a while. Despite everything, you must know you thoroughly deserve them.'

The squadron was flying above the white tablecloth of cloud that was obscuring their first glimpse of enemy territory in almost a year.

The last time Jox had been on this side of the Channel, he'd very nearly stayed permanently. He'd got bounced by a Me 110 that had outmanoeuvred him at every turn. It was sheer luck that got him home, to crash above the white cliffs of Kent.

Following that, he'd had a painful stay in hospital and his back still twinged as a legacy of that bruising dogfight. His one consolation had been Alice, as they'd been starting their romance. It all came back in a rush of black grief. He had to shake it off. Damn it, he had a job to do. His men needed a leader, not someone wallowing in self-pity.

They'd left North Weald in pairs, heading first southwest over Epping Forest, then flying parallel to the reservoirs on the river Lea towards London. They kept below the cloud, as Jox wanted them to see what they were defending: the great burnt swathes and shattered tracts of the devastated city; people's homes and lives reduced to bleak rubble, with a few fires still burning. Their jet-black Spitfires flew over the ruins like sinister bats.

As they neared the coast, they climbed with tail assemblies emerging from the swirling cloud like the fins of reef sharks skittering after baitfish. Keeping to the clouds when approaching the French coastline, the choice was between being physically seen or heard or getting picked up by the radar stations that dotted the shoreline. The systems weren't as advanced as those on the British mainland, but Jox was still keen for his eight aircraft to remain undetected. During the pre-flight briefing, he'd insisted on radio silence, flying within sight of each other and using hand signals as required.

Crossing Cap Gris Nez, the prominence near Pas-de-Calais, they were over the closest point between France and England, just twenty-one miles from Dover. Here the guns and massed concrete of the Atlantic wall were grim and plain to see. Three to four miles due east was the fighter aerodrome at Audembert, home of JG26, led by Adolf Galland himself. According to intelligence reports, some thirty-nine Bf 109Es were stationed here, more than enough to chop the flight to pieces.

They headed south towards the port of Ambleteuse, built by Napoleon Bonaparte when preparing for an earlier invasion of their homeland. This was where they were hoping to find the railway shunting yard that Jox had selected as their target.

Jox glanced portside. The movement was seen by his wingman, Cam Glasgow, who turned his leather clad head towards him. Jox pointed to himself and then to Glasgow, then directed two fingers downwards. Glasgow gave the thumbs-up. Jox then looked starboard, where Chalmers and Green Section were in a finger-four formation slightly to the rear. He clicked the throat mic under his rubber oxygen mask, the agreed signal for 'pay attention'. Chalmers looked his way as Jox indicated that he and Green Section should stay in the clouds.

Up ahead, a raised crest breached the flatness of the cloud cover. Jox recognised the effect of a plume rising from a steam train. He banked and dropped through the cloud like a kingfisher piercing the meniscus, followed faithfully by Glasgow.

Below the grey ceiling, an armoured freight train chugged unworried across the French *campagne*, assuming that with fighter cover nearby, their precious cargo was safe. The huge green locomotive had the letters SNCF emblazoned across its large tender, loaded up with black boulders of coal. Behind it and again at the rear of the train were armoured carriages, bristling with a pair of quad-firing 20mm guns. They began twinkling in their direction. Between the two sets of guns were twenty to thirty flatbed carriages loaded with squared-off shapes, covered in tarpaulins but identifiable as some sort of armoured fighting vehicles.

The Spitfires' .303 guns and even the 20mm cannons could do little damage against the thick armour of tanks, but it was the locomotive that was most vulnerable. The tanks could be destroyed if the train was catastrophically derailed.

Jox pointed a gloved hand at the locomotive, then to himself and then indicated that Glasgow should tackle the rear of the train. They parted, dramatically arching in separate directions. Jox lost height and angled towards the locomotive anxiously puffing away. It was straining against its load, great jets of steam pushed from either side, as steel wheels ground against iron rails. The tracks veered to the right, towards a wooded area, where the *cheminot* hoped to find some cover amongst the dark belt of forest. The guns defending his charge were blasting thumb-wide projectiles at the twisting raiders coming at them. They were stark crosses against the low cloud, but too swift to get a bead on.

Glasgow fired first and the weight of his shells smashed the wooden carriage of the rear guns to matchwood. Their crews had some protection behind steel plates, but the weight of fire on the rearmost bogie of the train ripped it from its rails, gouging into the trackside gravel and sending a bright fan of sparks from dragging wheels.

The air around Jox's Spitfire was filled with fire and fury. There were shuddering impacts as chunks were taken from the leading edge of his portside wing. He charged on regardless, dead-eyed, simply focused on revenge. He fired once the targeting rings on the plate before him had passed over the forward AA guns. He wasn't interested in them; he was after the locomotive. Like some rapacious bird after a scrambling beetle, he targeted the coal tender and saw it shudder with impacts, then carried on through to the locomotive. It juddered, as if catching its breath, then exploded spectacularly.

A powerful blast of smoke and steam burst from the funnel for a brief moment before the engine's long sides burst into a ball of fire. It seemed to stumble over itself, like a hare caught by a shotgun at full pelt. Disintegrating into component parts, it dragged the long line of carriages with it. A groaning, grinding noise was audible all the way up to the fighters as the carriages and shedding loads concertinaed into one another. Great loads spun end over end, the momentum far too catastrophic to stop. Leaving the carnage behind, Jox executed a victory roll.

'Dinnae be so bloody daft,' said Glasgow in reprimand, breaking radio silence in his inimitable way. 'Your wing is too knackered for that nonsense.'

They broke through the cloud cover to find the rest of the flight engaged in desperate air combat with a dozen enemy fighters, including several powerful new FW190As that they'd been warned about. As soon as Jox was spotted, two of the bulbous-nosed *Würgers*, Shrikes or 'Butcher Birds', peeled off in his direction. They were more than a match for Jox and Glasgow, markedly superior to their Spitfire Mk Vs in the dive, climb and rate of roll, but most importantly were also faster at all heights by 25-35mph. This was going to be a tough contest.

Still unnoticed, Glasgow pulled some hard Gs trying to get onto their tails as they focused their attention on Jox, whose aircraft was trailing a thin line of coolant. He shook his head to clear the spots in his vision, determined to come to the rescue of his foolhardy young wingman before he became an appetiser for the 'Butcher Birds'. Likewise, another Treble One Spitfire broke from the safety of the defensive circle they'd formed against the swarming enemy interceptors.

Jox was in real trouble, as his pursuers came hurtling at him with powerful radial engines. He didn't have much ammunition left and was jinking desperately from side to side, never straight and level for a moment, knowing that only aerobatics could save him. He caught glimpses of his pursuers looming in his overhead mirror, spectres of death on his shoulder.

When the blows came, they were juddering thuds to his tail assembly and a resounding thump to his back armour. Cold whistling air came through a jagged hole by the side of his left leg. Miraculously, he was untouched, but *Marguerite IV* couldn't take much more. He glanced back and in the corner of his eye saw the aircraft directly behind him explode with a cataclysmic bright flash. He didn't know who or how, until he recognised Glasgow's Spitfire banking hard to loop around again.

He was being chased by the second Focke-Wulf, presumably the wingman of the aircraft falling from the sky like tangled tinsel. In turn he was pursued by a pair of sleek black Spitfires, Chalmers in the lead from his identifying letters, JU-M. As Jox struggled to control his misfiring aircraft, he was oblivious to anyone behind him. Chalmers pumped fire into Glasgow's pursuer until a dark line of smoke appeared from the gaping mouth of his large radial engine. The electrically controlled canopy of the FW190 slid back and the enemy airman tumbled away in a flash of black leather and riding boots. Whoever he was, he'd come to the fight elegantly attired.

Chalmers and his wingman formed to the left of Jox, with Glasgow on his right shoulder.

'Right, boys, let's head for home,' panted Jox. 'I'm sorry we left you to face that circus. I'm afraid my kite's had it.'

When the rest of the flight caught up over the glassy waters of the Channel, one of the Aussies, Roo James, was missing. His wingman, Kanga Reeves was rambling on the R/T, obviously distressed. Bubbles Broughton was slow to catch up, flying uncharacteristically erratically. When he spoke, it was barely above a whisper.

'WAGON Section Leader this is ... B ... Blue Four. I've been hit. It's ... it's my shoulder. I can't move my left arm and there's blood all over the cockpit. So much blood.' He paused as if concentrating. 'I can't ... can't manage the throttle, just my feet and the stick. I don't feel right. I'm not sure I can make it back.'

'You'll make it back, Basil Boy. Miroslav is watching you. You just listen to my voice, nothing but my voice. I'll get you down.'

'Roger, Blue Three,' said Jox. 'I've got trouble too, but Blue Two and I will manage.'

'Roger wilco,' growled Glasgow, evidently still unhappy about Jox's cavalier flying.

'Green Leader, Flight Leader here. Mogs, you and Big Stick hang back with Kanga. Sounds like he's had the wind knocked out of him...'

An Aussie accent interrupted. 'I'll be all right, mate. It's just rough seeing Roo getting clobbered. One of them bloody Fokkers was all over him.'

'Hang in there, Kanga,' said Chalmers. 'We can talk about it when we pancake. Wilco Flight Leader, see you back at COWSLIP. God speed, out.'

Jox and Glasgow were on their own with a good fifteen minutes of flying time before reaching Blighty. Jox's engine was running a bit more smoothly than earlier, but he was frozen at the controls with wind whistling through the hole in his cockpit. Flying a Spitfire was chilly at the best of times, but he'd never been this cold.

'I'm going to struggle to keep this up all the way over London, Cam. I don't want to risk the kite going down into the city,' said Jox. 'I'm so bloody cold, I can barely think straight. You better find somewhere this side of the Big Smoke for an emergency landing. You lead and I'll try to follow.'

Glasgow settled on Tangmere, callsign SHORTSTACK, near Chichester in West Sussex, due west of their current location. He called in the request and moments later the airfield came into view. The emergency landing bell was ringing, with fire engines and an ambulance already on standby. A few nervy moments later, especially as one of Jox's wheels was stubborn in dropping into place, they were down, counting their blessings that they were more or less in one piece.

*Marguerite IV* had half of her tail assembly missing and a deep gouge down the side of her fuselage. Where her portside cannon was located looked like something had taken a big bite out of the leading edge. The duty crew chief at Tangmere said she could be patched up, but it wouldn't be quick. He was unsure if there was structural damage to her tail struts or the hidden cabling within.

'You're lucky to have made it back, sir,' said the grimy rigger. 'If you were a cat, I reckon you'd be down at least one life, mate.'

Jox gave him a weary smile. 'I think I may be down rather more than one, Flight. Can't have all that many left.'

Glasgow glared at him. 'Stop talking so soft. There's nothing wrong with you that taking less daft chances wouldn't cure. Having some sort of death wish is paying your wee lassie no respect at all, Jox. I need you to buck up. We all bloody do. Leading us into a hornet's nest like that was just plain daft.'

Cam had never spoken to him like this. His trust and support had always been unwavering.

'Well, that was a bloody disaster, Jox. Why the devil did you choose a target so close to a fighter base?' asked Brotchie, once they'd limped back to North Weald. 'I know I said to go have a stooge over in France to see what trouble you could stir up, but there's a difference between being brave and foolhardy.'

Badger Robertson was standing by the CO's desk, carefully packing his pipe. Once satisfied, he pointed the stem at Jox. 'Your foolishness has cost us two pilots. Roo's either gone or is a prisoner, and young Bubbles has a hole the size of my fist in his shoulder and may be out of action permanently, which would be a bloody shame as that boy's really got talent. We've lost one brand new Spit and three more may escape the scrapheap but are certainly no longer new.' He fixed Jox with cold eyes. 'What the bloody hell is going on? You've acted daft before, but I've never had to question your judgement.'

'I don't know, Badger,' replied Jox. 'When I get close to the enemy, I just see red. All I want is revenge for Alice.'

The pair of squadron leaders stared at him. Something had changed, something was broken, and that something was him.

The signs were ominous. Trouble was brewing on the other side of the Channel, and it wasn't long before the radar stations along the south coast reported signs of the enemy boiling up. This advance warning had been useful last summer, but now it only served to say that some poor city or town was going to cop it. It was a deadly guessing game, the result of getting it wrong being all too harshly felt by victims in widespread towns like Coventry, Bristol, Cardiff, Plymouth and Belfast.

On the 10th of May 1941, indications were that the night's target was London again. It was almost a year to the day that Jox had first flown to France with the Treble Ones as part of a composite squadron. He'd seen the war for the first time and had failed to save a little girl, Marguerite, from the rapacious Stukas attacking columns of refugees. The porcelain arm of Marguerite's doll was his now not so lucky talisman, but was always in his tunic pocket, a reminder of his failure that day.

Returning to North Weald after the Rhubarb mission over Cap Gris-Nez, Jox was met by sullen faces, unhappy about the debacle he'd led them into and how much it had cost the squadron. He was grateful at least for the welcome he got from wee Georgie, who was always happy to see him. With recent events he'd been rather neglected, but Jox treasured that pup, the only tangible link to Alice that he had left. Cuddling the wriggling terrier was his only comfort, since even Pritchard's jovial banter had become rather clipped.

The squadron ground crews sweated all day to get a maximum number of aircraft to readiness for that night's interceptor operations. The aircrew were fed and by seven o'clock were waiting for the enemy's next move. Tension in the dispersal was palpable, the sweat of anxious men mixing with the fug of chain-smokers. They were trying to be nonchalant, but the tell-tale signs betrayed their nerves. Solly Solomon was reading the evening gazette but upside down. Olivier de Ghellinck and Axel Fisken were playing chess, but neither had moved a piece in over ten minutes. Scanning the room, Jox imagined he could only see hostility and disappointment on their faces. Whether it was true or just in his head was unclear.

The dispersal telephone rang and was snatched up by an anxious Brotchie. He nodded, then spoke calmly, though his expression was anxious. 'Squadron scramble, lads. Wheels-up in ten minutes. They're coming in from the east, over the water.'

Jox shuddered, recalling the mauling the squadron had suffered over the same brown Thames estuary waters on that terrible Sunday when they'd lost five pilots: Jack Copeman, Wolfie McKenzie, Rob Roy Wilson, Robert Sim and Toby 'Jugs' Carmel-Connolly. All lost without a trace, but he could picture each of their faces perfectly.

The room erupted with men scrambling for equipment: Mae Wests, flight helmets, rubber oxygen masks, outer boots, and thick woollen jackets — whatever they thought they needed.

Each man had his own pre-fight rituals. There were few more superstitious men than fighter pilots, each with his own foibles and lucky charms. For one it was a Star of David, for another a favourite school cricket jumper. A pressed shamrock in a wallet brought the luck of the Irish, an ivory Buddha hopefully some good karma. Some clutched photographs of lovers, mothers, sisters, or wives, but for Jox it was still his cracked porcelain doll's arm. Today he'd paired it with a string of pearls, worn with his RAF identity discs. They'd been a wedding gift from a bridegroom to his lost bride. He swallowed a wave of grief, catching a worried look from his wingman.

'Right then,' he said. 'Let's get this done.'

On the nights of the 10th and 11th of May 1941, taking advantage of a full moon and low tide, the Luftwaffe increased their attack over London. In a blow to the nation's morale, Westminster Abbey and the Law Courts were badly damaged, and the House of Commons was burnt to the ground. London was burning, and the Treble Ones were sent out to punish those responsible.

# CHAPTER TWENTY

After their night mission over London, the Treble Ones returned to North Weald in ragged dribs and drabs. The dawn skyline was marred by several shifting columns of smoke from the burning city, and the air was acrid in their throats.

The aircraft were streaked, soot on metallic black, with surfaces pitted and ragged from projectiles. This wasn't generally because an enemy gunner had been lucky, nor was it due to unlucky strikes from their own AA, but because *Staffel* of German fighters were now accompanying the raiders for the first time. Night fighters were stalking night fighters in a deadly new game of cat and mouse, a worrying new development and the enemy's latest countermeasure to the growing effectiveness of the RAF's defences.

Jox stumbled onto the dewy grass along the ragged line of scarred aircraft, ticking and cooling after the night's exertions. Mike Longstaffe's Mark V, with 'Big Stick' in Chinese characters painted on it, was missing the tip of a starboard wing. He'd done well to get it down in one piece. Longstaffe was an odd chap, always a bit of a loner. Jox wondered at the horrors he'd seen in Asia and if it had made him that way. Perhaps he was headed that way too.

Squatting on the wet grass in his sweaty flying gear was an exhausted Pritchard. His bad leg was stretched out in front of him and his face had the waxy sheen of a runner who'd given his all in a race.

'Where the bloody hell did you get to?' he asked Jox. 'Oh, you know what, it really doesn't matter.' He rubbed his troublesome knee, missing a patella since he'd gone down at

Dunkirk. 'This leg of mine. I wish they'd just chopped the bloody thing off.'

'Be careful what you wish for,' replied Jox.

'Yeah, sorry. I'm being stupid. Seriously, though, where did you get to? One minute we're all together, the next you're gone. You had me worried, matey.'

'I needed to be on my own. I was with you, just a bit higher up.'

'How d'you get on?'

'Two heavies, Heinkel 111s.'

'Bloody hell. Definite kills?'

'Yeah, both done for,' said Jox, a steeliness creeping into his voice. 'They weren't getting away this time.'

'Good job. I got a piece of one, then got jumped by his mate. That's when having you around might have come in useful, you plonker. Got the shock of my life when he started taking great chunks out of my tail. Look at the state of it.'

Jox could see that Pritchard's tail assembly could only be described as seriously chewed up.

'Jerry's sending night fighters up against us,' said Jox. 'Modified Me 110s with onboard radar interception, but also some of those long thin chaps.'

'What, flying pencils? Dornier 17s?'

'No, the fast ones. The Ju 88s they call *Schnellbombers*. I saw one last night.'

'Saw one? Christ, I copped a lot more than that. They bagged old Ghillie too.'

'What? Are you sure?'

'Well, no, not really. There was a lot of noise on the R/T. I heard his accent saying he was getting out. Hope he made it down all right. There really weren't many spots to safely land in a chute. The whole city was in flames.'

'He's a survivor, that one,' said Jox. 'You look terrible — are you sure you're all right?'

'Just tired. More to the point, how are you holding up? Been acting strangely lately.'

'I know. It's all getting a bit much. I need a break. A chance to sort my head out.'

'I don't think anyone would begrudge you that. We need you firing on all cylinders, and frankly, mate, you've been off lately. I know you've had a lot on your plate, with Alice and everything, but up there we don't get second chances. You need to be on your game. I'm sure the CO would understand.'

'I don't want to let anyone down.'

'You're not letting us down, Jox. We're all worried about you.'

'I'll think about it. Come on, let's get some breakfast.' He helped Pritchard up, who groaned as he put weight on his knee, taking a moment and breathing hard.

'Maybe just a cuppa. I'm not sure I can stomach anything else.'

*Chevalier* Olivier de Ghellinck was back that afternoon. His clothes were charred, and he was unrecognisable as the man who'd climbed into his cockpit the previous evening.

It wasn't that he was burnt or particularly disfigured, just that the elegant Belgian aristocrat's hair, eyebrows and eyelashes had been singed to stubbly bristles. His thin face, fine features and aquiline nose were unblemished, still identifying him as one of Europe's blue bloods, but now he was more Jean Valjean, Victor Hugo's *bagnard*, than a descendent of Godefroy de Bouillon, the one-time King of Jerusalem. Even his usual scent of *eau de cologne* had been replaced by the acrid stink of burnt hair.

'It was terrible, *mes amis*,' he croaked after taking a swallow of the pint of bitter placed before him. 'When Pritch and I were attacked, we split. He was lucky, I was not.' He ran a sooty hand through his ruined coiffure. 'We were too close together, *mon brave*,' he said to Pritchard. 'Side by side in the darkness, looking for reassurance above the burning city. Maybe subconsciously seeking companionship when confronted by such horror. The Boche crept up on us. I saw him as I floated down on my parachute into the inferno. He was twin-engined and we really should have seen him. He must have hidden in our overlapping blind spots. He was up above; then he swooped and fired *et voilà*. It is embarrassing but we were, how you say, sitting ducks, *n'est-ce pas*?'

Pritchard nodded reluctantly.

'From then onwards, the night was one stink after another. My instrument panel was shattered, and the cockpit filled with glycol fumes. It was only then that I realised I had lost this.' He held up a bandaged hand with a missing little finger. He looked at it. 'I didn't feel a thing. It hit my signet ring. Eighteenth birthday present from my father, but I didn't care, I just needed to escape the smell. I have a sensitive nose.'

'Take your time,' said Robertson, who had joined to listen. He handed de Ghellinck a tartan handkerchief, noticing that the usually fastidious Belgian was distressed at being so grubby. He nodded his thanks, wiping his unhurt hand and face.

'Hanging from the parachute, I was in a different stink. Boiling air rising from the fires seared off my hair. Like an idiot, I had ripped off my flight helmet and mask when I'd jumped. The thermals reeked of burning oil, timber and coals, and I kept being lifted and dropped, drifting west for a long time. I could see from the moon on the Thames that I was being pushed away from the flames.'

He groaned at the sudden pain in his hand. The painkiller was wearing off. 'The men on the ground found me on a church roof on Fulham Palace Road, near Bishop's Palace, hours later. I was tangled up under the canopy, trapped by the cords of my parachute. I could see nothing. I could just hear the sirens, the exploding bombs and the howling of the fires. All around me there was a revolting smell of corruption and decay. I could not understand it; I was trapped beneath the canopy. Silk is very strong, you know. I tried to rip it, but I couldn't with this.' He held up his hand.

'So, I am trapped in a putrid new hell of rotten meat. I could do nothing but sit until someone came. The morning light shone through the cloth, and I sensed movement, then I heard the cawing and squabbling of crows. The smell became more overpowering, I vomited and *voilà*, I had another stink to contend with. I was feeling very sorry for myself, thinking this ordeal would never end, when I heard something scrambling on the metal gutter of the roof. I heard a voice, part of a UXB crew.'

He laughed acidly. 'At first, they thought I was a Nazi, but once they cut me out, they recognised my RAF wings, even covered with the vomit. *Dieu merci*! I asked what the terrible smell was. My new friend explained, "We were called out to deal with a 50-kilo bomb sticking out the church roof. We wouldn't have known it was up here, but for the fins hanging over the guttering. There's a school on the other side, so we needed to get it sorted out quick. We couldn't leave it hanging."'

'I asked how that explained the execrable odour and he told me it was the vicar. Seeing my puzzled expression, he explained that the local priest had disappeared four days before. The community had searched everywhere for him.

When the workmen came up here for the bomb, they found not only me, but also what was left of him, not two metres away. The odour I had endured was a rotting man of God, caught by an explosion and flung onto his own church roof. He'd lain there for days, until I landed beside him. God moves in mysterious ways, *n'est-ce pas?*'

This last revelation, and imagining what de Ghellinck had gone through, stunned his comrades into silence.

The CO, never the most delicate of individuals, said, 'That's a hell of a tale, Olivier. Glad you're back with us. Better let the MO take a look at that finger. I'll sign you off Ops for a bit. Give it a chance to heal up. Tell you what, though, you really need a shower and a change of clothes, old boy. You stink and you're putting people off their lunch.'

Someone gave an embarrassed laugh. De Ghellinck frowned and muttered, '*Ah, quel fumier!*' before wearily getting to his feet and heading for the washrooms. De Ghellinck's war was shelved for a bit and Jox felt rather envious.

Jox wasn't given time to dwell on it, as new reports were coming in that the enemy was boiling up again across the channel. It appeared they were squaring up for a return match and the Treble Ones would be waiting. Back when the squadron had been equipped with Hurricanes, their primary targets had always been the bombers, but now with nimble Spits, they were tasked with protecting re-purposed Boulton Paul Defiant 'bomber destroyers', Bristol Blenheims and radar-equipped Bristol Beaufighter twin-engine heavy fighters.

Images of the Wild West came to mind, each separate posse assigned to protecting their own particular homesteaders. Jox wondered if he was wearing a hero's white hat or a villain's black.

The squadron was airborne before the bombers reached the outskirts of London. At altitude, last night's fires appeared to be mostly under control, the tide having turned, physically and metaphorically. Tidal seawater had flowed back into the Thames, refilling tanks, reservoirs and hoses, ready for what the new night might bring.

London's twinkling lights were extinguished, as blackout was again in force. It was as if a sea of candles had been snuffed out all at once. Jox led his sections through low cloud northeast of the city. A Flight had been shuffled about to make up numbers, with Broughton and de Ghellinck out wounded, and Roo James 'Missing in Action' over France. The CO had decided to join them for tonight's patrol. Was he there to check on whether Jox was coping?

Searchlights probed the night sky, beams crossing as they sought the intruders. Occasionally, the dozens of plump silver barrage balloons were lit up, clustered over green spaces and along the river shoreline. Released when the enemy was overhead, their long trailing steel cables were designed to tangle up low-flying aircraft. Explosives attached to the cables were set to detonate when pulled. They pushed the raiders to higher altitudes, so they would come into the range of the anti-aircraft guns. Here again, the odds were in the enemy's favour, with the typical AA gunner needing to strike a moving target, flying at several hundred kilometres an hour, constantly altering course and elevation. In addition, he or she, since many AA emplacements were crewed by young women, had to aim kilometres ahead of the target with shell fuses set to detonate within range after several long seconds of flight time. It demanded the ultimate deflection shot.

In an ideal world, the balloons would also make the bombers fly higher, where they could be detected by the radar stations.

The searchlights were then given their location, and they found and illuminated them so the guns could shoot them down. Added to the mix now were Jox and his merry men, bringing more targeted firepower, but in reality they were also very much at the mercy of any one of those moving parts.

The enemy, of course, needed to be factored in, and were unlikely to collaborate, firing back all the while and dropping tons of high explosives and incendiaries.

Coordination of the disparate parts appeared to be working tonight. Several bulky silhouettes were already coned, and the Treble One Spitfires were vectored onto their targets in pairs. Glasgow and Jox were focused on the hulking form of a Heinkel 111, the beams piercing through its distended bomb-laden belly and reflecting off the glasshouse canopy of the bulbous nose. Pulling towards it, Jox saw shadowy forms moving in the cockpit, then a spiralling trail of red tracers as a gunner tried to get a bead on him.

Jox angled the Spit and delivered a glancing burst. Glasgow was a beat behind him, on his shoulder on the starboard side. All around, dirty smudges of AA fire burst and buffeted their light aircraft, adding a crude rhythm to their strike.

The bomber's glass cockpit collapsed like a crushed egg. A headshot mallard caught by a fowling piece. A split second later the aircraft's internal bomb rack, directly behind the crew cabin, exploded. It held two thousand kilograms of high explosive in eight separate 250 kg bombs, stored vertically with their fins pointing towards the ground. This arrangement usually led to the characteristic tumbling of bombs from the He 111, but not this time.

The bomb load exploded cataclysmically, triggering the bomber's secondary load, a further three thousand five hundred kilos attached to external hard points. It was like

Thor's own lightning had burst inside the aircraft, creating a destructive force that shattered the Heinkel into a million pieces. Jox and Glasgow were swatted aside like flies by a rolled newspaper. Glasgow's Spitfire spiralled off, trailing a dark streak of smoke and then deployed a parachute, reflecting bright white in the searchlights. Another Treble One had joined the Caterpillar Club, grateful to the distant silkworms of India for saving his life.

Jox had no such luck. *Marguerite IV*, already damaged by the Fokker-Wulf incident over Cap Gris-Nez, had her weakened skeleton twisted like a hunchback by the force of the blast. All power was lost and the propellor windmilled as the aircraft fell.

Thanking providence for no sign of flames, Jox reached to pull back the canopy to escape the dying aircraft. Jammed shut, however much he tugged, it refused to budge. He was losing altitude and gaining speed, hurtling towards the ground in a dramatic curve. He had to do something, and do it fast, as bailing out wasn't an option.

The reflection of the moon showed the twists of the river. Jox strained to recognise any landmarks to find somewhere to get the kite down. Finding a place in the dead of night, albeit one lit by a thousand burning buildings, was never going to be easy, especially over one of the largest cities in the world.

Up ahead, a cluster of barrage balloons bumped against each other, buffeted by hot winds. They were grouped around a large sprawling edifice with a familiar outline. He was puzzled why it needed so many balloons, but got his answer when he recognised Tower Bridge nearby, backlit by the docklands in flames.

The words of the submariner, Matt Pye, who had saved Jox and Alice from the flames at Christmas-time, came back to him.

'I spent my childhood mud-larking and swimming around here. There's even a beach down by Tower Bridge.'

With what little control he still had, Jox edged *Marguerite IV* towards where he hoped to find the promised beach. The tide was in and there wouldn't be much of it exposed, but at least it would be long, clear and flat, not an unreasonable place to attempt a crash-landing. Frankly, he had no alternative.

Edged down one side by a sheer stone wall, protecting the White Tower's battlements from the water, and on the other by old Father Thames, Jox's wet landing strip was suicidally short and narrow. Wheels up, his radiator scoop made first contact with the shallow water, scraping a jagged scar in the river mud. Running a ragged course, it veered towards the ancient wall of Portland stone. A long tail of bright sparks flared from the starboard wing, grinding along the sheer wet surface, friction fighting momentum.

The dying Spitfire tumbled over with the propellor blades frothing in the muddy water. Upside down and hanging from his Sutton harness, Jox felt a thudding impact across his chest, arm and shoulder, then a sharp, searing pain and everything went black.

## CHAPTER TWENTY-ONE

Jox had no recollection of the days directly after his crash. He wasn't sure whether it was from the bump to his head or pain medication, but he had scant memory of arriving at the Officer's Hospital at RAF Uxbridge.

The last time he'd been at the station, he'd been square-bashing as a raw recruit in 1939. He recalled the training cadre of professional NCOs had treated the student pilots with utter disdain. In complete contrast, the care he received from the nursing and medical staff couldn't have been kinder or more devoted.

His first conscious memory was a conversation with a grey-templed consultant, with a name that escaped him. 'Well, Mister McNabb,' he said, 'I'm glad you're back with us. You'll be feeling a bit groggy and disorientated for a while, as you've taken quite a blow on the noggin. I'll get the sister to bring you a looking glass, so you can see those first-class shiners. Things may well be uncomfortable for a bit, as your injuries include a shattered collar bone, a fracture to the ulna of your left forearm and a few cracked ribs. Your shoulder is in the worst state, which explains the metal rig you're wearing. Bones will mend, but it will take a while, and I'm afraid that in the future, you'll be one of those grumpy old fellows that say, "I can feel it in my bones" when inclement weather threatens.'

The doc gave an odd barking laugh at his own joke. 'I've got to tell you; you gave me quite a fright when I saw that blue foot of yours. I was convinced I needed to amputate before I realised the contusions were in fact only dye or paint. You must tell me the tale one day.' He flicked through Jox's medical notes. 'You've been with us for a few weeks, and I think you're strong enough to be transferred to Babbacombe, the Officer's Convalescent Home. You'll love it; it's an excellent facility set in a converted hotel with lovely views of the sea.'

'I have a friend who spent some time there after Dunkirk,' croaked Jox.

'Good show, so you'll know what to expect,' said the doctor. 'I don't mind telling you, we won't miss the queue of chaps coming to check on you every other day. That warrant officer, the Scotsman, is really quite terrifying. The nurses scarper whenever he appears.' He chuckled. 'You must be a popular chap.' He took his glasses off and his expression changed. 'Listen, I've had the opportunity to have a chat with your CO, Squadron Leader Brotchie. He's told me about the troubles you've had recently and I'm very sorry for your loss. We've agreed that you could do with some time out. You'll see that in addition to being a convalescent and physical rehabilitation centre, Babbacombe has an excellent reputation for providing psychotherapeutic treatments. Many wounded airmen have found it helpful in getting over the trauma of injury and combat. I understand your CO has a good friend who he served with in France who is currently there, and the treatment has done him a power of good. It'll help get your mojo back, firing on all cylinders again, what?'

The transfer from RAF Uxbridge to the Palace Hotel, Babbacombe in Devon involved a long, bumpy and rather painful journey. The discomfort was exacerbated by Jox's travel companion, an American airman called Zatonski, lying on the other gurney with a leg in plaster and giving off a stomach-churning odour of charred flesh. He groaned continuously and whilst Jox counted his blessings that he wasn't in the same state as this poor beggar, the sentiment wasn't making the journey any easier or quicker.

Since their destination was a converted hotel, there was no shortage of rooms, with individual suites catering for up to two hundred and forty patients. They were cared for by a complement of two hundred staff: doctors, nurses, dentists, admin personnel and locally recruited civilian staff who'd previously worked at the hotel.

Apart from the convalescent facilities, the psychotherapeutic programmes were the legacy of treatments that had evolved since the First World War, when the armed forces had been overwhelmed by servicemen suffering from 'shell shock'. Battle-weary RAF personnel were now being treated using ground-breaking physical and occupational therapies, designed to rehabilitate both the injuries and mental health of wounded and exhausted aircrew, whose experience was still in demand after two years of torrid air war.

On the second day at his new home, Jox was sitting in his room with the metal rig over his shoulder set up over an old Victorian bathchair. He'd been parked before an open window with a view across the hospital lawns, mature trees and then over the sea. It was supposed to be therapeutic, but he couldn't help thinking that the water, variously sparkling blue, steely-grey or just plain mud brown would always represent the watery grave of so many of his friends. He doubted he would ever enjoy a seaside holiday again because of the melancholy association.

Lost in his dark musings, he didn't immediately notice the two RAF officers who had entered his room without knocking. When he looked over, he saw that both had bandaged heads. One was built like a burly rugby player and the other had burn scars on his face and hands. He was also walking with a stick, as his leg was plastered up to the knee. Smiling self-consciously, he appeared to be the more reserved of the pair.

'Hello, McNabb. Can I call you Jox?' said the burly one. 'I'm Peter Ayerst. Wee Brotch asked me to look you up.' He shook Jox's hand. 'This is Eric Nicolson, but we call him Nick. I thought the two of you ought to meet, as you're the celebrities.'

Nicolson appeared embarrassed. 'Come off it, Peter.'

Jox had no idea what they were talking about.

Ayerst continued, 'Why, yes, Jox, you're the only George Cross at Babbacombe and Nick here is our only Victoria Cross. Come to think of it, he's the only one in Fighter Command. You see, my dear boy, at this exclusive clubhouse for recuperating gentlemen aviators, a plain DFC simply doesn't cut the mustard. Hell, even I've got one of those.' He bellowed with laughter. Jox still didn't get the joke. 'Seriously, though, you'll meet all kinds here. Good fellows who have been hurt and suffered one way or another. Rather embarrassing, but I'm here for a bump on the head after a car accident. Keep getting these bloody headaches and fainting at the most inconvenient moments. Not really ideal for a fighter pilot, is it? My fault for drinking then driving. Bit of a silly sod, you see.' He became pensive. 'The worst you'll see are the burnt fellows. Old Nick here's not in great shape, but he's an oil painting compared to some of the chaps you'll meet. Many come up from the Burns Unit at Queen Victoria Hospital at East Grinstead. They call themselves McIndoe's Guinea Pig Club. McIndoe's this terrific Kiwi surgeon who has done wonders with their burns. "Airmen's burns", they're rather blandly called, but that hardly covers the horrors we've seen, eh, Nick? Pretty ghastly, but just remember they're all splendid chaps who have sacrificed a great deal.'

'Yes, I'm sure,' said Jox. 'I came down from Uxbridge with an American chap. He was in a bad way. Had a Polish-sounding name.'

'Actually, he's probably past the worst of it. The Guinea Pigs who arrive have usually already had many treatments and come down to recover from surgeries on their burns.'

'Here, take a look at my hand,' said Nicolson. He held out his left arm, palm down. The back of it was mottled and lumpy, with the fingernails like melted lumps of metal. 'That's about the nastiest bit that I've got. The hand's still fairly useless, but I'm hoping they'll get it working again. I'm desperate to get back to operations, but first I need to get back to Muriel, the wife. We've just had a baby and she's still rather cross with me. Damned inconvenient, getting shot down like I did.'

'Congratulations,' said Jox. 'Don't worry, it does heal. I burnt my hands quite badly trying to rescue a chum from a crash a while ago. Actually, that's how I got my George Cross. Don't think I really deserved it; I was just trying to help a pal. I guess these are the price I paid.' He held up his own scarred hands.

Nicolson gave a lopsided smile and looked down at his. 'Yes, I suppose these are the price I paid too. The price of stubbornness.'

'What do you mean?'

'Well, my VC story is pretty unremarkable. I just stuck to my guns. We were on patrol near Southampton when I got jumped by a Bf 110. I got hit in the eye and the foot. The engine was alight, so I prepared to jump. That's when I spotted another one of them just in front of me. All I really did was get back into my now rather hot seat and fire a long squirt at him. He went down, then I got out, but by then I was rather charred. On my way down, some Home Guard idiots shot at me, but eventually picked me up from a field.' He fingered the signet ring on the gnarled little finger of his right hand. 'Apparently, by being stubborn, I "displayed exceptional gallantry and disregard for the safety of my own life".'

'Who said that?'

'My medal citation. It's all been a terrible fuss and I rather hate it, but my Muriel seems to like all the attention from the newspapers. I just want to get better and get back to work with No. 249 Squadron.'

'No. 249 Squadron? You must know Ginger Neil. I trained with him at Montrose,' said Jox. 'Great fellow.'

'Yes, he flies in my section. Lovely chap.'

Jox was pleased they had found some common ground.

Ayerst interjected, 'Don't tell me you're another one of these bashful heroes. If I was you, Jox, I'd be using that medal to get the maximum free drinks and attention from the lovely nurses, let me tell you.'

'No, I'm not interested in anything like that,' said Jox, a cold wave of grief hitting him. 'I … I lost my fiancée in a raid not long ago, so I just want some peace and quiet to get my head straight. I'm sorry, I just can't…' He began to cry. Ayerst and Nicolson looked on in stunned silence. They exchanged glances and shuffled away from the room.

Jox didn't even notice they'd left. His broken body was hurting again, but not as much as his broken soul. Silent tears fell down his face as his gaze went back to the shifting surface of that endlessly moving sea.

The next morning Jox was handed a letter from Pritchard.

*111 Sqdn, North Weald,*
*Sept. 1941*

*My dear Jox,*
  *How are you, old boy? You gave us such a fright, you silly sod! Glad to hear that you're on the mend. The boys send you their best wishes. Please don't worry about wee Georgie. He's doing fine and is never short of attention. That little mutt does more for squadron morale than anyone else. Even the C.O., who's being a real ball-breaker these days, is putty in his hands — well, paws.*
  *I hope things are going all right for you. I never did tell you about my time at Babbacombe, beyond trying to paint a rosy picture. The truth is I got quite a dose of the funk after that frightfulness at Dunkirk. The head shrinker chaps did a good job on me, otherwise there's no chance I would have made it through last year. Take your time and do what it takes to get back into shape, physically and mentally. You've done more than enough and deserve a rest. We miss you, of course, but we'll be here when you're ready to come back.*
  *Things have changed a fair bit since you've been away. It's like a revolving door with all the new bods in and old chaps being promoted and heading off. Miro has finally been commissioned and is now training on Blenheim night fighters. Otmar is joining a new Czech No. 313 Squadron. Bubbles and Ghillie are back from sickbay, more or less in one piece. We've also had a bunch of replacements: some Fleet Air Arm chaps plus a few Sergeant Pilots, including a Pole with an unpronounceable name, who we call Mika — he has joined my flight. Oh yes, I forgot to say, both Mogs and I have finally been promoted. You know Pete Simpson has moved on to take over No. 66 Squadron, so Mogs and I are now flight leaders. I've taken your spot as Blue One, with Cam covering my back. I'm not sure how happy he is about that. Who'd have thought*

all those months ago in the back of that truck in Woking that we'd be here? We've come a long way together, my friend.

Ops are relentless, but we haven't seen many night-time raids. Wee Brotch is getting impatient for action and we're going on more Rhubarbs, looking for trouble. Every time we go over, it's like rattling a stick in a wasp's nest, and we're immediately covered in bandits in no time. We lost one of the Fleet Air Arm midshipmen and a Welsh sergeant — a black-haired chap, rather unoriginally called Taffy — just last week. Hopefully they got down safely and are now 'guests' at a Stalag Luft, rather than the alternative.

Better sign off so I can catch the postbag. You're in our prayers, old boy. Badger sends his best wishes and Cam Glasgow misses you so much that he's like a bear with a sore head. He's absolutely terrorising all the new sergeant pilots.

Chin up and get well soon,
Yours affectionately,
Pritch

Babbacombe, Dorset,
15th December 1941

Dear Pritch,

First of all, apologies for not replying to your letter much sooner. It's taken me a while to shake off the blues that have been grinding me down since I lost Alice. Even admitting what has happened is a big step for me. I spent the first weeks here feeling sorry for myself. I was in a lot of pain, but it was my head that was in the worst shape. There's a marvellous chap here called Maskell who runs the gym and is helping me regain my coordination and build up my strength, but it's bloody hard work. The facilities are remarkable and I'm enjoying sports for the first time since school. They get us all moving, encouraging competition and generally keeping our eye in. The grub's great and there are always celebs and starlets from ENSA coming down from London to put on shows, but of course you know all that.

As for me, there are endless sessions with the headshrinkers, but to be honest, it's seeing the others that has done me the most good. It's very hard to feel sorry for yourself when there are chaps with such terrible injuries, who remain upbeat and optimistic. You should see how excited the badly burnt fellows are about the Christmas decorations and flirting with the nursing staff. Come to think of it, the ladies remember you fondly, so you must have made an impression, you old rascal.

We've got chaps from all over: Canucks, Aussies, Kiwis, Yarpies, Frogs, Clogs and Belgies, Poles, Czechs and even some chaps from India and the Caribbean. I expect, now that the Americans have joined the war, we'll be seeing more of them too. If there's ever been any doubt we're fighting a world war, the price being paid in the torn flesh, broken bones and the melted faces of these poor boys is clear. One must learn to look past their injuries to find the person within.

The other day I was introduced to the family of an air gunner called McIntosh. I was struck by what a lovely family they were, how handsome the two boys were and their pretty little sister. Their mother was fine-looking, but it was clear from their colouring that they took after their father. My mistake was to think they'd somehow look like him now, rather than how he must have been. Poor chap has a way to go. His face is covered in scars which need to be cut away, then replaced by skin grafts. The doctors will eventually rebuild his nose too. I got away awfully lightly with the burns on my hands. What's remarkable to see is the children knowing that he's still in there. Their joy and gratitude for that is heart-warming.

I've been putting a lot of thought into what I should do next. I know the Treble Ones will always welcome me back, but I need a new challenge. I need to put the life I'd planned with Alice behind me. I've been in discussions with the patient welfare officer and with his contacts in the Air Ministry. I understand they're after experienced fighter pilots for some

Top-Secret push. Looking at the papers, I'm sure we can both guess where that might be. I understand they're desperate and I've thrown my hat in the ring. The request is with the C.O., so be a pal and see if you can't massage it along.

In any case, I won't be in any decent shape until after the New Year. Frankly I don't want to spend the anniversary of my last Christmas with Alice anywhere other than here. I'm surrounded by those who can help chase away the dark thoughts when they come. I'm sure there'll be some re-familiarisation flights involved, with perhaps a view to Ops in early spring. Don't worry, I don't expect it'll be a long-term posting and I hope to be back with the Treble Ones in good time.

All the best, chum. Have a very happy Christmas and Hogmanay. If I don't see you, give my best to the boys and tell Cam Glasgow to cheer up — it might never happen!

Yours aye,

Jox

# CHAPTER TWENTY-TWO

Dawn broke over *Jabal-al-Tariq*, the Mountain of Tariq, named for the Moor who established a foothold for Islam in Europe. To the current holders it was simply known as 'The Rock'. It dominated the Strait of Gibraltar, its reflection clear in the teeming turquoise water.

It was Jox's second day on Gib and he was shaking off the nausea that had dogged him since leaving Greenock aboard the freighter, SS *Queen Victoria*, a week earlier. Escorted by the Royal Navy destroyer HMS *Airedale* and corvette HMS *Petunia*, the churning voyage was interminable, and it was good to finally be on *terra firma*. He was starting to feel human again and more optimistic than he had in a long time.

The view was breath-taking, across the wide mouth of the Mediterranean to the other legendary Pillar of Hercules and beyond to the dark smudge of Morocco's Rif Mountains. It was clear to see why the Rock dominated access in or out of the Med and the Atlantic beyond.

To the north, the Rock's angled peak was steep on one side and sheer on the other. Down below, the short runway of RAF Gibraltar held nine crated Spitfire VBs, being assembled by ground crews with the unlikely name of the 'Special Erection Party'. Once complete, they would be loaded aboard the aircraft carrier HMS *Eagle*, from which Jox and eight other pilots would take off for the besieged island of Malta. Before then, *Eagle* and its escort would need to reach within range of the island.

The Royal Navy Captain briefing the pilots advised that they would be 'ferried' to a position south of the Balearics and would then fly the rest of the way over the tip of Tunisia and onto Malta. It was a three-hour flight at the extreme of their range. They would be flying high to avoid detection and hopefully interception, but Jox was still stupefied to discover that to lighten the load and maximise flight time, he was being asked to fly into the hotly contested Mediterranean warzone with empty guns.

'It's a choice between bullets or fuel if we're to get these vital machines to Malta,' said the ruddy-faced captain. Like many senior sailors he was on the portly side, the result of years cooped up on ships, benefitting from the hospitality of the ship's mess. 'There'll be ammunition and fuel on the island, just not enough fighter aircraft. There are other convoys heading for Malta, assuming they make it in one piece, but quite frankly, I'd rather be up there with you than running the gauntlet down here. Mind you, steer clear of that nasty nest of Me 109 vipers based on Pantelleria.' The veteran sailor added grimly, 'Once you land, the aircraft will be re-crewed, re-fuelled and armed, and sent right back to provide air cover for whichever convoy is approaching Valletta. They help you get there, so it's only fair you see them in safely.'

'That big ape looks exactly like you did when I found you at the train station,' said Jox's companion, interrupting his train of thought. They were killing time before the convoy was set to sail, a last chance to stretch their legs before being confined on yet another wretched boat. Climbing the steep face of the limestone peak was proving harder than either of them had anticipated.

'Well, you can hardly expect me to be anything but surprised at seeing your mug emerging from the freezing murk at Glasgow Central.'

Out of breath and red-faced, Jox was being likened to the large male leading a troop of Barbary macaques that were swarming towards them. Mehmet, their tour guide, had lured them across with some shelled peanuts. It was obviously part of the usual tourist show that he'd orchestrated many times.

'I take a picture, you pay,' he prompted. The macaque was very obviously male and about the size of a three-year-old child wearing a furry Inuit suit. Pale-eyed, he had the facial expression of a cunning old man. A seasoned performer, he swiftly clambered up Jox's arm, sitting astride his shoulders with his unmentionables resting warmly against a sunburnt neck.

This was the funniest thing that Cam Glasgow had obviously seen in a long time. He hooted with laughter at his flight leader's discomfort. The predicament was bad enough, but Jox's shoulder still wasn't a hundred per cent, and the bloody ape was heavy. Reacting in pain, Jox reached for the primate, pushing him aside. This was clearly not what the guide nor the star performer had expected, and both reacted indignantly.

'Calm down, calm down,' said Jox, handing the Gibraltarian a handful of coins. 'Here, feed the blasted monkey, but keep it away from me!'

Glasgow was laughing so hard that he couldn't catch his breath.

'And you can bloody well stop that too,' said Jox. 'Show the uniform some respect, if not the man.'

It was good to see his friend laugh, though. There hadn't been much of that over the last six months. Sure, there were moments of bonhomie with the others at Babbacombe, but there was no disguising the pain and appalling suffering that many were going through. The fragile morale of the injured airmen wasn't helped by reports of their erstwhile squadron mates failing to return from the fighter sweeps and bombing runs over occupied Europe. In their letters, Pritchard, Chalmers and Robertson invariably spoke of the disappearance of such and such. One bittersweet aspect of being away for so long was that eventually, the names became more unfamiliar.

It certainly was a shock to find Glasgow amongst the pilots gathered on that platform, waiting for transport to Greenock and the dubious comfort of the SS *Queen Victoria*. Their subsequent conversation went broadly along the lines of Glasgow having told Brotchie and Robertson that he'd made a vow to watch over Jox, come what may. The tough NCO and former 'Trenchard Brat' was the longest serving and surviving pilot within the squadron. He was well within his rights to rotate off Ops, but instead his request was to serve alongside Jox, and if it meant 'going to bloody Malta, so be it.' He rationalised that 'I could do with a tan anyway', although truth be told, Glasgow was the fish-belly white variety of Scotsman with a deep suspicion of the sun, born from a childhood in the tall dark tenements of Tayside Dundee.

Finding that Glasgow was to be his wingman again was a great comfort, but it was not the only shock reserved for Jox. The next was a discovery neither welcomed nor desired, and only promised to deliver trouble.

Just over the ridge line was the massive, white-washed Rock Hotel, Gibraltar's finest establishment. It had been built by the fabulously wealthy 4th Marquess of Bute, John Crichton-Stuart in 1932. His father had reputedly been the richest man in the world for a period, thanks to the family's coal mining and transport interests. Legend even said that he was responsible for building most of Cardiff.

The opulent hotel was the venue for the RAF Gibraltar station commander's welcome dinner for Jox's flight of pilots. The wags were calling it 'a last supper for the condemned men', but the great and the good from this stubborn little bastion of the British Empire were out in force to wish the brave fellows well, flying as they were to the rescue and crewing the life-saving convoy to their besieged sister island of Malta.

Queuing to shake hands with the dignitaries, Glasgow had time to shoot Jox a warning glance before he came face to face with the station's commanding officer. He recognised him immediately; it would have been hard not to.

Towering over him were the scarred features of Wing Commander D.D. Drummond, Jox's nemesis when he'd been the ops room controller at RAF Kenley during the desperate days of the Battle of Britain. The pair had crossed swords and in fact had come to blows as the battle had raged. Drummond's sneering face, damaged during the battle of Norway, had been significantly worsened by a badly broken nose, the result of two perfectly executed 'Glasgow kiss' headbutts delivered by Jox, poleaxing the obnoxious senior officer. Jox had escaped court martial for the offence, but only because he'd been due to be decorated by His Majesty the King. The dossier against Drummond for bullying, sexual harassment and intimidation had also gone a long way in brushing the incident under the carpet. Nevertheless, the bad penny had turned up and was now glowering down at Jox. This did not bode well.

'I've been looking forward to seeing you again, McNabb, ever since I spotted your name on the manifest.'

'Good evening, sir,' replied Jox, as noncommittally as he could. 'It was kind of you to organise this evening for my men.'

'These airmen belong to the RAF,' said Drummond. 'And on the Rock, I am the RAF. I'd advise you not to forget that.'

Before Jox could respond, he was nudged down the waiting line of dignitaries by Glasgow, finding himself unexpectedly shaking the hands of a lady in an emerald-coloured frock. She was the wife of an official in the Governor's office and seeing the decorations on Jox's chest, she twittered excitedly about 'brave boys flying towards danger, when everyone else is running for cover.'

He thanked her for her kind words, but his ears were attuned to the discussion between Drummond and Glasgow. The wing commander clearly outranked Glasgow, but there was no doubting the past valour and experience behind the warrant officer's DFM and bar, plus the row of long service ribbons. In addition, everyone knew that in the services it was really the senior NCOs that ran things.

'A very good evening to you, sir,' said Glasgow. 'It's good for me to finally put a face to a voice.'

'I don't follow you, Warrant Officer,' Drummond replied coldly.

'Glasgow's the name, sir. Been with No. 111 Squadron since 1937. Right through the Battle of France and Battle of Britain, and until just a few weeks ago I was leading fighter sweeps over the Continent. I'm one of Lord Trenchard's boys, you see. Father of the RAF, so he is.' Glasgow smiled, the icy menace in his pale eyes very evident. 'Aye, your voice is familiar, all right, from when you were leading the controllers, tucked up away in the ops room at Kenley. It was awfully reassuring to hear you and your clever young ladies, when me and the boys, like young Flight Lieutenant McNabb over there, were up there doing the business. It's good to know you'll be tucked away here, when we're getting stuck in again in Malta.

Leading us from the rear, shall we say?' He chuckled mirthlessly, making quite sure that Drummond got his full implication. 'I'm minded of that day we came to Kenley's rescue. That was a bloody shambles, was it not? Every one of us heroes, wouldn't you say? Well, maybe some more than others.'

'Quite right, Mister Glasgow,' replied Drummond, fully realising that his behaviour on that fateful day had left much to be desired. 'Must carry on, must say good evening to the rest of the chaps.'

'Aye, right you are, sir. Most civil of you,' chuckled Glasgow. He was not terribly tall, compared to the hulking Drummond, but he still managed to exude pure threat and deadly competence. 'If that'll be all, sir...'

Drummond steered well clear of Jox and Glasgow for the rest of the evening, but every time Jox glanced over, he found him glaring and mumbling to himself. It was hard to tell whether his scowl was continued antipathy or if it was the scar running down his hairless right eyebrow and over his cheek to his lip, giving him a permanent sneer and blindness in one eye.

It was the demands of the service that meant that a senior officer with Drummond's technical skills, however blotted his copybook might be, still had a part to play in the vast war machine pitted against the Axis. It was just lousy luck that their paths had crossed again, giving Drummond the opportunity for revenge. The question was how would he strike and when? His window of opportunity was limited, and this was really the last thing Jox needed to be worrying about right now. Sadly, he knew the man well enough to know he wouldn't miss an opportunity to strike. To Drummond, Jox was an insubordinate parvenu who had slighted him and disrupted the plans he'd had for Alice, one of the WAAFs that he considered as his own personal harem. Jox had put paid to that.

The commodore co-hosting the evening with Drummond gave a speech.

'Welcome to the Club, gentlemen. That's what we Royal Navy Force H boys call this command, with responsibility for the western Mediterranean. You have volunteered for hazardous duty, which we like to call Club Runs, and I want to thank you for that. We've already had several successful runs delivering Hurricanes to Malta earlier in the war, but now we need to get Spitfires there, if we're to hold Jerry back.' He gazed at the group of assembled aviators, as if trying to memorise their faces.

'I want to stress the importance of getting your kites through. They are all that stand between Malta and defeat. Mister Churchill may well call the island his unsinkable aircraft carrier in the Mediterranean, but let me assure you, it can be sunk. What is at stake is the entire civilian population of the island, plus of course all the RAF, Army and Navy personnel, and the facilities, equipment, aircraft, and vessels that are based there. Your Spitfires and the other kites delivered so far are all that keep the bombers at bay. The island has been ravaged and our losses are heavy. Let's be clear: we're barely hanging on. That is why you are so important. Once on the island, you and your aircraft will defend subsequent convoys bringing in more vital supplies and war materiel, and crucially, even more aircraft. You will sustain the war effort and preserve the morale of the martyred populace.'

The commodore looked tired. 'I know some of you are veterans of the desperate air battles earlier in the war. I fear things are every bit as desperate over Malta. We are grateful you are here, and I wish you all the very best on your Club Run.'

The next morning, the nine designated pilots were inspecting their newly assembled Spitfires, parked inside brick and sandbag blast-proof pens dotted across the airfield. They had none of the usual markings or embellishments, standing in the Mediterranean sunlight like bolted-together Frankenstein beasts, all clumsy joins, raw welding, metal patches and lumpy fuselages. The assembled airmen were trying to be professional, but many had sore heads from the night before.

'Christ, they're ugly enough to give Jerry a fright,' said Glasgow, suffering in the morning's heat. 'I'd be terrified. Hope they're more air worthy than they appear.'

'What do you think, Flight?' Jox asked a Cornish crew chief called Pengelly, the leader of the 'Special Erection Party', who'd assembled the beasts.

'She'll serve all right, sir,' he replied, rolling his Rs as he wiped his oily hands on a rag. 'She won't win any beauty pageants, but she'll serve.' He looked a bit uneasy. 'Mind you, my armoury plumber doesn't like the idea of you going off with empty guns.'

'Well then, what's he doing fiddling with the 20mm magazine? What's he up to?'

'Just following the CO's orders, sir. Packing the empty magazine compartments with cigarettes and leaf tobacco. Apparently Wing Commander Drummond has some sort of arrangement with a station commander in Malta. It don't weigh much, and you can pack a lot of snout in there. Chief in charge of maintenance here says it's all above board and is just a little treat for the troops sweating it out on the island. I'm not sure I entirely swallow that. My family's been in the smuggling business for long enough to recognise it when I sees it.'

'Let me get this right, Flight. Not only are we flying to Malta unarmed, but we're also being used as tobacco mules?'

'That's about the size of it,' said the laconic Cornishman. 'Excepting, that is, the modifications we've carried out for desert conditions and the fact you're taking off from a bloody short carrier deck. Has anyone explained that to you, sir?'

'No, not at all.'

'Oh Christ,' said Pengelly. 'I'm not sure I should be the one explaining. That's way beyond my paygrade.'

'I'd rather get a straight answer from you, Flight. There's a lot about this mission that we're learning about for the first time.'

'Come on, laddie,' chipped in Glasgow. 'Spit it out.'

'Right, well, two main things are fairly obvious. That big old upturned mouth under the nose is called a Vokes tropical filter. Over in Malta and pretty much everywhere you'll be flying, it'll be from dirty airstrips covered with dust, sand, and other flying bits of debris, all of which can seriously wear down your engine parts and aircraft performance. That bloody great thing filters most of it out.' He pointed at a thickened portion of the fuselage, between the aircraft's spatted front wheels. 'That there's a ninety-gallon slipper tank extending your range to reach Malta. It can be dropped off if you get into trouble and need some extra speed, but standing orders are to avoid doing that, since they're scarce on the island.'

Glasgow and Jox dipped their heads to see what Flight Sergeant Pengelly was referring to. The shade under the aircraft's wings was cool, in contrast to the blistering sunlight beating down onto the airfield. The air was warming, and wobbling thermals were rising from the tarmac. The men were sweating out last night's excess.

'None of that looks particularly terrifying,' said Glasgow, his face rather redder than usual. 'Does it affect performance at all?'

'Not too much. The nose is a bit top-heavy and she'll fly lumpy with the additional drag, but most of the extra weight is offset by the missing ammo.'

'Right, anything else?'

'Yeah, but that's not the worst of it, sir,' replied Pengelly. 'Your biggest problem is this.' He held a fist in front of Jox's face, who jerked back in surprise. 'No, no, hold your hand out, sir.'

Jox did as instructed, and Pengelly dropped something into his palm. Jox peered down at a wooden wedge about three inches long. 'What the devil is that?' he asked, turning it over in his hand.

'I'm not telling you that, sir, but it's definitely something you need to be worrying about.'

# CHAPTER TWENTY-THREE

The ships of the Operation PICKET taskforce steamed into the azure waters of the Bay of Gibraltar, looping around Europa Point, bristling with gun positions. The tall lighthouse semaphored 'Good Luck', as the winds picked up on the open sea.

At the heart of the convoy was the battlecruiser HMS *Malaya* and aircraft carrier HMS *Eagle*. The cruiser was an intimidating sight, dull grey and top-heavy with a tower, funnels, and formidable guns. A scarred veteran of the first war, she'd served at Jutland. At almost two hundred metres long, she was equipped with eight fifteen-inch guns in paired turrets fore and aft with a firing range of almost twenty miles. A further twelve six-inch guns were mounted down one side of the ship and a further pair were on the ship's forecastle, meaning she packed quite a punch. Below the waterline she even had hidden torpedo tubes. Sunlight glistened on her seal-like skin, the breeze whipping her ensign to tatters, and there was no doubting she was a thoroughbred of the seas and a reassuring presence amongst them.

In contrast, the carrier HMS *Eagle* was a converted South American dreadnought, normally equipped with Fairey Swordfish torpedo bombers. Two thirds the length of HMS *Malaya*, she was an ungainly vessel, a squat metal ironing board with a lozenge shaped island. Like some travelling blacksmith's caravan, her steep sides were festooned with equipment, inflatable life rafts and heavy netting, hardly reassuring to Jox and his flight of landlubber airmen. Within the escort were also the light anti-aircraft cruiser HMS *Hermione* and no fewer than nine E and F-Class destroyers from 'H' Force's Eighth Flotilla. Finally, the tugboat HMS *Salvonia* and the motor launch *ML-174* were there as rescue vessels, should the need arise.

The taskforce were protection for a dozen or so merchant ships, laden with supplies for the besieged island, including a grimy tanker, which wallowed in the swell. Despite the number of escorts, the sense amongst the Navy men was that the convoy was underweight for what lay ahead. That anxiety was heightened by the sight of the flotilla of destroyers, perpetually circling nervously like white-moustached terriers anticipating predators. Never still, they cut through the waves, sometimes disappearing entirely into the deep troughs of the ocean.

Officially, they were bound for 'destinations unknown', but it was common knowledge that the convoy was heading south of the Balearics. A briefing was called on their first morning out of Gibraltar.

'Welcome aboard, gentlemen. My name is Newton-Taylor and I'm what our American friends call the "air boss" on HMS *Eagle*. I have some good news and bad news for you.' He gave them no time to choose. 'The good news is the weather conditions are pretty much ideal for this run, particularly to avoid detection over enemy territory in Tunisia. Sandstorms inland have sent a lot of particulates into the atmosphere, with conditions hazy up to twenty thousand feet. That gunk won't do your engines any favours but will muffle your signature with enemy tracking stations.'

'And the bad news, sir?' asked Jox, articulating what his men were already thinking.

'Glad you asked, McNabb. The last club run of Spits we attempted a few days ago ran into problems with the seals of their slipper tanks. We've had to send them back to Gib. My ground crews have been checking the seals on your kites and we're fairly confident that seven are fit for purpose, but I'm afraid two have perished seals.' He was a bit embarrassed, galled at being a senior service man admitting failure to the junior service. 'It's not a decision we've taken lightly. Without those tanks, you simply won't make Malta. A tough call, McNabb, but you'll need to drop two of your chaps.'

'That's not a problem, sir. These chaps are all sound, but we need to prioritise experience. It's no reflection on your abilities, Sergeant Douglas and Pilot Officer Goodwin, but you're the freshest here, so we'll have you make the next run.' Jox looked from one to the other until they both nodded their acknowledgement. The sergeant was a tough Scouser who didn't seem too bothered, but young Goodwin, from Farnham, was newly qualified and keen as mustard. There was no disguising his disappointment.

'Right then, that's set,' said Newton-Taylor.

'Perhaps then, sir, it's time for you to explain what this is for?' said Jox, holding the wooden peg that Pengelly had given him.

'Ah, quite so,' replied Newton-Taylor. 'I've been meaning to get to that.'

Sometime later they were gathered with the ground crews beside the seven fated Spitfires, strapped down onto the heaving carrier deck. Without folding wings, they were too big to fit in the lifts to the hangar holds below. Since Jox had last seen them, the Spits had been painted: sea-blue on top and sky-blue below. He ran his hands over the fuselage and at first thought the paint was still wet, but realised it was sticky from wind-blown spray.

Newton-Taylor stood, arms clasped behind his back, impassive as the breeze tugged at his bulk. He was happy to let his chief engineering officer do the explaining.

'Gents, you'll notice the ramp at the end of the flight deck. It's designed to propel aircraft off this carrier, but not something as heavy as your Spits. This flight deck is exactly 652 feet long, and from your training manuals you'll recall that for take-off in zero wind and standard conditions, a Spitfire Mark V requires 990 feet, which you simply do not have.' He gave the pilots a nervous smile. 'What you do have is about 18 lbs of boost with the tit pulled out, equivalent to 30 knots into a 10-knot wind, so effectively 40 knots over the wings.' He could see he'd lost most of them. 'Our intention is to start you parked far aft of the flight deck to have the longest possible run. We'll have some ratings holding onto your tails while you build up the revs. Once you're set, lower your flaps to maximum, when wedges like this cut to an angle of exactly twenty-five degrees will be inserted into just the correct position. Then you'll select flaps up and they'll jam into place to give you an automatic twenty-five degrees of flaps from the off. Once you're safely aloft, flaps down a touch and the pegs simply fall away. An elegant solution to a complex problem, and it seems to work most of the time.'

'What happens if it doesn't?' asked Jox.

'Well then, you're in the drink with a bloody great aircraft carrier thundering over you. Don't fancy your chances against the propellor. Fish food, I'd say.'

That certainly gave them something to think about as they completed their inspections of their respective aircraft. Jox's Spitfire looked much better for the new paint job, but something was bothering him. It wasn't the bulbous dust filter nor the chunky drop tank, as he scanned over the otherwise familiar lines of this new *Marguerite*. He fiddled with the porcelain arm in his trouser pocket, which had once belonged to the original Marguerite. It came to him: he needed to name the Spit. The mission was really just a ferrying trip, but she still needed to carry the name or else he risked falling foul of all kinds of fighter pilot superstitions. He turned to Pengelly, who was discreetly following him as he checked over the aircraft's flaps, hatches and fuselage.

'Flight, I've got a favour to ask. My kites have always been named in memory of someone important to me. I don't mind if it's just scrawled on the side in chalk, but I'd feel better if you'd scribble the name *Marguerite V* on her. While you're at it, add a rough sketch of an arm like this one, but holding a sword.' Jox opened his hand to reveal the pale piece of ceramic, repaired several times.

Pengelly smiled. 'No worries, sir, I've been asked some pretty daft things by officers and that's by no means the worst. If it gives you confidence, of course, but I think we can do better than chalk. Young Arthur is always sketching in his little book and I'm sure he's a painter too. What was it you wanted, an arm holding a sword?'

It took a few days to reach the launch point, and they passed without incident. Each passing day was much the same, windy with lurching decks, ceaseless vibrations and hollow clanking from deep within the vessel. The first opportunity for excitement came when the convoy commodore decided to drill the guns before approaching action. The resulting cacophony from guns of every conceivable calibre firing into the waters of the Med was exhilarating, spectacular and utterly deafening.

Ships rocked with the recoil, wreathed in cordite smoke before it was snatched away by the breeze, to be replaced by the drifting spray from the towering columns of white-water explosions. Jox couldn't help but wonder at the cost of these pyrotechnics, achieving little other than soaking personnel and scattering litter onto the seabed. It did make a glorious racket, though, leaving crews grinning like excited boys, which frankly most of them still were.

The morning of the mission dawned, and the seven chosen aviators faced the prospect of their first carrier take-off with trepidation. Jox was adamant the men shouldn't attempt something he hadn't tried first, so was determined to lead the way.

A brisk breeze whistled across the deck, as the ship turned to maximise airflow over their wings, creating additional lift and lowering required take-off speed. This wind was stronger than forecast, so that was encouraging but bracing.

Jox taxied to the far end of the flight deck, hand-guided by naval ratings holding onto either wing. Two more were tasked with gripping the tail and two senior men with inserting the all-important wedges at the right moment. Once in position, Jox asked for tower clearance. He glanced up to find the flight deck officer waving green flags at him. He gave the start-up signal by slowly rotating one flag, as a flare shot up into the air, advising the convoy that take-off was imminent. Jox throttled up but kept his brakes on. The flight deck officer gave the thumbs-up. Jox did the same, then watched the flag rotate more rapidly, indicating that he should continue raising revs.

At near enough full power, he activated his pneumatically controlled flaps, first one way and then the other. He waved the chocks away, released the brakes and heard the deep throaty throb of the Merlin engine propelling him down the deck. Reaching the ramp, he was flung into the air, but with insufficient speed. The aircraft bounced on the deck with a worrying crunch, then appeared to drop off the front of the carrier in a terrifying semi-stall.

With an agonising roar, Jox managed to skim the heaving surface of the sea, slowly and ever so painfully gathering speed as he climbed away. Exhaling into his mask, he realised he'd been holding his breath. Down below, the ships were suddenly very small, tracing white-water wakes like the tails of comets.

'Bloody hell, that was close.'

He circled the carrier group like a mother mallard anxious to see her fledgelings take flight. Their take-offs were neither pretty nor elegant, but he marvelled at just how well the wooden wedges had worked. There were some close calls, but none were any worse than his far from perfect attempt. He was relieved they'd all got off without loss.

The flight rose into the hazy sky stretching over the seemingly endless ocean. The sole suggestion of land was a smudgy shadow on the horizon indicating the Balearics. Gaining altitude, visibility worsened, but Jox reasoned that was a good thing as they were heading into harm's way.

He clicked the switch of his radio-telephone. 'PICKET Flight, this is PICKET Leader. Form on me. Cam on my portside. Second element starboard. Rear trio, I want you above us. Climbing to Angels Twenty now. Get your masks on, boys, and keep checking them as we're going to be on the bottle all the way. I don't want anyone conking out. At the risk of stating the obvious, you're expendable, but your kites aren't.'

He swung his head to check everyone was complying. Glasgow gave the thumbs-up.

Jox addressed the capable Fleet Air Arm Sub Lieutenant Cochrane, who was leading the rear trio of Spits. 'Stay tight, Cocky, and keep an eye out for the Hun. There's pretty much nothing else up here but bloody sun. This glare's a killer, so be careful.'

'Roger, Skipper,' replied Cochrane.

Jox glanced at his directional gyro, partially hidden behind his gloved hand grasping the spade grip of the stick. On his lap was the map with their journey pencilled on. 'Heading and altitude as per the briefing. Settle in and let's get this done, and for God's sake keep your eyes open. We're in bandit country all the way, so radio silence except for emergencies. Good luck, chaps.'

They were sixty miles off Algiers, three hours from Malta, the largest of an archipelago of islands south of Sicily. The island was halfway between Gibraltar and Alexandria in Egypt and had been an outpost of the British Empire for almost two hundred years. It was a crucial base for British naval and air operations striking at the supply routes between Italy and North Africa, depriving Axis forces of vital materiel. It had been besieged since June 1940, when Italy had declared war on Britain and the *Regia Aeronautica* had begun operations against the tiny island, just eighteen by nine miles, yet large enough to be a thorn in Rommel's side.

The aircraft defending Malta's harbour, airfields and submarine pens were dwindling through attrition and obsolescence, facing the best the Luftwaffe and *Regia Aeronautica* could throw at them. Fuel reserves were also at a critical low, explaining the vital but vulnerable tankers sent in successive convoys to the island and always the prime targets for the enemy.

Two routes had been discussed. One over water all the way, skirting around Cap Bon in Tunisia, then heading southeast. This was dismissed, as it meant getting too close to the German fighter *Staffel* based on the Italian island of Pantelleria, a scenario which was rather too close to the mauling Jox had received off Cap Gris-Nez, not least since they'd be flying unarmed. Counterintuitively, the alternative meant landfall over Bizerte in Tunisia, passing Tunis and the ancient city of Carthage, before doglegging over Hammamet and approaching Malta between the islands of Linosa and Lampedusa. They would be in the airspace of Tunisia-based Vichy French fighters, but they were generally believed to be more apathetic than Pantelleria's aggressive fighters, especially under the midday sun. Flying high, the hope was the hazy conditions would also mask their progress.

Jox checked his wristwatch, then the flight time indicator on the instrument panel. They were making good time. He tapped the compass and then the fuel gauge. It would soon be time to refill the main reservoir from the external fuel reserve in the vaunted slipper tank. On cue, the warning light blinked on and Jox flicked the switch of the electric pump. There was a soft purr and a brief moment of anxiety before the Merlin coughed, then continued humming sweetly. He checked his oxygen and noted the tank was half full.

The sprawl of Tunis was below and yet nothing moved. Their luck seemed to be holding, and it appeared that as in Noel Coward's words, only 'Mad dogs and Englishmen go out in the midday sun'. Reaching the coast again, Jox led the flight over the resort of Hammamet. Kriegsmarine and Luftwaffe personnel were doubtless cavorting in the waves with *Pied Noirs* lovelies down there, enjoying their leave in the African sunshine, unaware of what was passing overhead.

Approaching the corridor between the Pelagie Islands of Linosa and Lampedusa, Jox discerned the first signs of enemy activity. The glassy surface of the sea was broken by the feathery wake of a narrow vessel. It was unlike any ship he'd seen before, and with curiosity overriding discretion, he lost height to investigate.

His section were in a loose finger-four formation and followed him down. Glasgow clicked his R/T button several times, gesticulating and wanting to know what he was playing at. Jox pointed at the vessel, then to his eyes and back at the sea. Glasgow shook his head but reluctantly complied. The second element did too, followed by Cochrane's rear three.

They dropped towards the intriguing silhouette, still oblivious to their presence. Whatever it was, it was clearly confident it was well within enemy-controlled waters. The 'toothless' flight of Spitfire Vs swooped towards it, and it soon became clear it was an enemy U-boat recharging its batteries on the surface. A sitting duck, if they'd only been armed. Falling from the sun, they remained unseen as the sub scratched a long white line into the glassy surface of the water. They couldn't have missed and Jox seethed with frustration.

'The least we can do is give them a fright. Follow me in pairs. Cocky, keep your boys up top on lookout. Right, Cam, come on.'

They fell onto the foe, who, suddenly alerted, panicked and started firing back with a double-barrelled AA gun behind the conning tower. Bare-chested crewmen, who moments earlier were sunbathing and performing callisthenics on the deck, scattered in every direction. A dive klaxon brayed as they bottle-necked at the hatches. Glasgow uttered an exasperated expletive. The golden target was sinking below the waves.

'That certainly spooked them,' said Jox. 'Back up to Angels Fifteen. We're due to meet our escort beyond the islands.'

They entered the final phase of the mission, the rendezvous with two long-range Bristol Beaufort torpedo bombers and a trio of Bristol Blenheims that had flown directly from

Gibraltar. Their crews were familiar with this final leg into Malta and would show the newcomers how to approach RAF Luqa in the south of the island. The bombers guided the fighter pilots in exchange for the semblance of a fighter escort to dissuade opportunistic raiders. PICKET flight orbited the RV point for less than ten minutes before the larger aircraft appeared, wobbling like mirages in the heat haze.

Forming around the bombers, Jox welcomed them. 'BEAU element, BLENHEIM section, PICKET flight leader. Good to see you, chaps. We may have found some trade for your tin fish, BEAU leader.'

'Very glad we found you,' replied the lead Beaufort. 'Where away on that trade?'

'U-boat on the surface about three nautical miles due west, between the islands. Probably long gone, but it may be worth a shufti. Oppos like that don't come along all that often. I tell you, my boys are fuming we didn't have a pop at it.'

'Roger, PICKET leader, but that's not your mission; delivering your aircraft is. We'll circle back and take a look. Stick with BLENHEIM flight. We'll catch up.'

'Wilco,' replied Jox tersely, irritated but knowing the other man was right.

After twenty minutes the Bristol Beauforts were back, torpedoes still hanging pendulously between their twin engines. They had found nothing but empty sea.

Up ahead, Malta was about the size of the Isle of Wight, lying like a giant coconut frond floating on the ocean. Smudgy brown, it was arid with towering dust devils that rose from the dry land surface, twisting high up into the sky. They'd been briefed that dust often indicated that enemy activity was in progress, so after their long flight, it appeared they were landing onto a hot airfield.

Dropping to five thousand feet, Jox raised Luqa tower. It responded immediately, warning them off. Their escort were instructed to press on in the hope of distracting any raiders, whilst Jox's Spits were told to orbit offshore until it was safe to approach.

Once the coast was clear, they were ordered to pancake and vacate their cockpits immediately. Ground crews would refuel and arm their aircraft. Fresh pilots would then take the kites back up to defend the airfield. The lesson was hard-learnt, as a few weeks ago, a squadron's worth of newly delivered Spitfires had been destroyed on the ground.

As soon as his wheels touched the dusty tarmac, Jox was relieved that he'd fulfilled his mission. The sharp bark of an ack-ack gun shook him from his reverie as he powered down. The Spit was manhandled towards a blast pen where a crowd was waiting with a starter trolley, fuel bowser and an armoury truck. As soon as he'd switched off, riggers, armourers and fitters crawled over the aircraft. Glasgow was parked in the next pen along. Unhooking his mask, he slid back the canopy and asked a ginger-haired mechanic standing on his wing, 'Where are those replacement pilots?'

'Stuck on the other side of the station, sir. Be here in a jiffy, I expect.'

'Sod that,' replied Jox. 'I've not brought this kite all this way to see it flattened.' He called to Glasgow, 'I'm going back up. You coming?'

# CHAPTER TWENTY-FOUR

They were on the dusty tarmac at RAF Luqa for no more than ten minutes. The nautical paintwork of their grimy Spitfires was streaked with oil, and, in places, worn to bare metal by the abrasive power of the airborne silica particles.

Parked within an 8-shaped blast pen, made of sandbags and earth-filled four-gallon petrol cans, Jox was also shielded by a mob of frantic ground crew. A battered static bowser on bricks snaked a fuel line over the wing of the latest iteration of *Marguerite*, held in place by a sunburnt lad in boots, shorts, a tin helmet and little else. Cam Glasgow's Spit was in the other half of the pen beyond the bowser's reach so it was being filled from a combination of sturdy metal jerry cans and tin plate British 'flimsies.' It puzzled Jox as to how on earth the jerry cans had made it onto the island.

He hopped down from the cockpit, anxious to stretch his legs after the long flight. Wobbling like a new-born lamb on the tarmac, he waved to Glasgow and watched him waddle off wearing his parachute harness to have a pee in the corner. Returning, he lit a cigarette rather too close to the petrol can-wielding crew, but then again the chap doing the refuelling had a butt between his lips. They lived dangerously in Malta.

Jox ran his hands over 'new' *Marguerite*'s dusty fuselage, grateful that she'd got him this far. He enjoyed a quiet moment of gratitude amidst the frantic activity. Glancing at her name in elegant calligraphy above the drawing of a beefy arm holding a claymore aloft, he smiled. None of his previous aircraft had been so elegantly personalised. Pengelly and Arthur, back on

HMS *Eagle*, had done a fine job. A pair of armourers draped with linked belts of .303 ammunition elbowed him aside.

'Sorry, sir,' mumbled one. The other was already on the wing by the ammo bin. 'What d'you want done with this?' He held up a padded package that Jox could only assume was Drummond's tobacco.

'I don't really know,' replied Jox. 'Chuck it in a corner. I'm sure someone will come looking for it.' Turning to a grinning red-headed sergeant standing by, he asked, 'What's the prognosis, sergeant?'

'Oh, she's grand. Here, I'm sure you could do with this.' He handed Jox a canteen of tepid but very welcome water. He drank deeply and was about to thank him when the gun position by the pen began firing. It pounded shells into the clear blue sky, as the sinister shape of a green Ju 88 swung over with a dull roar. It was low enough for its shadow to flicker across the pen, wiping the grin from the sergeant's face.

Men scattered, as the *Schnellbomber* fired from every one of its gun positions. Rounds skittered across the concrete and brick, sparking and dinging off equipment and into the hot tarmac. One of the 'plumbers' pirouetted off the wing, his ankle a bloody mess when he landed on the ground. The same round had banged a neat hole through the left aileron.

'Bloody hell,' said Jox, cowering under the doubtful protection of the Spitfire's wing. The red-haired sergeant was long gone. Jox searched for him across the clearly not so blast-proof pen and saw that he was dragging the wounded armourer, leaving a crimson slug trail in his wake.

'Right, get me back up there,' roared Jox to no one in particular.

In times of stress, well-trained military men react to orders instinctively and there are very few as well trained as fighter ground crews. Jox was given a leg up and strapped in, as his aircraft was made battle-ready with renewed intensity. Her domed canopy, glaringly bright in the sunshine, was given a final wipe. The ginger sergeant was back, hauling a starter accumulator on big rubber wheels. He slotted the lead into the engine mounting U-frame under the starboard wing and the trolley began to whirr.

Jox went through his starting procedure: throttle lever to half-inch open, mixture to rich, radiator shutter open. He pumped fuel then switched the engine on. It roared to life, thanks to the supplied charge. It vented orange flames through the exhaust stubs like an awakening dragon. The start-up procedure was complicated but executed instinctively in mere seconds.

He checked if Glasgow was ready. He waved back, as Jox clicked his R/T switch. 'Right, let's get at them. Follow me.' They taxied out of the pens, as a fuel store somewhere on the airfield boomed with secondary explosions. A towering pall of black smoke was rising into the haze of an impossibly blue sky.

They got off the deck without seeking any clearance, desperate to get the kites up and out of harm's way. Jox wondered how the rest of the flight were faring, realising that in his haste to save *Marguerite* from destruction on the ground he'd been foolhardy. The flight was his responsibility, and in his thirst for action he'd completely forgotten them. It was behaviour unworthy of his new rank.

He was at fault, but the frustration of the U-boat sighting had awakened a hunger inside him. His grief, though constant, burned a little less fiercely, but the red rage was back. Witnessing the carnage inflicted on the airfield with apparent impunity infuriated him. 'Not on my watch,' he said, raising revs and steadily gaining altitude.

On the far side of RAF Luqa's three crossed runways, a mustardy-olive Ju 88 was making a low sweep across the airfield. It had a blue underbelly, visible from the ground, and forward-facing guns that blasted anything in sight. An M/T car park was bearing the brunt of the fire with lorries, armoured cars and miscellaneous utility vehicles collapsing onto their axles, igniting with dramatic bangs, or simply falling to pieces under the lash of armour piercing projectiles. The raider was oblivious to the two Spits rising towards it, swinging arrogantly from side to side to maximise its cone of fire and confident he was unchallenged.

He never knew what hit him when Jox's first burst stitched up the side of the fuselage, shattering Perspex and drilling through the aluminium siding. The armourers hadn't had time to reload the 20mm Hispano cannons, leaving Jox with only his four .303 machine guns, under-gunned considering the hulking size of the Junker Ju 88. Fortunately, Glasgow's armourers had escaped the first *Schnellbomber*'s murderous pass and had been faster on the case.

Jox jinked aside as the throaty roar of Glasgow's Hispanos ripped into the wounded raider, sending some thirty cannon shells at him at a blistering rate of 650 rounds per minute. The fire from the three-second burst raked the doomed bomber from end to end. It had already dropped its load and none of Glasgow's shells struck a fuel tank, so there was no explosion, just a slow drop, almost lazily falling to the ground with its crew torn to pieces. She was a 'Marie Celeste,' a ghost ship, by the time she scraped into the dusty ground beyond the airfield's wire fence. Only then did she burst into a mass of burning fuel.

Jox and Glasgow banked to observe their fallen foe, climbing above the haze and searching for more trade.

'Unidentified aircraft, this is Luqa tower. Identify yourself,' demanded the ops room.

Jox took a deep breath before answering, continuing his search of the horizon for more raiders. He found nothing but the pyre from the smoking ruin beyond the fence.

'Luqa Tower, this is PICKET One and Two,' said Jox. 'PICKET leader here. We are inbound from Gib. We took the kites up to avoid being sitting ducks.'

'PICKET leader, Luqa Ops Room. Following whose orders?' asked a different voice.

'PICKET Leader to Ops Room. Our own initiative. I can report one bandit brought down beyond the perimeter.'

'Initiative! Who the bloody hell do you think you are?' screamed the incensed ops controller.

*What is it with these chaps? I can't seem to put a foot right*, thought Jox.

The controller was still ranting. 'This isn't the wild west. You can't just turn up over my airfield and start banging away because you've got some hero complex.'

'Hero complex?' said Jox, his R/T mic still on.

'Aye, that's a bit harsh,' added Glasgow. 'I'd remind you we've just bagged one of those beggars that were beating up your airfield. A simple thank-you would have done just fine.'

'A thank-you?' roared the voice, which might even have belonged to the station commander. 'I'll give you a bloody thank-you! Get those kites down immediately. Once you're on the deck, report directly to the ops room. Ask for Keneally, Wing Commander Keneally. Consider that an order.'

*Damn*, thought Jox. *I haven't been here five minutes and the wing co's gunning for me already.* Not terribly helpfully, Glasgow, who was clearly enjoying himself, began humming the opening lines of Irving Berlin's 'Let's Face the Music and Dance'.

'Shut up, Cam, you're not helping.'

They taxied their aircraft into some pens on the opposite side of the airfield. They were upwind now and the air was clear. They could smell the sea and the island's baked earth and rock in the warmth of the Mediterranean sun. It was exactly as one might imagine a pretty island in the Med should be, the air scented with wild flowers and fragrant herbs. It was deceiving, though, for what the nose couldn't discern, the eyes could see. Everywhere they looked lay debris, charred equipment, and a cratered moonscape of shattered buildings. The airfield, like the island, had endured months of siege and was worn, tired, and evidently teetering on the verge of collapse. Perhaps that explained the short fuses and temper of the irate controller on the R/T.

Climbing down from their respective cockpits for the second time, the ground crews swarmed again. They unclipped their chutes and straps, handing them to a crew member, then began stripping off flight gauntlets, leather helmets and masks. It was getting hot under all those layers.

Once free of their stifling clothing, they were unexpectedly seized by a pair of blue-clad RAF gunners wearing white peaked caps, blancoed Sam Browne belts and white spats.

*Snowdrops! They've set the bloody snowdrops on us*, thought Jox. These were the men of the Royal Air Force Provost and Police.

'Oh, come on,' said Jox, as he and Glasgow were handcuffed. 'This is completely unnecessary. We were just doing our jobs. The only ones actually fighting back, by the look of things.' He was starting to lose his rag.

The officer in charge was wearing the standard peaked cap of an RAF officer but had the same black and red armband as his men.

'Flight Lieutenant Jeremy McNabb, I'm arresting you on suspicion of smuggling contraband. You are not required to say anything, but anything you do may be held against you in a court-martial for these offenses. Do you understand me, sir?'

Jox couldn't believe what was happening. He'd expected to get some trouble for an excess of zeal, but being arrested on some trumped-up charge of smuggling? *Smuggling what, for Christ's sake?*

It hit him like a ton of bricks. Tobacco. Drummond's bloody tobacco. He'd been stitched up like a kipper.

Glasgow came to a similar conclusion at the same time but reacted quite differently. He'd just shot down an enemy aircraft and was justifiably proud at having done so. In recompense, he'd been nicked. The usually dour Scotsman began roaring with laughter at the situation they found themselves in. His laughter was so infectious that soon Jox was laughing too, and even the coppers couldn't help cracking a smile. What truly finished Jox off was when Glasgow asked sweetly, 'I don't suppose any of you laddies have got a tab? I could really do with a wee smoke right about now.'

Jox, his flight of men and the Spitfires they'd successfully delivered, were now involved in a peculiar three-way tug of war. The protagonists were Keneally, RAF Luqa's Ops Controller, who wanted his pound of flesh, the station's Provost Marshal who believed he had cracked a major conspiracy involving seven pilots guilty of smuggling and finally the Head of Flying Operations for the island of Malta, who was desperate for the aircraft, not to mention fresh and experienced pilots. His need was all the more urgent since the Royal Navy were begging for fighter escorts for their beleaguered convoys, running the gauntlet towards Valletta's

Great Harbour.

Jox and his men were bewildered and bemused by the shit-storm they'd flown into. Innocent of all accusations, they'd fallen foul of a vindictive superior officer who'd taken the opportunity to take his revenge on someone he felt was an insubordinate upstart. Wing Commander Drummond had neither forgiven nor forgotten Jox's transgressions against him. It was a measure of the man that he should stoop to engineer this sort of situation when there were so many larger considerations that should have been the focus of his attention.

This was the world of pettiness that Jox had glimpsed with Brotchie, but he realised that here in the Med, siege mentality and the strain of being under constant attack was expressed as jealousy, private fiefdoms, and delusions of self-importance. Jox and the rest of the flight had no choice but to ride it out.

The voice of reason came from an unexpected but very welcome quarter. The island of Malta had three principal airfields: the RAF Luqa wing, nearest to Valletta, where AHQ Malta was headquartered, RAF Hal Far, also known as HMS Falcon to the southeast of the island and close to the sea, and finally RAF Ta Kali, recently established on a dried lake bed in the interior of the island. This bleak site was where a new Spitfire wing was being formed and earmarked to receive the Mark Vs that Jox had just delivered.

It's newly appointed wing commander instantly recognised the madness of detaining what amounted to half a squadron of experienced pilots whilst the battle for Malta was at its height. Tommy Thompson was also delighted to recognise his old comrades amongst their names.

# CHAPTER TWENTY-FIVE

Considering how far from Blighty they'd travelled, it was surprising how many familiar faces Jox found on the island. The RAF was still a small family.

Thompson was their saviour and was of course most welcome. The big bear of a chap had come to their rescue, immediately cutting through the red tape that threatened to lock them up and promised even worse. He had dealt with Drummond's plotting and scheming before, the last time again coming to Jox's rescue.

Jox and Thompson had an almost father-and-son relationship. They'd survived the Battle of Britain together, when the squadron had been decimated by the loss of irreplaceable men and cherished comrades. They were also together when His Majesty the King decorated them both at the palace, in the presence of Thompson's talkative wife, Sylvia and, of course, Alice.

The big man's eyes filled with unexpected tears when they spoke of Alice. He was devoted to his own little wife and knew how much darling Alice meant to Jox. The men had an emotionally charged stand-off, until Thompson enveloped Jox in his arms. They stood in silence, until Thompson spied Glasgow, a welcome opportunity to lighten the atmosphere.

'Cameron Glasgow, you great reprobate,' said Thompson, a beaming smile not quite hidden by his walrus moustache. 'By golly, I'm pleased to see you.'

'My respects, Wing Commander Thompson. I'm pleased to see you too, sir,' said Glasgow, ever the professional NCO, but grinning back.

The men embraced. They were of a similar age and experience, one a career officer, the other a career NCO. Both were older than most of their contemporaries and had a comradeship tested in the white heat of battle.

'Any word about your brother?' asked Thompson, referring to Glasgow's twin, Anthony, also a long-serving Treble One. He'd been shot down during the Battle of France and was last heard of languishing as a prisoner somewhere in Austria.

'An occasional postcard. Don't really know how he's doing, but I've no doubt he'll be giving them hell.'

'I'm sure of that,' said Thompson. 'By God, it's good to see you two. I'm afraid I can't promise things are terribly rosy here. We're in trouble, and I need your help to get morale and operations back up and running again.'

Thompson explained that the beleaguered island had suffered terribly. Public and military mood were at rock bottom in Malta's shattered towns and cities, the battered port and harbours and the dusty air stations and auxiliary fields. In fact, the entire island had already struck Jox as rather ancient and worn-out.

According to Thompson, Malta had pretty much been 'bombed back to the stone age', but what was remarkable was the sheer number of locals living in the ruins. In multi-generational families, the Maltese subsisted like troglodytes amongst the shattered buildings, in makeshift shelters and dank caves carved over the centuries from the very rock of the island. They were generally good-natured, chattering happily amongst themselves, but became sullen and defiant in the presence of British soldiery.

*Who could blame them?* thought Jox. *We've come uninvited, bringing nothing but death and destruction.*

'It's hardly surprising they're hacked off,' said Thompson. 'This place has the dubious honour of being the most bombed place on earth. I admire how stoic they remain, but I just don't understand it.'

The opportunity to catch up with more old friends provided one of the few bright spots in the otherwise depressing atmosphere of the island. The Spitfires of No. 603 (City of Edinburgh) Squadron had also recently arrived from Gibraltar, taking off from the American aircraft carrier USS *Wasp*. The 'Scottish gentlemen aviators' were based at RAF Luqa and Jox knew the unit well.

Amongst them was another of Jox's course mates from Montrose, Andrew 'Sally' Salvesen. They had a warm reunion, just what the doctor ordered to shake off the doldrums. Salvesen was the scion of a wealthy Edinburgh family and a technically superb pilot even when they were trainees. To those he didn't know, he could seem aloof, but that was just to hide his shyness. Tall, thin, witty and elegant, he fitted the Edinburgh squadron's aristocratic mould perfectly. He was delighted to see Jox and had grown in confidence since they'd last seen each other, with five kills to his credit and the DFC. He was now No. 603's A Flight leader and confident in the role.

Salvesen introduced Jox to 603's CO, Squadron Leader Lord David Douglas-Hamilton, another Scottish aristocrat, and one of four brothers serving in the RAF. He was tall and self-confident, a charismatic leader with the bent nose of a heavyweight boxer who'd won Bronze at the 1934 British Empire Games. He had a braying voice and laugh, a bit intimidating for Jox, but Salvesen clearly doted on him, and if he was all right by Sally, then Lord David was all right by Jox.

After an excellent, if somewhat frugal lunch at the Luqa mess, Thompson gathered his posse of replacement pilots together. Jox and Salvesen promised to keep in touch and to listen out for each other during operations. They also agreed to a night out in town as soon as that could be managed.

Bumping down the arid road to RAF Ta Kali, the Bedford trailed dust in its wake. Jox worried it might attract the attention of enemy fighter-bombers, but Thompson and the driver seemed unconcerned. He was struck by how run-down everything was. Broken buildings, dwellings and even the crops and vegetation were unkempt and apparently abandoned. Sallow-faced urchins stared hungrily, as old women in black dresses and headscarves poked through roadside rubbish, scratching for anything useful or edible. The towns were overrun with feral cats and scrawny dogs, abandoned by their hungry owners and risking the pot at every turn.

Only half of the pilots in Jox's flight from HMS *Eagle* were assigned to Ta Kali; the rest would stay on at Luqa, to join the ranks of the already depleted 603. In the back of the Bedford with Jox were Glasgow, Sub Lieutenant Billy 'Cocky' Cochrane and an excitable young Canadian sergeant pilot called George Beurling, nicknamed 'Screwball'.

It was a new expression to Jox, but one the sergeant enjoyed using to describe just about anything that was unfamiliar to him. By all accounts, there were many things on Malta that were totally 'screwball' to Beurling.

Arriving at the much-cratered Ta Kali airfield, the Bedford pulled up outside a tatty timber hut serving as No. 249 (Gold Coast) Squadron's dispersal. Out on the dust runway, actually a dried-up lakebed, ground and air crew were playing cricket. Jox recognised the tall red-haired bowler straight away.

It was Tom 'Ginger' Neil, another No. 8 FTS graduate. Thompson had briefed Jox that he was B Flight leader but was due to rotate back to the UK soon, having been in Malta since May 1941. They'd last seen each other before the Battle of Britain and Jox was struck by how gaunt he was. Neil had notched up seventeen kills during the battle and been awarded the DFC and Bar. He'd also been involved in a mid-air collision with North Weald's Station Commander Victor Beamish, very nearly killing them both. Beamish, a legendary character in the service, had since been reported Missing in Action over the Channel, like far too many others.

Ginger Neil shielded his eyes, trying to identify the newcomers. He watched them disembark, then, recognising Jox, came loping over with a big grin on his face. A tall, handsome chap, his gaze seemed dead, the strain in his eyes quite evident. Neil was clearly at the end of his tether; even multiple aces had their limits. Jox introduced Glasgow, Cochrane and Beurling and Ginger Neil reciprocated by presenting the CO of 249, Acting Squadron Leader Percy 'Laddie' Lucas.

Lucas was a bright, energetic fellow, who had been a sports journalist on the *Sunday Express* before the war. Playing wicket keeper, his love of the sport was evident, and he invited the newcomers to join in the fun. Jox was delighted to pad up and have a go, considering himself pretty handy with a bat, having played at school. Glasgow was less sure, but unsurprisingly proved to have an excellent eye and was a fearless fielder. Beurling insisted on holding the bat like a club, swinging at every bowl like a lumberjack and insisting that bouncing the ball was unfair. They rather suspected the excitable Canuck was playing an entirely different game. Cochrane declined to join in, insisting he was more of 'a Wet-bob, than Dry-bob,

Skipper. Navy man and all that. Anything to do with boats or the sea, I'm your man.'

After an hour's play under the beating sun, ears and noses were pink and rosy, and they'd sweated out the local Cisk beers from lunch. They retired to the NAAFI tent, hastily erected in lieu of a mess, which had been bombed just yesterday and had resulted in the loss of several lives.

At a table under the warm canvas, Jox asked, 'So, what's the gen, Ginger?'

The pair were nursing tepid gin and tonics. Neil gave a weary smile and ran long fingers through even longer red hair. He was sunburnt and scratched at an infected mosquito bite on his neck. 'It's a tough old road, Jox. We keep putting scratch teams in to bat and the damned rotters keep knocking them for six. They've pretty much got air superiority. Our old Hurricanes just don't cut it anymore, but it's the poor chaps in the Navy biplanes I feel sorry for. They've been chopped to bits. Still, with your Spits coming through, maybe now we stand a chance.'

'Sounds like you've really been through the mill.'

'Yes, rather. For my money it's been rougher here than during the Battle of Britain. Maybe back then we just didn't know what we didn't know. Now, it's very clear we're undermanned and undersupplied, flying clapped-out aircraft and completely outnumbered. Frankly, Jox, it's taken its toll.' He lifted his chapped hands with bitten fingernails. They shook like a centenarian's. 'I need a rest, but don't want to let the side down.'

'Listen, you've done more than your share, Ginger. No one can reproach you. I got pretty banged up during the Blitz and it took time to recover. I'm back now, so you can do the same.

There's no shame in letting others pick up the slack. Where are they sending you next?'

'On a bit of a tour apparently, before heading home. Something about war bonds and telling people about what's happening here in Malta. Egypt first, then across Africa and finally onto Canada. About a quarter of the pilots on the island are Canadians, so they're very interested in what's going on here.'

'Beurling's Canadian, and two of the others I came over with are Canucks too.'

'Yes, we have many chaps from the Dominions here. Not quite sure why — maybe the Brits all copped it during the Battle. We've got Aussies, Kiwis and South Africans too, but most are Canadians. There are even some Americans too. Ossie Wolf over at the bar is a Yank. Joined the RAF in thirty-nine, but before that he fought in Spain.'

'In Spain? On which side?'

'We don't talk about that,' laughed Neil. 'A few of us have been here for a while, others are still quite new, but the turnover is frightful. We lose people almost every day. Just yesterday, Johnny Booth, and our spy, Art Waterfield were killed when the mess got hit. Over at No. 126 Squadron they've lost four chaps, with many more injured. The place got flattened and they all died in the rubble. What a way to go.' He glanced around the canvas tent buzzing with quiet conversation. 'They're a good bunch and a great laugh. A touch undisciplined, but always game to mix it up with the Boches and Eyeties. Quite an eclectic bunch, you'll see. I'll introduce you, but the key ones to know are "Buck" McNair, Canadian and taking over B Flight from me; Erik Hetherington, Norman Lee and Raoul Daddo-Langlois, who are all Brits; Johnny Plagis and Dougie Leggo, who are

Rhodesian and inseparable; Jimmy Waerea from New Zealand and then "Mac" McElroy, Jean Paradis, Basil Butler and Wally Macleod, who are more Canucks. Paradis is French-Canadian and often refuses to speak English. He's a character all right.'

'Should get on with Beurling, he's … how does he describe himself? A screwball.'

Neil laughed. 'There's certainly plenty of those about.'

'What about ops? What can we expect?'

'You'll be busy. Patrols most days, but with all the raids, most are interceptions. We also provide escorts to convoys heading into Grand Harbour and Marsaxlokk Harbour. That means fighting off enemy bombers, torpedo-bombers and fighters, but also fast torpedo boats and occasionally even U-boats. You certainly won't get bored, just utterly exhausted. This damned heat, the flipping mosquitoes and fleas certainly don't help. Not to mention the dreaded "Malta dog". Don't worry, you'll find out what that is soon enough.'

Despite the best efforts of the Army Engineers, Ta Kali was struggling to get operational again after the recent attacks. In the meantime, Convoy MW10, consisting of four merchant ships and a naval escort of several light cruisers, an anti-aircraft cruiser and eighteen destroyers was running the gauntlet from Alexandria in Egypt.

Protecting the convoy was a priority, so a detachment of No. 249 Squadron's newest pilots were ferried back to RAF Luqa and would operate alongside 603's ageing Hurricanes. Jox would lead with Glasgow as his wingman, Cochrane and Beurling providing the second element. Designated Green Section of VIKEN, No. 603 Squadron's callsign, they were tasked with tackling any fighters over the convoy, whilst the Hurricanes would deal with the bombers.

On arrival, they were allocated Spitfires still in the light and dark blue livery of the transfer flight from Gibraltar. Knowing it was unlikely that he would be reunited with his personalised *Marguerite V*, Jox grabbed a stick of chalk and scribbled *Marguerite VI* on the side of his 'temporary' bird. Climbing into the cockpit, he gave the doll's arm in his pocket a quick squeeze for luck and was strapped in by the ground crew.

They then proceeded to sit in the sweltering heat in cockpit readiness, and Jox was very grateful for the cardboard sunshade his rigger propped up over the Perspex canopy. The dry air was heavy, with the smell of fuel fumes and something rotten coming from some nearby ruins. RAF Luqa and the surroundings hadn't escaped the deadly attention of the raiders either.

Jox waved at a bluebottle that buzzed around his head, when a red flare arced across the oddly coloured sky, a pale orange striped at high altitude with purple cloud. He pulled the lid shut and was surprised at how hot the handle was. The accumulator trolley whined, Jox throttled up and Green Section were soon airborne, vectored onto the convoy's last position. Gaining altitude, Jox realised the fly was trapped in the cockpit. It bumped about irritatingly when he needed to concentrate. He considered pulling back the lid to flush it out, but they were already too high.

*Bad luck fella, if I go down, you go down.*

They found the convoy from the smoke rising up from it and the snarling aircraft overhead. Hurricanes from No. 126 Squadron were heavily outnumbered by Me 109s, their radiator dust covers making them look like smiling assassins. Other aircraft that Jox didn't recognise were also present. He assumed they were Italian.

At their pre-flight meeting they were briefed on the three merchant freighters, *Pampas*, *Talabot* and *Clan Campbell*, in addition to the fast naval supply ship HMS *Breconshire*. Of these, *Breconshire* was the priority, as she was carrying a cargo of precious fuel oil, which made her the equivalent of a floating time bomb. Convoy MW10 had been relentlessly pursued by Axis naval forces since leaving Alexandria in Egypt, but their attacks had been successfully driven off by her naval escort. Approaching Malta now, it was the turn of the opposing air forces to step up.

In his earphones, Jox recognised Salvesen's voice sending his flight in with a Morningside-accented, 'Tally-ho, tally-ho.' He could also hear Lord David, roaring with glee on R/T. The fighting Scots of No. 603 Squadron were going in.

Jox split his Green Section into pairs, he and Glasgow going after the Ju 88s targeting the freighters, whilst Cochrane and Beurling had a go at the escorting fighters. Getting amidst the *Schnellbombers*, they disrupted their attack, scattering the giants like the petals of some monstrous flower.

Beurling's Maltese baptism of fire saw him burst into a formation of eight Me 109s with only terrified Cochrane by his side. His burst blew the tail off a first victim, but it fell unseen amongst the melee, so could only be recorded as 'damaged'.

Despite this success, the convoy suffered. SS *Clan Campbell* was finally sunk by a torpedo fired from a CANT Z.506 *Airone*.

# CHAPTER TWENTY-SIX

The Eyetie gunner in the top cockpit of the CANT Z.1007 *Alcione* tracked Jox's descent towards him. Crossing the leopard-spotted bomber's flight path, Jox noted the unfamiliar *Fasci* of the *Regia Aeronautica* on each mottled wing. Flashing by, they looked remarkably similar to the Treble Ones' squadron badge, just rotated ninety degrees. The Spitfire shuddered as the stream of fire struck home. There was a curious series of hollow thumps followed by fizzing sparks behind the dashboard of the cockpit, then came a horrible smell detectable even through his mask. Like a game bird bracketed by shot, he'd taken several solid hits. His goggles were misted with white glycol spray and the Perspex canopy was streaked with black oil. Hot liquid stung the unprotected skin of his face.

He rolled his dying aircraft, resulting in the dust and sand collected in the Spit's footwells dumping straight onto his sticky face. The instrument panel was a shattered ruin, and every instinct told him to get the hell out. Praying the airframe hadn't been bent by the impacts, he reached for the hood handles with his leather gloves. He pulled and it slid back smoothly, as the control column sagged worryingly between his knees. Ready to jump, he reached for the Sutton harness release with his right hand, gripping the spade handle with his left. This time the Spitfire reacted, and it appeared he had a modicum of control. He was losing altitude at a terrifying rate, so he eased the nose up, levelling to about two thousand feet, but he was guessing, as his dials were useless.

The choppy green sea stretched before him under a tiger-striped sky, purple blue on warm orange. Up ahead were some rocky cliffs teeming with seabirds. A strike now would make a bad situation worse, so he sheared away towards a larger island, reasoning it must be Gozo, northwest of Malta. It at least promised some level patches if he could just find them.

Searching the skies, Jox expected the *Alcione* would come looking for him, but to his utter relief saw nothing. It was short-lived. There was an alarming noise coming from the engine; something was rattling about in there. He suspected his oil pressure was dropping and the radiator temperature was going through the roof. The compass and R/T were useless, so he was on his own and God only knew where.

He was running out of options. Time and gravity were against him, and he was already too low to jump. The only choice left was whether to hit the deck wheels up or down. He didn't fancy the low rock walls that criss-crossed the terrain, and feared there were too many nooks and crannies to catch his wheels and tip him onto his face, so he opted for the former. He'd faced this choice before, above the cliffs of Kent and again on the banks of the Thames. He didn't relish a repeat performance, but there was no escape. The ground here looked a good deal harder than the forgiving chalk and soft mud of Blighty. Whatever happened, this was going to hurt. He could already imagine Thompson's fury at his pranging one of the precious few Spits.

He braced for impact as he roared towards the rock-strewn surface. A stream of black fluid caterpillared off his portside wingtip. It would maybe provide a dotted line on the ground for others to follow to find his lost wreckage. The landscape was a confusion of dusty pastures with sheep or goats. Separated by low stone walls it would be a hard landing, but perhaps he could find a fortuitous patch of prickly pear cactus that might prove softer.

He dipped a wing towards a yellow meadow, as the ground reached for him, slowly then very swiftly. Should he reconsider wheels down? Before he could act, the aircraft yawed, as his damaged tailplane violently gave way. He throttled back as much as he dared, the usually smooth Merlin gargling and coughing to its death.

Cactus plants raced past, as he pulled back and stalled. The slipstream whistled through the open hood, then was drowned by a grinding roar. In a split-second, the props shattered, splintering and disappearing over his shoulders. His stomach lurched as the Spit somersaulted, wing stub over stub, before coming to a brutal halt against a gnarled stump.

Hanging from his straps, blood rushed to his brain, and Jox felt incredibly thirsty from all the dust raised. His leather helmeted head was resting on hard ground, and he could feel a crick in his neck. Surely a good sign, he reasoned. At least he could feel something.

Close by came the sound of agitated voices and tinkling bells. His nose filled with the dangerous smell of aviation fuel and then a country stink of manure. Inside the cockpit, liquid was dripping everywhere, and the cooling wreckage ticked ominously like a timebomb.

An old man's tanned face appeared through the scratched Perspex. He began to shout, then disappeared, leaving Jox hanging, heart in his mouth, expecting the Spitfire to blow at any second. The man returned with an axe and began swinging at the side of the cockpit, half buried in sandy soil. The axe head flashed worryingly close to Jox until a ragged hole appeared, large enough for strong peasant arms to reach through. The old man was joined by a young boy whose adolescent voice was shrill with alarm. Together they managed to unclip Jox, supporting his weight to avoid damaging his neck. They manhandled him through the gap, carrying him away with some difficulty, the old man struggling with the torso and the boy his feet. They pushed through scrub as the wreckage behind them caught fire with a soft crump. In moments, the cockpit was a mass of roaring flame, providing a fine impression of a fierce wood-fired oven.

Jox panted with relief as he observed his rescuers. They wore rough peasant clothing and tattered straw hats. Both were brown as berries from the sun and smelt of animals and sweat. Around them were dozens of goats, darting every which way, alarmed by the strange sounds and smells. Each had a little bell around its neck marking its progress.

The old man smiled, revealing a missing front tooth, then spoke in a language that sounded vaguely Arabic. For an awful moment, Jox feared he was so horribly off course that he'd landed in enemy-occupied Tunisia, but then realised it was surely Maltese. The man helped him to his feet and the boy slipped beneath his arm to help support his weight.

'*Merhba. Jisimni* Elias,' said the boy. He pointed at his chest and repeated, 'Elias.' He then pulled Jox away from the spreading circle of fire and towards some felled vegetation, happily grazed upon by several goats, their bells tinkling as they clambered over it.

The old man indicated he should sit and then spoke to the boy in rapid Maltese. The boy nodded but before leaving, he pointed at his chest again and repeated, 'Elias.' He gesticulated towards Jox quizzically, who croaked back in response, 'Jox.' Elias beamed, gave a military salute and ran towards some low buildings on the ridgeline.

In no time, the old man had some water boiling and handed Jox a glass of piping hot sweet tea. It was surprisingly invigorating and Jox soon felt strong enough to get to his feet to stretch his aching back. He delicately touched his blistered face as he watched his aircraft burn, the chalked words *Marguerite VI* lifting as the paint bubbled.

*Christ, she barely lasted twenty-four hours on the island.*

He was thanking the old man for a second tea, when Elias appeared with a young woman in tow. She looked concerned.

'Your nose is bleeding,' she said, a frown on her pretty face. 'Are you wounded?'

'I … I don't think so,' spluttered Jox, thrown by her unexpected beauty. He wiped his nose on his sleeve, leaving a claret stripe across it.

'No, stop, you're making a mess,' she said, then smiled. 'It does make you look quite heroic, though,' she teased.

'Heroic?'

'Of course. You are an *Ingliz* pilot. You are heroic and brave, and my brother Elias idolises you for it.'

A persistent fly buzzed around Jox's face. He waved it away, wondering if it was the same indestructible insect as before. 'Elias is your brother?'

'Yes, and this is my grandfather, Giovanni Vella. My name is Julianna Vella. I'm pleased to meet you.'

'Very pleased to meet you too. I'm Jeremy McNabb, but people call me Jox.'

'Should we call you Jeremy or Jox?'

'My friends call me Jox.'

'Is that what we are? Your friends?'

'I certainly hope so, considering your family just saved my life.'

'They did, didn't they?' She shrugged. 'It is normal, but now you owe us a debt of honour. This means a great deal to the Maltese, Mister *Ingliz* Jox.'

'I'm not English. I'm Scots, and honour means a great deal to us too.'

She cocked her head, tucked a strand of dark hair behind an ear and thought about his response. She smiled and it was like the sun coming out after a long period of rain. 'I'm glad to hear it. My family will surely call on the debt one day.'

'I'd be happy to honour it. In the meantime, I'd be grateful if you could help me get in touch with the authorities? They must be wondering what's become of me.'

'Of course, there is an airfield on Gozo, just a few miles away. I can take you.'

'Could you perhaps first thank your grandfather and brother for me?'

'Thank them yourself. They understand English. They are just proud to speak our language instead. Pride is all we have left with this war.'

The old man and boy grinned and Jox felt rather foolish. He could see that pride in their eyes. It burned fiercely and was humbling to witness. Perhaps it went some way to explaining how the Maltese were stoically coping with this war. It fuelled their resilience and defiance in the face of Armageddon.

By the time they'd reached the farm buildings, Jox was really feeling the effects of the crash. His old back injury had been put out, his recently set arm and shoulder were aching and his blistered face was aflame. Hobbling like an old man, he was grateful to be offered a shaded *pultruna*, a day bed covered in a throw. It was under an awning in the van of the largest of several low, flat-roofed stone buildings that made up the farmstead. Jox was familiar with dry stone dykes from a childhood in rural Scotland, but the construction of these squat buildings appeared to involve the use of no mortar at all, and yet they sat solid in the landscape, appearing almost fortified. Warmed by the afternoon sun, the walls wriggled with long-fingered lizards scrambling for insects.

Jox dozed in the soporific heat — perhaps an effect of delayed shock — as Julianna and Elias were sent to alert the airfield of his whereabouts. It was becoming increasingly clear that he wasn't getting there under his own steam. He was awoken by flies buzzing about his face. He opened his eyes to be greeted by their grandparents saying, *'Bonswa.'* To Jox's schoolboy French ear, it sounded very like *'Bonsoir.'* The Vella grandmother fussed over him like an mother hen, bringing him some unsweetened grapefruit juice, evidently grown on the farm, then some grilled fish and a delicious dish called *kapunata*, fried aubergine and celery. He then tried some sweet sliced prickly pears for the first time.

All the while, the grandfather, Giovanni, sat smoking, sipping tea and watching him with a world-weary gaze. His hand-rolled cigarettes smelt awful and glowed malevolently. Occasionally he would check on his goats, but mostly sat rubbing the ears of one of the skinny mutts that wandered about. Otherwise, he remained silent and impassive like a lump of Maltese rock.

Jox was relieved when Julianna and Elias finally returned, their chatter breaking the awkwardness of their grandfather's scrutiny. The airfield at Ta Lambert was sending a vehicle to collect him and would arrange a flight back to Ta Kali on the mainland.

'Are you feeling better?' asked Julianna. 'How is your appetite? Have you enjoyed my grandmother's cooking?' She appeared irritated. 'We will go hungry tonight because of her generosity.'

Jox was stung by the unexpected venom in her words, but realised just how thin the family all were. Supplies in Malta were scarce, not just in terms of fuel and ammunition, but even basic foodstuffs. The civilian population were always at the back of the queue for what was available and often had to subsist on what could be grown, hunted or what the sea might provide.

'I had no idea, I'm so sorry,' spluttered Jox. 'I'll make it up to you, I promise.'

Julianna was embarrassed, her temper wilting under her grandfather's glare.

'My granddaughter shames her family,' he said. 'You are a guest, Mister Jox. You are welcome. Please think no more of it.'

Julianna apologised. 'I'm sorry, my temper is like a fire. My tongue is sharp. It has always been my weakness. I speak without thinking. Please forgive me.'

'There's nothing to forgive. I'm the imposition here. I've been utterly thoughtless and intruded on your day. Your family have been nothing but gracious.'

He was struck again by her dark beauty. She was utterly bewitching, but it was her fiery spirit that appealed most: tempestuous one instant, shy and vulnerable the next. This woman was really getting under his skin.

As the Bedford bumped down the track to the farm, Jox found himself forlorn at the idea of leaving her. He couldn't leave things like that. 'I hope to … ah, see you again,' he spluttered. 'I'm keen to repay your family's kindness to me. Perhaps I could find you some supplies? What would give your grandmother pleasure?'

Julianna frowned. Her mood had swung again like a weather vane. 'We did not help you to be paid off like servants,' she said angrily. 'You do not understand us at all.'

'I'm sorry, I didn't mean to offend you. I'd just like to help. Please forgive me,' said Jox. How the hell had he managed to put his foot in it again?

Just as quickly, her faced cleared and she smiled. She put a warm hand on his arm. It was like a jolt of electricity. 'You are kind, Jox. I'm sorry. My grandparents would appreciate some tea and Elias loves sweets. He's had so few treats because of the war.'

'How can I find you again? Do you ever come over to Malta? I'm stationed at RAF Ta Kali airfield. Do you know it?'

She laughed. 'Yes, I am often there. I work at the Point de Vue Hotel, the RAF officers' mess at Rabat. It was hit a few days ago and is shut at the moment, as they try to get things cleared up. I'll be back soon. You can find me working there most days.'

Jox brightened. There was a way forward. He was jubilant, despite his body aching all over. 'I better get going, before I fall over. I'll come to find you, I promise. Please thank your family again.'

Rather awkwardly, he tried to shake her hand. She giggled, seized his shoulders and kissed him on his stinging cheek.

'Yes, I will see you again, Mister Jox McNabb.'

# CHAPTER TWENTY-SEVEN

The large man reached the outcrop of rock high above Ta Kali's scarred airfield. His hair caught the wind as he scanned the arid landscape stretching before him. High above, a hunting raptor gave a plaintive cry.

He was wearing the slate-blue tunic of an airman, with the stripes and crown of a flight sergeant. He took a deep breath, as if steeling himself for some endeavour. He then laid down the six-foot staff he was carrying and began unbuttoning his tunic, folding it neatly onto the rock. He removed his sky-blue shirt.

He was solidly built and had dark swirling tattoos on his right pectoral, over the shoulder and down the arm to the elbow. His skin was a mass of geometric patterns, ocean waves, feathers, and fern fronds. Placing meaty hands on his hips, his face suddenly contorted as if he was angry. His eyes bulged, showing their whites, and his tongue flicked in and out like a lizard's. He stamped his feet and slapped palms against his illustrated torso. He cried defiantly at the sky, calling the Gods to come and face him, then grunted disdainfully at their inaction.

It was an extraordinary performance that the sergeant presumed was unobserved, but he was in fact being watched by two others.

Unable to sleep, Jox had risen early and found Ginger Neil languishing in the NAAFI tent. He was having trouble sleeping too. They decided to go for a walk around the airfield before the cool of the morning turned unbearably hot. Jox was still stiff after his prang, nursing a bruised nose, a black eye and some scabby blisters. He could do with the exercise to loosen up. The pair were due on 'readiness' from eight o'clock, to face the inevitable raids the day would bring. It meant another day of sitting in stifling cockpits or running the distance to their aircraft from the airless dispersal tent. So, an opportunity to get some fresh air was very welcome.

For once, Jox's insomnia hadn't been caused by his dreams of violent battle in the skies. Nor was it their more recent replacement, a deep sense of melancholy and longing for Alice. Since her death, he would often wake reaching for her and was then unable to get back to sleep. Last night, though, his dreams were haunted by something new: visions of that dark-eyed, dark-haired woman whom he'd only just met. Perhaps it was the guilt over these unexpected feelings that had woken him.

Bleary-eyed and exhausted, he'd still agreed to the stroll around dry Ta Kali. There were scars of recent raids plain to see, but the army's engineers had performed miracles in getting the airfield operational again. The wing's aged Hurricanes and newer Spitfire Vs were parked ready for action in makeshift bomb-proof pens. Others were sheltered under new arched hangars made of concrete, impervious to all but the heaviest of what the enemy could throw at them.

'What on earth is that man doing?' asked Jox.

Neil looked where he was pointing. 'That's Jimmy Waerea. Red Two in your section. He's a Māori man from New Zealand and one of the squadron's best pilots. He's lost six friends in the last two weeks. That's his way of honouring his fallen comrades.'

Up on the hillside, Waerea continued what Neil explained was called a *haka*, a ceremonial ritual central to Māori culture.

The flight sergeant stood frozen, breathing hard from the exertion. He acknowledged Neil and Jox with a nod of the head. He picked up the wooden staff he'd laid on the ground. Jox could see it had three distinct parts: a pointed head, broad shoulders ringed with feathers and an oar-like blade at the bottom. Waerea began spinning and thrusting the weapon with great skill. The movements combined the drama of a pipe band drum major tossing his staff and what Jox imagined a Japanese samurai warrior might look like brandishing his sword.

'That staff is called a *taiaha* and is a weapon in *Mau rākau*, the Māori martial art,' said Neil. 'Jimmy is a master at it.'

'How d'you know so much about it, Ginger?'

He shrugged. 'It's not the first time he's had to pay his respects like this. We've had far too many losses. Last time, I just asked him, and he explained the significance.'

Jox peered back at the proud Antipodean warrior bellowing at the skies. He was certainly impressive and quite terrifying but now had tears streaming down his chiselled features. It felt disrespectful to be watching him cry.

'Let's go,' said Jox. 'I'm knackered, and I'm sure he'd rather be left alone. Maybe we can catch some breakfast before we're off.'

The raiders appeared in ones and twos during the morning, but it wasn't until midday that numbers swelled to double figures. The delay gave Jox the opportunity to check out his new aircraft before taking off. He was delighted to discover that he was reunited with *Marguerite V*, the Spit he'd flown over from Gibraltar. He was unsure quite how that had happened but suspected the hand of Flight Sergeant Pengelly. The sergeant and his crew of 'erectors' had finally reached the island.

The Spitfire was resplendent in yet another new paint job of mustard and khaki desert camouflage, but with a bright red spinner. Because of the frequent interchange of aircraft between the squadrons on the island, she had no ID letters, but otherwise Jox's personal touches had all been carefully reapplied. It was great to see her, despite the new clown's nose.

After his inspection, Jox caught up with the rest of Blue Section: Glasgow, Cochrane and Beurling. He was then introduced to the other half of A Flight by the squadron CO Lucas. Red Section was led by F/O Victor Buchanan, a tall Yorkshireman with dark hair standing on end and baggy eyes that made him seem older than he was. His number two was Jimmy Waerea, who held Jox's gaze and nodded his recognition.

Red Three was a taciturn Northumbrian called Erik Hetherington, a sergeant during the Battle of Britain but recently commissioned, with his second element the French-Canadian Jean Paradis. Jox had been warned that he was quite a character, so addressed him directly in French, eliciting a broad grin, then an effusive welcome in heavily accented English.

As Jox had predicted, Beurling and Paradis got on like a house on fire, sharing the same sense of humour and disdain for authority. Jox didn't mind their horseplay on the ground but expected tight discipline on operations. He left them in no doubt about that.

No. 249 (Gold Coast) Squadron were airborne by lunchtime and vectored over to RAF Hal Far on the southeast tip of Malta. All of the airfields on the island were being targeted at once, including Ta Kali, but the main thrust of the day appeared to be on Hal Far where many of the island's bombers were based.

It was being attacked by Me 109 fighter-bombers, followed by two *Staffel* of Ju 87 Stuka dive-bombers, targeting the aerodrome with high-explosive bombs. The naval officers' mess was demolished and an entire barrack block flattened, along with damage to several other buildings.

The vulnerable gull-winged Stukas were escorted by Fiat CR.42 biplanes led by Capitano Antonio Larsimont Pergameni, a decorated ace with the Republican forces that had fought in Spain. Their aircraft appeared archaic compared to the monocoque design of the Spitfire but were in fact deadly and highly manoeuvrable adversaries.

The Stukas and the escort of six 97a Squadriglia's Fiat CR.42s were making strafing runs on a Bristol Blenheim bomber and seven Gloster Gladiators left foolishly parked on the concrete aprons. The Blenheim was already alight with flames licking over its bulbous nacelles. The naval biplanes were shattered wreckage, like mosquitoes squashed on a pane of glass. So focused on their attack were the Axis airmen that they made easy prey for Jox and his approaching flight.

Beurling was first to break formation, behaviour that would soon prove characteristic of the Canadian. He nailed a shrieking Stuka as it pulled out of a dive. He dealt with the rear gunner with a few well-aimed shells from his Hispano Mk. II cannons, drenching the interior of the cockpit with a bright scarlet wash. The heavy rounds must have burst through the Ju 87's rear cockpit and struck the pilot too, for the aircraft dropped like a dead bird, ending entangled in some powerlines along the perimeter of the airfield.

Paradis scored some good hits on a second Stuka, jabbering on the R/T in frantic French Québécois. However, he didn't escape the accurate return fire from a far cannier rear gunner than the first. The battling opponents separated, both trailing smoke, with Sergeant Paradis going on to make an emergency landing on Hal Far's littered runway. The fate of his foe was unknown, but he had sixty miles of sea back to Sicily to face with smoke pouring from the gaping underslung mouth of his damaged aircraft.

The rest of A Section followed orders and focused their attention on the *Regia Aeronautica* biplanes, who scattered like rodents set upon by terriers. The swift little aircraft were lucky to only lose two in the first murderous pass. A kill was shared between Glasgow and Cochrane, the other falling to Waerea's vengeful fire. Its tail was sheared off but remained attached by control cables, flapping like the tail of a diving fish as it fell. The surviving CR.42s, including their decorated leader, made good their escape.

Returning to Luqa to refuel and rearm, there were already gaps in the squadron roster. Thankfully, Paradis telephoned from Hal Far, but Rhodesian Dougie Leggo who'd gone up hungover, hoping a whiff of oxygen would see him straight, was caught by a predatory Bf 109. He brolly-hopped through skies filled with swirling belligerents, under the anxious eyes of his squadron mates McNair and Lucas. His parachute was deployed, but then collapsed as an enemy fighter deliberately shot through it. To the horror of his friends, Leggo fell and hit the ground with a brutal impact.

The raiders were back in force later that afternoon, this time targeting Grand Harbour, the island capital of Valletta and the residential neighbourhood of Floriana. The Grand Master's Palace, centre of the Knights Hospitaller Order of St. John, who ruled Malta for three hundred years, was hit by several high explosive bombs. So too, were Custom House, the Combined War Headquarters and the Lascaris Barracks.

Fires raged through the alleyways of Floriana, as the weather worsened, and the enemy switched focus onto Marsaxlokk Harbour to the south. Their target once again was the naval supply ship HMS *Breconshire*, incapacitated but under tow by the tugs trying to get her to the comparative safety of the harbour.

For the last thirty-six hours she'd wallowed off Zonqor Point, her ship's company and passengers stranded on board and at the mercy of constant air attack. Her only protection, because the island's aircraft were busy defending their home airfields, were the guns of the destroyer HMS *Southwold*, standing solidly beside her throughout. In the heavy swell, however, the escort ship struck a mine and sank, leaving HMS *Breconshire* to drift unprotected towards the minefield too. With five thousand tons of precious oil aboard, she was rescued by the tugs *Ancient* and *Robust*, and the destroyer HMS *Eridge*, finally allowing her to reach a mooring in Marsaxlokk Harbour. Throughout that night and into the next day, HMS *Breconshire* continued to be harassed piteously. Poor weather and drifting smoke shielded her visually from enemy raiders, content to drop their bombs blindly through the clouds, hoping that intensity rather than accuracy would destroy their target.

Ta Kali's fighter squadrons operating from RAF Luqa were repeatedly scrambled in a desperate attempt to defend hapless HMS *Breconshire*. It was a battle of attrition against seemingly countless opponents, and yet the corkscrew trails and blazing wreckage within the city's ancient walls proved that their foes were suffering too. By nightfall, the enemy was still targeting the shipping in Marsaxlokk Harbour, using parachute flares to illuminate their targets. Explosions amongst the swirling cloud and smoke provided a dramatic and deadly light show. By morning, No. 249 Squadron was stood down but in the harbour, HMS *Breconshire* was still more or less in one piece.

Landing back at RAF Luqa, Jox sat exhausted in his sweaty cockpit, having lost track of the number of sorties he'd been on. The wail of bagpipes drifted through the still air as Lord David of No. 603 Squadron played homage to his returning warriors in a manner befitting their gallant actions. The primal skirl of Jox's homeland stirred something within him, but he was just too tired to react. If anything, it brought back halcyon days at school and he felt an unexpected pang of homesickness.

Still at 'dispersal readiness', Jox sat in his flying gear ready to go at short notice. He was hollow-eyed with exhaustion as he nursed a cup of sweet tea, hoping it would be as invigorating as Julianna's grandfather's brew. If he was honest with himself, it was actually Julianna that he hankered for. He'd resolved to seek her out but really needed rest first. His boys had done well over the last, what was it, thirty-six hours? How many ninety-minute sorties did that represent? They'd certainly dished it out and hadn't been too badly clobbered in return.

He was contemplating some shut-eye, when a mess sergeant began distributing post amongst the grey-faced pilots scattered around the NAAFI. He handed Jox an official-looking letter, addressed in purple ink with his name, rank and the alphabet soup that came with his decorations. He opened it with a grubby finger. It was from Robertson:

*RAF Debden,*
*19th March 1942*

*My dear Jox,*
*I hope this letter finds you well. Please pass on my fond regards to Cam. I assume he was able to track you down and get assigned to Malta too. Frankly, I can't imagine anyone getting in his way once that fellow sets his mind on a course.*

How are things? We keep hearing such dreadful news about conditions out there. Do keep your head down, dear boy. I'm rather fond of you and would hate to hear the worst. I got a note from Tommy telling me he had to pull some strings to get you and your chaps out of a bit of bother. He was his usual gruff self, but I can tell he's thrilled to have you and Cam back under his wing. I hope you're settling in with your new squadron. It's rather hard for me to accept that you're no longer a Treble One, although of course you'll always be one really. Tommy tells me you're with No. 249 Gold Coast Squadron. They've got a good rep. I expect they must have been in the thick of it during the Battle of Britain, for that chap Nicolson to earn his VC. Pritch tells me you met him at Torquay. I'm sure they're more than capable, but if not, I've no doubt you and Cam can sort them out.

Rest assured the Treble Ones are missing you. We've had a rum time of it lately. There's no point beating around the bush: I'm afraid we lost the C.O. in a senseless accident. One of our excellent Czech sergeant pilots, Laddy Zadrobilek, collided with Wee Brotch's aircraft. No one's quite sure how it happened, but the C.O. was the middle Spit of three taking off, followed by three more with Laddy in the middle. For some reason, the front trio aborted without telling those behind. The chaps on either side pulled away, but Laddy, already wheels-up, pancaked onto Brotchie's aircraft. The whole lot went up with Laddy escaping burnt, but the C.O. didn't make it.

We've been knocked for six. That man was a pain, but no one deserves that fate. We did what we could for the family, but I had to leave instructions for a closed casket. Pritch, Chalmers and I attended a ceremony at the crematorium in Dundee, where I understand he went to school. I'm glad it was a cremation, otherwise they would have been burying mostly rocks. He was only twenty-five, you know.

Pritch and Mogs are feeling the strain. With so many chaps moving on, it's been left to them to hold things together. Miro's off to become a twin-engine night fighter and Otmar Kucera has joined No. 1 squadron at

Kenley. Tom Wallace is transferring to a non-ops role and finally getting his commission back. That leaves just Ghillie, Axel Fisken and Mike Longstaffe as senior men. Georgie is a great comfort. He seems to know that we're all rather sad. That dog has done more for this squadron than anyone. When all this is over, there will be medals and monuments, but not, I fear, for that little soldier.

Operationally, we've been doing less night work. Jerry's not raiding much and seems to be concentrating on the Russians and your lot in the Med. We've even ditched that horrid black get-up and are now camo-striped up top and dark grey below. Much better, in my view. We've been taking the fight to occupied France and Belgium with fighter sweeps on Rhubarb missions, Mandolins after ground targets and occasionally working with the bombers on Circus missions. I understand there is a big op in the pipeline, and we've been pencilled to get involved. I've no details, but I expect I'll get the gen once the powers assign a new C.O.

Which reminds me, I ran into your pal Moose in town. His lot have been renumbered as No. 401 RCAF Squadron and are at Biggin Hill. I was with Pritch, Fisken and Longstaffe on a bit of a jolly, courtesy of the Norwegian Embassy. Moose was there with a redhead called Stephanie. They were getting on like a house on fire. I think she knew your Alice quite well.

I hope things are getting easier on that front. I fear it will always hurt, but hopefully feels less raw. After the last war, it took me a long time to believe there could be a life after what I'd seen, but there was. You and the boys are testament to that. I don't think you realise what a blessing you are to old Badger. Look, I better sign off before I start blubbing; one too many malts, I fear. Take care of yourself, Cam, and that old buzzard Tommy. I've written to him with an idea I've had. Let's see if it works.

Chin up.

Yours,

Badger Robertson

# CHAPTER TWENTY-EIGHT

It was a warm evening on the piazzas of Marsaxlokk fishing village, east of RAF Luqa, but cooler down by the harbour. It was several weeks since Jox and Salvesen had originally planned a night out together, but both squadrons had been kept rather busy.

Jox was pleased to see that Salvesen was in one piece. Both squadrons had suffered in the intervening weeks and even Glasgow was covered in sticky plasters and purple blotches of gentian violet. Suffering in the heat, he'd chosen to fly in shirt sleeves and shorts, when his supposedly bulletproof canopy was shattered by a tenacious Italian in a Macchi C.202 Folgore. Glasgow described the mauling by the green monocoque fighter as 'a bloody great pike determined to make me a fish supper.' Like the others, the tough Scotsman was twitchy and showing the strain, furtive glances searching for threats betraying a constantly racing mind.

Salvesen had brought three chaps from his flight with him: Hamish Newlands from Edinburgh, who had been to school with him at Fettes, a lively Kiwi chap called Bert Mitchell and a softly spoken Englishman, Kit Curtis, wearing a cravat despite the heat. Jox had persuaded Glasgow, Cochrane, Waerea and Red section leader Victor Buchanan to come along. There was potential for quite a party if they could get into the mood and Jerry cooperated.

The airmen strolled down the alleyways of Marsaxlokk old town, heading for the harbour, all too often a target for the enemy. The waters of Malta's second port were no deeper than ten metres but hid a junkyard of broken ships and wrecked aircraft, often with aircrew still strapped in their chairs. Unexploded ordnance of every calibre littered the sandy bottom, blanketed with debris, shrapnel and twisted components testifying to the intensity of battle.

On land, signs of the fighting were even more obvious. There were great glaring gaps between the port's limestone buildings, the grand and ancient, but also the humbler and more contemporary in origin. The group navigated the dark cobbled streets followed by hordes of hungry cats. Electricity was intermittent, and blackout threatened if a raid were to materialise.

They'd agreed to meet in Marsaxlokk, rather than the usual boozy haunts of Strait Street in Valletta, known as 'The Gut'. Alcohol held little appeal, as most would be flying in the morning. Someone suggested going to the flicks but was then reminded that the Regent Cinema had been hit, collapsing on the audience and resulting in great loss of life.

Salvesen suggested a visit to a Turkish barber down by the port. He promised that they'd feel like new men, following the restorative effects of hot perfumed towels, a massage and a close shave with a cutthroat razor.

Making their way down the improbably named Immaculate Conception Street, they attracted the attention of some painted ladies plying their trade in the dark corners. Declining their attentions brought on some catcalling, but they were soon left alone as the women focused on more enthusiastic soldiery.

Antonio the barber was delighted at the unexpected bonanza of customers. '*Bonswa*, hero *Ingliz* pilots. Noble defenders of our blessed Malta's honour. You are the new Knights of St. John and I am your unworthy servant.' He ushered them into his salon, outside of which a sign defiantly proclaimed, 'Business as Usual'. Walking through the doorway, Jox sensed movement and spotted a scrawny cat meowing at him from the wooden balcony above the sandbagged shop window.

Antonio quickly called for reinforcements from the shops of his nearest competitors and switched on the Bakelite radio, which had pride of place in the salon. Tuned to Radio Belgrade, it played that melancholy tune about the girl waiting beneath the lamplight, popular with servicemen on all sides of the Mediterranean conflict. Antonio identified the senior rankers from the flight lieutenant rings on their shoulder straps and settled Jox and Salvesen in a pair of tatty reclining chairs.

Jox wasn't particularly hirsute, so the shave was a swift operation, but he took the opportunity to get a haircut and a fresh application of hair pomade. After all, fighter pilots still had to keep up appearances, even in Malta.

Since Montrose, Salvesen had affected a little moustache with waxed upturned tips. He was inordinately proud of it and kept poor Antonio busy for half an hour, trimming and applying hot curling tongs. In the meantime, the others lounged about, snoozing under hot towels, playing Backgammon or enjoying the devilishly strong Turkish coffee with some honey pastries of undoubtedly contraband origin. Only Glasgow, with his arms and face covered in plasters, was unable to have a shave, and complained about being bored and hungry.

Outside the shop, a siren began to wail as the sound of engines throbbed across the water, reverberating off the harbour walls. Ack-ack guns from the destroyers moored in the port began firing and were joined by the 'tonk-tonk-tonk' of several gun emplacements dotted along the quayside. A 40mm Bofors gun on a wheeled carriage was positioned directly outside the shop, rattling the window and pulsing the air in their eardrums every time it fired.

Panicking, Antonio bustled his customers to a cellar hewn straight from the island's bare rock. In the darkness was a thin black-clad woman, presumably his wife, surrounded by a gaggle of skinny children who stared wide-eyed at the soldiers. The flickering candlelight accentuated their thinness, prompting Jox to surrender the few biscuits he had in his pockets. Their mother nodded her gratitude, as the noise outside got louder.

There was an angry snarl of an engine followed by a tremendous splash. Outside, the Royal Malta Artillery gun crew cheered after sending another foe to join his *Kameraden* on the sea bed. A sudden cataclysmic boom delivered an even more brutal change in air pressure, which left their ears ringing and brought on waves of nausea. The shopfront glass was shattered, sandbags flung aside like discarded toys and the contents of the salon had been sucked onto the wet quayside.

Down in the basement, the air was rank with a child's vomit, as the ringing began to subside. The airmen looked at one another, relieved to still be in one piece. Outside, the gun had stopped firing, but fresh explosions could be heard across the water and were getting closer.

'Sod this,' said Jox. 'I'm not sitting here just waiting to get snuffed out.' He searched for his sticky-plastered Number Two. 'You coming up, Cam?'

'Aye, always,' Glasgow replied, a murderous gleam in his eyes. He'd been equally unhappy at being cornered in the cellar like a rat.

'Let's see what's going on. Maybe we can make ourselves useful.'

The others agreed with varying degrees of enthusiasm, but Jox wasn't waiting for consensus.

Wading through the debris piled outside the shop, Jox saw that the wooden balcony above the doorway had been ripped off the wall. At his feet was a pile of smashed timber and a dead cat. The rest of the quayside was revealed by the sweep of a searchlight. It was utter carnage. The limestone wall against which the ladies of the night had leant earlier was pitted with fresh blast marks and splashed with a dark crimson arc. On the cobbles, like scattered skittles, were the remains of the women and their would-be Romeos. Clothing was blasted aside, but it was the brutal finality of their postures that was most shocking. Flies were already buzzing over the sticky corpses.

The Bofors gun emplacement had been swept clear of its crew. The gun was toppled over with shredded black tyres pointing skywards and splattered with gore. What was left of the gunners was floating in the murky waters of the dock.

'Let's get this thing on its feet,' ordered Jox. The men righted the gun; beyond slashed tyres, it appeared undamaged. 'Cocky, you're a Navy man,' said Jox. 'Do you know how this thing works?'

Cochrane stood out amongst the others in his Fleet Air Arm white shirtsleeves. He'd been mid-shave when the sirens had sounded and ran a nervous hand over his bristly chin. 'Yes, Skip, I think so,' he said, peering at the complicated apparatus. 'First, we need to get the outrigger legs out and get the gun settled flat on its pads. These tyres are knackered and aren't steady enough for a gun platform.'

The others laboured as Cochrane directed, pulling levers and clicking parts into position.

'Cam, you're Number One, in the left-hand seat. That crank in front of you traverses the gun left to right. Aim through that spider sight in front of your face. Give it a go.' He turned to Jox. 'You'll be firing the gun from the Number Two position on the right. You control the elevation with your crank. The barrel depresses to just below the horizontal, then up to ninety degrees. When you're on target, stamp the foot pedal to fire. Take it easy, though; these things go through a hell of a lot of shells, firing two four-pound 40mm explosive shells every second. I'll be standing between you and will be feeding the rounds into the hopper. Jimmy and Victor, I'll need you to scramble about and find as many of these shells as you can. Keep feeding them to me. This is going to get rather frantic, my boys.'

There were aircraft swirling above them, making low passes at the vessels across the harbour.

'Jox, I'll call out the targets, but you're in control and the one firing. Aim at something, then punch your foot down. There's already a shell in the breech.'

Jox and Glasgow began cranking in unison, tracking an Italian torpedo-float plane with pelican feet. Jox fired and the gun kicked like a mule. There was a bright explosion just behind the target's tail, as if something had taken a big bite out of it.

'More deflection, Skipper,' shouted Cochrane. 'Come on, you know that!' He heaved a four-round clip into position. 'Again!'

Jox stamped his foot and this time his aim was just ahead of a looming Messershmitt-110. He recognised the double-tailed silhouette, having tangled with them before. They were fast, with deadly nose armament of four 7.9 mm MG-17 machine guns and twin MG-FF cannons, but it took them time to get up to speed and their wide turning circle made them vulnerable to the nippier Spitfire. The Me 110 was at its most dangerous when diving from height, exactly what he was doing now.

This one's under-nose had a yellow wasp figure with a bulbous white eye painted on it. Sweeping over the water, it strafed the naval port and dockyard. The *Zerstörer* was clearly confident that the dockside AA guns were out of action, his nose hosing fire with impunity at the shipping moored down one of the creeks. Jox fired too low and missed with his first shot, fearing the round might have struck one of the ships. He lifted the gun's flared barrel and tried again, encouraged by Glasgow's cursing beside him. The big twin-engined fighter staggered, caught in the bright beam of a searchlight. A wheeled undercarriage dropped unexpectedly.

Jox was getting the hang of things and the boys had set a good rhythm of loading, spotting, and firing. Further up the dock, Salvesen's chaps had followed their example and had another abandoned gun up and running. Kit Curtis had lost his cravat and was firing a .50 cal HMG, while the rest of his mob worked the Bofors. *Not as smartly done as my lot*, Jox noted with a touch of pride.

A second *Schwarm* of waspy Me 110s swung towards them. Jox was unsure why he singled one out in particular — perhaps because it had a black arrow on its fuselage, indicating a *Staffelkapitän* and a worthwhile target. More likely, though, it was Waerea pointing at him, screaming in defiant Māori. The weight of fire from the heavy fighter flailed Jox's position. Sparks and shell fragments dinged off the gun's shield. Waerea fell in a crumpled heap and Buchanan was snatched away. Waerea rose unsteadily, his left arm hanging useless by his side. Buchanan did not. Half of his head was missing, and his long body twitched and shuddered, limbs sprawled on the quayside like a squashed spider.

Glasgow yelled at Jox, 'It's getting too hot out here. We've done what we can. Jimmy's hurt and we're running out of ammo.'

'You take Jimmy down to the cellar. Cocky and I will manage for a bit. We'll catch up when we've run out. Right, Cocky?'

The naval sub-lieutenant nodded and loaded another four-shell clip into the hopper. He slid into Glasgow's vacant seat and traversed the gun. Jox peered through the spider-web at the black arrowed fighter coming back around for another pass. This time he was ready and applied every instinct he'd honed over years of shooting clays and pheasants, and more recently Jerries.

He let the sight pass through the raider, above and in front, then fired in what felt like slow motion. The trails of shells rose like the fingers of a comb and two explosions bracketed his target. The starboard engine was enveloped in flames and the aircraft began corkscrewing towards them. The fiery wing slammed brutally against the stone edge of the dock, shearing off at the shoulder and sending the flaming remains skidding across the cobbles, with sparks and burning fuel scattering in its wake. It slid screeching into a burnt-out butcher's shop, perhaps an appropriate final resting place for these bloodthirsty Nazi raiders.

Cochrane lugged another clip into place. He pointed at a V of three-engine CANT Z.1007 *Alcione* bombers lumbering towards the largest and most tempting target in the harbour. It was the supply ship HMS *Breconshire*, damaged but still containing some of her cargo of precious petroleum. Alongside was the Hunt-Class destroyer HMS *Eridge*, blasting with all guns.

Jox followed suit, aiming for the nearest attacker, hoping that he had the range. He fired four quick rounds and hits registered on the mottled green skin of the Kingfisher medium bomber. It seemed to catch light from within, like a lightbulb when the current is gradually turned up. Flaring sodium-white, it exploded cataclysmically, revealing both Royal Navy ships in the flash. A shower of debris plopped and hissed into the harbour water, reminding Jox of the sound of feeding trout on a Scottish loch.

'That's it. We're out,' said an exhausted Cochrane, dripping with sweat, his shirt wet through. 'I'd say you got a couple of them.'

'Two and half, I reckon,' said Jox, his ears still ringing from the gun. 'Let's be clear: they're not mine. They're ours. I couldn't have done it without you lot.'

Cochrane grinned and rubbed his palm over his half-shaved chin. 'You can always depend on the senior service. Britannia rules the waves and all that, Skipper.'

'Right you are, Cocky. I'm certainly grateful tonight.'

'It rather appears the senior service is grateful to you too, sir. Look at *Breconshire* and *Eridge* signalling.'

Jox looked to where he was pointing. Blinking lights on the decks of both large ships were sending persistent Morse thank-yous.

# CHAPTER TWENTY-NINE

After what would come to be known as 'The Battle of Marsaxlokk Harbour', Jox and Cochrane were stood down from duty as the squadron was reorganised. With Red Section decimated by the loss of Buchanan and the wounding of Waerea, Glasgow and Beurling were teamed up with the recently commissioned Erik Hetherington and Jean Paradis. Glasgow was unhappy about leaving Jox's side but was placated by being told it was only temporary, and that he should be flattered that the section needed his experience.

The Royal Navy were making quite a fuss about what Jox and his improvised crew of AA gunners had achieved, especially when they discovered that one of the crew was Fleet Air Arm. Their Bofors gun was credited with three kills, the 'half' hit on the Italian CANT Z.506 *Airone* having been confirmed as the floatplane crashed over the city. The other two kills were easier to prove, one smeared across the quayside, the other scattered in smithereens over the graveyard waters of Marsaxlokk Harbour, with more than enough witnesses.

Their reward for sticking it out to the bitter end was to be given a day off 'to recover from their exertions'. Jox was using it to visit Julianna, and Cochrane had nothing better to do than play gooseberry. Actually, he was doing Jox a favour since Julianna had told him that her younger brother Elias was coming along to act as a chaperone at her grandmother's insistence. Cochrane was tasked with keeping the young chap distracted, whilst the couple spent some time alone.

Jox had managed to convince Pengelly to lend him his squad's lorry to visit Julianna in Rabat. He'd agreed on the condition that he and his crew be first dropped off at the Boneyard and picked up on the way back. They called it the Boneyard because it was the central repository for all aircraft wrecks that fell onto the island. Friends and foes deemed beyond repair were collected and dumped here in great tumbling piles. Jox expected *Marguerite VI* was probably here somewhere, although Gozo was a fair distance to have brought her from.

The scrapyard was a forlorn sight but was really just a sloping stony field amongst the cactus groves growing in the middle of the island. Earlier in the island's siege, the Boneyard had provided vital scavenged parts and spares, in spite of the harrowing nature of their origins. With the arrival of more aircraft from carrier-borne ferry flights or shipped over in crates, Pengelly's crews had less need for the 'very used' parts the site could provide. For these technicians, though, it remained a site of pilgrimage: somewhere they could pay respects to fallen machines but also feed an insatiable curiosity about the enemy's technology and weaponry.

It was a lonely, windswept place with burnt and smashed aircraft wreckage lying about in bits. Remarkably, there were also some that were seemingly unmarked. The wrecks were spread across the site haphazardly, depending on how respectful the salvage crews had been when unloading. Some were parked, as if ready to take off, and others were piled on top of each other as if tipped from some monstrous bucket. The persistent breeze kept most smells at bay, but when still, the air was rank with aviation fuel and charred metal, paint, plastics, fabrics, and cabling. In some dark nooks and pockets, the stench of carrion seeped from crushed cockpits and bent fuselages, betraying the body parts that still lay trapped within.

The aircraft were piled pell-mell, with hulking carcasses of Allied behemoths like Sunderland flying boats tipped onto dainty fighters like Sienna-nosed Me Bf 109s, various leopard-spotted Italian fighters and some tattered old Hurricanes.

It was a melancholy place, like an elephant graveyard or the ruins of some extinct civilisation. Foes that had inflicted such violence upon each other lay side by side or more likely piled on top of one another. There was nothing noble, humbling, or impressive here, and to Jox it was all such an utter waste. He hated it and couldn't wait to leave.

Pengelly's crew were like children in a sweetie shop, collecting souvenirs for salvage or personal collections. One rigger with a ghoulish streak gathered enemy clothing. His booty included a German officer's leather jacket complete with decorations, a bomber crewman's gauntlets and goggles, and a pair of brown cavalry boots, which some aristocratic Italian must have worn to his untimely death. Jox marvelled at the idea of flying in knee-length boots and wondered at the fate of the blueblood legs within. The whiff of corruption rising from the leather suggested an answer he didn't want to contemplate.

He told Pengelly he had to get going, and called over to Cochrane, who was riding shotgun to Rabat. He asked for ten minutes to finish the film in his Box Brownie. He was snapping some pics for his younger brother at home in Liverpool.

'I'll wait in the cab, but hurry up,' said Jox. 'This place gives me the willies.'

Jox had scoured the market and cajoled mess sergeants to fill a crate with supplies for Julianna and her family. It didn't amount to all that much, just some flour, sugar, tea and a few contraband chocolate bars and a little tobacco. He hoped it would be enough to please her as it had cost him a small fortune, in both favours and currency, but he was determined not to turn up empty-handed after her family's kindness and hospitality.

Jox and Cochrane were heading for a beach between the cliffs south of Rabat, chosen by Julianna for its views. It was also a good place to walk and visit the nearby ruins of a Hospitaller castle. It had been a bit chilly at the Boneyard, but as they neared the coast, the day warmed, and they were grateful for the light clothing.

Jox was feeling nervous and appreciated the distraction of Cochrane's chatter. He spoke of his family in Liverpool and his younger brother, who he was clearly devoted to and missed terribly. He was looking forward to spending time with a youngster of about the same age.

Julianna and Elias were waiting for them outside the Hotel Belle Vue. She was beautiful, her hair wrapped in a headscarf, wearing a simple cotton dress and strappy sandals. Jox and Cochrane were a bit late, having got quite lost in the myriad of unmarked roads across the interior of the island. The map Pengelly provided had proved next to useless, particularly when it emerged that the able mariner, Cochrane, was neither a useful map-reader nor a competent navigator, but they got there in the end.

Jox was uncharacteristically tongue-tied as Elias, obviously taking his role as chaperone very seriously, watched him like a hawk. This was where Cochrane played a blinder. Having anticipated the scenario, he had swapped a full packet of Players for a black leather flying helmet and a pair of RAF goggles with the rigger with a penchant for 'used' clothing. The boy was enchanted with the gifts, and the pair were soon running about, the boy with arms akimbo, mimicking an aircraft in flight, whilst Cochrane provided the target, complete with the sound effects of engine noises, firing guns and whistling bombs.

Julianna found their antics hilarious and her laughter was the balm Jox needed to calm his jitters.

'He loves your gifts,' said Julianna. 'Thank you.'

'I can't take credit for that. It's all Cocky. He has a brother about the same age and seems to know what makes them tick. Don't worry, he's having the time of his life too.'

'Yes, he is. Let's go for a walk. I want to show you the ruins on the cliff. They'll be fine here on the beach, and we can keep an eye on them from up there.'

They walked in silence for the short distance up the steep path.

'But what about you, Jox?' she asked. 'Why do you look so sad? Are you not happy to see me? I was so impatient to see you.'

'I was, too,' he stammered. 'You have no idea. It's just…'

Julianna peered at him with her dark brown eyes, deep pools pulling him in. 'I know you are sad. Please, Jox, tell me about her.'

'How do you know?'

'I asked around. I work at the officer's mess. People like to talk, especially lonely men, far away from home. I just listen, smile, and then ask questions.'

'Sounds like you'd make an excellent spy.' He laughed nervously, but wasn't being remotely funny.

She frowned but realised he was just being clumsy. 'Yes, I suppose so, but I'm on your side, no?'

He smiled, relieved that she wasn't angry.

'You see, I can make you smile. Please tell me about her.'

Jox took a deep breath and steeled himself. 'Her name was Alice. We were engaged to be married, but she was killed in an air raid on London. I was devastated. It's taken me a long time to even be able to talk about her. I don't think I can ever forget her.'

'Who's asking you to forget? We can never forget those we cherish. We just need to make room in our hearts for others, so we can go on living our lives.'

'But I feel so guilty.'

'Guilty of what? Of loving her still? There's surely no crime in that.'

'No, just guilty for feeling something new.'

'Would she wish you not to? Surely, your Alice would want you to live your life. Especially when everything can be snatched away in just an instant; you know that better than most. I do not think we live in times that allow us the luxury of pondering every decision, every choice. We can only choose to live. None of us know how much time we have, and we must fill it with what we can. That is truly what I believe.'

Jox's head was spinning. They were in a dark, vaulted hall of the ruined castle. Who knew what dramas had unfolded here over the centuries? Some ancient carved stone effigies seemed to be mocking him, and emotions were swirling through his mind. The room smelt of vegetation, roots growing through fissures in the rock, and also vaguely of urine. He needed some air.

Things were moving faster than he'd expected and with a growing intensity that left him breathless. He bolted up some steps to a balustraded balcony that overlooked the sea. Julianna followed him, gently taking his hand, then turned towards the majestic cliff-top view. A cool sea breeze came off the water, perfumed with wild herbs from the land. Crickets sang noisily in the long grass.

'Sicily is on the other side of the island,' said Julianna. 'But this way are Linosa and Pantellaria, both volcanic like Sicily. Malta has no volcanoes of its own but is surrounded by them. The ancient people settling on the slopes of Mount Etna have a saying: "Those who live at the mercy of the fire must live intensely, for the Gods may awaken at any time." In Malta, we fear the eruptions too, not because of fire, but the huge waves they send us, destroying everything in their path. We know what it is to be at the mercy of things we cannot control. Our history has always been like that; the Turks, the Knights of St John, the Italians, the French, and the English have all brought their troubles to our shores. Now, once again, it is the *Inglezi*. War is not new to us; we endure and find joy where we can. Do you understand?'

'I think so,' stammered Jox. 'I'm not very good at this sort of thing.'

'I don't think anyone is.' She was holding both of his hands. 'Maybe we can learn together.' She stood on her tiptoes and kissed him on the lips. She paused, checking his reaction, and kissed him again.

His head was spinning. She had completely taken the wind from his sails, but he felt this was exactly what he needed to reset his life. To stop living in limbo. He took her in his arms and kissed her longer and more deeply. Now, it was her turn to be left breathless.

'We must slow down,' she said. 'My grandmother would be scandalised. Let's find Elias or I'll be in trouble. My brother is loyal but incapable of lying to his *nanna*.'

They found Cochrane and Elias paddling in the rockpools, searching for fossils and seashells. The leather helmet hadn't left the boy's head and the goggles were around his neck. Cochrane was taking snaps of their finds and neither had missed them, nor were they in any particular hurry to leave.

After a simple picnic lunch on the beach, Jox and Julianna paddled in the clear water, whilst Elias showed Cochrane the castle.

'It's so beautiful here,' said Jox. 'And peaceful. Hard to believe there's a war on.'

'The war gets everywhere,' Juliana replied. 'Even here, I'm afraid. At the beginning of the siege, when the carrier HMS *Illustrious* was in Grand Harbour for repairs, it was terribly bombed and suffered great loss of life. Her dead sailors were given sea burials, but their bodies were not weighted down enough. Those poor boys washed up on this beach and were bobbing all along the bottom of the cliffs like grim buoys. It was heart-breaking to see. For many months, I couldn't face returning here, the favourite beach of my childhood. I'm glad we came together, to create some happier memories.'

Jox smiled and took her hand.

On the beach and then walking back to the lorry, Cochrane was taking pictures of Julianna and of them together, Jox with his arm around her, the sea glittering behind the ruins of the Hospitaller castle. Hand in hand, they chatted as Elias observed them, but said nothing.

Since they had a vehicle, a rare thing on the petrol-starved island, it seemed a good idea to make the drive to the grandparents' farm. Julianna reasoned that offering the supplies Jox had collected in person would make the best impression. It involved taking a ferry, and most probably a late pick-up for Pengelly and his mob, but Jox was feeling invincible and willing to take on all comers. Cochrane was less happy but had no choice but to go along with his excitable flight leader's instructions.

The reception from Julianna's grandparents was muted. After a burst of rapid Maltese between the grandfather and Elias, there was a lengthier exchange between a suspicious grandmother and her granddaughter.

Jox was bewildered and Cochrane was amused by the dramatics. Julianna seemed embarrassed and clearly irritated. The discussion grew in volume and heat. Giovanni cut through the noise with brutal finality, brooking no argument. He crossed over to Jox and Cochrane and shook their hands.

'Thank you for bringing my grandchildren home. We are grateful for your generous, but completely unnecessary gifts. Mister Jox, I am glad to hear that you have behaved like a British officer and gentleman. Mister Cochrane, you have been very kind to my Elias. It is good for him to play like a boy again. It is so rare with this war. I would be pleased to welcome you both again.' He smiled, exposing his missing front tooth. 'Perhaps with a little more notice next time.' He indicated they should sit on some armchairs in the shade. 'These old *pultrunas* are worn but comfortable. Come, let's drink some wine. It is not very good but comes from my own grapes. Be careful, not too much — you must drive home.' He chuckled. 'Let's see if we can get these bickering women to prepare something from the bounty you have brought us. It is better, I think, than arguing over what did or did not happen. Don't you agree, Mister Jox?'

The old man was smiling, but his eyes were firing off a warning. Jox took careful note of it. He'd heard all about the feuds and rivalries of the Maltese, referred to as *pika*, often triggered by someone feeling slighted, then things escalating out of hand. Jox reasoned he had more than enough enemies in Maltese skies; he didn't need more down here. Jox nodded respectfully. They had come to an understanding.

Any remaining tension was relieved by the arrival of the drinks. Julianna had transformed into the dutiful granddaughter, keen to please her grandfather. She served some spicy fried sausage and soft white cheese pastries drizzled with olive oil she'd rustled up. It showed Jox a new side to her.

Her grandfather began cutting up the sausage with an evil-looking blade. 'This meat and cheese is from my goats. You see we live simply, close to the land. Here, Mister Cocky, take this *trabuxu*, how you say corkscrew, and open the bottle.'

They proceeded to have a very pleasant tea-time, with Cochrane enthralling the family with his retelling of the Battle of Marsaxlokk Harbour. He had them clapping with admiration and Elias was beside himself with excitement. Giovanni was impressed, and even the grandmother grudgingly patted Jox's bare knee in approval. Julianna's face was a picture; her family were warming to her new beau. For Jox, it was a homecoming that he'd longed for, for months.

Flight Sergeant Pengelly was unamused when Jox and Cochrane turned up at the Boneyard well past nightfall. Despite his crew's fascination with the place, it wasn't where you'd choose to spend the night. The fitters and riggers had collected firewood and were clustered around a bonfire, trying to fend off swarms of buzzing mosquitoes.

Jox placated them with the crate of red wine Giovanni had pressed on him as a parting gift. Cold and hungry, the wine barely touched the sides, and the men were soon singing lustily, chasing away any lonely spirits that may have haunted the graveyard of aircraft.

By the time they got back to Ta Kali, half the airmen were asleep, and the rest watched the lightshow of Valletta being bombed once more. Someone was humming the song about 'meeting again' by that perky blonde singer, and everyone except Pengelly had forgiven the wayward officers. The Cornishman remained silent, driving the lorry and brooding darkly about people taking liberties.

# CHAPTER THIRTY

The next morning, the duty sergeant stuck his head into the dispersal hut and said to Jox, 'Glad I found you, sir. The CO would like a word. Asked that you pop up to the squadron office at your earliest convenience. He's with Wing Commander Thompson, visiting from Group.'

*Oh Christ*, thought Jox. *I know Pengelly's pissed off, but I hope he hasn't dobbed me in. I was only a bit late and all in a good cause. His boys didn't seem to mind too much, by the sound of their sing-song, after a belly full of old Giovanni's gut-rot red.*

He angled his forage cap at not too jaunty a tilt and straightened out his uniform in the mirror that hung by the hatstand. It wasn't easy trying to smarten up baggy khaki shorts, socks that wouldn't stay up and a shirt that was already sweat-stained. *Never mind, I don't suppose they'll be coping with this heat any better than I am.*

The corporal in the front office told Jox to knock and go straight in. They were expecting him. He had a touch of the jitters, like when he'd been called up to the rector's office at school.

He knocked and entered, finding Squadron Leader Lucas standing by the familiar moustachioed bulk of Thompson. With them was Jox's friend and fellow flight leader Ginger Neil. By the look on Neil's face, things didn't bode well.

'Ah, Jox, there you are,' said Thompson. 'Understand you've been getting into some bother with the maintenance erks. Mustn't upset them, you know; we depend on them far too much.' He grinned. 'I hear there's a young lady involved. Glad to hear it. I know losing your poor Alice was a terrible blow.

She was so lovely. You'd have liked her, Laddie. Absolutely top drawer. Very kind to my wife when we visited the palace together. That was a grand day, eh, Jox?' He shook his head, saddened by the memory. 'Still, we who remain must soldier on. Now then, we've got a bit of a situation. We need your help to figure it out, Jox.' He turned to Lucas. 'Laddie, do you want to explain?'

'Right sir,' said the CO. 'You've been doing a cracking job with A Flight, Jox, and that business at Marsaxlokk Harbour the other night was first-rate. I'll come back to that. The trouble is your Red Section took a hammering, with the loss of Victor and Jimmy. Jimmy will get patched up — tough as old boots, that one, but it'll take time. So, we're down by two in your Flight and B Flight are down by three, once Ginger here heads back to Blighty. I'm afraid we lost Reggie Round and Baz Butler yesterday. Both of them went down over Grand Harbour. The rescue launch searched for hours but found no sign of either. Terrible shame, good chaps.'

'Yes, and now I've come in and thrown another spanner in the works,' said Thompson. 'Let me explain. I received a letter from Badger Robertson the other day.'

'Yes, I got one too,' said Jox. 'Things don't sound great back at No. 111 Squadron.'

'That's exactly it. Look, my heart will always be with the Treble Ones, and I owe Badger more than you'll ever know. I'm sure you feel the same.' Jox nodded. 'They're in a terrible funk and have lost quite a few pilots during sweeps over the continent. Losing Brotchie has rather tipped them over. Their new CO is a solid enough chap called Peter Wickham, but he's struggling to get a grip. He'll get there, I'm quite sure. He's got plenty of experience in North Africa and the Med, but it's taking too long to get the squadron sorted, according to Badger.'

Jox listened, concerned for Pritchard, Chalmers and his former comrades, but not really understanding how this had anything to do with him.

'The long and the short of it, Jox, is that they want you back,' said Thompson. 'You'll be second in command, the next flight lieutenant in line to get the step up to squadron leader. Pete's got plenty of experience but is quite new in the role and needs a solid number two. He's also got a wild streak that needs tempering, but the two of you should get on. I have every confidence.'

'But I just got here,' said Jox. 'Surely there must be someone else that fits the bill.'

'They want you and I've made my decision,' replied Thompson. 'You should be flattered.'

Jox was flabbergasted, then resigned. 'Right then, when do Cam and I leave?'

'No, I'm afraid Warrant Officer Glasgow stays here,' said Lucas.

'What? He's not going to like that.'

'He's a professional soldier and he'll do what he's bloody told,' snapped Thompson, but then he softened. 'Look, I know how protective of you he is. To sweeten the pill, he will be commissioned. The next time you see him, he'll be an officer. He's more than capable and is technically without equal. God help us with that temper of his in the mess, though!' He guffawed. 'Joking aside, we can't afford to lose his experience from the wing.'

'It's bad enough that I'm losing the two of you,' added Lucas. 'Buck McNair takes over B Flight from Ginger as planned, but we'll ask Erik Hetherington to step up for A Flight. Is he up to it, Jox?'

'I don't know him that well, but he seems solid enough. What do you think, Ginger?'

'He'll get there. That's when having Cam Glasgow will really count. Jimmy Waerea will help when he gets back, but for now he'll need Cam's experience.'

'Screwball and Paradis have talent but are hotheads,' said Jox. 'Cocky is solid and should be a good influence on them. Then it'll depend on the replacements we get in.'

'You needn't worry about that. Laddie and I will figure it out,' said Thompson. 'There's a bunch more Spits and pilots due in. You two just need to sort your affairs out on the island. Ginger, we've got you on a ship to Alexandria, and Jox, be sure to be on that Sunderland we've got you booked on back to Gibraltar.'

'Ah, then there is one more fly in the ointment, sir,' said Jox hesitantly. 'As you know, Wing Commander Drummond and I don't see eye to eye. I'm sure he'll be waiting for me in Gib with daggers drawn.'

Thompson gave a sly smile. He wasn't a fan either. 'Oh, I shouldn't worry too much about that. You see, I really didn't appreciate him making trouble for my boys with all that tobacco business. It appears he's been running that racket for a while, but rather foolishly he also used it as a way to get at you. Let's just say he's had an uncomfortable conversation with the Snowdrops, and I think it's safe to assume he's no longer a problem. For what it's worth, I understand that scar-faced chap has been demoted and posted to some arse-end training school in Rhodesia. Fanny Barton's the wing commander there and he'll doubtless be hard on his case. Drummond's far too busy picking tsetse flies from his teeth to come looking for you.'

'Right ... er, well, thank you, sir,' said Jox. 'It's a lot to take in. Will you tell Cam, or should I? He's bound to go off on one. What about the other chaps?'

'I'll deal with Cam,' replied Thompson. 'We go back a long way. Laddie, will you brief the others?'

'Yes, of course, sir.' Turning to Jox, he said, 'I'm sorry to see you go, Jox. You've not been with us very long but achieved a hell of a lot in that time. No. 249 Squadron is grateful. I hope you'll remember the Gold Coasters with affection.'

'You're a sound fellow, McNabb,' said Thompson. 'Service needs more like you.'

'Speaking of which, sir, there is also that other matter,' added Lucas.

'Ah yes, of course,' said Thompson. 'It's all a bit hush-hush, so keep it under your hat, Jox. There's a bit of a top-level reshuffle going on with Malta Command. I'm getting kicked upstairs and will be working with the new boss, Lord Gort. "Tiger" won the VC in the first war and saved the BEF during the debacle in France. He's taking over as Governor of Malta, tasked with holding the island together and getting a grip on flagging morale. Part of that will be a gong-fest, principally to recognise the contribution of the local Maltese troops. All three services have been asked to put some names forward. It seems the Royal Navy have taken the unexpected step of recommending some airmen for gallantry awards.'

Jox wasn't following.

'You, you damned fool!' said Thompson. 'You and your chaps shot down three aircraft, which were attacking a strategically vital supply ship. Therefore, in recognition of "an act or acts of exemplary gallantry during active operations against the enemy on land," you are awarded the Military Cross. There aren't that many airmen that can say that. Sub-lieutenant Cochrane is being promoted and will receive the Military Cross too. As discussed, Cam Glasgow will be commissioned, but before that he will receive the Military Medal, as will Flight Sergeant Jimmy Waerea. An impressive haul of medals for an evening's work, I'd say.'

'What about the chaps from No. 603 Squadron? They were there too.'

'Yes, they were, but they couldn't hit a barn door. It took two of my Treble Ones to do that,' said Thompson, with evident pride. Abruptly, he turned serious. 'I'm afraid these new orders rather scupper things with your new young lady. I'm sorry for that, Jox, but it's in the interest of the service. You've got three days to get things straightened out. I do hope she waits for you, but I know it's rough. I'm terribly sorry, but needs must.'

Lucas was good enough to lend Jox his little Standard Flying Eight so he could get across the island to meet with Julianna in Rabat. The plan was to pick her up from work after her morning shift at the now partially rebuilt Point de Vue hotel, already restored as an officers' mess. Bombed on the day before Jox arrived in Malta, a thousand-pounder had collapsed a section of the 17th-century villa, resulting in great loss of life. The damage was still very evident on the limestone façade, with cracks and gouge marks from shrapnel visible on the honey-coloured rock.

Up on a ridgeline, the hotel had a sweeping view over the lakebed of Ta Kali aerodrome and the patchwork of vineyards beyond it. Driving up the avenue of mature palms to the hotel, there were several trunks lying by the roadside like bowled-over wicket stumps. That the bomb damage should include such ancient trees struck Jox as horribly tragic. He wasn't relishing the task ahead.

When Julianna came out, seeing her shook him from his dark funk. She was dressed for work in a black and white uniform, approximating a chambermaid's outfit, and was carrying a bag of beach things, since they planned to return to the cliffside beach near the Hospitaller castle. As she walked down to him, she stopped and put on a headscarf, a bright contrast to her drab uniform.

'I'm not very elegant for you,' she laughed, getting into the car. 'Maybe just from the neck up.' She took his chin between her hands and kissed him tenderly. His heart thumped in his chest. 'Come, let's go,' she said. 'It's too hot to sit in the car. I need some air.'

They talked about banalities, how Elias was doing at school, how some of Giovanni's goats and his favourite dog had been killed in the latest bombing and how Cochrane had come down with the dreaded Malta Dog, nasty local dysentery that had grounded him for the last few days.

Arriving by the castle ruin, Julianna turned shy and ordered Jox to the other side of the car. 'Look at the view or something,' she instructed, as she slipped into her swimming costume and beach dress. Jox had on his trunks under his shorts, and a towel and a bit of a picnic in the boot of the car. His mind wandered as he scanned the blue horizon. It was a perfect day in a perfect spot, an ideal place to bring your gal under any normal circumstances.

Imperceptibly at first, he could hear what sounded like the hum of a beehive. He frowned, trying to trace its origin, then realised it was distant aircraft. Somewhere on the island was getting hit again.

Julianna emerged from behind the car. Now she looked like a French starlet, her dark hair tied back in her scarf. She wore a pretty strappy dress in a colourful print with espadrille pumps and sunglasses. She kissed him on the cheek. 'Come on, why are you so grumpy?'

Shying away from the truth, he replied, 'Oh, it's just the raid. Another bloody raid.'

'Jox, by now you should realise that in Malta, there's always *anuther bludy rayed*,' she said, mimicking his Scots accent. 'Let's eat. I'm starving.'

They found a shaded spot on the beach, not too close to the damp rocks so as to keep the sandflies at bay. They stripped to their bathing costumes, then laid out towels and a picnic of bread, olives, goat's cheese, and wine. They drank from the bottle and ate with their fingers. They chatted and laughed, until she finally frowned.

'What is it, Jox? I can read you like a book; something has happened. Tell me, so we can get on and enjoy this perfect afternoon together.'

Jox realised it was futile trying to keep anything from her. Even accepting that truth was somehow telling. Here was someone that already knew him so well, perhaps even better than he knew himself. 'I've had new orders. I'm going to be leaving the island,' he said with more bluntness than he'd intended. He watched the effect of his words. The carefree smile of a few seconds ago was replaced by hollow bereavement, as Julianna realised the implications of what he'd just said. She turned away and scanned the waves, the sea breeze moving her long hair. With a sad smile, she looked back to him with tears in her eyes, but a new determined look on her face.

'You came to me from the sky in an instant, Jox. Now you will go the same way. It is the reality of our life. It is war. Come, let's live in the moment. Let's go swim.' She took his hand and led him to the water's edge. Here she stopped, slipped out of her costume, and waded naked into the clear water like Aphrodite returning to the sea.

Shocked by her boldness, he followed suit, embarrassed by his arousal. Reaching chest height, she held out her arms for him, offering a tantalising glimpse of her sleek body through the translucent water.

'I must give you something, so that you don't forget me,' she said huskily. They embraced and began exploring each other, gently rocked by the current. Entwined like otters, they made love in the ocean and as he entered her, she moaned, 'Remember me.'

Satiated, they emerged from the sea, sleek and shiny, to lie on their towels. They didn't care if there were onlookers.

As they lay in each other's arms, she ran her long fingers through his hair, her eyes welling up, salty lips on his. 'My darling, I will never forget you.' A single tear slipped down her tanned cheekbone.

'I'll be back, Julianna. I promise you that. Nothing can keep me away.'

'You cannot say that. There is so much that can be taken from us. Let us be content with what we have right now. Know just this: I love no other like I love you.'

It was Jox's turn to cry. How could life rob him of this second chance to love? She soothed him like a mother would a child.

'You must be my brave soldier,' she said, kissing his forehead, nose, then lips. 'What is it that girl you soldiers love to listen to says? "We'll meet again … some sunny day."

Remember that this was a sunny day and there will be others, Jox. You must remember me.'

Walking arm in arm back to the car, the sun was drying the salt on their skin as distant sirens sounded over the capital. The rumbling of another raid began with ragged lines of JU 87 Stuka dive-bombers and JU 88 twin-engine multi-role *Schnellbombers* appearing at stepped intervals. Above them, Messerschmitt Me 109s were in their usual finger-four *Schwarms*.

Jox and Julianna shielded their eyes as they watched the island's fighters get in amongst the bombers with inelegant haste. With neither height, nor the sun's glare to disguise their approach, their Merlin engines roared in protest. Stressed fuselages shuddered and wings flexed as G forces sucked at the pilots' bodies. The controls would be feeling stiff, and approaching their closing speed, raking tracers would be punching back from bomber gunners reacting to their sudden proximity.

Criss-crossed vapour trails appeared like claw marks on the azure sky. Lazy puffs of black flak punctuated the aerial ballet, when unexpectedly one chord struck home and flame enveloped an enemy fighter. It slowly rolled onto its back, before a dark speck of a man could be seen falling. Tumbling and flailing, his streaming parachute filled with a loud crack. Like a delicate dandelion seed, he floated in the thermals, in stark contrast to his aircraft windmilling earthwards like a fat sycamore seed.

A Ju 88 traced a graceful curve in the sky, smoke pluming from dying engines as three more parachutes popped. The aircraft's bombload gave a thunderous boom, when it eventually slammed into a desolate patch of cactus, blasting earth and rock skywards and creating a crater like the mouth of a volcano.

Jox was all too familiar with this world. What he couldn't see, he could imagine perfectly. It had been this way for pretty much his entire service life. He was simply changing location but doing much the same — something he was born to do and was bloody good at. And now, once again, he had a reason to do it.

# CHAPTER THIRTY-ONE

The slab-sided Short S.25 Sunderland dwarfed the seaplane slipway in Marsaxlokk Bay. A shadowy group were gathered by the quayside of RAF Kalafrana on the southernmost tip of Malta. They included the nine-man Fleet Air Arm crew, but also several well-wishers seeing off the dozen or so passengers.

The blunt-nosed four-engine flying boat was kitted out for anti-submarine operations and could carry two thousand pounds of bombs, nautical mines, or depth charges. It had a forward-firing 37 mm gun and defensive armaments in powered turrets in the nose, dorsal and tail positions, plus a manually operated pair on either side of the fuselage. So well defended was it that the Germans called it *Das fliegende Stachelschwein*, the flying porcupine.

Tonight, it was ferrying passengers to Gibraltar on the six-hour flight through a Mediterranean night fraught with danger. Gathered on the dockside were Jox and his fellow passengers. Some were walking wounded, returning to convalesce, others pale from the dreaded Malta Dog. Still others were haunted with broken spirits after many months of siege.

The flight promised to be an interesting one, given how any one of them might react to the tension of the long journey. In case of trouble, a burly medical orderly and a tough-looking matron from Queen Alexandra's Imperial Military Nursing Service were in attendance. She wore a cape against the night air, grey with scarlet piping, the red lining covered with the shoulder patches of her grateful patients.

Seeing Jox off was Cam Glasgow, skulking and ill at ease with his new pilot officer stripes on the shoulder tabs of his khaki shirt. Their newness contrasted with the ancient pilot wings on his breast. He was unhappy about their parting, his loyalty offended. The bond between them had always been strong. Glasgow would do his duty and follow orders, but he didn't like it and it showed. Earlier, he'd tried to explain how he felt but had struggled for words. In the end, they simply shook hands, holding each other's gaze, unsaid words expressing volumes about the friendship between them.

Cochrane had wanted to be there too but was still laid low by The Dog. He'd lost about a stone in a week and was too weak to travel, unwilling to stray too far from his commode. As a goodbye gift, he'd asked Glasgow to let Jox have an envelope. It contained a few black and white prints of the afternoon spent on the beach with Julianna and Elias. Jox had them in his tunic pocket with Marguerite's dolly's arm. He'd take a look later as he didn't think he could bear seeing her face right now, feeling as low as he did.

Their parting was hard. Earlier he'd cycled to Rabat, and they'd spoken on the hotel terraces with a view of the airfield and vineyards. The sun was setting, and the view was magnificent, but neither had any interest in it. They'd held hands, kissed a bit and she began to cry. He tried to console her but was hopelessly ill-equipped. After a while, they sat quietly, until she finally said, 'I have a gift for you from my grandfather. He says he is sad to see you go but understands it is the nature of war. He hopes this will protect you.'

Julianna held a folded knife, about four inches long. It had a black ebony handle and was silver at either end. On the butt, etched in red was a Maltese Cross, and on the hilt there was a silver button in the handle. It looked brutal in her hand, but she handled it deftly. As she pressed with her thumb, there was a click and a silver stiletto blade flicked from the handle.

'My grandfather makes these Maltese switchblades. They are highly prized, and he is considered one of the best. The blades are from Maniago in Italy, but everything else is by him. He has signed it for you, with his best wishes.'

Etched into the base of the blade was the word MANIAGO. Above it, larger and more florid, were the initials GV — Giovanni Vella. The knife was elegant and terrifying. Jox folded it carefully and then pressed the button to release the blade again. It jumped in his hand, poised for action, for violence, ready to defend him against all comers.

'My grandfather has marked this weapon with the cross of our island. It has been our identity for centuries and defines our proud little nation. He says that when you use it, you must remember us and know we are waiting for the day when, God willing, you return to us ... to me, my darling Jox.'

She brushed her fingers down his cheek, raised the shawl over her lustrous black hair and ran. His instinct was to chase after her, but perhaps this was a better way. Down the sloping street, she slowed to a walk, and he could see that her shoulders were heaving as she sobbed. Clad in black, shrouded in her shawl, she was like one of the many grieving widows that filled the streets and markets of Malta. It was an image that chilled him to the core. The knife flipped open in his hand, of its own accord.

Standing now on the pontoon, under the giant wing of the Gibraltar-bound Sunderland, he could feel it in his pocket, pressing against his sweating thigh. He was unaccustomed to wearing trousers after weeks in shorts and was grateful for the breeze making the behemoth bob on its deep belly and twin lateral floats. He looked up at the four large Bristol Pegasus engines and the rows of portholes down the side, marvelling and wondering how on earth this monster would ever get off the water. He hoped the trail of circular portholes didn't foreshadow a more sinister pattern from a night fighter's guns.

The take-off was smoother than he'd expected. It was past midnight, and the island was shrouded by cloud and the dark of night. Up north, some flashes in the clouds indicated another raid. The aircraft banked to starboard, before settling on a heading broadly eastwards.

Jox was sitting by a porthole with a portly Pongo major in the canvas seat beside him. He was in no mood to talk, no doubt also reflecting on having survived his tour on the island. There was no artificial light allowed in the cabin, but once they were above the clouds the moon was bright enough for Jox to see the photographs Cochrane had left for him. There were six in all, annotated with 'Malta 1942'.

One was of Juliana and Elias at the rockpools, another of Jox with the two of them. There were three beautiful candid shots of Julianna on her own. In one, she was laughing at her brother's antics, mouth open, teeth showing and the wind in her hair. In the other two, she was pensive, almost wistful; in one she was looking out to sea, and in the other her eyes were hidden behind her sunglasses. Jox's favourite was the one of the two of them together, the sun glittering on the sea and the castle ruins in the foreground. He was smiling, sun-tanned and bony-kneed in shorts, his arm around her. He was facing the camera; she was gazing at him adoringly.

He stared at the photo, absolutely resolved to get back to her one way or another. He had come a long way and suffered a great deal, but she was his salvation. His friends and comrades of No. 111 Squadron needed him now, but he would be back. He had a reason to live again, a reason to return to the island for this woman who had got under his skin.

Something flickered outside the porthole. He glanced and could see only wispy clouds, bathed in eerie moonlight. The sky above was clear, mackerel striped with anthracite and granite, but he felt his night fighter instincts kicking in. Something didn't feel right.

He slipped the photographs into his pocket and leant his nose up against the Perspex porthole. His movement attracted the portly major's attention.

'What's up?' he asked.

'Not sure. Something doesn't feel right.'

There it was. The dullest flicker beneath them. Innocuous enough, but to a night fighter, it was gold. A bit of luck had betrayed a predator's presence through the flash of an engine backfire.

Jox called the nearest waist gunner, further down the Sunderland's cavernous hold. 'Petty Officer, you better get busy. I think we've got company.'

Beside him, the major's eyes widened. An anxious boy wearing a bulky Sidcot flying suit and a yellow Mae West came scrambling towards Jox.

'What have you seen, sir?'

'I think it's a Ju 88S.' Jox knew it was the fastest variant of the high-speed bomber, adapted for night fighting with a smooth glazed nose, perfect for night vision, and equipped with onboard radar. This would be a tough proposition to cope with.

The petty officer peered through the porthole, then swore under his breath. He plugged the jack of his headset into the nearest comms net socket. 'All crew, action stations. Tinker here, Skipper. We've got a bogey at eight o'clock low. A sharp-eyed passenger spotted him on the portside. Looks like a Ju 88 big job, a night fighter.'

'Roger, Tink. All crew, stand by for action,' said the crew's captain, his voice tinny through the petty officer's headpiece. 'Fire as he comes to bear. Everybody latch onto him as soon as he's coned, then hit him hard. Tink, let the passengers know it's going to get bumpy and rather loud. Make sure everyone's strapped in, then get back to your gun.'

Petty Officer Tinker spoke to the nursing officer, who was alarmed but then nodded.

The throbbing of the Sunderland's snowflake-shaped Bristol engines was cut by heavy machine guns being cocked and powered gun turrets whirring into position. Before stepping away, Tinker put a gloved hand on Jox's shoulder. 'Thanks, mate, we've got this. We're not some toothless transport. You watch and learn.'

The major swapped seats so that he could see out of a porthole of his own. In the cabin, the news had spread and one of the nervous cases was keening like a frightened child. The orderly was doing his best to calm him down. Jox peered into the darkness, feeling redundant and desperate to catch another glimpse of the predator stalking them. He scanned the clouds, filled with excitement, trepidation, and no little fear.

There it was, an indistinct dark cross now almost level with them, just behind and below. It was porpoising through the cloud, dorsal tailfin knifing through cotton wool softness. The key thing was for the Sunderland's gunners to fire first, and once they did, for the aircraft to execute evasive manoeuvres to avoid retaliatory fire.

Tinker and his mates didn't hang about. The tail turret fired first, swiftly followed by the handheld mid guns and the dorsal turret. Jox was frustrated at being unable to help, but wasn't given time to ponder, as the giant aircraft tipped and lurched about violently. A few solid impacts were felt rather than heard, and the portly major flew up, bouncing off the curved cabin ceiling. He came down with a crunch, as did Matron, landing across Jox's lap. It was chaos in the cabin, but the guns kept up their fiery tempo, the engines roaring as the Sunderland skidded and jinked, surprisingly manoeuvrable considering its size.

Outside the darkness was punctured by a pulsing light, above and to the left of them now. In its glow, a prehistoric-looking creature was revealed, with grotesque antennae spread across its nose like gnarled antlers. Closer now, its throaty wing nacelles and twin props were discernible, the fuselage leopard-spotted in tropical grey-green with white-edged black crosses on either wing and a hooked swastika on the tail. Halfway down the aircraft body, twin cannons projected upwards at an odd ninety-degree angle. Jox's blood ran cold. He'd heard about these — a devastating new gun system, *Schräge Musik*, developed for German night fighters, firing automated 20mm cannons directly upwards into the body of vulnerable bombers or transports. The Sunderland was bristling with guns but had a large vulnerable belly. The interceptor was positioning itself downwards.

He'd clearly taken some hits and was wary of the larger aircraft's defences and of getting too close. His nose antennae were more twisted than usual, and a thin trail of smoke seeped from the portside engine mounting. He wouldn't risk it much longer but would make at least one final pass.

The Sunderland had enough fuel to stay airborne for up to fourteen hours, so could keep manoeuvring like this all day long. That said, it made for a nauseating experience for the panicked passengers, not to mention the fear of living their final moments. The roar of outbound fire was interrupted by the higher pitched zip of incoming rounds. The cabin's decking shuddered with impacts, as half a dozen cricket ball-sized holes appeared in the floor. Freezing cold air whistled through like a giant ocarina, accompanied by the groans of the wounded. Matron was struck in the elbow and there wasn't much left below the joint. Arterial blood seeped into her cape, which one of her patients wrapped around the stump after fixing a tourniquet. Further up the cabin, one of the long-suffering victims of the Maltese Dog slumped even paler than before, strapped into his chair. A 20mm shell had passed through the flimsy seat and up through his body. He didn't stand a chance. His suffering was over, but for him in death all dignity was lost.

As the Sunderland levelled, through the porthole Jox could see that the night fighter had dropped away. His trail of smoke was larger, the affected engine throwing off sparks which didn't bode well. Petty Officer Tinker and a fellow crewman staggered into the cabin, carrying a wounded colleague and followed by a pall of acrid smoke. The gut area of his pale overalls was soaked a deep burgundy.

'Matron! We've got a patient for you,' said Tinker. 'Oh shit,' he added, seeing her pale face and bloodied wrapped stump.

Her burly medic colleague replied. 'Put him down here. I'll do what I can. Here, you two, give me a hand.'

Jox and the major reacted automatically, easing the waist-gunner to the floor and covering him in a blanket.

Petty Officer Tinker surveyed the damage to the cabin, the wounded, and the dead. He took in the whistling damage to the floor, which had already lowered the temperature in the cabin to the point of their breath showing, but also helped clear the smoke. He crossed to the comms socket he'd used earlier.

'Skipper, this is Tink. I'm with the passengers. We've got one dead and one wounded. Jack's been hit too. It looks pretty serious. The medic's working on him, since Matron's hurt too.'

'Understood, Tink. We're an hour from Gib and the ship's handling okay. Thank God that bandit has cleared off. You boys took a chunk out of him. What's the damage at your end?'

'We've got problems, Skipper. The keel is peppered with holes and we're on fire somewhere. There are half a dozen in the passenger cabin and God knows how many elsewhere. We've lost the starboard float, so the minute we land, we'll tip over and water's going to come rushing in. We won't stay afloat very long and will need to evacuate sharpish.'

'Damn!' replied the aircraft's commander. 'Right, can't be helped. Secure the wounded, then get the rest of the passengers organised to stuff those holes as best you can. Won't solve the problem but may delay the inevitable.'

Dawn was breaking as the Rock appeared low on the horizon. The sea was choppy with white horses on the surface, and the water looked cold. They'd spent the intervening time frantically stuffing fabric, kapok from life belts and even shredded clothing into the whistling holes of the keel. There were more holes outside the passenger compartment. It was a miracle the big aircraft was still holding together, but there was no doubting the Sunderland's reputation as a tough flying porcupine.

Gibraltar stood proud, offering sanctuary to the battle-weary traveller. One of the Sunderland's Bristol Pegasus engines began to falter, a persistent blue flicker of flame appearing amidst a strengthening plume of smoke. In the cabin, the Queen Alexandra's matron had gone worryingly quiet. The remaining passengers were warned to brace for impact and of the likelihood of the aircraft tipping on landing. Once in the water, they were to evacuate through the escape hatches as quickly as possible. There was scant prospect of reaching Gibraltar without first getting spectacularly wet.

With the distraction of survival filling his mind, Jox had no time to dwell on what lay ahead, nor what he'd left behind. New battles and perils awaited him now that he'd found something or rather someone to fight for again. How would he make it back to her? He didn't know, but there was no doubt in his mind that he would see Maltese skies again.

# EPILOGUE

## *London, April 1990*

The hulking building on the Richmond Hill was bleak in the wintery rain. The last time she was here, Melanie McNabb was filled with the hope of discovery. Now it held only the finality of death.

Mrs Cunningham from the Royal Star & Garter Home had explained on the phone that her uncle Pritch had passed away during the night. The old warrior had died peacefully in his sleep. Melanie was listed as his sole family and the beneficiary to whatever estate he might have. She was asked to come by that evening to collect any items, documents or possessions that might be of personal or historical interest, given her professional expertise. Pritch's particular friend, Nancy, was keen to speak with her.

Melanie was shown to Nancy's room up a creaking lift and down several labyrinthian corridors. The hospital smelt of fried food, the burnt dust of electric fires and of disinfectant. The room was smaller than she'd expected, but was neat and tidy, overheated in the way of the elderly. It smelt of gin and Nancy was a little unsteady. She'd been crying and, seeing Melanie, was moved to do so again.

'He loved you so,' said Nancy, planting a boozy kiss on her cheek. 'Come, sit, sit. Pritchy darling has got me in such a state. Why is it that the men leave and die?'

She sat back in her armchair, moving like a bewildered bird. It was hard to equate this frail old lady with 'The White

Mouse', the scourge of the *Gestapo*, heroine of the *Maquis* and saviour of countless downed airmen in occupied France.

'He didn't suffer,' said Nancy. 'Just faded away. "Off to see my boys," he told me. It was a blessing.'

Melanie took her hand and the two women sat quietly for a while.

'He got agitated a few days ago. Wanted me to tell you, well, it doesn't make much sense. He said, "The Poles know about Alice. Tell Melanie, the Poles know. Miro went to a party and saw her."' Nancy looked confused. 'Does that make any sense? Do you know this Miro?'

'Yes, I think I do. It's Miroslav Mansfeld, a Czech pilot that flew with Uncle Pritch and my grandfather. Quite a famous night fighter, on Mosquitoes, I think.'

'Oh, that's excellent news,' said Nancy. 'Maybe you can follow up with him?'

'I'm afraid he died. I went to his funeral at Brookwood Cemetery, to represent my grandfather. I met his wife Bobina at the reception. She might know something. I've got her number somewhere.'

'Excellent, that sounds like a plan,' said Nancy. 'I'm so relieved that I got the message to you and that it makes some sense. I was worried it might be nonsense, just his mind wandering, but he was very insistent. I hope you find some closure.' Her hands fluttered in her lap.

'How are you holding up, Nancy?'

She ran trembling fingers through her grey hair. 'What must I look like?' She gave a sad smile. 'Not terribly well, to tell you the truth. I'm going to miss the old rogue. I know time's catching up with us all, but it gets terribly lonely seeing your pals dwindle away.'

Melanie glanced at the green bottle of gin on the nightstand. 'You must take better care of yourself, Nancy.'

'Me? Fit as a fiddle. A seventy-eight-year-old gin-soaked fiddle, perhaps, but fit nonetheless,' she cackled. 'It's everyone around me that keeps dying. Like I made some pact with the devil to survive back in the day and just keep going. I'm running out of friends.'

'I'm your friend, Nancy.'

'I know you are, darling, but it's not the same. We've lived through different times, and frames of reference.'

It took Miro Mansfeld's wife, Bobina, a moment to recognise Melanie's voice on the telephone as that of Jox McNabb's granddaughter. To her husband, who had retired from the RAF as a Squadron Leader and had been promoted to Major General by the Czech government, Jox was always the boy, barely a man, that led Blue Section during the Battle of Britain.

Bobina recalled the conversation between Pritchard and Mansfeld. It was at one of the innumerable reunions that were the highlight of the ageing flyers' twilight years. Some weeks earlier, Mansfeld had been invited to an anniversary celebration at the Sikorski Polish Institute in Kensington. The fighting Poles and Czechs in the RAF had a particularly strong relationship, with several serving in each other's squadrons. None more so than Czech Sergeant Josef Frantisek, who flew with the legendary No. 303 Polish Squadron as a 'squadron guest' with his seventeen kills during the Battle of Britain, making him the deadliest pilot in the squadron and indeed the RAF.

Perhaps stranger still for Mansfeld, whose own father had died of cholera whilst fighting in Poland in 1914, after the war the relationship grew even closer. Unsurprising, given the

Communist takeover of their respective countries, the pariah treatment of the heroes who had fought with the RAF, but worst of all the betrayal by the western Allies in accepting Stalin's puppet regimes for geopolitical reasons. It would always hurt to know that the war had been declared to protect Poland and Czechoslovakia, but both would end up under Stalin's heel.

Mansfeld and his Czech comrades were guests of their Polish counterparts. There was a presentation of gifts and a vodka reception that soon had everyone talking freely. A new exhibition was being launched celebrating Poland's military involvement with Britain during the war, each glorious episode brought to life with artefacts, uniforms, and photographs.

It was while standing in the cavernous stairwell of the Kensington mansion, which housed the Polish Institute and Sikorski Museum, that Mansfeld caught sight of a woman with a familiar face photographed with a group of Polish lancers. She didn't seem particularly happy about being in the picture, but there was no mistaking Alice, the soon to be Mrs Jeremy 'Jox' McNabb. Despite his advanced state of inebriation, Mansfeld had the presence of mind to ask the official photographer to snap a picture of him pointing at the image.

'Yes, I still have the photo,' said Bobina. 'I can let you have it — is it important?'

'Yes, I think it might be,' replied Melanie, breathing heavily. 'Thank you, that would be wonderful.'

As good as her word, the black and white snap arrived in the post a few days later. In it, an evidently well-refreshed Mansfeld was grinning at the camera, one hand resting on an iron balustrade, the index finger of his other pointing at a large group photograph mounted on the wall. It wasn't clear enough to make out the figures, but one of them was evidently female.

Protecting the precious photograph from London's rain in her coat, Melanie entered the impressive columned entrance of the Institute. As the black cab she'd just hopped out of U-turned through puddles, she pushed the intercom button on the door's brass plate and explained that she had an appointment.

She knew Andrej, the Sikorski's Director of Archives quite well. They had collaborated on several exhibitions celebrating the exploits of the fighting Poles over the years. Tall, pale and with an impressive moustache, he greeted her with a discreet click of the heels and a continental nod of the head, then kissed her on either cheek. It made her smile, reminding her that during the war those impeccable manners had melted many an Englishwoman's heart.

She'd explained the scenario to him on the telephone and he had promised to investigate. He listened attentively again as she repeated the details of her request, then smiled reassuringly.

'My dear Melanie, I'm so glad you called. I have a bit of a surprise for you. I want to introduce you to one of our volunteers, Rikard Zygmunt. During the war, Mister Zygmunt was with the 24th Lancer Regiment, part of the 1st Polish Armoured Division. He was invalided out after being terribly injured but has been a supporter of the museum for many years. I must warn you, his scars are quite alarming, but I think you will be interested in what he has to say.'

Andrej led Melanie through the grand foyer filled with militaria and artefacts, on to the airy central stairwell of the townhouse. The walls all the way up the steps were lined with portraits, photographs and paintings of derring-do, which appeared to involve a lot of horses. On one of the upper landings stood an old man, with dark sunglasses and a cane. As they approached, Melanie was confused.

'My apologies,' said Andrej. 'I didn't explain properly. Mister Zygmunt was the photographer that took that picture. He says he will remember that day for the rest of his life and the lady who saved them.'

The man on the landing shuffled forward, executed an approximation of Andrej's clicked heels and bow, then held out a frail liver-spotted hand. What was striking was that it was criss-crossed with the scars of lacerations. His aged face too, behind the dark glasses, was covered with tracks, like the contrails Melanie had heard described as Battle of Britain skies.

'Please do not be frightened, my dear,' said Mister Zygmunt in a reedy voice, his Polish accent still strong despite a lifetime in Britain. 'My scars look a lot worse than they actually are. It was flying glass, but I am long healed; thanks be to God for the *Aniol Kina*.'

Melanie glanced at Andrej, unsure what he'd just said.

'Our Angel of the Cinema,' clarified Zygmunt. 'This lady here.' He pointed his finger at a figure in the photograph on the wall.

Melanie leant in to look more closely and saw a tall woman in a military uniform, with striking eyes and long curly fair hair, which was pinned back. She looked stern but was undeniably beautiful. Melanie felt a flutter in her chest. She knew she had found Alice.

'We never discovered her name, but she saved us that day, when we foolish boys were running around like scared chickens.' Mister Zygmunt chuckled. 'Before the picture, she wasn't happy with our clumsy flirtation, nor that I took that photograph. When the raid started, she was magnificent, taking charge and showing us the way. When that cursed parachute came down and my comrades ran towards it, thinking it was a Nazi parachutist, she tried to stop them. I was further down the avenue. That's what saved me. Those that followed her orders lived, those that didn't, disappeared. Just like her.'

His eyes were hidden behind the glasses, but tears were following the raised tracks of scars down his face. Melanie gave him a hug, feeling the sobs through his thin shoulders as he relived the trauma.

'Thank you for telling me her story.'

Composing himself, Mister Zygmunt replied, 'Every year in the spring, we who survived meet to remember and pray for her. We never knew her name, but we remember our "Angel of the Cinema". Who was she to you, my dear?'

Caught out by the question and surprised by the emotion she was feeling, Melanie stuttered, 'She ... she was my grandfather's fiancée. The love of his life, I think. She stayed in his heart forever.'

Zygmunt smiled. 'And may I ask the name of our angel?'

'Alice. Section Officer Alice Milne.'

'Ah, *Alicja* in Polish, which means noble and exalted,' said Mister Zygmunt. 'Yes, that is appropriate for our angel.'

# A NOTE TO THE READER

Jox McNabb is a fictitious character who encounters an array of real historical characters and then others who are figments of my imagination. I hope that the 'join' isn't too obvious and that the reader will enjoy teasing them apart.

As is my habit, I have used the names of friends and relations in my fiction, as a sort of in-joke to keep myself amused as I write. I'm afraid, no one is safe, for which I apologise, but hope they will all accept that it is done respectfully and affectionally, with no intention to misrepresent anyone.

My stories try to be as authentic as they can be, by including the life stories of real individuals. I do this as an homage to their lives and deeds, hoping always to tell their story respectfully and in awe of their often-forgotten valour. To include as many as I can, I have on occasion had to be creative with timelines. I hope my readers will be forgiving of that.

In the style of certain film directors, I have also included some 'Easter Eggs' within my stories, referencing characters that I admire and some of my other novels. My hope is that readers will enjoy spotting them as much as I have including them. Again, it is done respectfully and playfully.

The horrors that Jox and Alice faced during the Blitz are all true, particularly the experience of the raid of the 29th of December 1940, which came to be known as the Second Great Fire of London. London was indeed burning, and her landscape would never be the same again.

The Clydebank Blitz, over the nights of the 13th and 14th of March 1941, were also as described, with proud Clydesiders experiencing Scotland's largest, most intense, and devastating air raid.

In marked contrast to the suffering endured by the British people, a gilded minority did lead the life as described in The Ritz London. King Zog the First of Albania and his family did occupy an entire floor of the hotel, with Albania's gold reserves in the hotel vaults. His many elegant sisters were the darlings of a world where London's demi-monde intersected with high society. The Ritz's La Popote night club also existed, as did The Coconut Grove, but the events described in the latter have been merged with what actually occurred at the Café de Paris nightclub near Piccadilly Circus on the 8th of March 1941. The café was bombed at the beginning of a performance and thirty-four revellers were killed and around eighty injured. The character of Curly Cummings is loosely based on the very real bandleader Ken 'Snakehips' Johnson, killed with all bar one of his orchestra on that fateful evening

Jox's breakdown after the loss of Alice, for that's what it was, was a very real issue with young aircrew stretched to their limits. Psychiatric facilities like those at Babbacombe in Torquay are also real, as was the innovative treatment of terribly burnt airmen by medical pioneers like Archibald McIndoe, his team, and many others.

During his travails, Jox meets aircrew from many nations, which is in keeping with the evolving international nature of the air war. Many of the characters and heroes that he meets are real, or otherwise are based on amalgams of real individuals. I hope that readers will enjoy recognising fact from fiction when meeting this revolving cast. It has been commented that the casts of my novels are large, but I believe that is the very nature of World War.

Squadron Leader George 'Wee Brotch' Brotchie, Commanding Officer of No.111 Squadron was tragically killed in a flying accident on the 14th of March 1942. For dramatic effect, he is described in the fiction as more of a martinet that he may actually have been, and was undoubtedly a fine C.O. and pilot, deprived of the accolade of being one of The Few on a technicality.

In early 1942, Wing Commander John 'Tommy' Thompson arrived on Malta to establish the RAF Ta Kali Spitfire Wing. He went on to command the Hal Far Wing and the Luqa Wing too, earning the distinction of commanding all of Malta's Spitfire Wings over a period of ten months.

On the 15th of April 1942, a handwritten letter was sent by King George VI to the Governor of Malta and her people:

*The Governor*

*Malta*

*To honour her brave people, I award the George Cross to the Island Fortress of Malta to bear witness to a heroism and devotion that will long be famous in history.*

*George R.I.*

*April 15th 1942*

In response, the Governor Lieutenant-General Sir William Dobbie replied:

*By God's help Malta will not weaken but will endure until victory is won.*

In May 1942, Prime Minister Winston Churchill replaced an exhausted General Dobbie, with Viscount 'Tiger' Gort, who brought Malta's George Cross with him, going on to decorate several other meritorious individuals.

In its history, the George Cross has only ever been awarded to an organisation three times. To the island of Malta in 1942, the Royal Ulster Constabulary in 1999 and the National Health Service in 2021.

For the Maltese, the George Cross is every much a part of their national identity as the Maltese Cross of the Knight's Hospitaller. It was proudly incorporated into the island's national flag in 1943.

This novel is respectfully dedicated to the memory of all those lost during the events depicted.

*Per Ardua Ad Astra* (Through Adversity to the Stars)

I hope you've enjoyed reading my second novel. More in the series are in the pipeline. Reviews are important to authors, so if you enjoyed *The Raiders and the Cross*, I'd be grateful if you would post a review on **Amazon** or **Goodreads**. Readers can also connect with me on **Twitter (@P33ddy).** Also, for anyone who may be interested, I have loaded some images on **Instagram (jox_mcnabb)** that inspired me to write the story of Jox's remarkable war.

Best regards,
Patrick Larsimont
April 2023

**Sapere Books** is an exciting new publisher of brilliant fiction and popular history.

To find out more about our latest releases and our monthly bargain books visit our website:
**saperebooks.com**

Printed in Great Britain
by Amazon